NEW YORK REVIEW
CLASSICS

PEACH BLOSSOM PARADISE

GE FEI is the pen name of Liu Yong, who was born in Jiangsu Province in 1964. He graduated with a degree in Chinese from East China Normal University in Shanghai, and in 2000 received a PhD from Beijing's Tsinghua University, where he has taught literature ever since. He first started publishing short stories during the 1980s and quickly established himself as one of the most prominent writers of experimental avant-garde fiction in China. Ge Fei's scholarly publications include *Kafka's Pendulum* and his fiction includes *The Invisibility Cloak* (available as an NYRB Classic); the Jiangnan Trilogy, of which *Peach Blossom Paradise* is the first volume; and the novella *Flock of Brown Birds*. He was awarded the 2014 Lu Xun Literary Prize and the 2015 Mao Dun Prize for Fiction.

CANAAN MORSE is a translator, poet, and editor. He cofounded the literary quarterly *Pathlight: New Chinese Writing* and has contributed translations of Chinese prose and poetry to *The Kenyon Review*, *The Baffler*, and other journals. He is currently editing two anthologies of Chinese literature and translating a collection of the work of the Taiwanese poet Yang Xiaobin into English. In 2016 he translated Ge Fei's *Invisibility Cloak* for NYRB Classics.

PEACH BLOSSOM PARADISE

GE FEI

DISCARD

Translated from the Chinese by
CANAAN MORSE

NEW YORK REVIEW BOOKS

New York

THIS IS A NEW YORK REVIEW BOOK
PUBLISHED BY THE NEW YORK REVIEW OF BOOKS
435 Hudson Street, New York, NY 10014
www.nyrb.com

Published by arrangement with People's Literature Publishing House Co., Ltd.
Originally published in Chinese as *Ren mian tao hua*.
First published as a New York Review Books Classic in 2020.

Library of Congress Cataloging-in-Publication Data
Names: Ge, Fei, 1964– author. | Morse, Canaan, translator.
Title: Peach blossom paradise / Ge Fei ; translated from the Chinese by Canaan
  Morse.
Other titles: Ren mian tao hua. English
Description: New York City : New York Review Books, [2020] | Series: New
  York Review Books classics
Identifiers: LCCN 2020010224 (print) | LCCN 2020010225 (ebook) | ISBN
  9781681374703 (paperback) | ISBN 9781681374710 (ebook)
Classification: LCC PL2872.F364 R4613 2020 (print) | LCC PL2872.F364
  (ebook) | DDC 895.13/52—dc23
LC record available at https://lccn.loc.gov/2020010224
LC ebook record available at https://lccn.loc.gov/2020010225

ISBN 978-1-68137-470-3
Available as an electronic book; ISBN 978-1-68137-471-0

Printed in the United States of America on acid-free paper.
10 9 8 7 6 5 4 3 2 1

Translator's Note

PEACH *Blossom Paradise* gives voice and presence to a brief span of Chinese history in which the millennia-old dynastic government had effectively died but the famous and brutal movements that we frequently weave into China's tortuous narrative of modernity (the Republican era, the fight against Japanese imperialism, Maoism, the Cultural Revolution, and economic reform) had not yet begun. To the reader, the specter of that history makes this novel's moment—the span between the failed Hundred Days' Reform of 1898 and the final collapse of the last dynasty, in 1911—feel like a quiet inhale, a calm before the storm. To that end, the author has blurred the lines between fiction and history even further by annotating significant places and people with information about their life and fate within the whirlwind of twentieth-century Chinese history. The author has placed these annotations in line with the main body of the narrative, as is customary in Chinese novels. We present them here as footnotes.

PEACH BLOSSOM
PARADISE

Part One

SIX FINGERS

I

FATHER came down from his studio.

He descended the stone steps and entered the courtyard with a white wicker suitcase in one hand and his cane tucked into the crook of his arm. Every room of the estate was empty, all hands called out for the wheat harvest. Sprigs of pine and poplar that had been hung over the lintels in celebration of the Tomb-Sweeping Festival had long since dried into brittle twigs beneath the summer sun. Likewise, the flowers that once covered the dwarf crab apples in the rock garden had been shuffled off by a flourish of green leaves, and the unswept petals lay wind-scattered across the courtyard.

Xiumi had no idea how to react. She had sneaked over here to dry a pair of underpants that she clutched in one hand. But now she'd run into Father.

This was her second time finding blood on her underwear. She had just spent ages crouched by the well, trying to scrub it away. Honeybees had tumbled and buzzed loudly by her head and intensified her anxiety. She had felt an unbearable pain in her stomach like a lead weight sinking right through her, but when she sat on the toilet, nothing came out. She pulled her pants down farther and looked for the source of the bleeding with a hand mirror; when she found it, embarrassment flushed her face crimson and set her heart racing. Confused, she tucked some cotton balls in place, yanked her pants back up, and ran to her mother's bedroom, throwing herself atop an embroidered pillow and whimpering, "I'm dying, I'm dying, I know I'm dying." Her mother was away visiting her sister-in-law in Meicheng, and the boudoir was utterly empty.

But the immediate problem was that Father had come downstairs.

This lunatic almost never emerged from his chambers. Only on the first day of the New Year would Mother ask Baoshen to carry him downstairs and install him in the stately armchair in the main hall to receive the family's blessings. To Xiumi he seemed a living zombie—his eyes and mouth weirdly offset; he constantly drooled, and was so weak that even a cough left him wheezing and exhausted. Could that be the same man who just now tripped nimbly down the stairs and stood before her with a bulky wicker suitcase in hand, looking the very picture of energy and presence? He paused under the crab apple tree and calmly took a handkerchief from his sleeve pocket to wipe his nose. It couldn't be possible that his disease had disappeared completely overnight, could it?

The wicker suitcase suggested to Xiumi that Father might be setting out on some kind of journey. She glanced reflexively down at the rust-stained wad of cloth in her fist, and in a jolt of panic, turned toward the front courtyard and yelled, "Baoshen! Baoshen! Cockeye Baoshen!" But no one was home, not even the clerk. The petals, dust, and lifeless afternoon sunlight carpeting the courtyard floor ignored her, as did the crab apples, the pear trees, the moss on the wall and the butterflies and bumblebees perched on it. The blue-green willow leaves outside the front door and the stiff breeze swaying them paid her no mind.

"What are you yelling about? Stop yelling," Father ordered.

Stuffing the filthy handkerchief back into his sleeve, he turned slowly and regarded her through squinting eyes with faint opprobrium. His voice sounded deep and gravelly, as if his throat had been scrubbed with sandpaper. This was the first time she remembered hearing him address her directly. Years of hiding from the sun had left a sooty patina on his skin and tinged his hair a fine corn-silk yellow.

"Are you going away?" With Baoshen not there, she knew she had to calm down and assemble the courage to deal with him herself.

"I am," Father replied.

"Where are you going?"

Father chuckled and raised his eyes to the sky. After a pause, he replied, "I'll admit, at this point, I still don't know."

"Is it somewhere far?"

"Very far," he said, his tone evasive. His ashen face stared at her without moving.

"Baoshen! Baoshen! Cockeye, where are you?"

Father paid no attention to her raised voice, but stepped slowly over to her and raised a hand as if to touch her face. Xiumi shrieked and dashed away from beneath his fingers. She leaped over the bamboo fence into the garden, then turned to peer at him from a distance, her head cocked and her hands nervously twisting and untwisting her soiled underwear. Father shook his head and smiled. His smile was like ash, or paraffin.

From her new vantage point, Xiumi watched Father pick up his wicker suitcase once more and shuffle his stooped body out the side door of the courtyard. Her heart was pounding, and her mind fluttered with activity. Moments later, Father returned, poking an otter-like head around the doorway and peering around the courtyard, an embarrassed half smile on his face.

"I need an umbrella," he whispered, "it's going to rain in Puji very soon."

Those were the last words Xiumi's father would ever say to her, though she didn't know it at the time. Xiumi looked up at the sky: not a cloud in sight, just a vast field of electric blue.

Father found an umbrella by the hen boxes and opened it up. Worms had riddled the oilcloth canopy with so many holes that the ribs showed through, and a good jostling would have left nothing but a skeleton. Father hesitated, then leaned it very carefully back up against the wall. Picking up his suitcase one more time, he retreated backward across the threshold, closing the door behind him as if afraid of disturbing someone. The double leaves of the side door folded silently shut.

Xiumi allowed herself a long sigh of relief. After hanging her washed underwear on the hedge, she scurried around the greenhouse and into the front courtyard in search of help. But Baoshen was gone, as were Magpie and Lilypad. The madman had excellent timing: the main hall, side chambers, woodshed, kitchen, and even the outhouse were all deserted, as if he'd planned it with the whole family. Finding no one at all, Xiumi had no choice but to run through the antechamber and out the front gate, where already she could see no sign of Father. Their neighbor, Hua Erniang, was drying sesame seeds in bamboo baskets outside her door, but when asked if she had seen Xiumi's father, she replied in the negative. When Xiumi asked about Baoshen, Hua Erniang merely laughed. "How should I know? You never asked me to keep an eye on him in the first place."

Then as Xiumi was leaving, she called out, "I thought your father was locked in his studio. How could he run away?"

"I don't know how he got out either," Xiumi replied. "Anyway, he's gone. I saw him leave through the side door."

"Then you need to send people to find him right now," Hua Erniang enjoined with obvious urgency. "He's so confused, he could walk right into an outhouse hole and drown, just like that."

As they were speaking, Xiumi caught sight of Lilypad walking back from the east end of the village with an overflowing basket of daylilies under her arm. Xiumi hurried over to give her the news. Lilypad showed no sign of panic, but remarked, "You said he's carrying a suitcase, so he couldn't have gone far. We'll run to the ford and cut him off. If he crosses the river, he'll be impossible to catch." Putting down her basket, she grabbed Xiumi's hand and took off running for the ford.

Lilypad's bound feet meant that running made her body shake hard and sent her breasts bouncing in all directions, a sight that drew open-mouthed, baboon-like stares from Wang Qidan and Wang Badan, the blacksmith's apprentices. Farther down the road the women ran into a couple of peasants returning home from the harvest; both said they hadn't seen old Mr. Lu pass. Xiumi and Lilypad turned and ran back, and they got as far as the fishpond before Lilypad's legs gave out. She flopped down onto the ground, undid the buttons of her vest, and slipped off her embroidered shoes to massage her feet, her chest still heaving from exertion. "Scrambling around like this won't do any good. If your dad didn't head for the ford, he must have taken the back road out of the village. But first we've got to tell Cockeye."

"If only we knew where he went," Xiumi complained.

"Oh, I know," said Lilypad. "I'll bet you anything he's playing mahjong at the old lady's place. Pull me up."

Lilypad put her shoes back on and tucked her vest under her arm; Xiumi helped her up, and the two women made their wobbly way toward a large apricot tree in the center of the village. Only then did it occur to Lilypad to ask a barrage of questions: When did the master come downstairs? What did he say? Why wasn't Magpie at home? Why didn't Xiumi try to restrain him? Having probed every corner of the case with questions, she felt a sudden anger well up inside her. "I told them not to go leaving the studio door unlocked, but your mother said she wanted him to get some sun out in the pavilion. Now look what's happened."

Beneath the apricot tree, Grandma Meng was spinning cotton. Her wheel was turning too quickly, nearly snapping the fiber, and she accompanied the movement of the machine with a constant stream of muttered curses aimed at herself. Lilypad called to her, "Rest a moment, Grandma, I have a question for you. Did Baoshen come by to play mahjong with you today?"

"What do you think? Of course he came," grumbled the old woman. "Won twenty strings of cash from me and then left. Can't save his own money, so he comes here to steal wood from my coffin. Wins a round and leaves, just like that. Tried to get him to sit for one more, but no dice. Even snatched a couple of my dried persimmons on his way out."

Lilypad couldn't keep from laughing at her story. "Well, Grandma, don't let him play next time and you'll be all right."

"Who will I play with if not him?" the old lady shot back. "No more than a handful of players in a place this size; if I lose anyone, I can't fill the seat! And my luck's just been bad anyway—can't even spin cotton without breaking the thread."

"Did you see where he went, Grandma?"

"I saw him walk off, eating my persimmons and happy as a clam, toward the far end of the village."

"Was he going to Miss Sun's?" Lilypad asked.

Grandma Meng smiled but said nothing, and Lilypad grabbed Xiumi and turned to leave. Behind them, they heard the old woman mutter, "I sure never told you he was going to Miss Sun's." And she chuckled.

Miss Sun lived at the far end of the village behind the mulberry orchard in a small house with a courtyard. Her home boasted a small pond ringed by wild roses and honeysuckle. An old man sat basking in the sun outside the front door, which was shut tightly and admitted no noise from within. When he saw the two women draw near, the man rose in alarm and scanned them both with narrow eyes. "Stand by the pond and don't move. I'm going in to get Baoshen," Lilypad instructed Xiumi, then strode forward as steadily as she could on her bound feet. Sensing her aggression, the old man raised both hands in a gesture to stop her. "Who are you looking for, Bigmouth?"

Lilypad ignored him entirely; she pushed open the door and started to walk straight into the courtyard. Caught off balance and out of position, the old man grabbed the lapel of her jacket. Lilypad turned and glared at him with a ferocity he didn't expect and spat at his feet. "Touch me one more time, you dried-up old bastard, and I'll drown you in the pond."

Though obviously both angry and frightened, the old man managed to screw his face into an ingratiating smile. "Lower your voice a little, my dear," he whispered.

"What, out here in the middle of nowhere? Your little whore in there could scream to high heaven and no one would hear her," Lilypad snorted, raising her voice even louder.

" 'Cursing the lily spoils the lady,' as the saying goes. Even if you're not afraid to offend our ears, don't you worry about soiling your own mouth?"

"Blow it out your grandma's ass! I swear, if you don't let me go, I'm going to burn this cathouse to the ground." The old man nearly stamped in frustration but had to let her go.

Just as Lilypad stepped into the courtyard, one of the inner chamber doors opened and a man stumbled out. It was, of course, the very man she was looking for. He approached the front door, making a passing attempt at doing up his buttons. Head cocked to one side as always, he giggled and asked, "Hey, Bigmouth, you think it might rain today?"

And rain it did, in a heavy downpour that lasted from early evening to midnight. Water collected in the open spaces of the skywell between the outer wall and the courtyard, finally rising beyond the edges of the flower basins and pouring into the hallway. Mother had returned from Meicheng, and was now slouched in the grand armchair in the main hall, staring at the rain and sighing.

Lilypad yawned constantly and could make no progress on the hempen weave she carried around with her. Magpie sat next to Mother, smacking her lips when Mother smacked hers and sighing when Mother sighed. No one spoke. Storm winds hammered the windows; the shushing of rain on the roof continued without end.

"The hell did you have to go picking flowers for?" Mother snapped at Lilypad, as she had done several times already. When no reply came, she turned to Magpie. "And you don't seem to have ears on your head either. I told you to wait until after the harvest to grind the flour, but there you go hurrying off to the mill anyway." Then her eyes fell on Xiumi. "Your father may have been crazy, but he's still your father. If you had held on to him tight enough, he wouldn't have bitten your arm off." Finally, she cursed Baoshen, the dumb cur, repeating the same insults over and over. "Where did that cockeyed bastard disappear to all day?" Magpie would only shake her head, Lilypad claimed ignorance, and Xiumi heard Lilypad's lie and didn't contradict it. She struggled to keep her eyes open; even the sound of the rain seemed a little unreal.

Baoshen did not return until long past midnight. He trudged into the main hall carrying a hurricane lantern, his pants rolled up to the knees and a look of defeat clearly visible on his face. He had led a search party across every inch of ground in a several-mile radius that stretched as far as the Martial Temple at the foot of the mountain, and questioned hundreds of people without obtaining a trace of useful information.

"Did he just fly away?!" Mother cried. "How far do you think a crazy man with a suitcase can go in half a day?" Baoshen just stood there in sheepish silence, water dripping from every part of his body.

2

WHAT DROVE Father insane? This unanswered question would weigh on Xiumi for years. Once she asked her private tutor, Ding Shuze, about it, but the old man merely frowned and chuckled, "Go ask your mother." She did, when she got home that day, and Mother slammed the table with her chopsticks so hard that all four rice bowls leapt into the air at once. Later, she would recall thinking that four rice bowls leaving the table at once might have been the reason Father went crazy. She went to pester Lilypad, who replied with an air of total confidence, "What else but all the fuss over that stupid Han Yu painting of the *Peach Blossom Spring*?"

Xiumi asked her who Han Yu was. Lilypad informed her that Han Yu was a great general who had defended China against a Jurchen prince who invaded from the north many centuries ago. He also had a wife, Liang Hongyu, who was famous the world over for her beauty. Eventually Xiumi read Han Yu's essay "On Entering the Academy" and realized that Han Yu was not the famous general Han Shizhong, nor was he married to Liang Hongyu, and Lilypad's explanation fell apart. So she went to ask Magpie, what happened, and her only answer was, "I guess he just turned out that way." In Magpie's mind, going crazy needed no explanation—insanity would come for everyone eventually.

At that point, Xiumi's only option was to coax answers out of Baoshen.

Baoshen had worked as Father's valet since the age of twelve. When Father's connection to the salt-tax scandal in Yangzhou cost Father his official position, Baoshen was the only one of his subordinates to follow him home to the south. Baoshen confirmed that the *Peach Blossom Spring* painting really did exist; it had been a gift from Ding Shuze on Father's fiftieth birthday. Ding Shuze and Father had become fast friends during Father's first few years home after his dismissal, exchanging poems and passing the cup with frequency. The painting, reputed to be the work of the Tang dynasty scholar and poetic luminary Han Yu, had been the crown jewel of the Ding family library. Even when the library burned down twenty years prior, the painting had miraculously survived.* That Ding Shuze could have made a gift out of the only surviving item of his collection, a cherished heirloom and a great masterpiece at that, clearly indicated the uncommon depth of his friendship with Father.

Then one day, Baoshen was carrying a kettle of boiling water for tea up to Father's study and heard the repeated strikes of flesh against flesh. He opened the door to find the two men fighting—Mr. Ding cuffing Father, Father punching Mr. Ding, both of them standing there hitting each other without saying a word. Baoshen was so shocked he merely stood and stared, without thinking to break it up; the fisticuffs ended only when Ding Shuze spat out a front tooth in a wad of bloody sputum and ran off howling with a hand over his mouth. Little time elapsed before one of his students dropped by with a written declaration of a terminated friendship. Father opened the missive and read it seven or eight times while shaking his head and exclaiming, "Those brushstrokes. Look at those beautiful brushstrokes." Both his cheeks were swollen, and it sounded like he had an egg in his mouth when he talked. Baoshen had no idea as to why their relationship had soured, but simply sighed, "Scholars all over are just a bunch of crazies, anyway."

That was Baoshen's explanation. Ding Shuze's own story went that Father had written a poem to him that misquoted a line by the clas-

---

*Allegedly painted by Han Yu, *Peach Blossom Spring* was passed down through the Ding family of Puji for several generations, then fell into other hands. In August 1957, a joint working group of experts from the antiquities departments of Beijing and Jiangsu determined it to be a forgery. It is currently stored in a museum vault in Puqing.

sical poet Li Shangyin—"Golden toad bites the lock; burning perfume enters"—accidentally replacing the character for "toad" with the character for "cicada."

"Both characters are pronounced the same—it was obviously an orthographical error. Your father's scholarship was amateur at best, but he knew Li Shangyin's poetry well, well enough, at least, to avoid such a silly mistake. I corrected him with the best of intentions, and I certainly didn't mean to ridicule him. But he blew up, and railed on and on about checking the sources. He knew he was wrong, but he played the imperious official and tried to shout me down. Well, since they fired him, he was no longer an official. He may have passed the civil service exam, as I never did, and held a provincial post, while I never served. But an exam score and a teaching post in the Imperial College still won't change a perfectly good toad into a cicada. And when I told him so, he stood up and hit me. Even knocked out a tooth." With old resentment clearly audible in his voice, Ding Shuze opened his mouth and exposed his pink gumline so his student could see the proof. Thereafter, Xiumi suspected that Father had turned crazy because of Ding Shuze's lost front tooth.

In any event, Father lost his mind.

When he first received the painting, Father locked it away in his study and rarely showed it to anyone. After the fight, Ding Shuze regularly sent servants to ask for it back, to which Father replied, "If he comes for it himself, I shall return it on the spot." While the mere thought of the painting made Ding Shuze's heart ache, it had been a gift freely given, and he could not bear the embarrassment of asking for it himself. Baoshen's opinion was that Father had gone mad looking at it.

Lilypad had been in the habit of making Father's bed in the morning after he got up. But one day, she entered his chambers to find his bed untouched, the owner sleeping soundly at his desk, on which lay piles of books and the Han Yu painting, speckled with soot from the lamp. Lilypad shook Father awake and asked him why he hadn't gone to sleep on his bed. Father made no reply, but rubbed his bloodshot eyes, turned to Lilypad, and stared at her fixedly. She caught the empty look in his eye, sensed his unnatural bearing. Tucking her hair behind her ear, she asked, "After all these years, aren't you sick of staring at me?"

Father held her in a motionless gaze for a long moment. Then he gave a small sigh and asked, "Lilypad, do I look like a cuckoo to you?"

At this, Lilypad turned and hurried her way back down the steps to tell Mother exactly what Father had said. Mother had been at the peak of fury with Baoshen for running off secretly to the whorehouses in Meicheng, and hadn't paid much attention. But that evening, as everyone sat down for dinner, Father strolled into the dining room (his first time coming downstairs in two months) without a stitch of clothing on. The sight of his naked body stunned the room into dead silence and a flurry of confused glances. Father tiptoed behind Magpie, covered her eyes with his hands, and asked, "Guess who?"

Magpie recoiled in fright, and the hand that held her chopsticks flailed about in front of her for a moment before she timidly replied, "The master."

"You guessed right," admitted Father, giggling like a child.

Mother's shock was so profound she forgot to swallow the food in her mouth. Xiumi was twelve that year. She would never forget the sight of Father's wordless smile and ashen face.

Mother didn't quite believe that Father could suddenly lose his mind; at the very least, she held out significant hope for his recovery, and the first few months did not distress her much. First she called the doctor, Tang Liushi, who force-fed Father herbal tinctures and covered him with acupuncture needles. Xiumi could recall witnessing Father being tied to a sedan chair by Baoshen in nothing but his underwear and squealing like a stuck pig as golden needles shimmered all over his body. After Dr. Tang, the Buddhist monks with their rituals arrived, followed by the Taoist priests with their exorcisms, the yin-yang geomancers, and the blind witches right behind them, trying every trick from ancient physiognomy to Heavenly Stem divination to Celestial Palace augury—everything short of pulling out his bones and boiling them. The parade continued from early spring right through late summer, during which time Father became more docile, as well as noticeably fatter, so much so that the extra flesh on his body jiggled when he walked and squeezed his eyes into slits.

That summer, while walking around the garden, Father leaned against a stone table to rest and immediately tipped it over. Baoshen summoned a few stout worthies from the village to lift it back up, but a solid afternoon of shouting and straining proved useless. When Father was in a good mood, he liked hitting people for fun; one heavy slap could send Baoshen spinning in circles. One day he somehow managed to get his hands on a halberd; he took it into the garden and started cutting down trees and flowers. Mother led a team of servants to see what was going on—the glittering blade flashed through the air, chopping down everything in its path. Eventually he felled a wisteria, a persimmon tree, three white poplars, and two young pagoda trees. Finally, Mother sent for Baoshen, who circled, dodged, and danced like a martial arts master as he tried to stop Father, but he couldn't even get near him.

The incident drove Mother to a courageous decision: she would hire the Wang brothers to forge her an iron chain with a heavy bronze lock, and tie Father up like a mule. She begged the Earth God's advice, and he readily agreed. She asked the Bodhisattva Guanyin, and the deity visited her that night in a dream, exhorting her to act quickly, and to make the chain as heavy as possible. Yet before the instrument was finished, disaster struck again: late one night, for no apparent reason, Father set his chambers on fire. By the time tendrils of acrid smoke jolted the household awake, the flames were already rising to the eaves. Baoshen displayed his undying loyalty to his master by charging into the inferno with a soaked cotton blanket over his head and shoulders, and miraculously returned with Father (who was three times his weight) on his back, a bag of books clutched to his chest, and Father's prized painting in his mouth. The scroll lost a corner to the blaze, but the building burned to the ground.

The unexpected fire woke Mother to the fact that every major disaster caused by Father's insanity was somehow connected to the painting. When she asked Baoshen's advice, he noted that since the painting was actually the Ding family's property, and Ding Shuze had repeatedly sent over servants demanding its return, they would do well to oblige and give the gift back. Though the fire had eaten up one corner and hardened the paper, turning it dark and brittle, a careful remounting could essentially allow for a complete restoration. Mother thought this a sensible plan, and went along with it: the next day, even as the ruins in the courtyard still smoked, she left through the side door and set off for the Ding family estate with the painting in hand. As she approached their western chambers, she heard voices and stopped to listen. The speaker was Ding Shuze's wife, Zhao Xiaofeng.

"And so the Lu family hoards *our* family treasure for no reason and refuses to give it back. And now look what's happened—it's all burned down. We kept that painting safe for how many generations, through difficult times, ill fortune and good, without so much as a scratch, and the day it moves to that horrible family, all kinds of strange things start happening. How can a dumb fool like him be able to look at a painting like that? He went crazy just trying."

That was enough for Mother. She turned and marched right back home, swearing she would torch the rest of the scroll right there. "Why burn it when I can cut it out for shoe soles?" exclaimed Lilypad. She snatched the painting from Mother's hands and marched to her room.

In September, Mother directed Baoshen to hire people to rebuild Father's studio. The changing seasons brought nearly constant rain, and the masons and carpenters managed to trample the well-tended rear courtyard garden into a pigpen. They wandered around the estate wherever they liked, and made no effort to avoid Magpie or Lilypad, but followed them with such hungry stares that Xiumi didn't dare go downstairs for over a month.

One of their number was a barrel-chested nineteen-year-old named Qingsheng, who was so solidly built he made the iron rings on the doors rattle when he walked. They called him Listen, because it was the one thing he couldn't do; he spent most of his time walking around the villa, and not even the foreman could control him. If Listen's fingers didn't listen, they'd find their way to Lilypad's hips for a juicy pinch; if his feet didn't listen, they'd take him right into the washroom as Magpie was bathing, causing her to leap out of the bath stark naked, and hide under her bed. When Mother and Baoshen complained to the foreman, the old man merely laughed. "He just won't listen to me. He'll never listen."

The day they finally finished, Xiumi stood by a window on the second floor and watched the workmen leave. Qingsheng continued his strange behavior: though the others all walked straight ahead, Qingsheng walked backward so he could keep his eyes trained on the villa, examining it top to bottom and nodding to himself. He caught sight of Xiumi standing at the window, and both of them started. He waved at her, made faces, and smiled mischievously. He kept walking backward and looking at her until he ran into a chinaberry tree at the far end of the village.

Once the mob left, Mother had the servants shovel the mud and filth out of the main hall, whitewash the walls, burn incense in the rooms to get rid of the stench, and send the master's chair, which the workmen had flattened, out for repair. It took over a week of constant work to restore tranquility to the estate.

The Wang brothers also delivered the chain, but now it had ceased to be necessary: the trauma of the fire had frightened Father so much he became as quiet as a sleeping baby. He spent his days sitting in the pavilion next to the studio, staring into space or conversing with a ceramic washbasin. He sucked on his fingers when he got bored. By his chamber's western wall stood a trellis of roseleaf raspberry bushes that bloomed every year in the early summer, at which time Father would order Baoshen to carry him downstairs so he could sit beside the small stone table among the flowers. He would sit there all afternoon, surrounded by the mosaic of white petals, and breathe in the faintly perfumed air.

That winter, Mother decided it was time to find a private tutor for Xiumi. They searched and searched, and ended up asking Ding Shuze anyway. The first few days of class, Ding Shuze gave Xiumi no lectures, taught her no new characters, and just complained about her father. He said that even though her father went on and on about leaving worldly troubles behind and swore to "pick wild chrysanthemums by his eastern hedgerows," as the poet-recluse Tao Yuanming had done, his spirit never left the magisterial hall at Yangzhou even for a second, just as the proverb says: "An ethereal white heron among the clouds, flying round and round the ministers' halls."

Xiumi asked her teacher, "Why did Father set fire to his study?"

Ding Shuze replied, "Your father was an unpopular man in the political world, and being excluded filled him with resentment. He had nothing to let it out on except his books. It seemed to him that reading and studying were to blame for his disastrous career. Even before he lost his mind, he used to carry on about wanting to burn every book in the village—all empty talk, of course, as he was still too attached to the glamour of the official's life. Why else would he keep a soft-skinned young trollop at home?" Xiumi knew he meant Lilypad. She asked, "So why did Father cut all those trees down?"

"Because he wanted peach trees in that courtyard," Ding Shuze answered. "He once told me his plan to plant a peach tree in front of every house in the village. I thought he was making a joke."

"Why would he want to plant peach trees?"

"Because he believes that Puji is the 'Peach Blossom Spring' utopia that Tao Yuanming wrote about fifteen hundred years ago, and the big river in front of the village is the stream that led the boatman to it."

"But that's insane."

"He's insane—you can't expect him to think rationally. And that wasn't even his most absurd idea, ha ha. He wanted to build a covered walkway to connect the entire village. He thought he could protect the people of Puji from sun and rain."

Ding Shuze's unrestrained ridicule of her father only strengthened Xiumi's sympathy for him. Moreover, she couldn't figure out why Father's desire to build a covered walkway was absurd.

"But..."

Seeing that a long stream of questions might continue to pour forth, Ding Shuze frowned and waved a hand impatiently. "You're still too young to understand these things anyway."

The night Father left, fifteen-year-old Xiumi lay wide awake in bed, listening to the rush of rain on the roof and smelling the soaked moss outside. She was aware that she might be too young to figure out the true cause of Father's madness; she was still too young to understand what was happening in the wide world beyond Puji.

3

A STREAM of visitors showed up the day after Father disappeared.

Tan Shuijin and Gao Caixia, the ferryman and his wife, arrived first. There had been no traffic at all at the ford yesterday, they said, and Shuijin had spent the whole day playing go with his son inside the ferry. They were both good go players, Shuijin told Mother. Skill at the game was passed down through the family. Apparently his own father had died at the go board, right after losing a whole field of pieces and spitting up blood. That afternoon, he and his son had played three rounds of the game; Shuijin won the first two, and the third was still going on when the downpour started. "Boy, that was a big storm," Shuijin said, his wife chiming in, "Big, oh boy, it was big." Mother sat quietly and listened to them babble for as long as patience would allow before finally interrupting, "Have either of you seen the man of this house?"

Gao Caixia said no, she hadn't, and Shuijin shook his head. "Not a single person crossed the river yesterday afternoon; no, I didn't even see a bird cross the river, much less a passenger. We came out here early this morning to tell you that. We haven't seen your old man. My son and I were playing go in the boat, played four rounds of it."

"Not four rounds, three, and you didn't finish the last one before the rain came," Gao Caixia corrected him. The pair went through the whole story backward and upside down one more time, lingering on until noon before marching off in a huff.

As they were leaving, Baoshen showed in an old woman who wore dirty, tattered clothing and whom nobody recognized. She swore she had seen Father leave with her own eyes. "Which way did he go?" Mother asked. "Bring me something to eat first," the old lady replied.

Magpie rushed off to the kitchen, returning with a full platter of sticky-rice cakes. The old lady ate hand to mouth, swallowing five in quick succession and pocketing three more. Then she burped heavily and turned to go. Lilypad grabbed her. "You still haven't told us where the master went."

The crone pointed to the ceiling. "Up to heaven."

"What is that supposed to mean?" Baoshen asked.

The crone pointed once more at the eaves. "He went up to heaven. You needn't wait for him. A crimson cloud appeared from the southeast and descended to him in the form of a magical *kirin*. He got onto its back, and rode off into the sky. As he rose, he dropped a piece of cloth..." With a shivering hand she drew an old handkerchief from her ragged clothing and passed it to Lilypad. "Have a look. Isn't this his?"

Lilypad took it from her and examined it closely. "It sure is, no doubt about it. It's an old one, but that's the plum flower I embroidered for him in the corner."

"Well, there you are." The crone tucked her hands into her sleeves and walked out.

Mother's face assumed a look of quiet shock, and her eyes turned confused and distant. After a long silence, she said, "It isn't very likely that he could have ascended to heaven. But where did that handkerchief come from?"

That afternoon, as Xiumi climbed the stairs to her room for a nap, a young woman in a red jacket arrived at their front door. She seemed to be in her early twenties, though her face was covered in pockmarks. She said she had been walking all morning, and had walked so far that the soles of her shoes were coming unstitched. She came from Beili, a village at least six or seven miles from Puji. No matter how Mother entreated her to come in for tea, she refused, claiming she had only a short message for Mother, and had to go back immediately. She leaned on the door frame and told her story.

It was the evening of the day before, after the rain had been falling for a while, when she remembered that she had hung a basket of soybeans out to dry from the roof of the pigsty, and ran out in the rain to fetch it. In the falling darkness she caught sight of a man, huddled beneath the eaves of the pigsty, holding a wicker suitcase in one hand and leaning on a cane.

"I had no idea that it was the master of your house. It was raining so hard. I asked him where he came from, and he said Puji village. I asked where he was headed, but he wouldn't tell me, and when I invited him to come inside to wait out the rain, he refused. So I brought the beans in and told my mother-in-law about him. She said that if he was from Puji, that made him a neighbor, and the least we could do was lend him an umbrella. So I grabbed one and went back out for him, but I couldn't find hide nor hair! And that rain coming down so fast. Later that night, when my husband returned home from drinking at his uncle's, he told me a couple of porters had come by carrying lanterns and asking for a lost old man, and I knew it must have been the man whom I had seen. That's what I came to tell you."

Having provided this news, the pockmarked young woman set off homeward again, refusing to stay even for a glass of water because, she said, they needed her for the wheat harvest. Mother immediately pressed Baoshen to send people in her direction in search of Father, but just as Baoshen was getting ready to leave, a smiling Hua Erniang brought someone else through the front door.

This last guest wasn't connected to Father's disappearance. He was a man in his forties with a short goatee and attentively coiffed hair, dressed in a traditional shirt of white cloth. Pince-nez spectacles sat on his nose, while a large pipe hung from his mouth.

The very sight of him instantaneously dispelled the clouds from Mother's expression. She invited him into the guest room, peppering him with questions the whole way. Xiumi, Magpie, and Lilypad all came in to be introduced. The man sat with legs crossed, smoking his pipe with an air of sincere self-satisfaction. It was the first time Xiumi had smelled tobacco smoke since the onset of Father's madness. The man's name was Zhang Jiyuan, and he had supposedly come from Meicheng. Mother initially told Xiumi that he was a cousin, but later instructed her to call him Uncle. To this, the man named Zhang Jiyuan spoke up. "Just think of me as your elder brother."

"But that would jumble up seniority," Mother said, smiling.

"Then jumble it," Zhang Jiyuan responded, carelessly. "Everything's jumbled up these days. Let's go ahead and jumble it all into jambalaya." He laughed loudly at his own joke.

One more lunatic. He pared his fingernails, jiggled his legs, and spoke with a powerful condescension. This elder brother made Xiumi deeply uncomfortable. His skin was pale and his cheekbones high, yet his narrow eyes were set deeply into his skull, giving him a sort of feminine delicacy. Though his aloof demeanor seemed to suggest arrogance, a closer look revealed a cold, deep-seated gloominess at its heart, as if he were a being from another world.

He had been staying in Meicheng to recover from illness, and would be in Puji for a short stretch. But if he were sick, why would he leave Meicheng and travel out here to the countryside? When Grandma was alive, Xiumi and Mother often visited Meicheng. How come she had never seen him before? According to Mother, he was a fine writer and a man of the world; he had been to Japan, and lived several years in both Nanjing and Beiping.

Mother ordered Lilypad to prepare Father's room for him, and sat and chatted with him in the living room until the lamps were lit and the call for dinner came. Baoshen and Magpie were very deferential at the dinner table, calling him Uncle. Only Lilypad seemed unimpressed by his presence, and watched him with a faint suspicion. Zhang Jiyuan talked forcefully and at length about the state of the outside world, touching on everything from reform and revolution to "piles of bones" and "rivers of blood." Baoshen shook his head and sighed, "The world has turned upside down."

After the meal, Xiumi sneaked into the kitchen to talk to Lilypad, who was washing dishes alone. They chatted about the crazy old woman's handkerchief, and about Baoshen's business with Miss Sun. Lilypad spoke on the latter subject with great interest, though Xiumi didn't always comprehend her. On the topic of their new guest, however, Lilypad was as much in the dark as Xiumi. "His family name is Zhang, but your mother's is Wen, and she doesn't have any sisters, so how could he be your uncle? There's a good chance he isn't a direct relation at all. I never heard his name once in all the years I've been in this house. He claims he's here because of an illness, but does he look like an invalid to you? Clopping around in those heeled shoes of his so that even the water in the basin ripples. And the weirdest thing"—Lilypad stretched her neck to peer out the window before continuing—"the weirdest thing is, your mother only just came home from Meicheng yesterday. If Mr. Mustache had planned to visit us, why didn't he come with her? Instead of just walking in here just as your father walked out, as if they planned the whole thing. Doesn't that seem strange to you?"

Xiumi asked if what he had said at dinner about "rivers of blood" was true. "Of course it's true," Lilypad replied. "The whole world is falling apart."

Hearing this, Xiumi fell silent, absorbed in her own dark anxieties. Seeing her lost in thought beside the sink, Lilypad dunked a hand in the water and flicked it at her cheek.

"If Puji fell apart, what would happen?" Xiumi asked.

Lilypad sighed. "Everything in this world can be predicted except for trouble. Every time trouble appears it's different, and only after it starts do you find out what it's really like."

Xiumi could see the studio through the north-facing window of her bedroom. It seemed small and threatening beneath the rich shade of the trees that towered above it. Those trees and the clear, reedy brook that once ran beside them were supposedly the reason Great-Grandfather had selected this ground for his estate, back when Puji was nothing more than a small fishing village. He raised a wall around the area so he could fish in the rear courtyard. When Xiumi was still very young, she once saw a charcoal drawing of the courtyard from those days, with wild ducks and migratory birds dotting the banks of the stream and roosting on the eaves and the courtyard wall. According to Mother, the stream had shrunk to no more than a trickle through the sunbaked pebbles by the time she and Father arrived. Only the reeds still thrived. Eventually, Father piled boulders from Lake Tai over the streambed to make an artificial knoll, on top of which he built his studio and the gazebo and put a woodshed at the base. A row of hardy impatiens bloomed along the woodshed wall, and every year Lilypad would grind some of the petals to dye her fingernails.

Zhang Jiyuan moving into Father's studio gave Xiumi the illusory sense that Father had not left. His lamp burned all night, every night, and aside from two meals a day (he did not eat breakfast), the occupant rarely appeared. Lilypad was responsible for cleaning up after him every morning, and when she came down she would find Xiumi to report the latest news.

"He's sound asleep," she reported on the first day.

"He's clipping his fingernails," she said on the following morning.

"He's moving his bowels," she said on the third day, and waved a hand before her nose. "Peeee-eww."

On the fourth day, her report was longer and more complex. "The idiot is staring at your father's old washbasin. He asked me where we had gotten it, and I told him the master had bought it off a peddler in exchange for a meal. The idiot just kept shaking his head and saying, 'Priceless, priceless.' The master always washed his face and hands in it; I don't know what's so special about it. He stopped me as I was going out, and said, 'Sister, wait a minute. I was wondering if you could help me find someone.'

"I asked him who he was looking for, and he smiled and asked, 'Might you know of a six-fingered carpenter living in this area?' I said, 'There's a carpenter in the village, but he doesn't have six fingers.' 'Could he be in any of the neighboring towns?' he asked. I said there was someone in Xia village known for having an extra finger, but he wasn't a carpenter, and he's been dead for two years. What's he hunting a six-fingered man for?"

On the fifth day, Lilypad came downstairs and said nothing. "What's the idiot doing today?" Xiumi asked.

"He's gone," Lilypad replied. "The lamp on the table was still lit, but he wasn't there."

This was Zhang Jiyuan's first disappearance. Mother didn't seem worried, nor did she ask many questions. When Lilypad pushed her, Mother scowled and said, "His affairs are no concern of yours. If he left for a few days, he'll be back."

He reappeared a few days later at noon, startling Magpie as she coached Xiumi on her needlework. "Whose pants are these?" Xiumi heard his voice ask from behind her. She turned around and saw her own underwear in his hands. She had left them drying on the hedge the day Father disappeared and had forgotten about them. By now, heavy rain and several days of full sunlight had stiffened them into a cloth board. The sight of the idiot shaking them loose and examining them closely set Xiumi quivering with angry embarrassment, and jumping from her seat, she ran over to him, snatched the underwear from his grasp, and ran straight upstairs.

On her way up, the faint clattering of hooves drew her to a window. A team of mounted police suddenly streamed down the high road beyond the village, following the river to the west, their hurrying mounts raising huge billows of yellow dust. Xiumi watched the red tassels on their official hats flicker and undulate with the horses' gait, the tassels glistening like fresh pig's blood.

4

SHE BLED again. At first it was no more than a dark trickle, the color of a freckle, but then it deepened in color and spread in a sticky mess all over her thighs. She changed underwear twice, but it kept coming. She spent the morning lying as still as she could in bed, afraid that the slightest movement would start a flow she couldn't stanch and eventually kill her. The last two times it had happened, the bleeding had stopped after three or four days, yet now it was back in full force again, along with the feverish nights and the twisting pain that felt like someone was turning a hot iron in her gut. She didn't dare use the mirror this time; she thought she would rather die than look at that hideous, bleeding fissure once more.

She thought about dying often. If she had to die, she wanted to avoid all the traditional endings—the silk noose, the well, the bottle of poison—but she couldn't think of any better way to do it. How should her death happen? She remembered the line from a Peking opera, "May golden sands cover my face, and my limbs be scattered," and wondered what kind of death that was; she knew that when she had heard the legendary general Yang Yanhui sing it, her legs shook and her eyes welled with tears. If she must die, it should be grand. The day before, when the horsemen had thundered past the village, the sight of their red caps and tassels, shining halberds, and strong horses churning up dust had exhilarated her. She felt a similar energy surging within herself, like an untamed and restless horse, ready to bolt off to parts unknown the second she loosened the reins.

Xiumi sat up in bed to change cotton balls. The first clump was soaked with black blood. She suddenly felt like everything in the room had turned black, even the sunlight filtering through the window. She sat on the toilet for a while, then tried to work with her needle on some embroidered flowers, but a wave of irritation drove her to grab scissors from the drawer and cut the red thread into pieces.

No, this wouldn't do. She had to talk to someone.

She didn't want Mother to know, and Dr. Tang was a lost cause as well. The old dotard never spoke during his visits, except to give bad news. He took pulses, wrote prescriptions, and took his payment in silence; if he did say anything, you were probably doomed. His favorite line was "Better get the coffin ready," which he always proclaimed with a barely visible elation.

The only three people left were Baoshen, Magpie, and Lilypad. Baoshen was good-hearted and trustworthy, but he was also a man, and how could she talk to a man about such a thing? Magpie was too timid, and she had a weak head that was easily confused. Xiumi thought the problem over thoroughly, and finally went to Lilypad for help.

Lilypad's first home was Huzhou, several hundred miles southeast of Puji. Her parents had died when she was only a few years old, and after she turned eight, her uncle sold her off to a family in Hangzhou. At twelve she ran away, finding refuge in a nunnery in Wuxi. One evening, the abbess led her down to the pier to steal silk thread from the merchant boats; the last boat they boarded wouldn't let them off. It carried them all the way to Sichuan Province in the west, a journey that lasted a full two years. The abbess made the best of a bad situation by getting pregnant on board. She had twins, officially became the captain's wife, and spent the rest of her life on the water. Meanwhile, Lilypad began a more arduous journey. She was sold to five different brothels and married four times, once to a palace eunuch. By the time Lu Kan paid her indenture at the last brothel, she had traveled across more than half the country, going as far as Zhaoqing in the deep southeast.

During their years in Yangzhou together, she tried running away three times, each without success. It had become an addiction. Lu Kan frequently asked her why she tried to leave, to which she replied, "I don't know. I like trying."

When he asked her where she was running to, she said, "Doesn't matter. You figure it out as you go."

After Lu Kan lost his position, he summoned her to his study to talk. "You need not bother running off again," he told her. "I'll give you some silver and you can go where you like."

He did not expect her to protest. "So you're driving me away?" she cried.

"Isn't that what you want? You're always running off anyway."

"But I don't want to leave," Lilypad replied.

Lu Kan finally understood: she didn't want to leave, she wanted to escape.

It happened one more time after they arrived in Puji. She returned an absolute wreck a month or so later, crying, her hair matted, clothes torn, feet shoeless. Biting flies and hunger had driven her back, not far from death's door. Her legs were red and swollen, and she had lost so much weight Lu Kan could barely recognize her. After she recovered, Lu Kan came to her room with a pot of tea. All smiles, he asked, "Not going to run off again, eh?"

"No guarantees," Lilypad replied. "If I get the right chance, I'll take it."

Lu Kan spat his tea out across the room.

In the end, it was Grandma Meng who solved the problem. She told Lu Kan that there was only one way to keep Lilypad home. Immediately curious, Lu Kan asked what it was, to which she replied, "Buy yourself another serving girl."

This made no sense to Lu Kan. "We could buy two if we needed them, but that won't stop her from running."

"Think about it. She's been running since she was a child. The tighter you fence her in, the more she wants out. It's not that she doesn't like life in your house; she just can't control her feet, just like an opium smoker can't control his hands. If you cut off her drug, you'll cut out the addiction."

"How do I do that?"

"Just like I said: buy another girl," Grandma Meng responded.

"Grandma, what on earth do you mean?" Lu Kan asked again, still lost.

"Buy another girl, then tell Lilypad that you've just bought more help, and she can leave whenever she likes, you no longer depend on her. Then, every time she gets the urge to run, she'll think, 'They said I could leave whenever I wanted, and nobody will stop me, because they have other servants, so what's the point?' Think about it: Why run off if she's already gotten permission to do so? After a while, the addiction will fade."

Lu Kan nodded. Brilliant, he thought, it was brilliant. Impressive that an illiterate old lady could come up with a plan like that. He asked her right then for her help in finding a girl, preferably someone strong and obedient. If the price was right, appearance wouldn't matter, and she could bring her by at her earliest convenience.

Grandma Meng chuckled and said, "I've already got the perfect candidate for you. As far as money goes, just give what you feel is right."

Having said this, she turned and left. A few hours later, she returned with a distant relative in tow.

Xiumi remembered Magpie's arrival at the house. She stood in the antechamber with her head down, biting her lower lip and toeing the moss nervously as she held a cloth sack with all her belongings in it to her chest. Grandma Meng tried to drag her inside, but she wouldn't budge. Irritated, the old lady slapped her twice across the face. Magpie neither cried nor flinched, but she refused to move.

"You hang around the house all day, eating enough for three people, and once that old bastard finally climbs on top of you, you'll be stuck to me like wet dough. But I've put my name on the line to persuade the master here to take you into his house, and it's a good home, and you're not going to bite the hand that feeds you this time, you little bitch." She slapped her again.

When Xiumi's parents appeared from the rear courtyard, the old lady put on an ingratiating smile, now fixing Magpie's hair, now rubbing her shoulders. "Now, my dear one, remember that for you to make it into a good house like this will have your mother and father crying with joy in the underworld." Grandma Meng tiptoed over to Mother and whispered, "This child is sweet and obedient. Beat her, curse her, make her do whatever you want, but just one thing: Master and madam should avoid mentioning arsenic in front of her."

"And why is that?" Mother asked.

"Oh, it's a long story. I'll tell you when I have the time." Grandma Meng took the bag of coins from Mother's hand, jingled it by her ear, and skipped out the doorway, all aglow.

Lilypad was in the middle of her afternoon nap when Xiumi burst into her bedroom. Finding the young girl standing by her bedside, red-faced and huffing with exertion, eyes brimming with tears, gave Lilypad quite a shock. She got up immediately, lifted the child onto her bedside, and poured her a cup of tea before asking what was the matter.

"I'm gonna die!" Xiumi cried out.

Another shock. "You've been perfectly fine, how is it that you're dying?"

"Well, I'm just gonna." Xiumi grabbed one edge of a bed-curtain and worked it with both her hands. Lilypad put a palm to her forehead: it felt a little warm.

"Whatever's wrong, tell me, and I'll help you figure it out," Lilypad comforted Xiumi as she got up to close the door. Her bedroom had no windows, and shutting the door threw the whole room into darkness. "Just speak slowly," she continued. "I'm here for you, no matter what."

Xiumi made her swear she would never tell anyone else. Lilypad hesitated, but closed her eyes and swore anyway. She swore five oaths one after the other, ransoming the honor of every family member she could remember. Yet Xiumi still said nothing, and simply sat on her bed and sobbed until the front of her shirt was soaked. It occurred to Lilypad that while she, in her impatience, had cursed a full eight generations of her family, she hadn't known a single one of them since she was old enough to remember. The thought pinched her heart and brought a tear to her own eyes.

A fractured memory surfaced in Lilypad's mind: Heavy rain the day her uncle came to Huzhou to take her away. Rain on the fishpond by her front door, falling droplets roiling the water like boiling congee. So she must have lived somewhere with a fishpond. The oath had proved her wrong about her own history: though she believed she recalled nothing at all from her childhood, it reminded her that she once had a home in Huzhou with a pond out front. She could almost hear the sound of the rain. The tears welled up again.

Lilypad cried quietly, allowing herself to be washed in sorrow. Sniffing, she said, "If you don't want to tell me, that's fine. I'll guess, and if I guess right, you nod."

Xiumi looked at her, then nodded furiously. "I haven't guessed yet, what are you nodding for?" Lilypad laughed, then began guessing aimlessly. After a string of failed attempts, however, her patience began to run thin, and she asked, "Why are you here if you're not going to tell me? I'm exhausted, and my lower back is killing me."

Xiumi asked her why her back hurt—had she caught a chill outside? "Oh, no. My you-know-what's come around again."

"What do you mean by 'you-know-what'?" Xiumi asked.

"You'll find out soon enough how a woman's body works," Lilypad said with a smile. Xiumi asked her if it hurt or not. "It's not that it hurts so much, I just get so bloated, and nothing comes out when I go to the bathroom. It's very frustrating." Xiumi asked her what it was that "came around," and whether it could be cured. Now she was irritating Lilypad, who replied, "It's only blood. It goes away in four or five days, so what is there to cure? It's the one annoyance about being a woman; every month, you have to go through it."

Xiumi stopped asking questions; now she sat on the bed, counting days on her fingers. After a while, she muttered, "So, it's already been two months since the master ran away?" Then nodded to herself: "I see."

Spying a hair band lying by Lilypad's pillow, Xiumi picked it up and asked with a smile, "Where'd you get this?"

"I bought it during New Year's at a temple fair in the village. If you like it, go ahead and take it."

"I think I will!" Xiumi slid the hair band onto her head, and stood up to leave. Lilypad yanked her back. "Hey, didn't you come here to talk about something?" she asked suspiciously.

"When did I ever say that?" Xiumi smiled coyly and blushed.

"That's strange, because you were just in here crying your eyes out and screaming about dying, making me swear on every grave in my family that I wouldn't tell on you."

"I'm fine, I'm fine." Xiumi started to snicker, and waved Lilypad off with a hand. "I'm going. Go back to sleep." She slipped through the door and dashed up to her own room, where she let out a long sigh, throwing herself onto the bed and laughing into the covers until her sides nearly split. The pressure of two months' anxiety and irritation evaporated instantaneously. Her stomach didn't hurt nearly as much as before. She ladled up water to wash her face; then she rouged her cheeks and powdered her face, slipped on a new set of clothes and a red hair band, and stood in front of the mirror, smiling at herself. Filled with an inexhaustible energy, she galloped around upstairs like a newborn calf and then down, zipping outside and weaving back and forth through the courtyards and hedges. She had never felt so perfectly at ease.

Magpie was in the kitchen preparing a pig's head, plucking out hairs with a large pair of tweezers, sunlight pouring in through the window. Xiumi blew in through the kitchen door without saying hello and snatched the tweezers from Magpie's hands. "Take a break, I'll pluck for you," she said while getting down to work. "Let me do it. You'll ruin your clothes," Magpie implored her, but Xiumi pushed her away, laughing: "I like plucking pig hairs."

Magpie couldn't imagine what was going on with Xiumi that day, to make the girl actually enjoy housework. She stood by the hearthside and stared at her in dumb disbelief. Xiumi continued for a spell, then turned to Magpie to complain: "I don't care if I can't pull his whiskers out, but even his eyelashes are so slippery, I can't get a grip!" Magpie snorted with laughter. Just as she returned to the table to show Xiumi how to do it, Xiumi tossed the tweezers into the bowl. "That's enough. I guess you should do it." And in a flash, she disappeared.

Just as Xiumi began to worry she had run out of places to wander, she heard the click-clacking of an abacus. Baoshen was working in the office. One hand flicked the beads of the abacus back and forth, while he licked the index finger of the other to turn the pages of the family ledger. Xiumi grabbed the door frame and poked her head inside. He saw her and asked, "Is Miss Xiumi not taking her nap today?"

Xiumi marched into the room without replying and sat down in a chair opposite him. She stared at him for a long while, then inquired, "Can you see what's written in the ledger with your head all cockeyed like that?"

"My head may be cockeyed, but my eyes see straight," he responded.

"What would happen if you tried pushing it straight?"

Baoshen raised a querulous eye, as if to ask where she got such a strange idea. He shook his cockeyed head, and replied, "So even the young miss is teasing me now? My head grew this way, you think it can be set straight again?"

"I'm gonna try it," Xiumi said. Circling around behind Baoshen, she grabbed his head in her arms and tried to wrench it over a couple of times. "It really won't straighten," she murmured to herself. "Baoshen, stop doing the books. Teach me how to use an abacus."

"What do you want to learn that for? How many girls have you ever seen using an abacus?" Xiumi sensed Baoshen's unwillingness, so she grabbed the abacus and shook it, causing him to yelp in surprise and frustration: "I had that all added, and now it's a mess!" She merely giggled.

Seeing that Xiumi had no intention of leaving immediately, Baoshen picked up his pipe and lit it. "Well then, young miss, you can give me some advice. I have a question for you."

Xiumi asked him what was up. Baoshen told her he was planning a trip back home to Qinggang to fetch his son. "Tiggie's already four years old. His mother can't get out of bed, and I worry he'll run off and fall in the fishpond. I'd like to bring him back here, but I fear your mother won't allow it."

"Go get him; it will be fine," Xiumi said with careless surety, as if she had already asked Mother, who had already agreed. Moments later, Xiumi seemed to have another thought, and asked, "What's your son's name again?"

"His mom likes to call him Tiger; I call him Tiggie."

"Is his head all cockeyed too?"

What has this girl had for breakfast, thought Baoshen, *that has her skipping naps and tormenting me like this?* He held back his impatience and irritation, and merely chuckled drily, "No, it isn't. It isn't cockeyed at all."

Xiumi left Baoshen in the office and made her way into the skywell, where she slid herself down the door frame and sat on the stepstone before the threshold. Looking through the far door, she could see a woman washing clothes in the courtyard pond. The repeated drumming of her wooden pestle echoed loudly in the empty skywell. A field of cotton plants, fully grown, tall and oily black, stretched down to the river; an occasional wind lifted their leaves to expose the white cotton bells. Not a single person moved in the field. A few sparrows bickered underneath the eaves, while moss grew in a thick carpet of verdant green along the walls. The powerful heat of the summer sun, together with the cool breeze that touched Xiumi's cheeks, was wonderfully delicious. She sat there for a long while, looking out in every direction, thinking of unrelated and irrelevant things.

5

IN THE morning, Mother reminded Xiumi that she had not been to see her tutor in the two months since her father ran away. Mr. Ding had come by the previous night to say that he wouldn't take money for not working, and he would return every penny the family had paid him if he had to.

"You're not doing anything just sitting at home. You might as well go back there, read a few books, and learn some new words. It will be good for you."

Xiumi had hoped that the mess caused by Father's disappearance would mean she wouldn't have to go back to Ding Shuze's classroom again. His memory proved sharper than she expected; he had sent people by two or three times by then to summon her. But now she was hearing it from Mother, and there was nothing for her to do but excuse herself from breakfast and prepare for her walk to Ding Shuze's estate.

Decades of study had never earned Ding Shuze an imperial posting—indeed, never even gotten him through the lowest level of the civil service exam. As he grew old, he set up a private classroom and admitted students, from whom he accepted a modest tuition to defray household expenses. Yet only a handful of families sent him pupils—not because the rest couldn't afford his tuition, but because they couldn't bear to let him beat their children. Ding Shuze's pedagogy was strict and unforgiving: improperly reciting one character earned the student ten strokes of the cane on the buttocks, and miswriting a character earned him twenty strokes, while even the student who spoke, wrote, and recited perfectly was hit because, in Mr. Ding's words, it would freshen his memory and remind him not to make mistakes in the future. During Xiumi's first day of school, she noticed several students studying standing up; upon further inquiry, she discovered that their behinds were too swollen to sit. Meanwhile, any boy who was turning pages with his lips most certainly had had all ten fingers caned stiff.

Mr. Ding never caned Xiumi, not because she was an excellent student but because she was the only girl in his school. Not only did he never beat her, he bent another rule and allowed her to eat snacks while she read. She still didn't like him. His stale breath, which reeked of garlic, was unbearable. She feared his guided readings, because every time he came to a word beginning with "t" or "d," little flecks of spit would shower onto your face. He liked touching her head, and sometimes even her face, with his dirty hands. She always turned her head to the other side whenever he neared her, sometimes turning so far that her neck cracked.

Ding Shuze loved sticking his nose into other people's business, especially when it involved an argument. He inserted himself into every single village affair he could uncover, save childbirth. His favorite endeavor was helping villagers solve legal disputes, yet every lawsuit he ever touched inevitably ended with a loss. Eventually, everyone in the village treated him like a useless bookworm; only his wife thought him a genius. Whenever a fight between him and anyone else came to an impasse, with both parties holding their own positions, Zhao Xiaofeng would strut in between them, with her floral handkerchief in hand and a smile on her face, and say, "Stop fighting! Stop yelling! Each of you make your case, and I'll be the judge." After each side had presented its argument, her reply would be, "You"—her husband—"are right, and you"—anyone other than her husband—"are wrong. We're done!"

The first thing Xiumi noticed upon entering Ding Shuze's classroom was the heavy bandage covering her teacher's right hand and his expression of intense pain. When she asked, "What happened to your hand, sir?" his face twitched violently at the question, then reddened. He replied with a smile that was not a smile, as he alternated low moans with a sharp sucking of air through his teeth. The injury was clearly quite serious. Just as Xiumi turned to ask Zhao Xiaofeng, Ding Shuze frowned and commanded, "Recite 'The Righteous Minister Refuses to Serve the First Emperor'! Whatever you wanted to ask, forget about it."

Xiumi sat down to recite, but memory carried her only to the end of the first paragraph. Ding Shuze called on her to recite the *Book of Odes* instead, but when she asked him which ode he'd like to hear, his constitution seemed to fail him. He simply stood up, held his right hand over his head, and draped his left arm over his wife's shoulder as she helped him back to his room. A puzzled Xiumi looked around the room for answers. Spying a young boy with a tuft of fair hair atop his head copying large characters at his desk, she went to him and whispered, "What happened to Teacher's hand?"

The boy, who was the youngest son of the ferryman Tan Shuijin, Tan Si, looked around to make sure no one else was listening before he replied, "He smacked it on a nail."

"What would he do that for?" Xiumi asked.

Fair-haired Tan Si snorted. "Dummies do dumb things, I guess."

When he wasn't teaching, Ding Shuze loved catching all kinds of flying insects. In time, he got so good at it that he could nab anything that flew—mosquito, moth, or housefly—right out of the air on his first try. If his target landed on a wall, he would simply smack it with his open palm; he never missed. Any six-legged creature that flew into his house was doomed. But the clay pot breaks beside the well, and generals die on the battlefield, so they say, and even the best are bound to make mistakes.

"A fly made it through the window this morning, and Teacher couldn't get it. I think his eyes are getting worse with age. But he got really aggravated looking all over the room for the fly. Then he spied it on the wall and slammed it with his hand as hard as he could. But guess what? It wasn't a fly, it was one of the big nails sticking out of the wall! It took him forever to pull his hand off the nail, the whole time howling with pain." Tan Si collapsed on his desk in a paroxysm of laughter. Xiumi laughed along with him for a while, but threw him a warning glance when she caught sight of Ding Shuze coming back through the skywell.

Her teacher wanted more recitation. She recited from the *Book of Odes* and the abridged *Comprehensive History* while Ding Shuze lay back in his rattan chair, whimpering and sucking his teeth, his heavy stomach rising up and down. Xiumi accidentally giggled. Ding Shuze frowned and asked her what she was laughing at, but Xiumi merely rolled her eyes at him. There was nothing he could say or do.

"Enough, enough, enough." Ding Shuze sat up in his rattan chair and looked over to the fair-haired boy, who was suppressing more giggles with all his strength. "Tan Si, come over here." Hearing his name called, Fair-Hair slid out of his chair and stood before his teacher. "You too," the teacher said to Xiumi.

Reaching into his inner pocket, Ding Shuze produced a letter, which he handed to Xiumi. "I need the two of you to take this letter to Xia village for me. You both know the way to Xia village, yes?" The two children nodded. Xia village wasn't far from Puji; Xiumi went to market days there with Lilypad.

Having just put the letter into Xiumi's hands, Ding Shuze took it back. The envelope hadn't been sealed yet; Ding Shuze blew the flap open and plucked out the contents with his good hand. He read the letter front to back one more time, nodding as he went, before returning it to the envelope and handing it again to Xiumi.

"Head east on the main road at the west end of Puji and go straight until the road curves hard. At the end of the curve you should be able to see Xia village. When you get to the village entrance, you'll see a pond with a burial mound like an island in the middle of it, covered in grass and reeds and whatever. But look past that to the three willow trees growing on the other side of the pond; the door that faces the middle tree belongs to the Xue family. I want you to give the letter to Master Xue personally. If he's not there, do not give it to anyone else, just bring it back here. Do not forget. Tan Si likes horsing around and getting into trouble, so Xiumi, you need to watch him: don't let him go play in the river. If the master wants to write a reply, just wait and then bring it back to me. If he doesn't, that's fine, just come straight back here."

Just as Ding Shuze finished his instructions, another thought crossed his mind and he asked Xiumi, "After I read that letter a second time, did I put it back in the envelope?"

"You did," Xiumi replied.

"I put it back?" Ding Shuze asked again.

"I saw you put it in. Do you want to check for yourself?" She handed it over. Ding Shuze pinched the envelope and peered inside before finally relinquishing it to Xiumi.

Xiumi led Tan Si eastward, along the avenue by the river. "This letter must be important," Tan Si said. "I saw the teacher writing it this morning. He put it in the envelope and took it out to read again four or five times."

Xiumi asked Tan Si if he had ever met Master Xue. Tan Si said he'd seen him twice at Ding Shuze's house. He was a rich man, and had a big mole on his face.

The first half of their route took them past the big temple at the eastern end of the village.* It had fallen almost completely in ruin; its grand hall sat like a half-plucked chicken, black rafters exposed beneath a scant patchwork of broken roof tiles. Only the side chambers were still habitable. Xiumi remembered stepping inside once with Lilypad on the way home from market day to get out of the rain. An outdoor stage made of earth once stood in the front of the temple, but no opera had been performed there for many years, the stage

---

*Black Dragon Temple: First built in 1621. Local legend states that in the days of the temple's construction, a huge black dragon appeared in the southwest corner of the temple grounds, lingering for three days. A lightning strike and resulting fire in 1842 significantly damaged the structure. Converted to a private school in the Republican period, it was rebuilt fully in 1934. In 1957, it became the Puji Primary School. In 1987, it was restored to its original state, and its name changed to Lasting Grace Temple.

overgrown with grass and weeds. No one had bothered with the temple for ages, and only beggars and itinerant monks found shelter beneath its roof. When locals wanted to burn incense or pray to Buddha, they went across the river.

Xiumi and Tan Si arrived at Xia village around noon. Just as their teacher had said, they found the pond, with three large willow trees on its opposite bank. Master Xue's front door was shut and didn't swing open when pushed, indicating the door bar was down. Tan Si knocked, but no one responded. Xiumi put an ear to the door and could hear the sound of voices though couldn't quite make out the conversation. She turned around and noticed someone in a wide felt hat fishing beside the pond. At the sound of knocking, the figure bent down and turned to look toward them, but when Xiumi tugged on Tan Si's sleeve and pointed to the pond, the figure ducked down into the weeds and disappeared.

Tan Si beat on the door several times and even yelled inside without eliciting any response. "Let's just slip the letter under the door and be done with it," he told Xiumi.

"That's no good, Mr. Ding told us to give it to the master in person."

"The door bar is down, so someone has to be home. How come nobody's answering?" Tan Si put his face to the door frame to peer inside. Suddenly he tumbled back, and sat right down with a surprised *Ai-ya!*

The door opened—not completely, just enough for a robed servant to lean out and look at them. "Who are you?"

"You scared me, you scared me!" Tan Si sat on the doorstep and wailed.

"We're looking for Master Xue," Xiumi replied.

"Where are you from?"

"Puji." Xiumi turned once more toward the pond. The fisherman was still there, crouched down, hat pulled low, but clearly staring through the reeds in their direction. In the bright light of the summer sun, Xiumi could see that he had a noticeable hunch to his back.

The servant looked them over carefully before saying in a low voice, "Follow me."

The outer door gave way to an extremely narrow vestibule with walls reaching so high they shrouded the interior in heavy shadow. A second door at the far end led to the courtyard itself, where the inhabitants resided. No wonder they had knocked for so long without anyone hearing.

Entering the courtyard, Xiumi saw two horses, one white and one chestnut, swinging their tails lazily beneath the tall locust tree to which they were tethered. The warm, sharp smell of fresh horse manure lingered in the air. There must have been several guests, as Xiumi could hear a commotion of voices from inside that sounded like an argument. They passed through the open skywell and reception room into a large rear courtyard, in the southwest corner of which stood an open pavilion that was packed with people. The servant stopped them beneath the corridor on one side of the courtyard, and told them to wait while he informed the master of their arrival. The servant's voice was soft and imploring like a woman's, though he was a man.

Once the servant left, Xiumi turned to Tan Si. "Why did you scream like that? You scared me to death."

"I was peering through the door and I didn't expect that idiot to be standing right there. His face got so close to mine that our eyelashes almost touched. Wouldn't you have been scared?"

Xiumi's gaze suddenly changed direction, and her expression darkened. "What's *he* doing here?"

"Who?" Tan Si asked, looking quizzically at Xiumi. Xiumi's face had gone from green to pale, and her jaw began clenching involuntarily as she shrank back. She said nothing but tugged insistently on Tan Si's sleeve. Looking across the courtyard, he realized she was referring to one of the three men who had emerged from the pavilion walking toward them. The servant was leading the way for a powerfully built man with a large black mole next to his eyebrow and Zhang Jiyuan, who was holding a teacup and saucer. The three men stopped in front of the children, and Master Xue addressed them in a booming voice: "What business do you have with me?"

A stupefied Xiumi pulled out her teacher's letter with a quivering hand, and passed it to Tan Si, who delivered it to the men. Xiumi never even looked up.

Master Xue took the envelope and looked at it with an annoyed expression. "It's this Ding Shuze again." He tore the envelope open and stepped into the sunlight to read the letter.

Zhang Jiyuan moved to Xiumi's side and placed a hand on her shoulder. "I'm here visiting friends," he said in a soft voice. "I didn't expect I would run into you; what a surprise."

Xiumi's heart pounded, and an awful nervous sensation filled her shoulder. She didn't dare look up at him, though her heart quietly screamed, *Get it off! Take your filthy hand off!* She wanted to squirm away, but her feet weren't listening to her. Her shivering grew more intense.

Finally, Zhang Jiyuan removed his hand. His body smelled faintly of tobacco. His cup and saucer clinked as he drank his tea. Moments later she heard him chuckle. Then he lowered his face to her ear and whispered, "Look at how frightened you are. Don't be scared, Mr. Xue and I go way back. We have some things to talk about."

Xiumi ignored him. His hot breath made her ears itch. She noticed that several people inside the pavilion were leaning against a pillar and talking in low voices. A pear tree next to the pavilion had been recently felled.

Finishing the letter, Master Xue laughed. "Ding Shuze. The old cur won't leave me alone."

"Let me guess, he wants you to help him find a post to fill in the capital?" Zhang Jiyuan asked.

"You got it. He keeps going on about how he was blood brothers with my father, then waxes poetic. But when I asked my father about it, he said he had never heard of the man." The master snorted again. "Unreadable crap."

"Little does he know that yesterday's imperial historian is tomorrow's target practice. He's really picked a great time to get in on the action," Zhang Jiyuan replied derisively.

"No doubt about it. And the man's over seventy—is it really worth it for him?" Master Xue pondered. Turning to Tan Si, he said, "Go back and tell Mr. Ding that I've received his letter, and will call on him personally at a later date." Then he cast a searching look at Xiumi and at Zhang Jiyuan. "Since your niece is here, why don't we let them rest awhile, and they can stay for lunch."

"My niece doesn't leave the house often," Zhang Jiyuan replied, "and I believe that seeing me here so suddenly has given her a bit of a shock. Why don't we let them return home posthaste."

"That's fine too."

The same servant showed them out. As they stepped through the skywell, they heard Master Xue and Zhang Jiyuan burst into laughter. Though she had no idea what the two of them might be laughing about, she could tell from their sniggering that it was something despicable. She hated him so much, she could taste it. Tan Si started peppering her with questions: Where had her uncle come from? How come he'd never seen him in Puji? Why was he here? If he was her uncle, why was she so frightened? Xiumi marched forward, head down, saying nothing, through the shadowy hallway and into the blazing sun outside. The servant mumbled, "Forgive me if I lead you no further," and slammed the door.

The area outside was completely deserted; even the old fisherman across the pond had disappeared. Tan Si asked, "Why would they bury a dead person out in the middle of a pond?" Xiumi knew he was talking about the mound in the middle of the pond, but the subject had already lost interest for her. She pushed his arm and pointed toward the water. "Did you see anyone out there fishing just a while ago?"

The fair-haired boy said he hadn't.

"He was just over there fishing when we arrived. Where did he go?"

"He probably went home to eat. Why do you care when he goes fishing?"

They circled around to the side of the pond where the fisherman had been. Through the reeds, Xiumi caught sight of a bamboo pole floating in the water, a light wind turning it slowly in the pond. She reached down and fished it out, only to discover that it was nothing more than the pole itself without line or hook.

Tan Si was pestering her to go; his stomach growled audibly. The two of them set off homeward, one following the other. Xiumi couldn't help but feel she was in the middle of a waking dream. Where had Zhang Jiyuan come from, and what had brought him to Puji? And who exactly was Master Xue? And the old man in the felt hat, crouching by the pond and pretending to fish without a line or hook?

She began to suspect that beyond the ostentation of her own house stretched an entirely different world, a silent world so large it had no end to it. They met no one on the road home. The sky looked higher and vaster than it ever had before, and the ditches, gullies, knolls, river currents, and even sunlight seemed like mirages.

Arriving back in Puji, Xiumi sent Fair-Hair back to Mr. Ding's place to deliver Master Xue's reply, while she herself went straight home. Seeing Lilypad washing mosquito nettings by the pond, Xiumi approached her, and asked, "Hey, Bigmouth, do you know if there's really a Master Xue in Xia village?"

"You mean Xue Zuyan? Of course. His dad is some high official in the capital," Lilypad replied.

Xiumi gave an absentminded "Oh" and headed upstairs to her room.

6

ONE EVENING at dinner, Zhang Jiyuan decided to tell his "three-legged chicken" joke one more time. Although he had told it just a few days earlier, he launched into the encore with enthusiasm, leaving most of the table in stitches. Magpie laughed because she really thought the joke was funny; Zhang Jiyuan could tell it fifty times, and it would still make her titter so hard her teeth would clink on her rice bowl. Mother laughed out of politeness, chuckling audibly a couple of times to indicate she was paying attention. Lilypad was most likely laughing at Magpie, and the fact that a dried-up old joke everyone in the village knew by heart could still amuse her. Baoshen laughed because he was good-natured, and laughed with everyone; besides, he was leaving the following morning to pick up his son at Qinggang. Still, his laughter sounded a bit forced.

Only Xiumi didn't laugh.

Zhang Jiyuan winked at her several times as he told his joke. His gaze was hard to read; it felt as if he sought some kind of understanding about their meeting that morning, or recognition of a commonly held secret. Though she kept her head down, Xiumi felt the glitter of his eyes, as though they were communicating in a language of their own that floated out from behind wet eyelids and hung midair in the evening light. With her eyes on her food, she endured Zhang Jiyuan's joke to the very end, when a confused Magpie blurted out, "But how could the chicken have three legs?" The table exploded with laughter again; she obviously still didn't get it.

Baoshen finished his dinner first. He set down his bowl and chopsticks, straightened his cuffs, and excused himself. Lilypad looked over to Mother and said, "You shouldn't have given him his travel money so early. You know he's just going to throw it down that bottomless pit behind the village."

"How do you know he's going to Miss Sun's?" Mother asked.

"Hah. That little kitten came by this morning to borrow a bamboo sieve. I saw them in the hallway, hands all over each other like they were right about to—"

Mother stopped Lilypad with a look, and then glanced at Xiumi, as if to determine whether or not the girl understood what they were talking about.

After Zhang Jiyuan finished, he sat back and didn't move, as usual. He cleaned his teeth with a toothpick, then cleaned his nails, and after he had dug under all ten of them, he put the toothpick in his mouth again. He fiddled with the lamp and stared through the skylight, as if he had something on his mind. Finally, he pulled his pipe and tobacco tin from his pocket, filled the bowl, lit it by the lamp flame, and started puffing away.

From out of nowhere, Grandma Meng burst into the kitchen, looking for Baoshen. "He can't play mahjong tonight," Lilypad said, laughing. "He's got another woman on his arm."

"Perfect," Grandma Meng replied. "Baoshen is the worst. He wins a few pennies, and then starts humming. It drives you so crazy, you lose even more!" She began pestering Mother to join her. Unable to fend off Grandma Meng's entreaties, Mother said, "Fine. I'll play a few rounds with you tonight." Before she left, she ordered Magpie and Lilypad to put bamboo screens on top of all the mattresses.

"That's the thing to do," Grandma Meng added. "You'll need those to sleep on, after a hot day like today." She dragged Mother away.

With Mother gone, Lilypad was in charge. She sent Magpie off to boil water to disinfect the screens; the bamboo would probably be wormy after a year of no use. Xiumi asked Magpie to add a little more water so she could wash her hair. "You wash your hair in the evening, you may never get married," Lilypad warned.

"Good. I don't want to get married!"

Lilypad laughed. "Men who don't want whores and women who don't want husbands are the biggest liars in the world, they say."

Xiumi replied that she wasn't getting married in any case, not to anyone. At this, Zhang Jiyuan pulled his pipe out of his mouth and interrupted, "In the future, you may not have to marry at all."

Lilypad reacted to this first with surprise, then with laughter. "That sounds easy enough, Uncle, but what's a girl to do who doesn't marry? Are Mom and Dad going to cook her for dinner?"

"You wouldn't understand," Zhang Jiyuan replied dismissively.

"We're all country bumpkins out here, and we haven't seen the world like you have," Lilypad teased. "But if all the women in this world stopped marrying and having children, everyone would be dead eventually."

"Who said anything about not having children? Of course you'd have children, you just wouldn't need to get married," was Zhang Jiyuan's officious response.

"Without marriage, where will you get the kids from? Under rocks?"

"Whenever you see someone you like, you visit them and have children, and that's it," Zhang Jiyuan replied.

"You're saying that whenever a man sees a girl he likes, he can just go over to her house and be with her?"

"Exactly."

"Without matchmakers and dowries? Or talking it over with her parents first?"

"Exactly."

"And what would you do if the parents don't agree? If they lock the door and don't let you in?"

"Well, that's easy; you just kill them."

Lilypad couldn't believe her ears. Zhang Jiyuan said crazy things all the time, but Lilypad couldn't tell if he was being serious or just having fun with her.

"What if the girl doesn't agree?"

"Kill them anyway," Zhang Jiyuan replied without hesitation.

"What if...what if three guys all want the same woman? What will you do then?"

"Simple: You draw straws to see who gets her," Zhang Jiyuan replied with a mischievous giggle. He got up from his chair to leave. "In the society of the future, everyone will be equal, and everyone will be free. Anyone will be able to get together with anyone else. As long as you're willing to, you could even marry your own sister."

"If that's how it goes, it'll turn Puji into one big whorehouse, won't it?"

"Sounds about right," Zhang Jiyuan said. "With only one difference: Nobody will ever need to pay."

"You're quite the pistol, Uncle. Sounds like you men would have a grand time then," Lilypad needled him.

"Wouldn't you too?" Zhang Jiyuan laughed out loud, laughed so hard he made himself gasp. Then he ran his fingers through his hair, turned on his heels, and left.

"What a load of bullshit," Lilypad spat after he had gone. "The bearded little troll doesn't have an honest thought in his head. He lies around all day with nothing to do, so he makes fun of us."

Lilypad washed Xiumi's hair for her beside the stove.

The tofu slurry she used had come from the seller's that morning and was already turning a little sour. Xiumi complained that it was sticky and smelled like moldy beans, and it didn't get rid of itching as well as wolfberry leaves. "And where am I going to get wolfberry leaves for you?" Lilypad asked her. The two were going back and forth when the sound of urgent speech and hurried footsteps came from outside the estate walls, sounding like crowds of people running through the alleys, past the pond, and through the trees. The commotion intensified until it whirled around them on all sides, then faded again.

"Uh-oh. Sounds like something bad has happened." Lilypad left Xiumi to peer out the window.

Xiumi's hair was heavy with water and slurry. She could hear it dripping from her hair into the basin below. Minutes later, Magpie appeared by the kitchen door, agitated and short of breath. "Something's happened!"

Lilypad asked her what it was:

"She's dead!"

Lilypad asked who "she" was:

"Miss Sun! Miss Sun is dead!"

"How can she be dead?! She was here just this afternoon borrowing a sieve, as bubbly as ever." Lilypad flicked the water from her fingers and ran out the door with Magpie.

The estate fell totally silent. The chunks of tofu in Xiumi's hair plopped into the basin below, where they floated on the surface for a moment before bursting with a soft *pop*. She closed her eyes and felt around on the stovetop for the ladle so she could scoop some water to rinse with. She heard the regular beat of approaching footsteps, and someone entering the kitchen. Her heart sank.

"What happened outside?" Zhang Jiyuan asked, leaning on the door frame.

Son of a bitch, of course it had to be him. Xiumi didn't dare look directly at him, and stammered, "They said . . . they said Miss Sun is dead."

Zhang Jiyuan replied with a faint "Oh," as if nothing could have been less interesting. He continued to stand there.

Go away, go away, go away now! Xiumi screamed at him with her mind's voice. Not only did he not leave, he stepped into the kitchen toward her. "Washing your hair?" he asked.

Xiumi managed a "Mm-hmm" through her anger. Catching hold of the ladle, she took a full scoop of cold water and poured it directly over her head and neck.

"Do you want some help?"

"No, no, that's fine." Hearing him say things like this made her heart beat even harder. It was the first time she had spoken to him alone.

"Don't you want some hot water?" he asked in a dry, rasping voice.

Xiumi paid no attention to him. She knew he was standing right behind her because she could see his white socks and cloth shoes. *Son of a bitch, he's watching me wash my hair. Disgusting! What's he hanging around here for?*

Xiumi finished rinsing, and began to cast around for her towel. Zhang Jiyuan reached out to pass it to her, but she wouldn't take it from him. Spying a dirty dishrag by the stove, she snatched it and rubbed it over her head a few times, ignoring the grease, and curled her hair into a bun. She did all this with her back to Zhang Jiyuan, as if expressly waiting for him to leave.

At long last, Zhang Jiyuan laughed derisively, shook his head, and walked off.

Xiumi breathed out a long sigh. She watched the thin figure pass through the skywell, waver in the shadows of the eaves, and disappear. Still standing by the stove, she shook her hair back out to let the southern breeze blow through it. Her cheeks still burned. Ripples on the water shivered the thin sickle of a new moon reflected in the basin.

Lilypad and Magpie came home with Mother, who said she had just finished a round of mahjong at Grandma Meng's place when she heard the news about Miss Sun. She noted, "Baoshen even had the nerve to cry out loud in front of all those people."

"How did Miss Sun die?" Xiumi asked her.

But Mother wouldn't give her a straight answer; she said she was dead, and that was all there was to it. Xiumi asked Magpie the same question, but Magpie wasn't about to say more than her mistress, and all she would do was mumble incoherently and exclaim, "It's horrible. Just horrible." Eventually, Lilypad pulled Xiumi into her boudoir, and whispered, "You and I have to be more careful in the future, there's a criminal on the loose in Puji."

"Didn't she just stop by this morning to borrow a sieve?" Xiumi asked. "How can she be dead now?"

"She came for the sieve to collect rapeseeds. If she hadn't gone out later, she wouldn't have died."

Lilypad told her that Miss Sun had ventured into her family's fields behind the village to harvest rapeseed and hadn't come home by nightfall. When Baoshen went out to look for her, he ran into her father, who had already gone out with a carriage lantern to try to find his daughter. The two of them searched the fields together, where they discovered the corpse—stripped naked, her mouth stuffed full of weeds, presumably to keep her from screaming. The weeds were pushed far into her mouth, to the back of her throat, and Baoshen couldn't clear everything out with his fingers. No knife wounds could be found on her body; her hands were tied behind her back. One foot still had a shoe on it, while the other was bare. She wasn't breathing—her body had long gone cold. She had gouged out a shallow hole in the earth with her heels. Blood covered her thighs. Doctor Tang performed an autopsy, and also found no lacerations on her body. Grandma Meng swore the killer wasn't local. Everyone in the village knew she took in any interested parties; anyone who wanted to top her could just give her father a few strings of cash at the door, and even if you didn't have money, he would let you in on credit.

"A local wouldn't go to so much trouble," she said. Hearing this, another onlooker—the local butcher, nicknamed Yellowtooth—blurted out rather simplemindedly, "Well, I'm not so sure about that."

"Unless you were the one who did it," Grandma Meng snapped at him.

"You never know, maybe I was . . ." Yellowtooth giggled, until his blind mother slapped him across the face. "Somebody's just died, and you're making jokes?"

"Maybe it was Yellowtooth who did it, don't you think?" Xiumi asked.

"Would you really believe a stupid joke like that?" Lilypad replied.

Xiumi asked why Baoshen hadn't come home yet. "He's helping Old Man Sun put up the funeral tent. Cockeye's spent a pretty penny on Miss Sun over the years. And now his kitten's dead, and he just can't stop crying." Xiumi asked why they needed to put up a tent. "That's the custom in Puji," Lilypad replied. When somebody dies outdoors, they don't bring the body into the house, so you have to set up a tent outside to shelter it. With the hot weather, I'm sure they're going to have to wake the carpenter up to make the coffin as soon as possible. It'll keep the cockeyed bastard busy for a while. It's just a pity the poor tramp had to die like that, her naked body tossed in the field. Old Man Sun nearly went insane, screaming about his daughter still being unmarried and that men shouldn't be gawking at her naked body. He kept trying to push them away from the crime scene, but there was no way around it, so he just sat down by the pond and cried."

Xiumi remembered standing beside the pond the day Father left, and how the honeysuckle dangled above the water like a curtain. She remembered Miss Sun's timid smile after Lilypad scolded her and Baoshen that afternoon, when she had come for the sieve.

"You and I need to keep a careful eye out in the future. They say a band of robbers have shown up not far from here. They kidnapped a couple of kids just a few days ago."

7

XIUMI brought up the rear of Miss Sun's funeral procession. Grandma Meng was handing out yellow flowers made of cloth from a basket for guests to pin onto their clothing. She gave out her last flower just before she got to Xiumi. "What bad luck!" Grandma Meng laughed. "I'm just short the one."

Xiumi caught sight of a regiment of imperial troops marching on the far side of the river. The soldiers looked exhausted and half-asleep, moving sluggishly under the noonday sun. Hooves kicked up huge clouds of dust, and the riders' red tassels bounced with the horses' gait. Their column slid past the low hills in the distance like a snake through water. Yet she couldn't hear the sound of the horses.

She looked around for Magpie and Lilypad to no avail. Miss Sun's coffin looked like the overnight job it was: unpainted white pine boards with a simple silk brocade shawl draped over the top. She could see the monks carrying the large ceremonial flowers, hammering cymbals, and playing other instruments, but no sounds reached her ears.

Strange. Why couldn't she hear anything?

The funeral procession passed through fields of cotton and headed east. As they left the village, dark clouds rolled in, a strong wind picked up, and the heavens opened. Raindrops falling on the thick dust of the roads made no sound; raindrops on the river transformed the water into a current of white flowers like chipped jade. The rain intensified, finally becoming so heavy Xiumi could barely open her eyes.

What was going on? How could such a downpour fall so silently?

Murmurs of unrest spread through the crowd. She saw the pall-bearers set down the coffin atop a stone bridge and scurry underneath the bridge to get out of the rain. The rest of the crowd dispersed like a retreating tidal wave. Baoshen and Old Man Sun in their hempen funeral robes and white hats tried to herd the crowd back together, their faces masks of bitter pain.

Xiumi began to run toward the old temple at the eastern end of the village, looking back several times as she ran. At first, she was among a group of people running in the same direction, but she soon realized that the others had disappeared, leaving her alone. By the time she arrived, gasping for breath, at the gate of Black Dragon Temple, she could see only the coffin still lying on top of the bridge. All the people, Baoshen and Old Man Sun included, had vanished.

Strange! How come no one else retreated to the temple?

Hurrying around to the rear gate, she found Zhang Jiyuan standing under the eaves, clutching a coil of rope and smiling at her.

"What are you doing here?" Xiumi started, covering her shirt with both hands. Her breasts hurt, and she felt slippery and exposed, as the rain on her new summer outfit had plastered the cloth right to her skin.

"I came to hear the abbot lecture on the sutras," Zhang Jiyuan replied in a low voice. Water had matted his hair into soaking locks.

"Why don't the funeral attendants come here to get out of the rain?" Xiumi asked.

"They can't come in."

"Why not?"

"The abbot won't allow them." Zhang Jiyuan peered outside, then bent down until he was right by her ear. "Because this temple was built especially for you."

"Who's the abbot?" Xiumi looked over at the Heavenly King pavilion: its roof tiles clattered in the storm, and a layer of fog already enveloped the exposed timbers.

"He's reciting sutras in the lecture hall," Zhang Jiyuan told her.

"This ramshackle temple hasn't had monks in it for years. How could there be an abbot now?"

"Come with me."

Xiumi obediently followed Zhang Jiyuan along a covered walkway toward the lecture hall. On the way, she passed broken and empty structures: the Heavenly King pavilion, the monks' dormitories, the ancestral garden pavilion, the Medicine Buddha pavilion, the Kuanyin pavilion, the kitchen and administration offices—everything was deserted, while the roof of the Kuanyin temple had already collapsed, walls tilted precariously, and what tiled roofs remained were covered in weeds. Moss, too, had conquered the walls, and yellow flowers bloomed from cracks in the stone. Xiumi caught the scent of snowbell resin and African arrowroot mixed with the heavy odor of earth and rainwater, and, of course, the air of tobacco smoke that floated around Zhang Jiyuan.

To her surprise, the lecture hall and the library were clean and in good condition. Arriving inside, they found the abbot, dressed in a red-and-yellow *kasya* robe, sitting in the lotus position and reciting sutras. Seeing them enter, he put his hands together in a gesture of welcome, then stood up. Xiumi, confused, wasn't sure how to reply to his greeting, and heard him ask, "Is this her?"

Zhang Jiyuan nodded. "It is."

"*Amitabha!*"

Xiumi felt like she had seen this abbot before somewhere, but she couldn't remember where. Slowly he clicked his heavy wooden prayer beads and chanted, occasionally raising his eyes to examine her. Completely at a loss, Xiumi simply stood and stared back at him. Then she noticed something—a pink and flaccid appendage that hung like a small sausage by the abbot's left hand. Fear followed recognition, and she opened her mouth to scream, but no sound emerged. So the six-fingered man her uncle was looking for had been hiding in the temple all along!

The abbot gave a barking laugh that made his face swell. "Jiyuan, since you've brought her here, what are we waiting for?"

"What are you going to do to me?"

"Don't be afraid, my pet," the abbot said. "No one comes into this life for no reason. We each have our own important mission to fulfill."

"What's my mission?"

"You will understand presently." The abbot's face creased with a brief but sinister smile.

Xiumi's entire body tightened as she came to realize the danger of her situation. She ran around the lecture hall searching for a door, knocking over the oil lamp on the incense table as she did so, but there was no way out. The two men merely watched her and laughed.

"Tell me where the door is!" Xiumi shouted at her uncle with imploring eyes.

Zhang Jiyuan grabbed her with one hand and pulled her close. His hand ran up her thigh, and he put his lips to her ear: "Little sister, the door is right here." As he spoke, he wrapped his rope around her wrists. When she felt her uncle tighten the rope, Xiumi gathered all her energy and screamed, "*Don't tie me up!*"

This time, she heard her own voice, followed immediately by a reply.

"Who's tying you up?"

Xiumi opened her eyes. Sunlight poured silently through the skylight above her. The parted mosquito netting around her bed smelled faintly of incense. An upset oil lamp lay on the floor by her bedside. She heard a sharp tinkling sound: Magpie was sweeping up broken glass. It had all been a dream.

"So who's tying you up?" Magpie giggled. "I came to call you for breakfast; you knocked the lamp right off the table."

Still breathing hard, Xiumi turned to the table. A stick of snowbell incense had almost burned out.

"How could I have dreamed all that?" she asked herself, still unsettled. "Nearly frightened me to death."

Magpie just giggled. After a while, she said, "You should go downstairs and have some breakfast. Then I'll take you to Miss Sun's place to watch the Land and Water alms ceremony."

Xiumi asked if Mother and Lilypad were going. Magpie said that they had left ages ago. Xiumi asked about Zhang Jiyuan. Saying his name made her chest tighten. Magpie replied that he was in the rear courtyard doing heaven knows what. Xiumi stared blankly into the folds of the mosquito canopy above her. After a long pause, she told Magpie that she didn't care about the alms ceremony, nor did she want breakfast; she would rather lie in bed for a while. Magpie closed the mosquito net for her and went downstairs.

Right after she left, Xiumi heard the song of a street vendor selling gardenias. A sudden impulse to buy a flower to wear got her out of bed, but by the time she had dressed and made it out into the alley, the flower seller was gone. She went back inside and retrieved some water from the well to wash her face. Then she ate breakfast and walked aimlessly around the courtyard. Magpie came to the well to wash clothes, and Xiumi went to speak with her but their conversation didn't get far before Zhang Jiyuan hurried over to them. Xiumi tensed and thought about running, but he was upon them in an instant.

"Hey!" Zhang Jiyuan greeted them excitedly. "The lotus flowers in the basins in the back have bloomed!"

"Have they?" Magpie replied, after glancing at Xiumi and realizing she had no interest in the conversation. "That's good to know."

What an idiot! Xiumi thought. *Who gets excited over a couple of lotuses blooming?* Thinking of the dream made her angry. She wouldn't even look at Zhang Jiyuan, who made ingratiating noises and asked if she would like to go with him to the rear courtyard to see. Xiumi wanted to reply, *I'd rather see you in hell first*, but instead she simply leaned on the wall by the stairs and asked, "So you like flowers and plants and stuff?"

Zhang Jiyuan appeared to think seriously for a moment. "I suppose that depends on the flower," he said. "The orchid grows in deep valleys, chrysanthemums cloister themselves in abandoned gardens, and the plum blossom scorns snowy peaks, but only the lotus swims in mud and yet never gets dirty. It symbolizes the highest, purest will, and thus earns the most affection . . . 'I made a coat of lotus petals, and wove a robe of water-chestnut leaves.'"

The line was from Qu Yuan's famous poem "Encountering Sorrow," though Zhang Jiyuan had listed the plants backward. Xiumi couldn't be bothered to call him on it. Seeing that Xiumi wasn't leaving immediately, Zhang Jiyuan continued, "The poet of Jade Stream has a line about lotus blossoms—do you remember it?"

Now he was quoting *Dream of the Red Chamber*, from the scene in which Lin Daiyu quizzes the young Jia Baoyu on Li Shangyin's poetry. It seemed the bearded little man was more bookish than he looked. Xiumi felt utterly uninterested in carrying the conversation further, and replied, "What could it be but 'leaving old lotuses to listen to the rain'?"

Zhang Jiyuan shook his head and smiled wryly. "Now you're calling me Lin Daiyu."

"Then which verse do you like best?"

"'Beyond the lotus pool echoes distant thunder,'" Zhang Jiyuan replied.

The quoted line reminded Xiumi of digging lotuses from the pond outside the village with Father, and a chasm suddenly opened within her. Father loved lotus flowers to distraction; all through the summer he would keep a miniature lotus in a bowl of water on his desk as a kind of offering. She remembered that its flowers bloomed crimson and bright as new peaches, though they seemed delicate and unassuming. Father called it "a twist of red," and would sometimes pluck a few petals to grind into ink for his personal seal.

Zhang Jiyuan asked her what kind of flowers she liked. "Peonies," she blurted out.

Zhang Jiyuan shook his head again and laughed. "Now you're just driving me away."

Wouldn't you know it, thought Xiumi. *This idiot might be odd, but he has obviously read quite a bit; perhaps I'm being too hard on him.* Yet her tone remained unsympathetic. "How am I driving you away?"

"You're well versed in the histories and classics, Little Sister, and your mind is always active. Why ask about what you already know? In his 'Catechism of Nature,' Gu Yuanqing notes that the peony has also been called the 'Two-Leaf,' as in 'to leave,' and is frequently given as a gift at parting. But then, it's time for me to leave anyway." At this, he straightened his cuffs, waved to Xiumi, and went out through the front door.

Xiumi followed Zhang Jiyuan's figure with a thoughtful gaze. After the previous night's dream, it seemed like something had passed between the two of them. She felt somewhat hollow.

Magpie looked up from her work at Xiumi. "What in the world were you and Uncle talking about? I've been here listening all along and I couldn't understand a word of it."

"It's all a bunch of empty posing anyway, why would you need to understand it?"

Magpie asked if she wanted to go see the Land and Water alms ceremony at Miss Sun's. Xiumi replied, "If you want to go, you should go. I'm going to see Mr. Ding."

8

MR. DING was writing calligraphy at his desk, his hand still wrapped in gauze. Seeing Xiumi come through the door, he told her, "No class today." Apparently he was too busy writing a tomb inscription for Miss Sun. He asked Xiumi why she hadn't gone to see the Land and Water ceremony; she said that she didn't want to. As she turned to leave, he stopped her: "Hold on a minute. I have a question for you."

Now that she was asked to stay, Xiumi flopped down into the wooden sedan chair by the window and began to play with the two thrushes in their cages. Mr. Ding wrote with such concentration that he had to mop his brow regularly with his handkerchief, his silk shirt already stained with sweat. As he worked, he muttered, "Such a pity, such a pity. Such a shame!" Xiumi knew he was referring to Miss Sun. Overpowered with distress, he paused now and then to wipe his eyes and nose. She watched him scrape the fingers he had just used to wipe his nose along the edge of his desk before shaping his goat-hair brush with his tongue; a wave of nausea passed over her. He kept abandoning his drafts and starting over, cursing his own illiteracy as he tossed crumpled-up sheets onto the floor. In the end he used all of his paper and had to climb the ladder into the attic to get some more. Grief for the dead young woman had swallowed him up—he completely forgot about Xiumi. Seeing his desperation and disorganization, she went to his desk to help him lay out new paper, grind ink, and rinse his sweaty handkerchief in a washbasin. The cloth turned the water black immediately.

Ding Shuze was a commendable literary stylist with a reputation for fast and decisive compositions. He liked to compare himself favorably to Yuan Hu, the ancient general who wrote a thousand words to the emperor on paper held against his horse's flank. Form was no object—he could produce a poem or a lyric, an essay or an exegesis, quickly and in full. Often when someone came to commission a formal invitation, a door-frame couplet, or a tomb inscription, he would produce the entire composition while still negotiating his fee. Moreover, once the piece was finished, he absolutely refused to change a single word of it. Asking for a second draft was like pissing in the wind. Once, he wrote a birthday tribute for a ninety-year-old man in which he accidentally misspelled his elder subject's name. When the man's grandson pointed this out and asked him to rewrite the piece, he exploded, "Ding Shuze's compositions do not bother with 'rewriting'! This is the piece; you can work with what I've given you."

"You didn't even get his name right—whose birthday is it?" the grandson complained.

"That's not my problem!"

Voices rose, and the two men jawed at each other until Mr. Ding's wife, Xiaofeng, swept into the room to arbitrate. Eventually, she pointed at the grandson and said, "You're totally wrong," before turning to her husband and saying, "Shuze, you're correct." Then she announced to both parties: "All done!" The grandson had no choice but to triple the fee and beg until Ding Shuze agreed to break his own custom and do a second draft with the old man's name written correctly.

So what was wrong with Ding Shuze now? Rubbing his cheeks and scratching his head, tapping his forehead, or pacing around with his hands clasped behind him. Either the tomb inscription must be too difficult to write, Xiumi thought, or Mr. Ding must have suffered too severe a shock when he saw the body the night before. Perhaps the suddenness of her death perplexed him. Grief was clearly visible in his face as he paced around the classroom. "Such a soft little thing, gone just like that. Alas, alas!" he muttered. Yet once he actually finished the inscription, he seemed fairly satisfied with himself. He called Xiumi over to read it, but fearing that she wouldn't understand, he read it out loud for her anyway. The inscription ran thus:

Miss Sun Youxue, of Puji village, Meicheng, daughter of Sun Dingcheng, well recognized for his filial piety and camaraderie, and his wife, née Zhen. Born on a day of heavy snows and blossoming winter plums, and named after snow, assuredly in reference to the purity of snow and frost, pines and poplars. As a child, she was clever, kindhearted, and careful, with the scent of orchids about her, and a gaze like distant mountains. Her faithful, upright character and her pleasing, womanly decorum were extolled by everyone. In her youth, she lost her tender mother, her father became sickly, and the family was frequently too poor to eat. Thus Youxue decided to make sacrifice of her own figure, pure as ice and clean as jade, and opened the door to guests. Though this was denounced as a soiling of the lotus, in truth, it was like the child cutting off his own leg to feed his parents. Both rough and elegant visitors received the benefit of her munificence, while salesmen and soldiers alike reposed in her fragrance. Kidnapped and brutally abused by an outlaw, she resisted his advances with the strength of the white cypress, giving her life for fidelity.

Alas, death remains the greatest trial in all our history, and we weep for more than just the kidnapped Peach Blossom princess. Poets of other centuries weep for the same tragic tales, here memorialized in stone that it may last forever. Thus we sing:

On ethics and precepts is founded the nation.
Who can change this? Oh, Miss Youxue.
Wondrous fidelity, sagely behavior:
different paths to a single end.
You served your family with the grace of the bamboo spear;
kept your house with the character of the blooming peach.
One fewer voice rings on the mountainside, as lovely bones
      lie in silence;
her deep morality here inscribed above this lonely mound,
never to be sung of in millennia to come.

"What do you think?" her teacher asked.

"It's good."

"What part is good? Tell me."

"The whole thing," Xiumi replied. "But normal people might not be able to understand it."

This elicited a joyful laugh from Ding Shuze, in which one could hear no trace of the sadness he had displayed before. Xiumi understood that in her teacher's mind, incomprehensibility represented the highest possible achievement for literature. It had become a maxim of his: "Good writing leaves people confused." If a hack driver or a tofu seller could understand your meaning, what was to love? Still, this particular inscription seemed fairly comprehensible to Xiumi. Mr. Ding explained the whole thing for her from start to finish, then asked her which parts she liked the best, to which she replied, "'You served your family with the grace of the bamboo spear' and the sentences after it show true genius."

Her teacher laughed out loud, praised her cleverness and precocity, and assured her that if she kept up with her studies, she would surpass him someday. He patted her head with his greasy, bandaged hand.

Just as Ding Shuze was at the height of his spirits, the door curtain rose and his wife stormed in, throwing herself into a chair by his desk and sitting speechless, as if frozen. Mr. Ding tried to pull her over to his side so she could see the inscription, and tell him if she thought it was good or not, but she batted his hand away and snapped, "Who cares if it's good? Looks to me like you've just wasted a whole morning's work. He won't take it."

"Not even for twenty strings of cash?"

"Never mind twenty, he wouldn't even give me ten."

"And why is that?"

"That Old Man Sun is tight as a drum." Xiaofeng's anger hadn't yet abated. "He said that his daughter's tragedy was so sudden, he didn't even know how he would pay for a funeral, a coffin, or the monks and Taoist priests for the service, let alone useless business like this. He also said that she came from a poor family, hadn't even gotten married, and had no real moral accomplishments to boast about, so they didn't need an inscription. He wants to bury her in a cheap coffin and get it over with. We went back and forth about it forever, and he still wouldn't pay."

"The son of a bitch was hiding lechers inside his house all day, letting his daughter make dirty money, and now that I offer to clean her name up a little, and spend all morning writing until I can't see straight, he wants to look a gift horse in the mouth?" Mr. Ding spat.

"And that's not the half of it!" Xiaofeng waved her handkerchief in the air. "I asked him for ten strings, and he said that even if you gave it to him for free, he wouldn't take it. Said he'd just have to spend more money buying a headstone and hiring someone to carve it."

Ding Shuze's face turned crimson and swelled like a ripe eggplant. He snatched the inscription and was on the verge of tearing it up when his wife held him back. "Don't tear it up in anger now; I'll send someone to talk to him later." She took the paper from him, read it all the way through, then gave her husband a look of deep feeling. "Shuze, your prose has gotten even better."

The distant but approaching wail of funeral horns reached Xiumi's ear. "They're carrying Miss Sun out," Xiaofeng said to her husband. "Shall we go see the affair?"

"Go if you want to, I'm not going." Ding Shuze slumped in his chair, still fuming. Xiaofeng asked Xiumi if she wanted to go. Xiumi looked at her teacher and asked, "Teacher, a minute ago you said you had a question for me?"

Ding Shuze replied with an exhausted wave. "We'll talk about that later."

Xiumi followed Xiaofeng outside. By the time they had stepped through the skywell and out the front door, the funeral procession was just passing by. While she had originally thought to go straight home, she instead fell into line with the others. The party reached the edge of the village; Xiumi brought up the rear. Looking up, she saw the coffin raised high above the heads of the crowd. It had been built in a hurry, and hadn't even been painted. A sudden realization made Xiumi tense: the whole scene looked just like her dream from the night before. There was Grandma Meng, standing under the apricot tree by her house and handing out embroidered flowers from a bamboo basket. Just as the old woman reached the end of the procession, she ran out of flowers. Turning the basket upside down and shaking it, she smiled at Xiumi and said, "What bad luck! I'm just short the one."

Xiumi didn't dare take another step. She stood dazed and motionless beneath the wide canopy of the apricot tree. Even though the flowers in the dream had been yellow, and the ones Grandma Meng had in her basket now were white, she couldn't repress the terrifying feeling that she was reliving the dream. The sky above was so high and so blue it might have dripped with indigo dye. She couldn't help but think that though she knew she was awake, she had no guarantee that this too wasn't just part of a vaster, more distant dream.

9

BAOSHEN returned from Qinggang with his four-year-old son, Tiger. The boy's head, unlike his father's, sat straight on his neck, but he was totally uncontrollable. His skin was almost as dark as coal, and so greasy it made him shine. He ran constantly and everywhere, wearing nothing but a pair of bright red underwear, and permeated the entire estate with his flashing presence coupled with the drumroll of his footsteps. Years without fatherly instruction made disaster inevitable after he arrived in Puji. During his first few days, he strangled a pair of the neighbor's barred roosters, which he carried into the kitchen and threw at Magpie's feet, demanding, "Now make soup for me!" The next day, he left a turd under Lilypad's bed, causing her to complain for days that a rat must have died somewhere in her room. Later, he poked the wasp's nest in Hua Erniang's backyard until it exploded; and while Hua Erniang had to deal with a swollen face for a month afterward, he escaped without a sting.

Baoshen spent most of his time in those days knocking on every door in the village to apologize, promising he would strangle the boy one day. In fact, he didn't dare harm a hair on his son's head; sometimes, when Tiger was sleeping, Baoshen would flip him over and kiss his little rear several times. Yet the day finally came when he almost killed his son.

Xiumi, Lilypad, and Mother had been doing needlework together in Mother's bedroom one evening when Magpie burst through the door. "Bad news!" she cried. "Baoshen's going to strangle Tiger. He's turning over everything looking for a rope. I tried to stop him. One of you has to go and do something!"

Lilypad immediately put down her scissors and stood up. But Mother spat, "Nobody goes anywhere!" with such force that Lilypad didn't dare move, and Magpie froze in the doorway. "The child needs serious discipline," Mother explained. "If he doesn't stop acting out, he'll be heading straight back to wherever he came from!"

Mother's words were meant for Baoshen's ears, and he heard her loud and clear from the courtyard. He had no choice but to prove his loyalty by doubling down on his commitment to punish his son. He tied Tiger to one of the pillars in the courtyard and started to beat him with a leather riding crop, slashing blindly as the boy screamed for his life and mother. Only when his cries started to weaken and fade into silence did Mother nod to Lilypad.

Lilypad went downstairs into the courtyard with Xiumi behind her. Tiger's head hung lifelessly, even as his father continued to whip his small body like a madman. Lilypad wrenched the riding crop from Baoshen's fingers, then untied the boy. Blood dripped down the child's face, his breathing faint through one open nostril. Chips of red paint from the pillar lay scattered all over the stone floor where he stood. Lilypad carried his small body to her own bedroom, worked his pressure points and spat cold water over his face until finally the boy took in a breath and screamed, "Daddy!"

Baoshen had already frightened himself speechless, and hearing his son call out to him caused tears to stream down his face. He knelt by Lilypad's bedside with his forehead on Tiger's chest and sobbed.

Xiumi wondered why Mother had gotten so angry with Baoshen. The kid must have done something really horrible for Baoshen to have whipped him so mercilessly. Xiumi asked Magpie and Lilypad about it, but both said they didn't know anything. Magpie seemed to be telling the truth; Lilypad wanted to say something but refrained, and instead added with a smile, "Some things are just better left unknown. Don't wear yourself out worrying."

Tranquility returned to the house the following day, and it seemed as if nothing had ever happened. Mother asked Baoshen to measure

Tiger's feet so she could make him a pair of cloth shoes. Meanwhile, Xiumi felt like strange and inexplicable events were occurring all around her, and yet the mystery refused to speak to her. Her curiosity fed on silence, grew stronger and more impatient, and frequently took flight with her riding its back. She swore she would get to the bottom of this incident, and after a few more weeks, she finally found her opportunity.

A caramel-candy seller announced his arrival in the village with the sound of his flute. Tiger, who was playing by the pond, watched him pass by with hungry eyes. His father's hard beating had deflated him completely; now he spent most of his time squatting on the ground and keeping silent. Xiumi walked over and squatted down beside him. "How would you like it if I bought you some candy?" Tiger grinned, but still said nothing. Xiumi ran to the vendor and came back with a square of caramel. She held it in front of Tiger's face; when he reached out, she yanked it away.

"Tell me: Why did your dad beat you so hard that day?" Xiumi winked at him.

"Daddy said I can't tell anyone, no matter what," Tiger replied.

Xiumi waved the caramel in front of his face until he drooled in spite of himself. He thought hard for a minute, then said, "If I tell you, you have to promise not to tell anyone."

"I won't tell anyone, I promise." Xiumi put a hand to her heart.

"You really want to know?"

"Of course I really do."

"You mustn't tell anybody."

"Pinky swear." The two of them swore. "Now can you tell me."

"If you give me the caramel, I'll tell you."

Xiumi gave it to him. The boy stuffed the whole candy into his mouth at once, chewed a few times, and swallowed with effort. Then he stood up, slapped the dust off his pants, and headed off.

"You haven't told me what happened!" Xiumi complained, grabbing his hand. But his greasy brown fingers slid right through her grasp, and he ran away. "Nothing!" he cried, and sprinted to the other side of the pond. Pointing a finger at the sky, he called out, "It's gone! It turned into a bird and flew away!"

On his way home to Qinggang, Baoshen had made detours through villages and towns in Shangdang, Pukou, and the Qingzhou area, searching for news of Father. He visited nearly every inhabited locality in the entire county without learning anything at all of Father's whereabouts.

Mid-autumn drew to a close. When Father disappeared, the cotton in the fields had just started to bloom; now the sounds of picking and carding could be heard in every household. Mother began talking to Baoshen about setting up a cenotaph above Father's personal effects. "Let's not jump to a tomb just yet. The master may have gone crazy, but there's no evidence he's dead. What's more, when he left the house he took a suitcase and quite a lot of money with him. He obviously wasn't going somewhere to die."

"But we can't keep sitting here and worrying ourselves sick about it," Mother replied.

"No need to worry, madam. Once the harvest work is over, I can hire people to carry out a thorough investigation. As long as he's still alive, everything will be fine. If you plant a headstone for him now without knowing anything certain, and one day he shows up at your doorstep with his suitcase, wouldn't that be a public embarrassment?"

Mother said that she had asked the Buddha about that already, and had been assured that it wasn't a problem. Moreover, according to local custom, a tomb should be built for anyone who had disappeared for more than six months, whether confirmed dead or not. "And besides, he's crazy, and the world is in chaos. Even if he were still alive, he could be far away from here, and how would we ever know? If we build him a tomb, we can at least have some closure for ourselves."

Baoshen wanted to argue, but Mother cut him off with a frown. "You just worry about hiring people to build it, and don't bother about anything else." Baoshen nodded and changed his tune immediately. "Yes, yes, of course, I'll find someone at once."

Yet a disturbing piece of news forced Mother to abandon her plan. One day in mid-November, a young man from Chen's Rice Market in Changzhou arrived to deliver a message from his employer. He arrived at the house just as the sun was setting. The young employee told them that two Buddhist monks in dark robes had come to the shop just that morning to buy rice.

"One of them looked exactly like the master. My boss has been to Puji before to buy rice, and was acquainted with him. He'd heard that Master Lu had been gone for almost half a year, his family desperate to find him, so seeing his resemblance in the monk surprised him. When he asked them what monastery they belonged to and where they lived before taking vows, they didn't answer his questions but just pressed him for the rice. It had been so long since my boss saw Master Lu he couldn't be sure it was him. But it so happened that we were sold out for the day, and the new rice hadn't been hulled yet, so he took a deposit from them and scheduled a pickup for the day after tomorrow. After they left, the boss thought for a while and decided this was no small matter, so he sent me over to tell you. He figured you might send a few people over tomorrow to spend the night in the store, so when the monks come the next morning, you could get a good look at them. If one of them is the master, my boss will have done a good turn; if it isn't, he hopes you won't blame us."

Mother sent Magpie into the kitchen to make dinner for the young man, which he accepted willingly. After food and wine, he begged for an oiled torch, and made his way back to Changzhou under the cover of darkness.

10

MOTHER rose early the next morning and gathered Xiumi, Lilypad, and Baoshen for their trip to Changzhou. Magpie and Tiger would stay home to watch the house. As they were about to leave, Zhang Jiyuan appeared from the rear courtyard, rubbing the crust out of his sleepy eyes, his face still unwashed. He slapped Baoshen on the shoulder and asked, "Mind if I tag along?"

Baoshen paused for a moment, then replied, "Do you know where we are going, Uncle?"

"I do. Aren't you going to Changzhou to buy rice?"

Mother and Lilypad couldn't help laughing at the exchange. Lilypad whispered to Xiumi, "Buy rice? We get more rice every year from our tenant farmers than we could ever sell, and this idiot wants us to go to Changzhou to buy it?"

"What will you do while we're buying rice?" Baoshen asked with a chuckle.

"I'll go for a walk. I've been feeling too shut in recently."

"If you could come, it would be a blessing," said Baoshen. "I fear that if the master throws a fit, I won't be able to handle him on my own." He looked at Mother, as if asking for her opinion.

Mother knitted her brow. "In that case, Xiumi doesn't need to go."

She had barely finished speaking when Xiumi threw her cloth bag on the ground and said in frustration, "I told you I didn't want to go, but you wouldn't let me stay, and now you're not letting me go. I don't even know what's going on!"

The force of her own protest surprised her. Mother said nothing, but stared at her like she was a stranger. The two women's gazes collided straight on and unavoidably, revealing the other's unspoken feelings completely and without pretense. Both were too stunned to speak.

"Let's everyone go together," exhorted Lilypad in order to break up the scene. "If the master really has taken orders and become a monk, he might be hard to persuade. If Xiumi goes, he'll at least have a chance to see his daughter."

Mother didn't argue, she simply started walking. After a few paces, she turned and glared at Xiumi with an expression in her eyes that said, *That little hussy has the gall to talk back to me in front of the family? I guess we can't treat her like a child much longer.*

Lilypad tried to drag Xiumi out the door, but Xiumi stood firm. Zhang Jiyuan picked Xiumi's bundle off the ground, brushed the dust off, and passed it to her. He made a funny face and said, "Want to hear my donkey impression?" He let out a wild, in-and-out hee-haw that sounded surprisingly real; Xiumi had to hold her breath and bite her lip hard to keep from laughing.

Mother led the way with Baoshen, while Zhang Jiyuan walked next to Lilypad, and Xiumi behind them. Puji lay among lowlands, only a mile or two north of the Yangtze River; as the party approached the water, the high embankment seemed to loom over their heads. Xiumi caught sight of patched sails crossing the river, and she could hear the rough sounds of the rushing current. The gray sky hung low, and an autumn chill pierced the air. Flocks of egrets landed and took off from the river. Xiumi listened to Zhang Jiyuan and Lilypad laughing and talking, though she could not discern their words. Sometimes Lilypad would laugh and punch his shoulder, and Zhang Jiyuan would turn back to look at Xiumi. The fire in Xiumi's heart grew again. She felt as if a steel curtain hung right in front of her eyes, letting her see only parts and pieces of things, but never the entire scene. Nothing seemed clear to her, even at this age. For instance, she knew that Zhang Jiyuan and Lilypad were joking with each other, but she had no idea what they were laughing at, and whenever she got close enough to hear, they suddenly stopped talking. Xiumi intentionally slowed her pace, as if she were upset with herself, but when the pair got too far ahead, they stopped and waited for her. When she neared them again, they turned and went on without saying anything to her, still chatting and casting an occasional glance back in her direction. Just as they got to the ford, Xiumi noticed that both were standing still. Mother and Baoshen had already climbed the tall embankment; Lilypad stood with a hand on Zhang Jiyuan's shoulder for balance so she could pull off a shoe and dump the sand out. How could she put a hand on his shoulder?! And Zhang Jiyuan was supporting her elbow with one hand. They were still laughing and talking. And when Lilypad was finished, they walked onward without even acknowledging Xiumi's existence. Xiumi started to curse the pair of them silently, every word touching the darkest and most malicious corners of her heart.

At the ferry dock, the wind was blowing strongly across the river, waves folding into each other and crashing violently against the shore. Tan Shuijin raised the sail, while Baoshen helped him on deck. Fair-haired Tan Si carried a stool out for Mother to sit on, and Gao Caixia brought out a plate of newly steamed sticky buns for her. Lilypad and Zhang Jiyuan stood beside each other on the far end of an upturned canoe, staring out at the darkened river. For some reason, the pair had fallen silent. When Lilypad saw Xiumi near the edge of the embankment, she waved to her. "What took you so long?" she asked.

Xiumi didn't reply. Lilypad's tone of voice sounded different. The blush on her cheeks looked different. Her energetic, easygoing demeanor was different.

Xiumi's heart sank again. *I'm stupid*, she thought, *they think I'm stupid. I'm just stupid.* She repeated the sentence in her head as her fingers played with her dress. Gao Caixia interrupted her self-loathing by offering her a sticky-rice cake as she exhorted her young son to call Xiumi Big Sister. The fair-haired boy merely giggled.

Tan Shuijin secured the sail and called the rest of the travelers aboard. The southwest gale continued, making the boats pitch and yaw. As Xiumi climbed the gangplank, Zhang Jiyuan reached his hand back to steady her, but she smacked it away angrily.

"I don't need your help!"

Her outburst drew a look of surprise from the entire party.

No one spoke on the ride over. When they reached the middle of the river, the sun appeared through the fog, penetrating the bamboo roof of the cabin and dancing across the floor like a bronze coin. Zhang Jiyuan sat with his back to Xiumi. Reflected light from the water flashed across his black cloth shirt in tangled lines, fluttering and waving as the boat moved.

They did not arrive in Changzhou until early afternoon. Chen's Rice Market stood beside a deep pool fed by a mountain spring; a thin mist hovered over the clear water. All was quiet, save an old mill wheel that clanked methodically as it slowly spun. A bamboo grove behind the shop extended a halfway up the mountainside. The shop owner, Chen Xiuji, and his employees had been waiting outside to receive them. Mother cued Baoshen to present the tael of silver they had brought as a gift, which Chen Xiuji refused to accept over Baoshen's prolonged protestations. After a round of small talk, Chen Xiuji led them through the bamboo forest to a separate courtyard, where they rested.

The courtyard was secluded and immaculate. A covered walkway surrounded a well in the middle of the open space. Red, ripe gourds hung from the interior eaves. Tea was served in front of the main hall. Mr. Chen said that the residence had been empty for over a year; he had sent people over that morning to clean up all the cobwebs. "Not the best living arrangements, but I hope it will suit you for a night or two."

Lilypad asked why such a lovely little place should stay empty for so long. Chen Xiuji stared at her blankly for a moment, as if unsure how to respond. Then he sighed and raised one cuff to dry his eyes. Mother shot Lilypad a look and changed the subject by asking how the rice business was doing, but Mr. Chen's sadness didn't dissipate; he held out for a few words of half-hearted small talk, then made an excuse about being very busy and took his leave.

Xiumi and Lilypad took the west bedroom; its single window faced the courtyard. A collection of items lay beneath a red silk blanket on top of an old-fashioned set of shelves that stood below the window. Xiumi was about to peek under the blanket when she noticed Zhang Jiyuan snooping around the courtyard.

He seemed to possess an intense interest in every aspect of his environment. He strolled under the covered walkway, tapping the gourds that hung from the rafters; he gently kicked a bamboo cradle that sat by one of the pillars; he uncovered the water basins by the kitchen and looked inside; he even lay down beside the well, peering inside it for a long while. *What an idiot*, Xiumi thought, *poking his nose into every corner. No telling what he is looking for.*

Lilypad plopped onto their bed and started babbling to Xiumi. Xiumi mostly ignored her. Her resentment from earlier that day had not died away completely, and she responded only when she had to or could say something biting, to the point where even she felt she was going too far. Lilypad yielded again and again, pretending not to hear her implications, and merely smiled at her from her supine position from the bed. When Mother came in to ask for a brush, Xiumi didn't move from her spot by the window, nor did she turn to look at her. Mother behaved differently toward her, now patting her head, now squeezing her hand, and finally putting an arm around her shoulder and saying, "Come, come keep me company in my room. This place really is a little terrifying."

Dinner was served inside the store. An eight-sided dining table had been set up next to the bellows for blowing chaff. Next to the bellows was a heavy stone mortar used to hull rice; screens and bamboo sieves of various sizes hung from the walls, and a round basket leaned against a rice crate in the corner. Fine particles of chaff floated thick in the air, making everyone cough as they ate. A feast had been prepared—Mr. Chen had even gone out of his way to cook them a pheasant. Mother chatted with him while picking out the best morsels of food for Xiumi's bowl and frequently casting a sidelong glance in her direction. Mother had never been so good to her before; it made Xiumi feel like crying. She looked up to find Mother's eyes sparkling.

After dinner, Zhang Jiyuan left the table first. Mother and Baoshen carried on endlessly with Mr. Chen, and finally Xiumi asked Lilypad if she wanted to go. Without looking up from the pheasant head she was sucking on, Lilypad replied she needed to stay and help with the dishes.

Xiumi left the table alone. Afraid she would run into Zhang Jiyuan on the way back, she dawdled beneath a large pine tree for a while, looking out at the lighted windows in the valley as the events of the day replayed themselves in her head. The lights floated in the dense darkness of the forest like golden stardust. She felt as if she were floating too, exacerbating her uneasiness.

Once enough time had passed for Zhang Jiyuan to have reached the courtyard, she set off in the same direction, following a path that skirted the outer wall of the rice shop. Yet as she made her way toward the heavy shadow of the bamboo grove, she found Zhang Jiyuan sitting on a stone, smoking his pipe. He was waiting for her, as she had half-sensed he would. And, behold, there he was! Her heart started to beat loudly. She held her breath and started to walk past him, but the idiot didn't move and continued to smoke, the ember of his pipe glowing red. It didn't matter how slowly she walked, he didn't say a word. *Does he not see me?* she thought.

As she entered the grove, Zhang Jiyuan finally sighed and stood up. "It seems that death has just visited this family."

Xiumi stopped. She turned to look at her uncle. "Who told you that?"

"Nobody told me," Zhang Jiyuan said as he walked over to her.

"Then how do you know?"

"It's plain as day," Zhang Jiyuan replied. "And it wasn't just one person, either."

"You're just making that up. How could you possibly know that someone has died?"

"Why don't you listen to my explanation, then tell me if it makes sense?"

Now they were walking side by side beneath the bamboo canopy. Dew had already condensed on the leaves; Xiumi waved away the fine, wet branches as they touched her hair. The distraction of talking about something totally unrelated to her instantly calmed her racing heart. Zhang Jiyuan explained: "You remember when Lilypad asked

Chen Xiuji why such a nice house didn't have anyone living in it, and he wiped away a tear?"

"I remember..." Xiumi murmured. She no longer felt embarrassed, even when Zhang Jiyuan's arm bumped her shoulder.

"This afternoon I found a cradle under the beams beneath the hanging gourds. It looked like it was recently in use, which means an infant must have lived in the house."

"So where did the child go?"

"It's dead," Zhang Jiyuan replied.

"How could that be?" Frightened, Xiumi stopped and looked up at her relative.

"Hear me out." A faint smile passed over Zhang Jiyuan's pallid face. The two of them continued to stroll.

"There is a well in the middle of the courtyard. I looked at it closely—it's been filled in completely with stones."

"But why would they fill the well up?"

"Because someone had died inside it."

"You mean the child fell in the well and drowned?"

"The outside wall of the well is too high, and there's a cover that's weighted down with a stone; a baby couldn't possibly fall in." Zhang Jiyuan reached out to push bamboo branches out of Xiumi's way, knocking her bun in the process.

"So how do you think the child died?"

"Disease," Zhang Jiyuan replied. "Someone stuck paper talismans against illness on the walls of the room Baoshen and I are staying in. So the child must have been sick enough that Mr. Chen paid for a shaman to perform an exorcism ritual. But the child died anyway."

"Then who died in the well?"

"The mother—she threw herself in—"

"And Mr. Chen had it filled in afterward," Xiumi concluded.

"So it goes."

He stopped unexpectedly and turned to look at her. They were on the verge of passing through the bamboo grove. The moon had been washed clean of its red haze. She could hear the trickling water of a spring somewhere beyond her sight.

"Are you afraid?" Zhang Jiyuan asked softly, his voice muffled as if he had something stuck in his throat.

"I am," she barely whispered.

Zhang Jiyuan put a hand on her shoulder. "Don't be afraid." She caught another whiff of his body odor, its mix of tobacco smoke and sweat, and then heard her shoulder blade pop. Her breathing got louder despite her best efforts to calm it. The rustle of the bamboo, the limpid shine of the moon, and the murmur of spring water running over stones were suddenly translated into a language that she could comprehend. She had already made up her mind that whatever Zhang Jiyuan asked of her, she would do, and whatever he did, she would keep to herself. She thought about her dream from several days prior: when she asked him where the door was, he slipped his hand into her dress and whispered, "The door is right here..."

"Little Sister..." Zhang Jiyuan seemed to be in the midst of a momentous decision. Xiumi watched his brow furrow and his expression grow uneasy; the moonlight showed her a face full of pain and anxiety.

"Yes?" Xiumi asked, looking up at him.

"Don't be afraid," Zhang Jiyuan finally said with a smile. He patted her shoulder, then took his hand away. They left the bamboo grove and arrived at their courtyard. After a pause, Zhang Jiyuan asked her if she'd like to sit on the doorstep for a while. "Okay," Xiumi replied.

The two sat side by side on the stoop. Zhang Jiyuan filled his pipe with tobacco, while Xiumi put her elbows on her knees and rested her chin in her hands. The mountain breeze on her face felt both refreshing and sad. He asked her what books she was reading, if she'd ever been to Meicheng, and why she always seemed so cranky and preoccupied. She answered each question in turn. Yet he did not reciprocate. When she asked where he really came from, why he had come to Puji, what he was doing that day at Master Xue's home, and why he was looking for a six-fingered man, he either replied evasively or simply chuckled and said nothing.

His expression suddenly changed when she mentioned the fisherman she had seen outside the house that day. Now he asked after every detail of what Xiumi had seen, and he noted that if the man had been there to fish, it was strange that he had neither fishing line nor hook.

"Did you see what he looked like?" Zhang Jiyuan stood up and looked at her with startling urgency.

"He wore a black monk's robe with a felt hat on his head. Hunchbacked. I saw him staring at us through the reeds…"

"Damn it!" Zhang Jiyuan hissed to himself. "Could it really be him?"

"You know him?" Xiumi asked. She was starting to feel genuinely afraid.

"Why didn't you tell me about this before?" Zhang Jiyuan snapped at her. He seemed to have changed into another person altogether. Xiumi said nothing. She realized that this was a crucial matter for him.

"This is no good," he muttered. "I have to get back immediately."

"But there are no ferries crossing the river this late," Xiumi said.

"Damn it, this could be a disaster…" He stared at her blankly, seemingly unaware of what to do next.

The sound of talk and laughter reached them through the bamboo grove, followed by the bobbing glow of a lantern on a cart. Mother and Baoshen had returned. Zhang Jiyuan said nothing; he turned and strode inside the courtyard, a black look on his face.

What an idiot! What right did he have to get so angry all of a sudden? Feeling abandoned, Xiumi went back to her own room, lit the lamp, and stood by the window. The memory rankled, and the skin on her face still burned hot. She regretted mentioning the hunchbacked fisherman. Lilypad brought in a basin of water so Xiumi could wash her face, but Xiumi ignored her. "Are you going to bed or not?" Lilypad asked. "We've been walking all day, and I'm as tired as a dog. I don't know what you want to do, but I'm getting in bed." She disrobed and crawled between the sheets.

Xiumi's hand accidentally touched something hidden under the red cloth on the shelves. Mr. Chen certainly was a strange one: Why cover regular old stuff with red silk? She touched the object again: it was soft and full, like the perfumed sachets women keep with their makeup kits. But when she lifted the cloth, the unveiling of the object gave her such an intense shock that she cried out.

It was a pair of baby shoes, traditionally embroidered with tiger faces on the front.

Lilypad sat up in bed and gaped when she saw what Xiumi had found. After a long pause, Xiumi asked, "Do you think this room gets haunted at night?"

"Haunted? It's just a room, why would it be haunted?" Lilypad looked at her with startled eyes beneath raised eyebrows.

"A child died in this room not too long ago," Xiumi replied. Her eyes caught his little shadow in every dark corner. She jumped into bed without even washing her face.

"You can't scare me." Lilypad smiled. "Everyone knows I don't scare easily. Most tricks don't affect me."

"You're not afraid of anything?"

"Nothing at all," Lilypad said.

She recounted one evening when she had run off and had to spend the night in a graveyard. Just as she was waking up the next morning, she felt something playing with her hair. Reaching out, she touched something smooth and tubular. "Guess what it was?"

"I give up."

"It was a huge green-and-black python. When I opened my eyes, its tongue was flicking at my face," Lilypad boasted. "If it had been you, that would have scared you to death, wouldn't it?"

"Who gets scared by snakes? If it had been me I wouldn't have been afraid either."

"But you're afraid of ghosts?"

Xiumi considered this for a while. She turned over to look at Lilypad, then turned back to gaze at the top of their mosquito netting. Almost as if speaking to herself, she said, "If it really were a ghost, I might not be scared. But I'd definitely be scared of something like a ghost that's not really a ghost, or a person who's not really a person."

"So you mean Zhang Jiyuan?"

The two of them laughed out loud and cuddled up closer. Goofing around with Lilypad drove the fear from Xiumi's heart and left her more at ease. After they had laughed a while, Xiumi had another idea. "I'm going to tell you a story," she said to Lilypad, "and we'll see if you get scared or not."

"Any story you want. It'll never happen."

"If you go to the toilet..."

"Why would I do that? I don't have to pee." Lilypad looked at her, suddenly confused.

"I'm not telling you to go now. I'm saying that at some point you'll get up to go to the toilet. Now, besides you and me, there's nobody else in this room, right?"

"Isn't that obvious? Who else could there be, other than me and you?" Lilypad glanced around the room as she spoke.

Xiumi continued: "In the middle of the night, you get up to use the toilet. You know that, other than me and you, there's nobody else in the room."

"Just tell me what it is." Lilypad gave her a shove. "My heart's already beating like a drum. Let me ask you this first: Are the lights on?"

"If the light's on, it's even scarier. If it's still dark it won't be scary," Xiumi said with a smile. "You wake up in the middle of the night and need to pee. So you get out of bed and put on your slippers. You see that the bathroom lamp is already lit, just like now. You pull back the curtain and someone is there, sitting on the toilet, grinning at you."

"Who?"

"Guess."

"How should I know?"

"Father."

Lilypad dove under the covers and whimpered audibly before sticking her head out and saying, "How could such a little girl come up with such a terrifying story? You've scared me half to death."

"I'm not trying to frighten you; he really is out there. Go look if you don't believe me," Xiumi replied gravely.

"Stop it, please, I'm begging you, I'm frightened enough as it is.

Uncle!" Lilypad panted for a long while before calming down. "To-night, neither of us is using the toilet."

They went early to the shop the following morning, so that they might meet the monks when they arrived to pick up their rice. Baoshen said that Zhang Jiyuan had left before sunrise, agitated and in a hurry, though Baoshen didn't know what the big emergency was all about. Mother didn't respond to this, but peered over at Xiumi. After a pause, she said, "I heard the two of you whooping and screaming all evening. Heaven knows what the ruckus was about." Lilypad and Xiumi repressed laughter with tight-lipped smiles. Chen Xiuji sent an employee over to them with a bowl of roasted pine nuts to help make the wait a little easier.

Yet the family waited from dawn to dusk without seeing the slightest trace of their quarry. As the sky darkened, Mother had no choice but to lead the party home. Chen Xiuji implored them to stay, saying, "The monks live up in the mountains, quite a distance from here. It's not an easy trip to make. And you've come a long way out here, too. Why not stay for a few days? If nothing else, I've got more rice here than you all could ever eat. What if they come back just as you leave?"

To this Mother politely replied, "Our visit has already caused tremendous inconvenience to you and your house. We are sincerely grateful to you, Mr. Chen, for such an expression of integrity and compassion, and we do hope you will receive our paltry gift of silver as a token of that respect, and a scant attempt at compensation for the trouble. Should you ever find it convenient in the future, I do hope you and your good wife will grace us with your presence in Puji."

Mother's mention of "your good wife" immediately aroused Xiumi's suspicion. Hadn't she died already? Baoshen took out the tael of silver once more, and went back and forth with Chen Xiuji until the other had no choice but to accept. Seeing that Mother was resolved to go home, he gave up trying to argue, and instead accompanied the family with a couple of his employees as far as the main avenue to the ferry before waving goodbye and turning home.

Once Mr. Chen's silhouette had vanished in the distance, Xiumi began to prod Mother indirectly about his wife: "Yesterday evening, he said she had taken their son back to her parents' house to help with the cotton harvest, and that's why we couldn't meet them." But if that were the case, she thought, neither his wife nor child had died. Xiumi asked Baoshen if he had noticed the well in the middle of their courtyard.

"Certainly," Baoshen replied. "I drew a bucket of water up this morning and last night to wash with. Why?"

11

BY THE time they got home, Magpie had long since been in bed and had to be woken up to answer the door. As she let them in, she whispered urgently to Mother that something horrible had happened in Xia village, words sputtering out in no logical order: When they cut the head off... the blood spewed everywhere... it started in the morning... they came along the riverbanks... imperial soldiers running everywhere through the village... some rode horses and others didn't, while some had spears and others had scimitars... they shouted and swarmed around like a hive of angry wasps. She mentioned Tiger: "As soon as the kid heard someone had died in Xia village, he started to pester me to take him to see the dead body. I wouldn't, so he had a fit and cried all day until I put him to bed."

Her scatterbrained answers put an end to Mother's patience. "Why do you never give me anything but worthless chatter? Who was it that died in Xia village?"

"I'm not sure," Magpie replied.

"Just tell us slowly; no need to rush," Baoshen comforted her. "Where did the soldiers come from? Whose head did they cut off?"

"Don't know," Magpie said, shaking her head.

"Then why did you say that blood spewed everywhere when the head came off?"

"That's what I heard someone say. Imperial troops from Meicheng surrounded the village. They cut the guy's head off right there, then chopped the body into a few pieces and threw it into the pond, and stuck the head on the big tree out in front of the village. Wang Badan, the blacksmith's apprentice, told me about it. He and his brother went with a few other brave souls from Puji to see what happened. The kid kept screaming about wanting to go with them, but I didn't let him, and heaven knows I didn't dare go myself."

Her report sent Baoshen immediately into the house to check on Tiger.

Lilypad snorted. "And here I thought something important had happened. People die every day in this country, and besides, why should we care if someone in Xia village dies? I'm starving, so let's just drop it and put some food on the table." She started to drag Magpie off to the kitchen.

"Wait . . ." Mother stopped them, her gaze focused on Magpie. "Have you seen your uncle Zhang today?"

"He came back at noon. I asked him why he'd come back alone and where you were, but he just scowled and said nothing. A little while later I saw him carry something down from the studio and shove it in the woodstove. When I asked what he was burning, he just said, 'It's over, it's over.' 'What's over?' I asked. He said, 'All of it.' Then he ran out again. I don't know where."

Mother had no more questions. She looked at her own shadow on the wall, then looked at Xiumi. She said she would go to bed now, no need to call her for the meal.

Xiumi didn't sleep that night. She stood stubbornly by the window, as if she were fighting herself, and stared out at the dark mass of trees surrounding the studio. No light emanated from those chambers all night. Xiumi stayed in bed until daybreak. She considered whether or not to go to Mr. Ding's house for news, but as she descended the stairs she heard her teacher and his wife speaking with raised voices to Mother in the front courtyard.

They moved behind locked doors in the grand hall; Grandma Meng and Hua Erniang followed on the heels of Ding Shuze and his wife; moments later they were joined by the owner of the pawnshop, Mr. Qian, and the Puji government clerk. Xiumi couldn't hear what they were talking about, but the conversation lasted until almost noon. Mother saw them off one by one. As Ding Shuze was leaving, he turned in the doorway and said to her, "I have to say, Xue Zuyan deserved it! A few days ago, I sent Xiumi to his house with a letter urging him to turn back and abandon the foolish path he was taking. But he thought his father's position in the capital made him untouchable, so he ignored me, and started assembling his own seditious band of rebels here in the countryside to plot against the government. And what do you think happened? The ax comes down and he goes belly up..."

From this, Xiumi learned that it was Master Xue who had been beheaded.* Later on, she heard that government spies had been on to him for a while; only his father's influence in the capital had delayed the inevitable. On the Double Ninth festival that September, imperial palace guards sent the old man a full jug of expensive wine as a gift from the emperor. Minister Xue knelt and knocked his head on the ground with thanks until his forehead bled, but the guards would not leave; hands on their swords, they told him they had orders to watch him drink before they could return. The old man then knew what kind of wine they had brought him. He tried faking insanity, weeping and crying out, refusing to drink. But the guards' impatience finally got the better of them, and they held him down, pinched his nose, and poured the wine down his throat. The minister's legs flailed and his orifices bled before he could take another breath. When news of the father's death arrived, provincial officials immediately deployed troops to capture his son. A brigade of mixed cavalry and infantry surrounded Xia village, forced its way into his home, and blockaded him and his concubine, Peach Pit, in his bedroom.

A Meicheng garrison lieutenant, Li Daodeng, had been a friend

---

*Xue Zuyan (1849–1901), courtesy name Xue Shuxian. Precocious as a child, he was a talented horseman with a strong-willed disposition, who successfully passed the martial service exam at the provincial level in the eleventh year of the Guangxu emperor. His plan to incite revolution against the Qing government by taking over Meicheng along with other members of the Cicadas and Crickets Society was leaked in 1901, leading to his execution. In 1953, his remains were moved to the Puji Revolutionary Martyrs' Cemetery.

of Xue Zuyan's for many years. Now acting on orders to bring him in, he thought he would do him a good turn. After his men surrounded the house, Li Daodeng left his guards at the door and went in alone. Sitting down in Xue Zuyan's grand armchair, he lay his halberd across his lap and cupped his fist in greeting. "Brother! A debt of gratitude built over years is repaid in this single moment. Run!"

When Xue Zuyan, who had been trembling under his blankets next to Peach Pit, heard that he could escape, he jumped out of bed stark naked and began to gather his valuables. Lieutenant Li watched the man toss his things around and just shook his head. Xue Zuyan packed everything he wanted without even putting on his pants; he even asked Li Daodeng if he could take his concubine within him. The lieutenant smiled and said, "You're an intelligent man, brother. What has made you so stupid today?"

"Daodeng, what you mean to say is—"

At that point, Peach Pit sat up in bed and jeered, "Strange that a man of lofty ambitions should think of sex while he faces his own death. If you run away, how could the lieutenant fulfill his orders?"

Xue Zuyan realized that even she had been eyes and ears against him; terror sent him round and round his dining room table like a mule around a millstone. Finally, he asked, "Daodeng, what you mean to say is that you're not actually going to let me go?"

Li Daodeng turned away, unable to look his friend in the eye. It was Peach Pit who impatiently explained, "What Lieutenant Li means is that if you run, he has a reason to kill you outright, instead of handing you over to be cut into five hundred and eighty pieces."

Xue Zuyan didn't move. He could neither go nor stay. Finally, Li Daodeng told him that whether Xue Zuyan got out alive or not was entirely up to him; if he ran farther and faster than the army could follow, Li Daodeng would keep them off his back. Hearing this, Xue Zuyan pulled on his pants and made straight for the door, forgetting his valuables entirely. No one appeared to stop him on his way out, yet Li Daodeng had long ago posted armed guards to the left and right of the outer door. The blades dropped just as Xue Zuyan ran through; his head soared into the air, his blood spurted all over the courtyard wall. Peach Pit sauntered out of the house after him as though nothing had happened, and remarked to the onlookers, "All this time I thought he was some kind of righteous hero, but instead he turns out to be an old, dried-up stuffed shirt."

Zhang Jiyuan reappeared that evening just as the family was sitting down to dinner, sauntering in lazily with pipe in hand just as he always did. His eyes had dark circles around them, and his hair, wet with autumn dew, lay stuck to his forehead. A long gash stretched down the back of his shirt. As Magpie ladled him a bowl of rice, Zhang Jiyuan pulled out a handkerchief to mop his face. With an obvious effort, he pulled himself together and assumed an air of nonchalance, saying, "Let me tell you all a joke."

No one responded. Every mouth stayed shut except for Tiger's: "Make a donkey noise for us first." But the request made Zhang Jiyuan even more uncomfortable. He looked first at Baoshen, then at Mother for support, but no one met his gaze—even Magpie kept her eyes on her bowl as she shoveled rice into her mouth. Finally Zhang Jiyuan looked at Xiumi, only to find her looking just as helplessly back at him.

While the rest of the table continued to eat in gloomy silence, Xiumi spoke up: "If you have a good joke, Uncle, you should tell it to us."

Pretending not to notice the severe glare Mother flashed at her, Xiumi put down her chopsticks and rested her head in her hands to listen. Her idea had been to lighten the mood a little by giving him a conversation partner, but instead she trapped him in his own performance. He made every effort to conceal his agitation, yet his gaze still darted back and forth, and he hesitated to speak. The joke came out disorganized and uninteresting, and even though it was clearly falling flat, he insisted on telling it to the end. The rest of the party looked at each other in shared embarrassment until Baoshen distracted everyone with a fart that was so noxious they all had to hold their breath.

Xiumi had already heard from Ding Shuze that Zhang Jiyuan was actually no cousin of hers. He was a convict wanted by the imperial court, and he had come to Puji not to recover from illness but to link up with his fellow conspirators and plot sedition. Ding Shuze's wife told her that Master Xue, Xue Zuyan, had been their leader, and even though he'd already lost his head, six or seven of his comrades had been captured alive and taken as prisoners to Meicheng. "And if even one or two of them cracks under the filleting knife, the first person they'll give up will be your cousin."

But if Zhang Jiyuan was a traitor, how could Mother have known him? And how could she allow a convict on the run who wasn't even family to stay in her house for six whole months? Xiumi could make no sense out of the situation.

Zhang Jiyuan finished his joke, ate a few more bites of dinner, then put his chopsticks down and addressed the table, saying that a full six months had passed since coming down to Puji from Meicheng to recuperate from his illness, and thanks to the boundless care everyone had shown to him, his recovery was complete. But all good things must come to an end, of course, and the time had come for him to take his leave. Mother, who clearly had been waiting for him to make this announcement, made no attempt to convince him to stay, but simply asked when he was thinking of setting off.

"I plan to leave tomorrow morning," Zhang Jiyuan replied, and stood up from the table.

"That sounds about right," Mother said. "Why don't you rest in your room for a while. I want to talk to you later this evening."

Only Xiumi and Tiger remained in the dining room after dinner ended. Xiumi absentmindedly played with him for a while until Baoshen came to put him to bed in the office. Xiumi made her way into the kitchen, intending to help Magpie and Lilypad wash up, but they had no space for her, so she kept getting in the way. Lilypad was so preoccupied she sliced a finger wide open on the sharp edge of a wok; she had no interest in entertaining Xiumi, who stood by herself next to the stove before removing herself from the kitchen. As she passed through the skywell, she saw Mother approach from the far end of the rear courtyard, a covered lamp in her hand. As Xiumi made for the stairs leading to her bedroom, Mother called out to her, "Your uncle wants you to go upstairs to see him. He has something to ask you."

"What could he have to ask me about?" Xiumi asked, surprised.

"He wouldn't tell me, so how should I know?" Mother replied sharply. "He asked you to go, so go!" She stalked off without even looking at her. Xiumi watched the glow from Mother's lamp flicker and slowly fade on the courtyard wall until she was left standing in impenetrable darkness. *What's her problem?* Xiumi thought resentfully. *Why is she taking her bad mood out on me?* Crickets filled her ears with a chorus of frenetic chirping, which only intensified her frustration.

The studio door was open; bright lamplight, shining in circles through a heavy autumn mist, illuminated the damp staircase. Xiumi had not been back there since Father disappeared. Fallen leaves covered everything—the corridor, the flowerpots, the stairs.

Zhang Jiyuan was sitting in Father's chambers, playing with Father's washbasin. Father had bartered it from a homeless panhandler, who had been using it as a begging bowl; Xiumi didn't know why the object was so interesting to Zhang Jiyuan. He turned it and flipped it over, examining every side and quietly exclaiming, "Priceless, priceless. It really is priceless."

Seeing Xiumi come through his door, he said to her, "You know, this antique has quite a history. Listen to the sound it makes." He rapped the bottom of the basin lightly with one finger—it produced a clear, almost crystalline chime that poured through the heart like water, and made Xiumi feel suddenly buoyant, as if she might be lifted off the ground by a breeze and carried over mountains, streams, and rivers to some unknown place.

"Not bad, huh?" Zhang Jiyuan proudly declared. Then he tapped the lip of the basin with a fingernail, and it tolled with the depth of a temple bell, sending out thick circles of sound that traveled outward like ripples across a pond, and persisted like a mountain breeze through the forest, the swaying of a flowering tree, the fluted rustle of bamboo, or the continuous sound of a stream. Xiumi could almost see the silent temple on the mountainside, and clouds chasing each other through the sky. For a brief second, she forgot herself, her thoughts, and her place in time.

Zhang Jiyuan brought his ear close to the lip of the basin with childlike enthusiasm, blinking at her as he listened. He in no way resembled a convicted criminal on the run from the government. "This beauty is called a 'carefree cauldron.' Originally forged out of copper by a Taoist adept at Zhongnan Peak who perfected the process over twenty-plus years. Southerners are unfamiliar with it, and only see an ordinary enamel basin. Diviners with perfect pitch used to use it to tell the future, saying they could foretell good or evil based on the sound it makes."

Xiumi considered how the sound had disoriented her, lifting her like a feather and finally setting her down in a place that felt like an empty graveyard. It seemed an unlucky omen.

"They say it has another, greater secret as well. Supposedly, when snow falls in the winter, the frost that forms on its surface will—" As he spoke, the door flew open and Lilypad walked in. The mistress had asked her to make sure he had enough oil in his lamps, she said. But the oil wells in the lamps were all full, so she pulled a hairpin out to trim the wicks and left, closing the door behind her before descending the stairs.

Zhang Jiyuan looked at Xiumi and smiled, and Xiumi smiled back, each as if knowing why the other was smiling but didn't care to explain it aloud. Xiumi felt a wave of inexplicable pity for her mother. Her hands and body prickled with sweat. She tapped the basin gingerly with her fingertips; its ringing reply felt pained. She imagined standing in an empty Zen temple. Few people ever visited. A stream bubbled outside the temple walls, and willow branches swayed by the road. The peach trees in the mountain valley behind were in bloom, every petal a snow-white windowpane filled with evening sunlight. Wild bees and butterflies danced and whirled;

flowers opened as if they were about to speak, then fell as if deep in thought. Something was vanishing, inch by inch, like tidewater retreating on a beach, or a stick of incense burning into ash. The bustle and noise of the human world seemed devoid of anything interesting.

Xiumi stood by the table, seeing nothing, utterly absorbed in her daydream. Looking up, she found Uncle looking at her with greedy energy: his expression was dark and shamelessly forthright, his face pale and his brows knit tightly together as tremors of pain seemed to twist his face. He licked his upper lip, as if he had something important to tell her, but couldn't decide if he should.

"Are you really a public enemy?" Xiumi asked him. She put her palm on the table and lifted it, leaving an imprint of sweat.

Zhang Jiyuan smiled bitterly. "What do you think?"

"Where are you going to go?"

"To tell the truth, I don't know myself," Zhang Jiyuan admitted. After a pause, he continued, "I can see that you have a whole string of questions for me. Is that true?"

Xiumi nodded.

"There was a time when I could have answered every single one of them truly and completely; in fact, before you came up the stairs, I was getting ready to tell you the truth. Whatever it was you wanted to know, I would tell you—you ask and I answer, with nothing held back or hidden. Who am I? How do I know your mother? Why did I come to Puji? What's my connection to Xue Zuyan in Xia village? Why are we fighting against the government? Who's the six-fingered man? You want to know the answers to all of these questions, don't you?" Zhang Jiyuan pulled out a crumpled handkerchief and mopped the sweat from his forehead before continuing:

"And yet, over the past few days, I've had a sneaking suspicion that all we've been trying to do has been fundamentally mistaken—or, to put it another way, that it is unimportant—possibly even meaningless—to me. Truly, even meaningless. Like when you're putting all your energy into some pursuit, and all the while you suspect that it might be a mistake, that it's been a mistake since the very beginning. Or when you're digging for the answer to some difficult question, and eventually you think you've found it. But then comes a day when you discover the real answer actually resides in some distant place far beyond anything you imagined. Do you understand what I'm saying?"

Xiumi shook her head in confusion. She honestly had no idea what he was talking about.

"That's fine. Enough of all that, then." Zhang Jiyuan slapped his forehead. "Let me show you something." He reached into the suitcase by the head of his bed and brought out a small box, beautifully wrought of silk brocade, which he placed in Xiumi's hands.

"Is this for me?" Xiumi asked him.

"No, it isn't," Zhang Jiyuan said. "This is something I can't carry with me at the moment. I need you to keep it safe for me. I'll be coming back to Puji in a month at the very most, and then you can give it back to me."

Xiumi examined the box. It was covered in sapphire-blue velveteen, like a lady's jewelry case.

"A month, at the very latest." Zhang Jiyuan sat down at the table beside her. "If more than a month goes by and I'm not back, then you won't be seeing me again."

"Why would we not see you again?"

"Because then it will mean that I'm no longer in this world. But when the time comes, someone else will come to you asking for it, and you can just give it to him."

"What's his name?" Xiumi asked.

"His name isn't important," Zhang Jiyuan said, smiling. "He has six fingers. But remember: the extra finger is on his left hand."

"What if he never comes?"

"Then it's yours. You can take it to the jeweler and have him make you a necklace out of it."

"What's inside? Can I open it?"

"As you wish," Zhang Jiyuan replied.

Lilypad once again walked through the door, this time with a foot-washing basin under one arm, a towel over her shoulder, and a kettle in her other hand. She entered without even knocking. Setting the kettle and basin on the floor and draping the towel over the back of a chair, she said to Zhang Jiyuan, "The mistress said to tell you that it's getting late, and you should wash up and get some rest. I've heated this water up twice already." She turned to Xiumi. "Time to say good night."

Xiumi looked over at Uncle. "Good night, then?"

"Sleep well."

Zhang Jiyuan stood up. His face neared hers for a moment as he rose. She saw that he had small pockmarks across his cheeks.

Xiumi followed Lilypad down the stairs. She could sense the studio door closing slowly behind her. Total darkness enclosed the courtyard.

12

XIUMI didn't hear the rooster crow at dawn. She opened her eyes to find her lamp still lit and the far wall of her bedroom drenched in the crimson light of the rising sun. The smell of cold air permeated the room—late autumn had arrived. She lolled under the covers and listened to Mother calling for Magpie. A summons from Mother always sent Magpie off in a flash, rushing to appear before the elder as quickly as possible. This time Mother sent her up to the studio to strip the sheets and blankets off the bed.

She knew Zhang Jiyuan had already left.

With his departure, the house returned to its old, tranquil rhythm. To Xiumi's mind, it seemed that more had happened in the short span from spring to fall than in all the years of her life before it. But to others the events came and went like frost on the rooftop, vanishing with the first touch of sunlight as if it had never occurred.

Baoshen began recording harvest tithes, leaving the house before daybreak and returning after dark. Trips to more distant villages sometimes took a day or two. Once he had gathered all the numbers, he buried himself in the office, the beads of his abacus clicking continually. Lilypad cleaned out the woodshed and lined it with reed mats to serve as a storage space for when their tenants brought their tithes of grain. Mother took Magpie with her on daily trips to the tailor as they made sure the family would be clothed warmly for the winter. Only Xiumi and Tiger were left with nothing to do but wander around the courtyard and occasionally accompany Mother to the tailor for measurements. When Xiumi got really bored, she would go to Ding Shuze's place to practice her reading. Ding Shuze had already sent his wife around to ask for the year's tuition.

On the first day of winter, horse carts and shoulder poles crowded into the courtyard. Grandma Meng came with her husband to help out. Wang Qidan and Wang Badan each held one end of a wooden pole that passed through the center of an iron scale, which Hua Erniang held at the center as she called out pounds and ounces. Baoshen worked furiously, writing in the ledger with one hand and working the abacus with the other. Mother beamed as she oversaw the whole affair, now running to the kitchen or checking the rear courtyard, now sending snacks out to the tenant farmers, many of whom had walked for miles to line up at her door. Lilypad and Magpie spent the day in the kitchen chopping meat and cooking rice, and the hammering of cleavers on cutting boards continued throughout the morning.

A line of farmers squatted timidly by the courtyard wall, their shoulder poles in their arms. Once a name was called, the farmer would hurry over to check the markings on the scale. Hua Erniang would smile at him and say, "Look carefully and tell me how much." The farmer deferentially reported a number to her that she would then repeat at a shout so that Baoshen, sitting at his desk in the sky-well, could hear it over the clicking of his abacus. Once he repeated the number back to her, it was entered in the ledger and the tithe was paid. Hemp sacks full of grain were carried one by one into the rear courtyard. Grandma Meng skittered back and forth on her tiny feet between front and rear courtyards on some strange business Xiumi couldn't comprehend.

One of their tenant farmers, Wang Aliu, was almost forty pounds short of his share. "Every year it's always the same with you," Hua Erniang scolded, and turned to Mother for advice. "He's been a problem year after year, even with a harvest as good as this one he's still short. I think you should just take his three acres back and be done with him."

Hearing this, Wang Aliu dragged his wife and young son before Mother to bow and smile imploringly. "To tell the truth, ma'am, my wife got sick twice this year, and we had the new baby, and half of those three acres were barren this harvest. I promise I'll make up this year's debt next harvest, just please don't take my lease away." He pushed his son's head and shoulders down, forcing him to kowtow. The boy stubbornly refused to kneel, for which Wang Aliu slapped him across the face. The child howled as blood oozed from his lips, and ran to the far side of the courtyard. He wore only a thin shirt and a pair of heavily patched pants; Xiumi could see his butt through the gaping holes in the back. Wang Aliu's wife really did look like an invalid, her face wan and yellowed. She wore a man's cotton coat with no buttons, secured across her waist by a makeshift cotton cord. She stood holding her baby and crying silently.

The sight of the family moved Mother to sympathy. "Just log their share," she told Hua Erniang. "Let them make it up next year." Wang Aliu thanked her effusively, kowtowing several times before calling his wife back over to pay respect to Baoshen. "Enough, enough," Baoshen stopped him. "This year's debt, plus last year and the year before, that comes to one hundred and sixty-eight pounds. I won't charge you any interest. Tighten your belt and work hard enough next year to bring it all in at once, so I can clear your account for you." Wang Aliu smiled, nodded, and repeatedly promised that he would as he backed away.

Grandma Meng was heading to the well with a basketful of arrowhead tubers to wash and trim; Xiumi, seeing there was nothing else for her to do, joined the old lady to work and chat.

"Wang Aliu really is a sad story," Grandma Meng said. "None of his land went barren this year, he just likes his liquor; once he opens a bottle, he can't stop himself. He's already pawned everything in his house not nailed down, and has tormented his wife terribly. Six children, and they've already lost three." The old lady sighed.

Xiumi suddenly asked, "How come these people have to bring the grain they harvested to us?"

Grandma Meng stared at her blankly for a second, then laughed out loud. Instead of replying to her, she turned to Baoshen and said, "Hey Cockeye, did you hear what this girl just asked me?" Baoshen appeared to have heard the question, and cracked a wry smile. As Mother happened to be passing by, Grandma Meng called to her, "Guess what your little daughter just asked me?"

"What did she say?" Mother inquired. Grandma Meng repeated Xiumi's question for the entire courtyard to hear. Hua Erniang laughed so heartily the counterweight slid off her scales and nearly fell onto her toes. Xiumi saw all the tenant farmers standing by the wall smiling at her. "Don't be fooled by how big my daughter's grown," Mother replied aloud. "She hasn't grown much sense yet. I've been feeding her all these years and she still doesn't know anything."

After Mother left, Grandma Meng turned seriously to Xiumi and said, "Silly girl, all of them are farming your family's land. Who are they going to bring their harvest to if not to you? Certainly not to me."

"Well then, why don't they farm their own land?"

"That's an even sillier question. Those beggars are so poor, they barely have a pair of sewing needles between them, to say nothing about land."

"Then how did we get our land?"

"Some of it you inherited, some you bought, and some you took when people couldn't pay what they owed you," Grandma Meng explained. "Silly girl. It's as if you've lived your whole life in the Peach Blossom Paradise—you don't know anything. And they say you can read?"

Xiumi wanted to respond, but Grandma Meng had already stood up, slapped the dust from her dress, and walked to the well to draw the water for her vegetables.

The tenant farmers were served lunch at a grand table set up in the skywell, as Mother feared they would soil her dining room. When sixteen or seventeen working farmers saw the table brought out, they quickly gathered around and sat down as the chairs appeared. Wang Aliu scooped himself a full bowl of rice, then piled portion after portion of meat and vegetables on top until he had made a large dome of food. Then he left the table in search of his son. The child lay asleep against his mother's knee amid the long grass at the foot of the court-yard wall. Wang Aliu hunted all around until he found the pair, and squatted down by his wife to offer her some food. She refused it, shaking her head as she woke her son up. When the boy opened his eyes and saw the food, he ignored the proffered chopsticks and dove in with his hands. A clear strand of snot reaching from his nose to the edge of the bowl got swept up and eaten with the mouthfuls of food.

Magpie and Xiumi watched the scene through the kitchen window and giggled. Lilypad laughed with them for a moment, then suddenly lost her smile and started to cry. Xiumi assumed she was thinking of her old home in Huzhou, or her dead parents, and felt pained for her. She did not expect that, after crying for a while, Lilypad would draw her into her arms and say, "Sister, if I come begging at your door one day, you'll give me a bowl of rice, won't you?"

"Why would you say something like that?" Magpie asked. "You have a good life here already, why would you need to beg?"

Lilypad ignored the question at first as she wiped away her tears. After a long pause, she said, "When I was in the deep southwest, I saw a fortune-teller walking down the street with a starving child. I felt so bad looking at them that I gave them a couple steamed buns; as I left, the fortune-teller stopped me. He said that a gift of food should be repaid as if it were the gift of life itself. He said he wasn't good at much, but the fortunes he told mostly came true, and so he asked me for the year, day, and hour of my birth. Of course I didn't know any of this information; I'd never even seen my parents' faces before, how could I know the hour I was born? So he read my face. In the end he said I would spend the latter half of my life on the street, that I'd starve by the roadside and dogs would eat my flesh. I asked if there were any way to avoid such a fate, and he said only if I married someone born in the year of the pig. But I'm only getting older every day—how can I possibly afford to be so picky?"

"The guy was probably just saying anything, why take him seriously?" Xiumi said. "It could even be that he was a pig himself, and wanted to scare you into marrying him."

Magpie added, "Now that I think of it, Baoshen's son Tiger was born in the year of the pig."

This interjection finally turned Lilypad's sadness into laughter. "Oh, so I have to marry him, now?" Eventually, her dark mood passed and she said to Magpie, "Where are you from originally? And how did you end up in Puji? Grandma Meng told us that we weren't supposed to mention arsenic around you. Why is that?"

Magpie began to shiver violently, her eyes staring straight ahead. Her lips pursed and turned purple; she shook until finally she closed her eyes and tears fell. She said that when she was five, her father had gotten into a dispute with a neighbor over farmland; the quarrel eventually went to court. The hearing went smoothly, but just as they were on the verge of winning, their neighbor managed to sneak arsenic into the family's soup one evening. Both her parents and her two brothers died. She didn't eat as much as they did, and her neighbors held her nose and force-fed her a spoonful of human shit until she vomited her guts out and held on to her worthless life. Afraid her presence would incite more retribution from someone they knew to be a killer, her relatives didn't dare take her in, so she ended up with Grandma Meng in Puji.

"No wonder I've seen you wash your bowl over and over before every meal," Xiumi noted. "Are you afraid someone's going to poison you?"

"A childhood habit; I know it won't happen but I can't help feeling suspicious anyway."

"Just another hopeless soul." Lilypad sighed before peering down at Xiumi. "How can we ever compare with you, all that good karma from a past life getting you reborn into a house like this one, everything seen to, everything done for you so you can go without a care in the world?"

Xiumi said nothing out loud. Her heart replied, *How could you all know my worries? I might scare you to death if I told you.* Even at that moment, however, she had no intimation of the disaster that moved steadily in her direction.

More than two weeks passed since Zhang Jiyuan disappeared, and few ever mentioned his name. Xiumi was woken in the late hours of a cold December night by the memory of the satin-embroidered box he had given her before he left. She had tucked it into her dresser without opening it. But what did it contain? The question danced through her head like the snowflakes on the roof. By daybreak, she could no longer contain her curiosity. She jumped out of bed, took the box from her dresser, and opened it.

Inside was a golden cicada.

Around that time, Zhang Jiyuan's body floated down the Yangtze River, skirted a sandbank, and turned into a narrow outlet that flowed under a dyke. A hunter from Puji found him. The river had long since iced over, and his naked corpse had frozen among a cluster of reeds. Baoshen had no choice but to hire people to chisel it out and drag it onto the land. Xiumi stared at the body from a distance; it was the first time she had ever seen a man's naked body. His brow was still furrowed, his body wrapped completely in ice like a candy apple imprisoned in sugar.

Mother ran down to the river and threw herself onto the body, completely oblivious to the cocoon of ice around his body and the growing crowd of onlookers. She wept loudly over him.

"I shouldn't have let you go. And even if I did, I shouldn't have wished you dead," Mother sobbed.

Part Two
HUAJIASHE

I

STILL clear. Met Xue Zuyan once more in Xia village. He claims the eighty-seven Mauser rifles are already on their way from the Germans. Zhang Lianjia announced his intention to quit the society, claiming he had to stay home after his mother's death. The real reason is simply terror in the face of the great moment. Zuyan pleaded with Lianjia unsuccessfully; his mood darkened and he became quite angry. Then he unsheathed his sword and pointed it at Lianjia, saying, "All this about quitting, quitting, quitting... I'll give you something to fucking quit for." One swing of his sword and the pear tree in Zuyan's courtyard fell. Zhang shut his mouth.

Noon: Xue's valet brought Xiumi and a fair-haired boy into the courtyard. They carried a letter from Ding Shuze. Xiumi noticed me and got scared; her face turned pale and she became too uncomfortable to speak. She stood under the covered walkway, playing with her clothing and grinding her teeth. When I put a hand on her shoulder she didn't withdraw, just trembled fiercely. Those eyes like autumn waters, hands like flower petals, along with her pitiable state gave her a coldly brilliant, intoxicating look. I wanted to pull her to me and squeeze her until her joints popped. Ahhh, well...

———

Three years later, as Xiumi reread this passage from Zhang Jiyuan's diary, she was only one night away from traveling to Changzhou to be married.

Magpie had discovered the diary hidden beneath a pillow as she stripped Zhang Jiyuan's bed. For the first time, she displayed the quiet cleverness that lay below her honest exterior: she neither said anything when she found it, nor reported it to Mother, but passed it secretly to Xiumi. Of course, the events that transpired in the diary's account far exceeded her expectations.

Xiumi had long suspected that while the world beyond held innumerable secrets, it consistently refused to reveal any of them to her. She felt as if she were trapped in a windowless room, and could barely make out the contours of the walls by the faint light that managed to sneak inside. But reading Zhang Jiyuan's diary ripped the ceiling off this room in one stroke, flooding it with such bright sunlight she could hardly open her eyes.

She spent three whole days reading it. Everything came too fast, and too unexpectedly. It caught her heart the way a river current catches a leaf, sending it now up and over the white crests of rapids and now into the depths. She thought she would go insane. She lay on her bed through the night without sleeping, discovering in the process that a human could survive four straight nights without a wink of sleep. Two weeks later, she made a new discovery, namely that a person could also sleep for six straight days without waking.

She finally opened her eyes to find Magpie, Lilypad, and Mother standing by her bedside looking at her, while Doctor Tang sat at her desk, writing a prescription. She looked at the people in the room as if she didn't recognize them, then spoke at great length in a way no one understood. In the month that followed, she hardly said a word to anyone.

Afraid that Xiumi would get pulled down the same path as Father, Mother once again hired monks and adepts to perform divinations and exorcisms. One day Xiumi wandered downstairs naked, and Tiger started calling her "the crazy girl." She began to talk more, and babbled without end whenever she bumped into someone. Mother didn't want to hear about Zhang Jiyuan in any case—the repetition of his name exhausted her patience. She had already thought up an excuse for Xiumi's descent into insanity: "The girl has always been a little off." Once she herself accepted this as fact, she let it slip out in conversation.

Only Magpie understood the real cause of everything. For a diary to have driven someone crazy meant its contents could not have been trivial. Clearly the scribblings of intellectuals had to be taken seriously. Knowing that vain regret and silent tears would be of no use to anyone, she decided to tell the truth. Yet the day she planned to spill everything to Mother was the same day Xiumi suddenly recovered her faculties.

That morning, Lilypad was carrying a bowl of medicinal broth to Xiumi's room when she happened upon a horrifying scene: Xiumi had inserted one tender thumb into the doorjamb and was slowly closing the door on it. The pressure of the heavy wooden door had already squashed the pad of her thumb; a trickle of blood ran down the frame. Xiumi turned to Lilypad and smiled. "Look. It doesn't hurt at all."

Lilypad was stunned. Instead of running over to stop Xiumi she raised the bowl of medicine to her own lips and drank it dry. The intense bitterness brought her back to her senses, and she muttered, "Good heavens, am I going crazy too?" She whipped out a handkerchief from the sash at her waist in order to tend to Xiumi's wound. The end of her thumb had been flattened completely, and beneath the broken nail was a mess of blood and flesh. Lilypad heard Xiumi repeat, "Now it hurts a little... I know it hurts now... Really, now it hurts really bad." Sharp physical pain lifted the cloud from her mind and miraculously restored her mental clarity.

One side effect of her recovery, however, was that she could no longer remember what Zhang Jiyuan looked like. His visage faded from her mind, and even the scene of his frozen body by the river began to blur. Forgetting is an irreversible action; a face melts from memory more quickly than ice, as if it were the most delicate thing on earth.

The first time she ever saw Zhang Jiyuan, she felt like that face must have been an abstract figure, something that didn't belong to the human world. Gradually, the face transformed into the green woolen cushion on the back of a chair, into the glittering stars over the empty courtyard at night, or the heavy scales of clouds on an overcast day; it became the peach trees in full bloom, with petals and stamens all soaked in dew. As the wind rose, the branches waved and the flowers trembled, and a bottomless grief opened in the deepest recesses of her heart.

Xiumi had been well for only a few days before Mother set to work on finding her a husband. Xiumi had zero interest in getting married, but she put up no resistance. When Mother sent Lilypad to test her feelings about it, Xiumi responded offhandedly, "Anyone is fine, I couldn't care less."

A match was quickly found. When Lilypad spoke to Xiumi about arranging a visit, she replied, "Any day is fine. It's all the same to me."

When that day arrived, Xiumi locked herself in her room. Magpie and Lilypad banged on her door until their hands swelled, but she wouldn't open it. Finally, Mother marched upstairs and pleaded with Xiumi through the door as tears rolled down her cheeks. "The matchmaker's brought the young man over," she told her. "He's standing in the courtyard. Just go and have a look at him, say a word or two. You don't want to reach the Hou family house in Changzhou and then regret it."

Only then did Xiumi learn that her betrothed lived in Changzhou, and his surname was Hou. "No need to see him," she told Mother from within her room, "as long as you think he looks all right. Have them send a palanquin over when the time comes and I'll join him."

"How can you talk like that, daughter? Getting married isn't some children's game."

"Oh, please." Xiumi sighed. "This body isn't mine anyway. If he wants to spoil it, let him."

Her response made Mother wail loudly; Xiumi wept silently on the other side of the door. A shared secret hung unspoken between the two of them. Mother cried herself exhausted, then continued to beg: "Even if you don't need to look at him, you can't refuse to let him have a look at you, can you?"

At this, Xiumi finally opened the door. She went to the upstairs railing and lackadaisically looked down into the courtyard, where an old woman and a man in a woven skullcap stood, their eyes raised to her. The man appeared neither young nor particularly old, and he seemed passably handsome. Xiumi had hoped he would be older or have some kind of noticeable flaw like baldness or pockmarks, to lend her marriage more tragedy. Over the past few days, she had become addicted to self-abasement; it felt like the only way to ease her rancor. The old lady grinned at Xiumi, while repeatedly asking the man beside her, "What do you think? Nice and pale?" The man mumbled, "Very pale, very pale. I like it, I like it." The man kept giggling as he stared at her—a short, idiotic laugh that sounded like hiccups. He licked his upper lip several times, as if chewing on something tasty.

Xiumi was truly indifferent about marriage. She had learned about "secret trysts" and the "pleasures of the bedroom" from Zhang Jiyuan's diary, and much more besides. The night before the wedding party came for her, she lay in bed alone beside her lamp and flipped through the diary. She had never been so close to someone else's naked soul. She fantasized that Zhang Jiyuan was sitting right next to her, talking and joking with her as if they were husband and wife. Even when she got to the salacious parts, she didn't feel embarrassed or nervous, but simply snorted with childlike laughter.

"Zhang Jiyuan, Zhang Jiyuan . . . you go on and on about revolution and unification, your worry for the world and the heat of your ambition, but all you really want is a piece of ass."

She giggled for a moment before her humor suddenly transformed into grief. She bit one end of her blanket and stared into space before tears welled up; she cried quietly, soaking both sides of the pillow. Then she let out a long, slow breath, and said to herself in her most determined tone: *Marry. Just marry. Doesn't matter who he is, as long as he wants it, I'll marry him and let him do with me what he likes.*

2

ONCE ABOARD her bridal palanquin, Xiumi drifted in and out of sleep. The bridal procession moved very slowly through the morning's thick fog. The pitch and yaw of the river ferry and the grunts of the palanquin carriers repeatedly woke her up. Lifting the window blind revealed her new husband riding an emaciated donkey alongside her; he must have been grinning at her, though his features were indistinct. The matchmaker followed behind them, her smiling face powdered and rouged. A barely visible disk of pale yellow hung in the sky. The fog thickened, gluing Xiumi's hair to her head; she could see no more than a few feet away. The clanking of the donkey's bronze bell was the only sound that accompanied her.

She thought of what Mother had said to her the night before: "When the bridal palanquin arrives tomorrow morning, just leave with them; you don't have to say goodbye to me. And make sure not to drink any water before you go so you're not too uncomfortable on the journey. Now, according to custom, a new bride returns to her parents three days after the wedding. But Changzhou is a long way away, and with all the trouble that's happening, you shouldn't try to come home." Her pursed lips trembled as she held back tears. Xiumi had seen Magpie and Lilypad crouched by the courtyard wall, crying as she walked to the palanquin that morning. Baoshen and Tiger had been with them, but they did not look at her. Only Hua Erniang and Grandma Meng made a fuss over Xiumi, stumping around on their bound feet and shouting orders. Ding Shuze had sent a servant around a few days prior with a handwritten couplet for their doorway: the word for "happiness" written in sixteen different calligraphic styles.

That morning he had stood by the village entrance, scratching his back with a wooden scepter as he watched the procession go by. To Xiumi, he had been little more than a shadow against the impenetrable fog.

A new anxiety overwhelmed her: she suddenly had a feeling she would never see Mother again. When the palanquin lifted, her heart floated off its moorings. The fog separated her from Puji almost immediately. She worried about more than just Mother. The golden cicada in the embroidered box was still locked in her dresser upstairs. Three years had passed, and the six-fingered man Zhang Jiyuan had spoken of had yet to appear.

Soon after they crossed the river, Xiumi's dreaming was interrupted by a commotion outside the palanquin. She figured that residents from the villages nearby must have discovered the wedding procession and come to cheer them on in the hopes of catching some wedding candy. The thought didn't interest Xiumi at all, and she continued to doze. It seemed strange that the clash of metal blades and a woman's screaming should suddenly pierce the general hubbub, but Xiumi didn't pay much attention to it. Yet the palanquin began to pick up speed, until it became clear they were moving at a full gallop. The rush of wind and the bearers' heavy panting filled her ears, and the palanquin jostled so violently she nearly vomited.

She finally drew the window blind to discover that the red-cheeked matchmaker, her dowry train, and her ostensible husband and his donkey with the bell had all disappeared; all that was left of the procession was the four palanquin bearers, who now carried her as fast as they could along a rocky path. One of the bearers in the front turned to face her and yelled breathlessly, "Bandits, it's bandits! Motherfucking bandits!"

Xiumi heard the sound of horse hooves behind them and realized the severity of her predicament.

Eventually, exhaustion overtook the four men carrying her; they dropped her on an outdoor threshing floor and ran for their lives.

She watched them jump away and scamper across the wheat field, then vanish in the fog.

Emerging from the palanquin, she found herself alone. One ramshackle hut stood unused at one end of the threshing area, its walls tilting precariously, the thatch of its roof already black with mold. A water buffalo lay asleep by the front door, while some white egrets perched across its back and along the hut's roof. A dark shadow in the fog signified a grove of trees from which emerged the cry of a cuckoo.

Xiumi watched a handful of men on horseback converge on her from several directions. Yet she didn't feel the slightest bit afraid. These highwaymen, infamous for being green-skinned and sharp-toothed monsters, looked a lot like ordinary farmers.

One of them, a middle-aged man with a bald head, sauntered up to Xiumi on a white horse and smiled as he reined in his mount. "Xiuxiu, do you remember me?"

The question shocked her. *How could this man know my nickname?* She scrutinized him for a moment. He did look familiar, particularly the long scar across his face, but she couldn't remember where she had seen him before.

"I don't know you," she said.

"What about me, then?" The question came from another one, a twentysomething young man riding a chestnut horse. He was broad shouldered and muscular, with a resonant voice. "Do you know me?"

Xiumi shook her head.

The two men looked at each other, then burst out laughing.

"Well, that's no surprise, after what, seven or eight years?" asked the middle-aged man.

"A full six years," replied the younger man.

"How come it feels like seven to me?"

"Nope, six years. Exactly six."

As the two riders argued, a young man who looked like a stable boy walked over. "Boss, the fog is breaking up."

The middle-aged rider looked up at the sky and nodded, then turned back to Xiumi. "You'll have to forgive us for this."

Before she could reply, a band of black cloth dropped over her eyes, while a salty wad of the same material was forced into her mouth. The men bound her hands securely and threw her back into the palanquin. Then they lifted the palanquin and continued on their way.

When the cloth over her eyes was finally lifted, Xiumi found herself seated in the cabin of a wooden boat. Everything in her field of vision was black: the cabin's roof, the table, the reeds they passed, and the water flowing beneath them, everything black. She closed her eyes, leaned back against the rail, and tried moving her arms and legs. She realized her pants were wet with urine but couldn't recall when that had happened. By this point, she no longer felt ashamed. She opened her eyes once more to examine the scene around her, a vague anxiety rising in her heart. Why did everything look black to her? She quickly found the answer: night had fallen.

She saw a sliver of moon and many stars. The boat was moving across a wide marsh in the company of other boats—she counted seven in total—all linked together with iron cable. Her boat was last in line. Someone on her boat lit a lamp, and soon, seven points of golden light stretched out in a wide arc across the water's surface, like a team of horsemen lighting their way along the road.

Where am I? Where are they taking me?

Only the wind replied, the creaking tiller, and the birds that cried as they skimmed the water. Two people sat across from her. She'd seen them both that morning in the threshing field. The bald, older man leaned against the rail, apparently fast asleep; the scar that crossed his face was deep, and so long it reached all the way from his cheek to his neck. He had propped up one leg on the table, his heel on top of her bag. *He even knows my pet name*, Xiumi thought. *Where could I have seen him before?*

Close beside the sleeper sat the stable boy. He looked like a young man of seventeen or eighteen, with a clear and well-defined face, but of slim build. He kept stealing glances at Xiumi with a timid look in his eye. All Xiumi had to do was accidentally meet his gaze, and he would immediately blush, lower his eyes, and begin playing with the red tassel on the hilt of his machete. Somehow, his gaze made her think of Zhang Jiyuan. He had one foot propped on the table as well, but his cloth shoe had two holes in it that revealed his toes. A lit hurricane lantern sat in the center of the table next to a long tobacco pipe. The lake water lapped the sides of the boat as they sculled along; the night felt as cold as the water. You could smell its decaying dampness in the air. Xiumi laid one cheek along the wet gunwale and felt the cold plunge into her.

What should I do?

She thought about jumping in and drowning. The problem was that she didn't want to die. And if they didn't want her to die either, they'd just pull her out anyway. She tried to avoid thinking about what would come next, but the memory of Miss Sun was a problem. The moment she envisioned Miss Sun's naked corpse as it had been described to her, her heart began beating out of control. Though she had no idea what kind of place this boat was taking her to, it seemed clear that her fate would not be much better than Miss Sun's.

She heard a heavy rustling as the boat slipped into a narrow lane of water between walls of river reeds that rose high above them. The reeds scraped the sides of the boat, and the noise of running water grew louder. The stable boy was still staring at her. He didn't look like a bandit at all; his face was slightly pallid, and while he seemed shy, his eyes twinkled. Xiumi tried asking him where they were and where they were going, but he just bit his lip and said nothing.

The middle-aged man suddenly stirred; he looked at Xiumi, then glared at the stable boy and said, "Pipe."

The frightened young man snatched the pipe from the table, filled the bowl with tobacco, and passed it with two hands to the other. Receiving the pipe, the middle-aged man commanded, "Fire."

The stable boy picked up the lamp and held it close enough for the other to light his pipe with the flame. The older man's visage glowed. Xiumi saw the boy's hands shake violently, and noticed the fine mustache around his lips. The older man sucked on the pipe, then turned to Xiumi and asked, "Do you really not remember me?"

Xiumi did not reply.

"Look closer and think again."

Xiumi instead cast her eyes down. After a pause, the man said, "I guess this means you really don't remember us. Qingsheng has been worried about you, you know."

"Who's Qingsheng?" Xiumi asked. Why did that name sound so familiar to her?

"He has a nickname: 'Listen.'" The older man chuckled. "How's that, do you remember now? Six or seven years ago, your father's studio caught on fire . . ."

Xiumi suddenly remembered. After Father's chambers burned down, Mother sent Baoshen out to hire a group of workmen; one of them was named Qingsheng, whom the others called Listen. She remembered seeing him on the day they all left, walking backward toward the village so he could keep his eyes on her until he finally walked into a tree.

"You're Qingsheng?"

"Me? No," the middle-aged man replied, "my name is Qingde. Qingsheng is in the boat ahead of us. You saw him this morning in the threshing field, riding a chestnut horse."

"But aren't you all tradesmen, how could—"

"How could we all turn into robbers, eh?" The man called Qingde laughed until tears came to his eyes. "Actually, to tell you the truth, we've been in this line of work all along."

Another pause, then he elaborated: "I am a tile roofer, and Qingsheng is a carpenter. We do work for hire, but that's all a front. Our real business is trying to figure out how much the client is worth. We're not interested in poor people; if we end up doing a job for somebody who turns out to be broke, we take our payment and call it bad luck and move on. In such situations, we really are tradesmen, and, generally speaking, we do decent work. But your house was different. After all those years working for the government in Yangzhou, your father had put together a small fortune in property alone."

As Qingde talked, the stable boy stared at Xiumi with a look in his eyes that said, *You're in for it now!* Noticing that Qingde had finished his pipe, he took it and dutifully refilled the bowl.

Qingde was in a talkative mood. He spoke slowly, with an air of world-weary arrogance. Taking a few hard drags on his pipe, he laughed again, and said, "But no matter if it's kidnapping or roof tiling, it has to be done right. I plastered the walls of that studio myself; they're as smooth as a mirror. I've never made prettier walls in my life. And I'll do good work with you, too—you'll see in a couple of days. Look at that, you're blushing. I didn't even say anything and your face is already red. I like girls that blush, they're not like whores. The whores just pretend to be into it. But I knew from the moment I laid eyes on you that you've got real spirit. We picked you up, and you never cried or made a sound; I've never seen that before. Even after we stuffed your mouth, tied you up, and threw you in the carriage, you fell fast asleep. If that's not a spitfire, I don't know what is." At that point, he turned and looked at the stable boy: "Hand."

The boy hesitated briefly, then offered him an upturned and trembling left hand, which Qingde rapped hard with the bowl of his pipe. A flaming ember fell out onto the young man's palm and smoked as the stable boy jumped up and down in his seat in agony. Xiumi caught a sharp whiff of burning flesh.

Qingde put a heavy palm on the attendant's shoulder. "What are you jumping around for? Stop it. I didn't drop it into your eye, what are you complaining about? Learn to control your eyes, so you won't go looking at things you're not supposed to look at." Looking back at Xiumi, he asked, "Aren't you going to go back to sleep? The boat won't arrive until first light tomorrow. Don't you want to get some rest? I know I'm going to."

Xiumi watched the night turn slowly into day.

Through the morning fog, she could discern a dark outline of mountains coming into view beyond the borders of the lake. Their slopes, not particularly steep, were populated with white birches, which gave way to pine trees and naked juts of stone in the higher reaches. She could hear lake water lapping against the shore, and the cackling of chickens from a nearby village. *We must be nearing shore,* she thought. Just ahead of them stood a thick grove of mulberry trees. The boats glided around the edge of the grove for another hour before finally coming upon a tiny village curled into the elbow of the mountain, now bathed in red by the rising sun.

3

LIGHT rain, clearing after noon. Zuyan went to Meicheng last night, but infantry lieutenant Li Daodeng refused to see him. Zuyan cursed his name all morning. The Mausers have made it as far as Zuyan's uncle's place in Xipu; storing them there for now. After dinner, Meiyun went to a neighbor's house to play mahjong. I chatted with Xiumi and Lilypad for a while before heading upstairs to bed. Just as I'd drifted off, chaos erupted in the village, and I heard shouting and running footsteps, like some catastrophe had occurred. I dressed in a hurry and came downstairs. Turns out that Miss Sun, who lives at the far end of the village, had been raped and killed by bandits.

The woman Sun was an amateur whore, and won't be missed. Had the revolution already succeeded, hers would still be counted among the Ten Capital Crimes. Dapples, Dapples, didn't you swear up and down that there were no robbers in Puji? What a load of shit. With the world falling apart, rebellion stirs in every breast. While outlaws may not lie as thickly on this side of the Yangtze as they do in Shandong and Henan, it's not as if there are none at all. I almost fell victim to them once three years ago, while passing through Danyang. That's why finding connections to local armed forces is of greatest importance. In this season of danger even the bandits may be of use to me. There will be plenty of time to get rid of them once the great project has been completed.

Still no word from Dapples.

Tonight a night of enchanting moonlight and perfect cold. As I stood in the courtyard, my heart wandered far from me, as if missing something. Seeing Xiumi washing her hair in the kitchen, I went in to talk to her. Water dripped down to her shoulders, and I could see the embroidered flowers on her dress in the moonlight. Her neck is so slender and so pale. As we chatted, I wondered what would happen if I simply walked over and embraced her. Perhaps she might have yielded to me. Zuyan is a sharp observer of the human heart; after seeing her in Xia village for the first time a few days ago, he said to me that even though the girl might be cold and aloof, she could still be brought easily in hand. He exhorted me to be bold. But would it really be feasible? What should I do? What should I do? No—I must hold back, must show restraint.

After lying awake for many hours, I sat up for a while, wrapped in my clothes, and composed a poem:

> Peach blossoms in hand are seeds of endless trouble;
> Breeze stirs my curtains in a long note of worry.
> A new moon knows nothing of the heart's old secrets;
> Yet it sends a pale face to visit the bedside.

———

They had brought Xiumi to a place called Huajiashe. That evening they took her out to a small island in the lake just opposite the village. The island was not more than an acre in total, and it stood only a short arrow's flight away from the village proper. The two had once been connected by a wooden bridge, which for reasons unstated was later torn down. A regular line of black wooden posts still poked through the water's surface, now serving as a resting place for birds.

The handful of structures on the island were old, their walls conquered by ivy and morning glory vines. The living quarters had a small front courtyard, enclosed by a hedge, as well as a garden. A number of peach and pear trees that stood before the house had already lost their blooms. The island lay very low, which kept the soil wet and allowed all kinds of scrub trees and climbing flora to flourish.

On days of heavy wind and rain, the lake water sometimes advanced as far as the walls of the house.

The lonely house was home to a single human inhabitant. Her head was shaved, and you could tell from the firmness of her breasts that she was a still a young woman, maybe between thirty and forty. Her name was Han Liu. She had been kidnapped from a Buddhist nunnery almost seven years earlier, and had even had a child, who died in its first month. Long years of solitude had given her the need to talk to herself constantly. Xiumi's arrival excited her somewhat. Yet she took pains to conceal her enthusiasm. Xiumi pretended not to notice, each woman cautious and guarded toward the other.

Strangely, once the bandits left her on the island, they appeared to forget about her entirely. No one crossed the water for a full two weeks. One day at noon, when Xiumi saw a small boat making its way toward the island, she felt vaguely excited. Yet the boat merely circled around to the south end of the island and stopped. Xiumi watched the boatman cast his nets into the water. She spent the days walking aimlessly around the banks of the island; when she got tired, she would sit underneath a tree and stare at the clouds.

She had read Zhang Jiyuan's diary several times already. Even though she knew that every reading of it was an exercise in self-torture, she was still able to glean new information. For instance, she only now learned Mother's given name: Meiyun. She attempted to connect the name to her mental image of Mother, which made her think of Puji. Less than a month had passed since she left, yet it felt to her like decades. It was hard to be sure that it hadn't all been a dream.

Xiumi could see the whole of Huajiashe across the mirror surface of the lake, and could even hear the laughter of small children on the other side. It surprised her to discover that every house built on that gentle mountain slope looked exactly alike: the same whitewashed walls with a black tile roof, same wooden doors and ornamentally carved windows. Each house possessed a hedged courtyard of exactly the same size and layout. One narrow lane paved with cobblestones ran straight up the mountain, splitting the town into eastern and western halves. A fleet of boats of various sizes floated at their moorings in the cove before the village, their unadorned masts like a forest of bare trees in winter.

One morning, Xiumi and Han Liu were playing with a nest of newborn chickens. Nearly freshly hatched, the chicks could walk only a few paces before tumbling to the ground. Han Liu minced vegetable leaves to feed to them, and crouched on the ground before the chicks, talking to them and calling them her babies. When Xiumi asked her why no one had come out to the island after all this time, Han Liu simply smiled.

"They'll come eventually." Han Liu scooped a chick into her palm and stroked the fuzz on its back. "They're probably out calling your number right now."

"Calling my number?"

"It means negotiating ransom money with your family," Han Liu explained. "Once your parents pay, they'll send you back."

"What happens if they can't agree on a price?"

"Oh, they will—they never ask for an impossible amount. Unless your family truly wants you dead."

"But what happens if they really can't agree?"

"Then they'll snip your ticket," replied Han Liu without a second thought. "Cut off one of your ears, or maybe a finger, and send that to your family. If your mom and dad still won't pay the ransom, then they'll tear your ticket accordingly. But they almost never do that. I've been here for seven years, and I've only seen them kill one person. She was the daughter of a rich family."

"Why did they kill her?"

"That one had an awfully fiery disposition. The moment they brought her to the island she tried to drown herself—tried to three times, then tried to kill herself by bashing her head into the wall. When they realized they were going to lose their mark no matter what, they killed her. Of course they gave her to the boys first for some fun, and after they'd had their way with her, they cut off her head and boiled it. Once the flesh boiled off the bone, they cleaned the skull and sent it to Number Two's house as a trophy. They hate suicides more than anything, and can you blame them? They spend all that time and energy choosing their mark, and let me tell you, it's not easy. From the scouting and the planning all the way to ransom and release takes them well over half a year. And when the mark dies, they get nothing for it, but you still have to pay the government its share."

"Why would they need to pay the government?"

"Governments and criminals have always been one family." Han Liu sighed. "Not only do you have to pay them, they take a full two-thirds of the ransom. It used to be half, but now it's forty-sixty. That is, sixty percent of the ransom ends up in the government's hands. Without their protection, they couldn't stay in business. And the minute they don't pay, the magistrate immediately sends the garrison after them, so there's no messing around. In the past, they only took one mark a year, usually sometime between the first frost and New Year's. Now, they have to go after at least five marks a year, mostly rocks and flowerpots—'flowerpots' being young ladies. Kidnapping children they call 'picking rocks.'"

Once Han Liu's mouth opened, it did not close easily. She said that the village was just like any other, for the most part. The people tilled the fields and fished the lake, and every spring, the men went out to work on houses. But the trade work was really a front; their purpose was to scout out rich households with good targets. They called the process "drawing lots." They maintained the utmost secrecy, and almost never tipped their hand.

Xiumi asked if she knew of a man named Qingsheng.

"He's Number Six," Han Liu replied. "The bosses here are split into two generations. The lower four are Qings: Qingfu, Qingshou, Qingde, Qingsheng. Qingsheng's the baby. The Boss and Number Two are Guans."

Han Liu looked closely at Xiumi, then smiled and continued, "From the looks of your clothing, your family isn't penniless. But don't worry. They're very good about following their own rules; as long as your family pays the ransom, they won't harm a hair on you. Think of it as being on vacation. Though to be honest I can't say that every negotiation has gone smoothly. For the children, they have a professional who takes them far away to be sold. For a young lady, especially a pretty one, things are more difficult. They'll want to 'loosen you up' first, then send you to the brothel."

"What does 'loosen up' mean?"

Han Liu said nothing at first, merely bit her lip and looked thoughtful. After a long moment, she sighed again, and explained, "They also refer to it as 'breaking fast.' Three of the brothers take turns coming to the island, and you do as they tell you. Once they've worked you hard enough, they'll sell you to the brothel. If it comes to that, it will be a hard thing for you; they know all kinds of tricks for tormenting women—who knows where they learned that from."

"But didn't you say there were six of them?"

"Numbers Two and Four never showed any interest. They say Number Two prefers men and won't touch women, though I can't say for sure. The Boss has been sick for the past few years, and he doesn't pay much attention to what happens in town. Some people even—" Here she broke off, then continued, "Some even say that Wang Guancheng is no longer with us."

4

WHEN XIUMI first set foot on the island a month earlier, the scene before her—the dilapidated house and garden, the flowers and trees, the clouds rolling unimpeded across the sky—inspired an unexpected sense of familiarity. She felt she must have been here before, as the whole scene, even the swallow nests in the eaves above, aligned perfectly with some part of her memory.

One evening, as Han Liu was ladling water out of the basin for dishwashing, the wooden ladle tapped the basin's lip and made a ringing sound that spread outward like ripples across a lake. Xiumi suddenly remembered the bowl in Father's chambers, and how Zhang Jiyuan had made that same metallic sound by tapping his finger against it the night before he left. She had felt weightless, as if she had been picked up by the breeze and carried over mountains, streams, and rivers toward a nameless place.

So this was where she had come to...

In that first vision, she had vaguely sensed an abandoned tomb on the island. To disprove this ridiculous idea, she hesitantly asked Han Liu if there happened to be an old tomb nearby, to which Han Liu offhandedly replied, "Sure, in the grove on the west side of the house. Why do you ask?"

The blood drained completely from Xiumi's face. She stood absolutely still, her eyes wide open. When Han Liu noticed her staring blankly beside the stove, transformed by fear, she hurried over and helped her into a chair. That enamel basin really was a treasure; could an object Father had bought from a beggar have some connection to the person buried out there in the woods? She didn't dare pursue the idea further. Han Liu tried her best to bring Xiumi back from her stupor, but Xiumi simply sat in silence, her eyes fixed ahead of her. When she explained everything moments later, Han Liu laughed and said, "So that's all it is! I couldn't imagine what could have scared you so much. That's just the shadow of your old incarnations—Buddha talks about this. What's so strange about you having been here in a past life?"

Xiumi begged Han Liu to take her to see the tomb, persisting until the other relented. Han Liu took off her apron, lifted a lamp from beside the stove, and led Xiumi out of the house.

A shadowy, secluded grove of trees stood near the western end of the house. The trees concealed a small vegetable garden that was strewn with yellow rapeseed petals; in the center of the garden was a tomb. Moss and vines had penetrated every crevice of its black brick walls; the fence around it had long ago fallen apart and was now replaced with reeds that rose taller than a person. Han Liu told her that this was the resting place of Jiao Xian, the Ming dynasty hermit, according to the black headstone she had read who knows how many times out of boredom. Xiumi snatched the lantern from Han Liu's hands and approached the headstone for a closer look. After brushing away a layer of dust, she saw that the engraved characters were still clearly visible:

Jiao Xian, courtesy name Xiaoqian. Originally from Jiangyin, became a recluse after the fall of the Ming. Built his hut from reeds and grasses on an abandoned island in the lake. His body, exposed to all the elements, became caked with dirt. When fire destroyed his hut, he slept outside; when people saw him lying naked in the snow, they thought him dead, but approaching, discovered he was alive. A man of expansive mind, Xian accepted earth and sky for his floor and ceiling. In perfect seclusion, he made himself one with the cusp of the Truest Way, passed through the facade of superficial difference, and entered the primal solitude of creation. Braving the elements did not injure his spirit, living in the wilderness did not torment his body, and meeting catastrophe did not quicken his anxiety. He escaped earthly cares, unburdening his mind, and renounced all beautiful sights and sounds, unfilling his eyes and ears. He was the only such man since the first Creator.

The signature on the bottom left corner read: "Wang Guancheng, the Dead Man Walking." So it was the Boss who wrote this epitaph. But why did he sign it "Dead Man Walking"?

Han Liu told Xiumi that Wang Guancheng had found this tiny island while searching for Jiao Xian's remains. He had passed the provincial service examination in 1867 and was selected for the Imperial Academy. They made him a senior minister and imperial overseer of Fujian Province, then sent him north to Ji'an, in Jiangxi. When he reached middle age, he developed a taste for Taoism, and decided to become a hermit. So he abandoned his wife and children and gave himself to the elements.

If his dream had been to become a hermit, then how did he end up the head of a gang of robbers? Xiumi thought.

The wind picked up. Xiumi sat on the stone steps of the mausoleum and listened to it rush through the trees. For some reason, she thought of her father. She had no idea if he was still alive or not.

Waves from the lake chased each other onto the bank, sending their white froth onto the land before retreating again in quick succession. The sky darkened fast, and heavy clouds rolled in with the sound of thunder. Rain followed soon after, pelting down until the whole lake boiled and bubbled like congee. A thickening mist obscured the mountain range in the distance; even the village disappeared in the rain. The sound of falling water surrounded them.

That evening, Xiumi went to bed early and slept more soundly than she had in many years. She woke up once, when Han Liu entered the room to make sure the window was securely closed, and sat up in bed and mumbled, "Today is the twenty-seventh of May."

Han Liu thought she was talking in her sleep; she smiled and closed the door on her way out. Xiumi drifted off again. But even asleep, she could feel the waves of cold that pressed inward through the cracks in the window and could smell the weight of the water.

Of course, she could not have known that at that same moment, a black-roofed fishing boat was moving through the rough water under cover of night toward the island. Its first several attempts at landing were rebuffed by the south wind. The sailors carried no lanterns.

When Xiumi woke again, her lamp was still lit. She could hear the rain falling thick and fast against the eaves outside. A person sat in the wooden chair opposite her. He was soaking wet; both feet were propped up on a square stool, and he held a nickel-plated water pipe in one hand, which made a gurgling sound as he smoked, like an obstructed stream. This wiry older man was none other than Fifth Brother Qingde. Lamplight shone off his oily pate, and his face was covered with wrinkles, like a dried apricot. His unbuttoned black silk jacket revealed the loose skin of his gut, which draped in folds over his belt.

"You're awake?" Qingde asked. He leaned forward to light a match by the lamp, then sat back and continued smoking.

Xiumi sat up quickly, grabbing a pillow and clutching it to her breast in terror.

"I've been here for a while, but I saw you were sleeping and couldn't bear to wake you." He jiggled his legs and did not look at her.

Xiumi sensed that the night she had imagined with dread so many times before had finally arrived. With no experience at her disposal, her mind went completely blank, and she forgot to be afraid. She twined her fingers nervously. The only other thing she could do was breathe hard. She felt her own chest rise and fall, and the skin on one side of her temple began to twitch.

"You! You, you . . ." She repeated "you" seven or eight times without knowing what she wanted to say next. Her breathing intensified.

"The man we sent to Puji just got back yesterday." The old man put his pipe down on the table, picked up a comb, and gently played over the teeth with his fingernails. "And guess what? Your mother won't pay up. Didn't expect that, did you? Not even I expected it.

"She said that marrying a daughter's like tossing a pail of water; since you're already married, you belong to your husband's family, not hers. So by rights, your husband's family ought to be the ones paying. She had a very good point, and our people had nothing else to say to her. So they spent a lot of time and money looking up your husband's house in Changzhou, but it turned out they didn't want to pay either. Your mother-in-law said that since the new bride had been snatched up before she even crossed their threshold, then her family ought to pay the ransom. And besides, they had already found a new bride closer to home, and the wedding was set to happen in a month. They wouldn't pay us anything. So your mother-in-law had a good point, too. It seems like our side remains the pointless one. When we took you, we thought we had a nice fat hen, but now it's like scooping water with a sieve—you're left with nothing. As we can't pay our bill to the government, we're going to have to pay with you.

"The district magistrate in Meicheng just lost a concubine, so you might as well take her spot. 'New shoes pinch the feet,' as the saying goes, so I'm here today to open you up and stretch you out a little, just to make sure you don't make the magistrate unhappy once you get there."

The old man's speech drained all the color and warmth from Xiumi's face and limbs; her teeth chattered. She even forgot to curse her mother.

"Don't be afraid," the old man coaxed. His voice came out raspy and hollow, like a sound traveling from afar. "Compared to my brothers, I'm the civilized one." He suddenly started coughing so hard he had to bend over. After hacking up a wad of phlegm, he was about to spit it out before turning to look at Xiumi and forcing himself to swallow. This was proof of his "civility."

Xiumi had already jumped out of bed and was running around with her feet half in her shoes and the pillow still at her chest, looking for her comb. Remembering that the old man had it in his hand, she started dressing herself in a hurry. The old man watched her tranquilly and laughed.

"Don't put that on. I'll have to take it all off again in a minute, why waste your time?"

Xiumi was conscious of a strong salty taste in her mouth. She realized she had bitten through her lip. She huddled at one corner of the bed, tears glimmering in her eyes, and said in a measured voice, "I will kill you."

The old man seemed stunned for a second, then burst out laughing. He stood up from the chair and started to undress in front of her. Naked, he walked toward her.

"Don't come any closer! You can't come any closer, you can't!" she screamed.

"And what if I needed to get closer?"

"Then you'll die!" Xiumi yelled, the hatred shining in her eyes.

"All right. Then let me die of pleasure in your arms." The old man walked over and almost effortlessly held both her arms behind her back, before bending over to suck on her earlobe and whisper, "They say heroes are buried in flowered fields, so please, kill me now."

She leaned as far back as she could to avoid his face and ended up falling backward onto the bed. It seemed like she had done it voluntarily. A deep sense of shame washed over her, and her body resisted violently. *What a humiliation! I can't make him stop! What is going on?* The harder she fought, the quicker she breathed, which was just what the old man wanted. *My God, he's taking off my clothes!* Xiumi's body stiffened as her understanding of what was happening intensified. The old man was as energetic as a bull. "Your skin is whiter than I thought. Only when the white parts are white, do the black parts really look black."

God, he . . . how could he say something like that?!

The old man forcefully pried her legs apart.

He's pulling my legs apart, is he really going to . . .

She heard the old man say, "Look at that, I haven't even done anything and you're already fucking wet." Now even more embarrassed and furious, Xiumi spit on his face; the old man smiled and licked it off.

"You...you...you really are..." Xiumi wanted to curse at him, but she had never cursed at anyone before. Her head rolled vainly on the pillow.

"Really are what?"

"You really are...a bad man!" Xiumi shrieked.

"A bad man?" The old man guffawed. "A bad man? Ha ha ha, a bad man, that's cute. Sure, sure why not, that's what I am."

He tied a brass bell onto her ankle. "A guy like me really doesn't have any strange kinks, but I do like to hear that bell ring."

Any movement of her leg and the bell clanged pleasantly. The harder she resisted, the louder it rang, like some kind of inducement or exhortation to the other. She was helpless, absolutely helpless. In the end, she stopped trying to fight.

Xiumi spent the second half of the night lying on her bed, open eyed and motionless, staring up at the canopy. The rain had long since stopped, and the frogs outside her window were singing. The sharp pain she had felt had already begun to dull. Han Liu sat beside the bed and talked to her; Xiumi didn't give any response. "Every woman has to endure this same trial," Han Liu told her. "No matter if it's your husband or someone else, you have to go through it eventually. Learn to accept it. At this point, it's the only thing left to do. When things like this happen, it's natural to think about death, but that's not what you want. Just grin and bear it, and you'll be fine."

The tea Han Liu had made for her had gone cold on the bedside table. Xiumi gave Han Liu a piercing look as she thought, *How is it that I have contemplated almost everything except death? In Puji, it seemed that any woman who faced this kind of crime had no other choice but suicide. Yet I have never wanted that, not even now.* Truly, she did not want to die. Besides, Zhang Jiyuan was long dead, and time could not run backward. She felt an inexplicable resentment toward Zhang

Jiyuan. *What an idiot! Idiot!* She bit her lip hard, and tears filled her eyes.

Han Liu said, "I'm going to go heat some water for you, so you can wash off." She gave Xiumi one more searching look, then went to the kitchen. Soon Xiumi could smell burning straw. *The old bastard got off easy*, she thought.

By the time Xiumi had bathed and changed her clothes, dawn was nearly breaking. Han Liu advised her to jump up and down vigorously several times. She said that would keep her from getting pregnant. Xiumi ignored her. Han Liu brewed another pot of tea, and the two sat down across from each other at the table.

"I can see from your clothing that your family isn't poor," Han Liu observed again. "Why wouldn't your mother pay a measly ransom?" Xiumi cried silently and didn't reply. After a long pause, she hissed, "God only knows."

"Still, I can't help but feel like something about this evening was unusual," Han Liu mused. "My guess is that something happened over in Huajiashe."

Xiumi said she couldn't give a damn about anything.

Han Liu continued, "The Boss is sick, and neither Two nor Four is interested in women. Even if your mother really did refuse to pay, then the first night should have been Number Three, Qingfu; why did Qingde come to the island first? Especially through such a heavy rain. None of his people carried lanterns, and they all left before daybreak. They were obviously sticking their noses in without permission. Qingde used to be one of Wang Guancheng's lieutenants when he was in Fujian. He may look like a dried-up old man, but they say he's an accomplished rider, archer, and swordsman. Even though Wang Guancheng put him at number five, he's closer to the Boss than any of the others.

"Ever since Wang Guancheng started pissing blood two years ago, he's rarely shown himself in public, and Qingde has used their relationship to issue 'decrees' in his name and order people around. He knows that no matter what, the day Wang Guancheng dies, he won't be the next person on top. Before you even got here, there were rumors that Wang Guancheng had already bled to death last winter, and Qingde had concealed the news and was hiding the body, all while sitting in for the chief and quietly bribing people for support. And once his opportunity arrives, he'll certainly burn the whole place down."

"So let them kill each other. What does it have to do with us? I think burning the whole place down would be the best thing for it."

"Silly girl, that doesn't make sense at all. There could be a bloodbath over there and it would make no difference to us. No matter how hectic things get, there will always be winners and losers, and no matter who ends up where, nothing good will ever come of it for us women. Outside of Wang Guancheng himself, the rest don't have a human bone in their body. Number Two keeps a whole harem of little boys in his house, and spends his days doing unspeakable things with them. He acts unconcerned about everything, and even goes out fishing on the lake like he has nothing better to do, but really he's just biding his time, waiting for his opportunity. He's as clever as they come—doesn't say much, but he's cunning.

"Number Three is a bookworm, and he's the worst of the lot. He has the airs of a useless, supercilious scholar. Even when he's on top of you, biting and snuffling, he'll still be reciting poetry. It's hard to imagine people like that really exist. If you spend a night with him, I guarantee you'll have to throw up two or three times afterward. You've already met Number Five, so I won't say more. Qingsheng, Listen, is the junior member of the group, but you have to be careful with him. He has no guile about him at all, and he may be kind of a simpleton, but he's immensely strong. They say he can lift a millstone over his head and spin it like a top. He has no problem killing people, and he acts on whim. Even Number Two is a little afraid of him. He's exhausting to serve because he won't rest until he's popped every one of your bones out of joint.

"Number Four is the only one I've never seen since I've been here. He's a loner, and rarely shows himself in the open. He does things his own way, and doesn't leave a trail. They say he keeps a parrot in his house . . ."

"How did you end up at Huajiashe in the first place? Where was your home?" Xiumi asked.

The question silenced Han Liu. Day had fully broken. She blew out the lamp, stood up, and said, "Plenty of time left for you to hear my story."

5

XIUMI slept the whole next day. Han Liu entered her room sometime around noon to speak to her briefly before leaving again. Xiumi could tell she was talking quickly and with urgency, as if informing her of something important, but Xiumi was just too exhausted to do more than look up at her, murmur a few words in reply, and roll back over.

But sleep returned lightly. She observed the color of the sky through the window: a rich yellow ochre, like a ripe apricot. A strong wind howled outside, tossing around a hail of sand from who knew where onto the roof, making a continuous hissing sound. Xiumi hated the wind. Every year in late spring, Puji would be visited by a torrential rain immediately followed by sandstorms. The wind whistled all day long, and the sand would get between your teeth. Now caught in the center of the storm, she felt her chest tighten and the sense of exile intensify. She remembered being a young child when Baoshen, Lily-pad, Magpie, and Mother had all gone out, leaving her home alone and huddled in bed, listening to the sand spatter against the window paper as she drifted between sleep and wakefulness. She thought herself lonely back then.

Now she felt as if she had become two people: The first was in faraway Puji, where night was falling, and Mother floated like a shadow up to her room to sit by her bed and ask softly, "Xiuxiu, why are you crying?" The second was imprisoned on a desolate island, her mother refusing to pay her ransom, giving her little chance of ever returning home again. As she often felt when standing before a mirror, it was hard for her to tell if the body or the image was more real.

Amid her delirium she heard someone open her door and walk in. A figure stood before her, stained head to toe in fresh blood. He walked noiselessly up to her bedside and regarded her, a look of extreme anguish on his face. She didn't know him. She saw he had a knife wound in his neck: it was deep and long, and blood still poured from it, down his neck and onto his clothes.

"My name is Wang Guancheng," the visitor said. "No need to be afraid, I've come to say goodbye."

"But I don't know you," Xiumi said suspiciously.

"That's true, we have never met before, however—"

"Did someone kill you?" Xiumi asked.

"Yes; by now I am already dead. The stroke cut deep, and almost took my head clean off. Honestly, you don't need that much force to deal with an eighty-year-old man like me. You have no idea how much it hurts."

"Who killed you?"

"I didn't see him clearly; he approached from behind me. I woke up this morning feeling stronger than usual, so I got up to wash my face. He stepped out from behind the standing screen and struck me down. I didn't even have time to turn and get a look at him."

"But you know who it was, right?"

"I can guess"—the visitor nodded—"but it's not important now. I honestly couldn't care less about it, because I'm already dead. May I have some of your corn? I'm starving."

Only then did Xiumi notice the ear of boiled corn on her nightstand. Tendrils of steam still rose from it. The figure didn't wait for Xiumi's permission before grabbing the ear and taking a hungry bite.

"But why are you here? I don't know you, nor have we ever met."

"Yes," the figure mumbled as he chewed the corn, "but the fact that I've never met you doesn't matter. I know that you and I are the same kind of person, or perhaps I should say we are one and the same person, because you are fated to carry on my labor."

"I don't know what I will do, except die," Xiumi replied.

"That's because your mind has been imprisoned by your body. Like a wild animal in a cage, it is by no means tame. Every person's heart is an island, trapped by water, sequestered from the world. Just like this island where you are now."

"You want me to become a robber?"

"Outsiders think of Huajiashe as a den of thieves, but to me it is the Peach Blossom Spring come to life. I have labored patiently here for almost twenty years, surrounded by mulberry and bamboo groves, clear ponds, every step opening out with nature's wonders. Here I found ease and amusement as my white hair grew past my temples. The spring sun called to me with visions of mist, while the autumn frost left me chrysanthemums and fresh crabs. My boat lolled in a breeze that tugged at my jacket; heaven and earth were one and together, and the seasons followed each other without incident. No one locked their doors, and lost purses were left on the road. Each home receives equal measures of sunshine. When spring opened its full richness, soft rains fell, and the peach and pear trees competed to be the most beautiful; even bees would lose their way. And yet still I became tired of it. As every day I watched the clouds emerge from the mountains and birds fly back to their nest, a sorrow arose and turned into a grief that would not dissipate. In those moments, I would think to myself, 'Wang Guancheng, Wang Guancheng, what are you doing?' I built Huajiashe with my own hands, and now with my own hands I must destroy it."

"I don't understand what you're talking about."

"You will eventually," the visitor replied. "Eventually, Huajiashe will be reduced to rubble. But someone will come to rebuild it and retrace my footsteps, and sixty years later, it will be a paradise again. Night and day will continue their succession, and the mirage will reappear. The second wave rises before the first has died. Pitiable and painful, but what can we do ... what can we do ..."

The figure sighed, and its form flickered and vanished completely. Xiumi opened her eyes and looked around; it had been a dream. An ear of corn, half-eaten, sat on her nightstand. The room had darkened. Outside, the wind still wailed, rattling the leaves of the trees in a chorus of noise like a crowd of bickering people.

Xiumi got out of bed, slipped her toes into her shoes, and padded over to the kitchen, where she filled the basin ladle with cold water, tipping it into her mouth. Wiping her lips, she headed to Han Liu's room. The bed was very neatly made, and Xiumi saw a pair of embroidered shoes atop a wooden stool below the bed, yet Han Liu was nowhere to be seen. Xiumi walked the borders of the island looking for her, to no avail. Finally, she looked toward the lake into the impenetrable chaos of rolling waves and hanging thunderheads, but there wasn't even a boat in sight.

Xiumi sat on a stone on the shore and stared at the line of old bridge posts sticking up awkwardly out of the water. No birds rested on them now. As darkness fell, her vision of the posts grew blurry, until they faded into curved shadows above the water, and eventually into nothing at all. She felt her arms grow cold and the weight of the moist air that gradually dampened her hair. Quiet had reclaimed the world after the storm's passing. The evening sky was utterly cloudless and a deep green, glowing with the faint light of new stars. Reeds along the bank swayed slowly against each other. Huajiashe was a silent twinkling of lights.

The moon had risen high. She noticed a boat moving out on the lake, like a lonely traveler on a journey. Yet its light appeared to stay still for so long that Xiumi assumed it must be someone fishing for shrimp. Only after a long while could she see it make its way toward her. The wooden rudder creaked as it sculled, and a wake rushed past the sides. The boat slid onto the shore, and a narrow gangplank was lowered. Han Liu emerged from the low cabin, a bamboo basket in her hand. Xiumi had been worried she would never see her again.

It turned out that she had been taken to Huajiashe that afternoon to recite sutras.

Back in the house, Xiumi asked her what sutras they had asked her to read. "*The Book of the Dead*," she replied. Xiumi asked why she had to read that one and if someone had died. Han Liu reacted with surprise and looked at her quizzically. "That's weird. Didn't I come to your room before I left and tell you what had happened?"

"I remember you coming in and talking to me, but I was just so tired I couldn't understand what you said," Xiumi said, laughing.

Han Liu told her that at noon that day, she noticed the corn she had hung in the kitchen was getting wormy and wouldn't be edible much longer, so she put the ears in a pot to boil. "Just as I took out the corn to have some, people from Huajiashe arrived to say that Boss Wang Guancheng had passed away, and they were burying him that evening. They knew I was a nun and wanted me to recite a sutra or prayer for him. The news shocked me; I asked them how the Boss could die so suddenly. The man said that there was an agitator in the village, and he almost cut the Boss's head off. He didn't say anything more, just pushed me to leave. I figured it was such a major event, I had to tell you, but you were so tired I had to shake you forever before you opened your eyes. I told you that the Boss had been murdered, and you nodded several times. And the man was still urging me to go, so I left you the corn and boarded the boat with him."

Han Liu asked Xiumi if she had eaten.

"Where would I get food with you gone?" Xiumi asked.

Han Liu laughed. "Isn't the rest of the corn still in the pot?"

Reaching into her bamboo basket, Han Liu removed a blue cloth covering a terra-cotta pot that contained cooked wood grouse. Not having eaten all day, a starving Xiumi grabbed the grouse and started to stuff her face. Han Liu watched her eat and smiled, occasionally patting her on the back and reminding her not to choke.

Han Liu said that she had arrived in Huajiashe during the wake. Wang Guancheng's body had been displayed on top of his coffin, but there was no cauldron or vase for incense, or candles or a ceremonial table. Two bowls on the floor contained enough lamp oil to sustain a few embers the size of mung beans; that was the extent of his funerary flame. An offering of a few pieces of ordinary fruit sat beside the bowls. The body was clothed in a tattered robe with patches, like a begging monk's cassock, and the cloth shoes on his feet had holes in the soles. The decor was embarrassingly spare. The handful of young boys and maids who stood in attendance were themselves dressed in rags.

It was Han Liu's first time seeing Wang Guancheng in the flesh, and she was shocked to see the chief was merely a wizened old man with a patchy beard and a worried expression on his face. Extensive blood loss had turned the face a paraffin yellow. Han Liu knelt on the prayer mat before the coffin, kowtowed a few times, and started to recite the sutra.

Soon, a woman in her mid-fifties emerged from the house with a heavy needle and a roll of thread. Han Liu recognized her as Wang Guancheng's governess. For some reason, perhaps out of fear, her hands began to tremble violently. The older woman handed needle and thread to Han Liu while gesturing with her head toward the body. Han Liu understood that she was being asked to sew up the wound on his neck.

The blade that struck him must have been dull, judging from the shards of bone she found in his long gray hair. By her own count, it took her sixty-two stitches to sew his head and neck back together. As she looked around for a place to wash her hands, the governess addressed her. "Teacher, if you could close his eyes while you're here."

Han Liu replied nervously, "Look at those eyes—they're open as wide as a water buffalo's. Only a close relation can close them properly. I am neither a friend of his nor family, how could I be so presumptuous?"

The governess sighed. "The Boss had no children and lived totally alone. Though a few of us served him for many years, he barely ever said a word. Besides, we don't understand the rituals. If you would take charge of the rites, Teacher, we would be very obliged."

Han Liu hesitated for a moment before agreeing. "Did he have a jade pendant?" she asked.

"The Boss was extremely frugal in his lifetime," the matron replied. "I never saw a polished rock in his house, let alone a jade pendant. Even the cheap timber for his coffin was paid for with donations from his neighbors."

"Did he have any prayer beads?"

The old woman shook her head once more.

Han Liu looked around the room and noticed a bunch of freshly picked cherries among the fruit offerings, beads of dew still shining on the ripe skin. She picked one, pried open his mouth, and dropped the cherry in before closing his mouth again, and then attempted to close his eyes. But Wang Guancheng's eyes would not close, even after six attempts. All Han Liu could do was remove a yellow silk handkerchief from her pocket and lay it over his face. When she asked the governess to bring her a clean set of his clothes, a maid stepped forward and said, "We've never seen the chief wear anything except the clothes on his body. He does have a heavy cotton robe for winter, but that would indicate the wrong season." Han Liu agreed.

Outlaws and villagers from all over gathered outside the courtyard to observe the funeral. The other leaders came to pay their respects, accompanied by a personal retinue of watchful bodyguards with hands on their swords. Each man made a hurried obeisance before the corpse, then retreated into the open courtyard. Han Liu could see from the dark suspicion etched in every man's face that Wang Guancheng's sudden demise had them all on guard. When the obeisances ended, Han Liu ordered the burial procession to begin. A handful of workmen awkwardly lifted the corpse into the coffin and were about to nail down the lid when Han Liu blurted out, "Where's Number Two?"

The matron stepped over to her and whispered, "He won't come. We sent people over there three times today. At noon, his servants told us he had gone fishing on the lake. No need to wait for him now."

Han Liu allowed the workmen to secure the lid by driving in the wooden nails and knotting the hempen ropes tight. When all was ready, a voice called out from the courtyard, "Raise the coffin!" She watched the pallbearers carry the casket slowly out the door, through the courtyard, and down the road west.

After Han Liu finished her story, the two women sat in dull silence for a moment. Then Xiumi told her in detail about her dream encounter with Wang Guancheng.

Han Liu smiled. "Everything turns into a ghost story when it passes your lips, doesn't it? Generally, we think of dying as no more than an unpleasant last thing you do with your life, so there's not much to be afraid of. But when you describe it, it all sounds terrifying, as if the whole world around us is fake."

"It's all fake to begin with, anyway," Xiumi morosely replied with a sigh.

6

Heavy rain. Meeting at the Xue estate in Xia village to discuss the Ten Capital Crimes in the afternoon. Current consensus is to kill (1) those who possess hereditary estates larger than five acres; (2) those who practice usury; (3) court officials with a history of corruption; (4) prostitutes; (5) robbers; (6) those afflicted with leprosy, consumption, or other infectious diseases; (7) those who abuse women, children, or the elderly; (8) women who bind their feet; (9) human traffickers; (10) matchmakers, witches, monks, and Taoists. All members present were in agreement over every item except number eight. The staunchest opponent was Wang Xiaohe, whose reason was that a majority of the women in Xia village and Puji bind their feet, including his own mother, wife, and two younger sisters. After group discussion, the item was changed to women who bind their feet after the success of the revolution.

Returned to Puji late in the evening as the rain continued. Felt an overwhelming bodily exhaustion. Meiyun came upstairs late in the night and pestered me until I had no choice but to muster my strength and give her what she wanted. I had lost interest in her long ago, and felt it poor entertainment. Forced intercourse without passion is truly the most unpleasant of activities. My spirit ailing, I came before my task was completed. Meiyun asked suspiciously, "What made you so soft? Did some vixen in Xia village suck out all your energy?" I swore up and down that had not happened, coaxing and cajoling her, but she was not convinced. After a brief respite, I gathered what remained of my energy to give her what she wanted and prove there was no one else. But the sight of the wrinkles on her neck, the hanging flesh on her back and arms, killed my ardor; it was like beating a dead horse.

Meiyun started to sob, then turned angry. "You're thinking of someone else, don't imagine I can't see it!" I tried to object, but she raised a cold eye to me and hissed, "If you so much as lay a finger on her, I'll tear your limbs off and feed them to the dogs."

My flesh turned cold and my hair stood on end. By "her," Meiyun obviously must have meant Xiumi. Strange. Xiumi and I have barely talked since I came to Puji, how could she have guessed my feelings? Truly astounding to see how connected a mother's mind is with her daughter's. A woman's eyes are a hundred times sharper than an eagle's talons; I must make sure not to be careless.

Thinking of Xiuxiu infused me with such thirst that I mounted Meiyun like a bull; she sweated and moaned, her eyes rolled. How magical it would be if this old lady should suddenly transform into Xiumi! Oh, my girl, my girl! As Meiyun breathed heavily, I teased her, "I wonder if the girl's body is as white and soft as yours, like a fresh-baked bun?" Meiyun pretended not to hear me and kept on whimpering. Then we heard a noise from the doorway; Meiyun opened her eyes and recoiled, pulling her clothes to her chest. Then she went to the window and looked into the courtyard. It was Baoshen's son, Tiger. The monster just arrived from Qinggang.

Zuyan and his concubine have become inseparable; they have eyes only for each other. I worry he will come to grief one day very soon.

Only when she read Zhang Jiyuan's diary did Xiumi feel she was living in the real world. Back in Puji, every rock and tree and blade of grass seemed be an impenetrable and inscrutable veil between her and a trove of dark secrets. Now she knew the truth about what had happened; it all seemed uninteresting, even distasteful to her.

A handful of questions remained. How did Mother know Zhang Jiyuan? Did Father know about them before he went crazy? Why did he miswrite the character for "toad" as "cicada" in the poem he sent to Ding Shuze? Did that connect in some way to the golden cicada brooch that Zhang Jiyuan had left for her? Though she read each page of the diary multiple times, she could find no clue to these mysteries.

The village was silent, no sign of activity. Xiumi lost track of time in the deathly quiet and had to guess the hours based on the shadows cast by the old bridge posts on the lake surface. The summer heat had become unbearable, and there were no bamboo sleeping mats or mosquito nettings in the hut. Even a short stroll in the evenings attracted clouds of mosquitoes around her cheeks. Nor did she have any summer clothes. Han Liu did the best she could for her by cutting the sleeves off her long robe. Summer could be endured, but what would she do when winter came?

Xiumi knew she probably didn't need to think so far ahead. Chances were good she would never see winter. It felt as if long centuries had passed since Wang Guancheng's death, yet Han Liu told her he had died just over a month ago. Utter boredom nearly suffocated her. One day at dawn, when she spied a fishing boat penetrate the morning mist, heading for their island, she cried out in excitement.

The boat made it to shore and several men disembarked, each carrying a sealed earthenware vessel of ale that they brought into the house and deposited in the kitchen before departing without a word. At noon, a second boat from the village arrived, this time with fresh fruits and vegetables, two green perch, brined pig offal, a basket of fresh shrimp, and two live chickens. A man with two cleavers wearing a white apron didn't leave with the boat but went straight into the kitchen and ordered Han Liu to clean the stovetop so he could start preparing dinner.

Han Liu immediately pulled Xiumi aside and whispered, "You're going to have a bad night tonight, my dear."

"Who's coming to the island?"

"Qingfu—Number Three," Han Liu replied, "the amateur intellectual. He only studied for a few years when he was young, but he puts on an act of being one of the greatest minds that ever lived. He has extremely refined tastes; even the water for his tea has to be brought from the village. Then there's the poetry recitation and the operatic singing. It's going to be a long evening."

The news made Xiumi nervous. She didn't move, unsure of what to do.

"But at least he's easy to satisfy. And he likes his liquor. So just make a few extra toasts this evening so that he gets really drunk; then it will be easier for you later," Han Liu comforted her, before heeding the call of the cook and hurrying off toward the kitchen. Yet a thought stopped her in her tracks, and she turned to whisper to Xiumi: "Just pretend it's someone else's body and let him do what he wants with it. I have a trick of my own, it's just too bad you can't use it."

"What's your trick?"

"Reciting sutras. The moment I start reciting, I go numb to the outside world."

Qingfu arrived just as the lamps were being lit. He brought no one with him, save two young maids. He was dressed like a Taoist priest, in a black cloth hat, an adept's robe tied at the waist with a tasseled belt of yellow silk, and straw sandals on his feet. He walked toward the hut with a slow, erudite swagger, waving a wide black fan embossed with gold leaf. Crossing the threshold, he didn't speak, but regarded Xiumi closely with beady eyes, then smiled and nodded. His smile grew until his eyes receded into slits and a glimmer of saliva collected in one corner of his mouth, as he said with a sigh, "Little Sister truly resembles an apricot tree in spring rains, a sweet olive bough hung with shadows, her spirit of autumn waters and her cheeks of hibiscus; sweet like white jade, a flower that understands speech, utterly amazing, utterly amazing..."

Stepping toward Xiumi, he made a deep and mannered bow. Her stony silence didn't appear to trouble him. Smiling foolishly, he took her hand and massaged it for a long moment, still murmuring. "Little Sister's quiet virtue and elegant gentility are matched with such austere beauty. I confess I am transported at first sight. Please accept your servant's rude invitation to take you to the lakes and marshes of paradise this evening, that I may quench my heart's deep thirst. What do you think, Little Sister?"

Han Liu interrupted his babbling with a tug on his arm, as she ordered the maids to set the table. He followed her obediently, leaving Xiumi behind as he found his place. He snapped his fan open once more and began fanning himself assiduously.

Xiumi refused to sit down at first, but after a series of hard tugs and dark looks from Han Liu, she tucked a pair of scissors into her robe and approached the dinner table. Qingfu's hungry gaze fixed on her, and she felt the shame growing inside her to the point of wanting to leap across the table and stab him to death with the scissors. One quick glance at his face was enough unpleasantness. The sight of his rude demeanor and the sound of his whispered "Little Sister, Little Sister" brought tears to her eyes.

Several dishes were spread on the table. Before the cook could place a cup of filtered ale before Qingfu, the latter raised his fan and snapped, "But stay!" with such vehemence that the cook spilled the drink all over his apron.

"Please stay," repeated Qingfu, who then turned to his maids: "Crimson. Turquoise. Which one of you will sing us an air to spice up our banquet?"

One maid bent close to him and asked, "Which play and scene would you like, master?" Qingfu considered for a moment, then ordered, "Sing 'I Sigh over Days That Pass as Cattails Sway.'"

The maid cleared her throat, opened her cherry lips, and sang in a high, girlish tone:

> Old rouge floats downstream;
> Slender the branch that holds the plum.
> At times like this, who will paint
> The faded brow?
> Spring heartache surely visited,
> But when spring left, why did it still remain?

At this line, Qingfu rapped his fan on the desk and reprimanded her: "Wrong, you're wrong again! 'When spring *died*, why did it still remain?' One wrong word ruins the whole image."

The flustered maid took a moment to regain her composure before trying again:

> But when spring died, why did it still remain?
> Now you're gone, rivers and mountains seem so far away.
> Counting days till your return, painting
> The edges of these brows.

> I sigh over days that pass as cattails sway;
> Everything, even imperial willows, empty.
> I don't know where I am, trapped
> Beneath a lowering sky.

Total silence greeted the end of the song; even Qingfu touched his cheek and looked mournful. The cook brought more drink over and was about to serve him when Qingfu raised his fan and commanded, "Stay." The cook trembled once more.

Qingfu picked up his ale bowl and inspected it closely beneath the lamplight before passing it to Han Liu. "I'll trouble you to wash this again, then rinse it with boiling water and bring it back." Han Liu paused in bewilderment, but got up and took the bowl into the kitchen without a word.

Upon receiving his cleaned bowl, Qingfu inspected it carefully again. Then, as if remembering something, he smiled and said, "No, I should wash it myself." He rose from the table.

"Could it be you fear someone has poisoned your cup, sir?" Han Liu asked facetiously.

"Precisely," Qingfu replied, and his expression darkened. "It isn't that I don't trust you. Trouble is stirring in the village, and everyone fears for their own safety. I have to take precautions."

Xiumi thought of Magpie, and how her fear of arsenic made her wash her rice bowl over and over. It was surprising to find a head outlaw with the same fear-inspired habit. She felt herself transported back to Puji again. The total darkness outside the window of the hut enveloped their solitary lamp and its flickering shadows, unbalancing her senses and creating an illusionary scene: Could it be that she had never left Puji, and that these people were really just animal spirits who had lured her into an empty tomb and cast a spell on her?

As she stared at the floor, lost in thought, Xiumi heard Han Liu say, "You're thinking too much, sir. No one ever comes to this tiny island, and the cook is your cook; nothing could possibly happen. Even if we take a step back and presume that someone did want to poison you, they would surely do it through the ale..."

Qingfu chuckled drily. "You're absolutely right. So I'll need the rest of you to have a sip first before I do."

The cook poured a bowl for everyone at the table before pouring one for himself and drinking it down. Qingfu pointed at Han Liu, and ordered, "You."

Han Liu drank. Qingfu waited a moment before lifting his own bowl and draining it. Wiping his lips, he sighed and said to Han Liu, "You'll have to forgive me. You know how clever a man Number Two was. His servants tasted every meal for him four hours before it was served, and he only ate when everything felt safe. Even then he died. As they say, the sage who thinks of everything will miss something eventually, and one in a million is more dangerous than a million and one."

"Number Two is dead?" Han Liu asked in surprise.

"Dead," Qingfu replied. "They buried him yesterday."

"But he was fine. What killed him?"

"When the Boss was murdered, I suspected that Number Two had moved against him in a bid for leadership. But his own death proves that he didn't do it. The killer is still out there, awaiting his chance to step forward."

"How did he die?"

Qingfu drank another mouthful of wine and said, "How else? Someone poisoned his bowl. The assassin was as inventive as they were merciless; they knew Number Two had people to taste his food before he ate it, and so applied the poison to the bottom of his bowl.

Once it dried, the servant who filled the bowl and tasted it was in no danger, but as soon as Number Two finished his meal, he vomited blood and his spirit ascended to the heavens. The assassin hides in the shadows and plans every move carefully. If he decides to kill you, you'll never see him coming."

"And this person . . . do you know who he might be?"

"Along with myself, the other three are all suspects. The Boss and Number Two dying in succession would suggest that I'm next on the list. But I don't want to spend my life seeing doom in every corner and guessing at unanswerable riddles." At this, Qingfu looked over at Xiumi and smiled. "So I hope Little Sister will take pity on me just this once. After this evening, I can die with no regrets. If I were to die on your pillow, it would be a reward beyond imagining." Turning to Han Liu, he continued, "But if heaven refrains from cutting my life's thread and allows me to keep drawing breath, I expect I'll have to beg you to accept me as a disciple, so that we might find a quiet temple and live out our lives reciting sutras beside the eternal flame. How does that sound?"

The poignant sadness of Qingfu's words caused Crimson and Turquoise to reach for their handkerchiefs and wipe their tears away. Han Liu filled the silence with an encouraging word: "Take a broader view of the situation. Everything is fate, they say, and beyond our power to change. 'Whenever there is wine, I drink, and count each day as twelve more hours lived.'"

"Well said, well said," Qingfu agreed. He downed three or four more bowls of beer in quick succession, then turned to his other attendant, who was standing by his side and fanning him, and said, "Let's have a song from you as well, to make the drink more pleasant."

The maid called Turquoise had just put a ripe bayberry into her mouth; hearing his directive, she spat it into her palm, thought for a moment, then sang:

> I have no heart to raise the altar lamp
> Or light the ornate incense cake;
> Enduring one day, I lie down,

And fear the hour I wake.
I yearn to know when disaster will cease,
when dawn will break.
Thinking of it eats up my heart.
O Mother, Father, I fear this trouble
Will be chased by more heartache.

Turquoise ended the song with a long, agonizing wail, followed by a fit of sobbing. Qingfu, at first mesmerized by this spectacle of pain, began to motion her to stop with a growing irritation that bordered on a verbal outburst. He grabbed the pitcher of liquor and poured himself a bowl but did not drink; he merely sat with his chin in his hands, lost in thought.

Afraid that Qingfu's sadness would harden into a fury she could not contain, Han Liu broke the paralyzed silence at the table by saying with a smile, "You know, Master Qingfu, when I was studying at the temple I learned a few tunes from Abbess Hua. If you can bear to listen, I can sing them for everyone now, and add some fun to the party."

One hand still on his chin, Qingfu regarded her with red, unblinking eyes and a smile that was not a smile. He appeared to be fairly drunk already.

Han Liu's song went thus:

Sakyamuni, Indian prince,
Abandoned hills of silver and gold,
Fed himself to an eagle above
The nesting dove, perfected himself
Until nine dragons bathed his golden form
And made him Mahayana Sagely King.

When she finished, she toasted Qingfu with two more bowls of ale.

"This drink must be poisoned," Qingfu declared. "Otherwise my heart wouldn't be racing so hard nor my chest feel so tight, as if I were about to meet my death."

Han Liu laughed and replied, "You've been drinking fast, and with so much on your mind to begin with, the alcohol is having a stronger effect, that's all. If the wine were poisoned, wouldn't all of us be dead already? Have a few bayberries and some tea to sober up—you'll feel much better, I'm sure."

Qingfu plucked a bayberry from the fruit plate and popped it into his mouth. Then he turned to look at Xiumi. "Did you do much studying at home, Little Sister? Can you compose poetry?"

When he saw she had no intention of replying, he continued, "Tonight's moon shines purely overhead, and a cool breeze blows. You and I may as well take a stroll beside the lake and recite poems, match couplets for one another. How does that sound to you?"

He stood up and walked around the table to Xiumi, reaching for her arm. Xiumi shrank away from his hand, Han Liu stood up quickly and hurried over to bring Qingfu back to his seat, saying, "Oh, but think of the weather outside. There's no cool breeze out there—it's suffocatingly hot; the bats are flying around in hordes, and clouds of mosquitoes and fireflies are everywhere. Imagine the two of you trying to recite those beautiful poems while you're slapping mosquitoes—wouldn't it be just awful, and such a waste of your literary talent? And what's more, it's pitch black out there; what if you tripped on something and broke your fan? That would be even more of a shame. Since the poetic muse is speaking to you, and the creative urge must be satisfied, why don't the three of us fill our bowls right here and compose together?"

Her suggestion inspired an assenting nod from Qingfu. Han Liu escorted him back to his seat and rubbed his shoulders a few times. Light returned to Qingfu's eyes; he straightened his cuffs and announced in a loud voice rough with phlegm, "None of you ladies will be a match for me when it comes to composing poems. How about we match couplets together? I'll give you the first half, and you match the second. I'll tap my fan on the table for ten beats, and if you can't match me before the time is up, you drink three bowls. How's that sound?"

"And what if we match you in time?"

"Then I'll drain a bowl myself."

Han Liu, Crimson, and Turquoise all agreed; only Xiumi looked at her feet and said nothing. Qingfu filled his own bowl and tipped it back all the way, then declaimed, "Orioles shuttle to and fro between the begonia's branches."

After giving them the line, he really did start tapping the table with his fan. After the third beat, Turquoise replied, "Swallows chatter back and forth in the shadow of bamboo."

"Good line, good line," Qingfu said admiringly. Then he shot Xiumi another rapacious glance and said, "Still, this 'oriole shuttle' of mine can turn hard as an oak sometimes…"

Crimson and Turquoise blushed in embarrassment; Qingfu laughed loud and long, as if he were alone. Then he gave them another line: "The hero carries a three-foot sword at his waist."

Qingfu raised his fan to begin the countdown, yet before the first stroke fell, Han Liu blurted out: "Wouldn't that be 'The true man holds five cartloads of books in his stomach'?"

"That's a fairly solid line, my dear, but far too conventional. And pairing 'man' with 'hero' makes for a boring couplet. Much better to change 'true man' to 'real woman,' no?"

"How would you use 'real woman'?"

"Perhaps 'The real woman bears two hills of snow above her heart.'" Qingfu giggled. "But 'The true man holds five cartloads of books in his stomach' is still a correct answer, so I must drink to it." He tipped another bowl down his throat.

As he was about to offer another line, Han Liu interrupted him: "You can't be the only one to test us. We ladies need to test him, too, and make him drink three bowls if he can't think of anything."

Qingfu cupped his fist with his hand in a gesture of invitation. "If that's the decision, I humbly await your instruction. Who will go first?"

"Miss Crimson, why don't you give the master a hard one," Han Liu suggested.

Crimson furrowed her brow in thought, then offered: "A lone swan loses its way on a moonless night, high clouds and the outskirts far away."

"You think you can stump me with such an ordinary line?"

Qingfu shot Crimson a condescending look. "I'll match it with 'A single dragon is lost in the cove amid dark peaches and pale pears along a smooth garden path.'" Snaking an arm around Crimson's waist, he pulled her close enough to stick a hand up her dress and grope around wildly as he whispered, "Let me see how smooth the garden path really is."

Crimson giggled, but her body wriggled and twisted hard in an attempt to free herself from his grasp. While he fooled around and she struggled, the sound of a low chuckle could be heard outside.

The spectacle of Qingfu's provocative words and lecherous demeanor had made Xiumi's cheeks burn with shame. She couldn't stay, and yet she couldn't leave; she felt like no hole could be deep enough to hide her safely. Not knowing what to do, she kept her eyes down and dug at the embedded dirt in the table with a fingernail. Hearing that pitiless laughter outside, she initially thought her ears had tricked her. Then, raising her eyes, she found the entire party frozen with fear, their mouths wide open as if paralyzed instantly by a magic spell. She felt goose bumps rise on her skin.

After a tense pause, Qingfu asked in a quavering voice, "Who just laughed? Did the rest of you hear it as well?"

Everyone looked at each other without speaking. A breeze blew through the window, extinguishing two of the three lamps inside the hut; Han Liu covered the table lamp with her hands just in time to save it from going out as well. Xiumi couldn't distinguish all the faces anymore. Before the guests could recover their calm, the sound of laughter repeated from beyond the door. Xiumi heard it with perfect clarity this time. It sounded like a decrepit old man who laughed with a toddler's mouth. Xiumi inhaled sharply and shivered with cold.

Qingfu had already unsheathed his sword and sobered up somewhat. The cook picked up his meat cleaver next to the hearth, and the two opened the door and walked slowly into the courtyard. Crimson and Turquoise hid behind the table, clutching each other and trembling so much that they made it rattle.

"How can anyone else be on this island besides the two of us?" Han Liu asked, looking steadily at Xiumi, though she clearly did not intend the question for her. Meeting her eyes caused Xiumi's heart to skip.

A few moments later the two men returned. Qingfu's body swayed unsteadily as he stepped inside; his sword left his grasp and clattered to the floor. With both hands he reached for one of the hut's wooden pillars; it guided him down as he slowly collapsed. His panicked cook moved to help him back up, but Qingfu fell to his knees and began vomiting loudly. Han Liu flicked her handkerchief out and, while dabbing his mouth clean, asked the cook, "Did you see anyone out there?"

"Not even a dead man's shadow," the cook replied.

Han Liu said nothing more. Once Qingfu recovered a little, she helped him into a chair, then ran to the kitchen for a basin of water so he could rinse and wash his face. Crimson and Turquoise stood behind him to rub his shoulders and chest. It took a long time for him to get his breath back.

"It couldn't be him. Is it really him?" Qingfu's eyes betrayed a deep uneasiness. He muttered to himself for a moment, then shook his head. "It can't be him. Can't be . . ."

"Who is the 'him' you speak of?" Crimson inquired.

Qingfu met the question with fury, shoving her violently to the ground. "How the fuck should I know?!"

Crimson toppled backward so hard she nearly hit the corner of the table. She stood up and dusted herself off, not daring to swear, protest, or cry. Han Liu brewed some tea and passed a cup to Qingfu; he sipped it lightly, never taking his eyes off the front door or halting the sotto voce conversation with himself: "The voice sounds just like him. I'm drunk and unprotected, he could kill me easily. Why hasn't he done it?"

"If he hasn't killed you, master, perhaps that means he respects you more than the others," Han Liu offered. "Perhaps you may find fortune through others' disaster."

"Certainly not." Qingfu waved her off, his tone and expression numb. "He simply wishes to play with me first. This won't do; I cannot stay a minute longer here." He stood up again, looked over to Xiumi, and nodded inexplicably. "No, it won't do," he sighed. "I must leave. He won't hold off, not even tonight."

He picked his sword up off the ground, bade them a quick farewell, and ordered his cook and maids to hurry back to Huajiashe.

"He's afraid," Xiumi said coldly.

It was around midnight. All was silent, and darkness concealed everything beyond the window. The two women had not bothered to clean up—plates lay in a messy heap on the table, the vomit remained on the floor, its stench permeating the room.

"Anyone would be in his position," Han Liu said. "I kept trying to get him drunk, just to make your night a little easier. I had no idea something like this would happen. Even now I feel like a kite in a strong wind, like I'll never come back to earth—"

"That man who…" Xiumi interjected, "that man he mentioned, could he be on the island still?"

Han Liu rushed over to lock the door, securing the crossbeam before jamming it tighter with a short wooden post. Leaning against the door and breathing hard, she said, "Judging by Number Three's tone, he seems to know who the murderer is but can't quite believe it himself. That suggests regular people like us couldn't easily guess who the murderer might be."

"Why bother guessing at all?" Xiumi took the scissors out of her robe and placed them on the table. "I was carrying these the whole time. If that old bastard had tried to jump me, I would have ended him right there. All this sudden drama at Huajiashe might seem terrifying, but it's all pretty simple when you think about it. This must be what's happening: Two of the six leaders are dead, and the third already has one foot in the grave. The others will die too, until there's just one left, and that will be the new chief. No need for us to exhaust ourselves with guessing."

"You have a point," Han Liu replied. "You think Number Three will make it till morning?"

7

Clear and cool. Yesterday, Chen Xiuji, owner of Chen's Rice Shop in Changzhou, sent an orderly to report that Lu Kan, missing for months, had been seen. Meiyun would set out at dawn with Baoshen and others to find out the truth. The prospect of several days at home with nothing to do inspired me to ask Baoshen if I could come along for a diversion. Who could imagine that just as we set off, Meiyun and Xiumi would get into a heated argument.

Xiumi didn't originally want to go to Changzhou; only her mother's persistent coaxing persuaded her. The moment Meiyun heard that I was accompanying them, she changed her mind and ordered Xiumi to stay home. How could Xiumi not get angry at such inconsistent behavior? Thinking back, I am sure that I was the cause of everything. Meiyun's real reason for dragging Xiumi off to Changzhou in the first place was to allow me no chance to be alone with her. The minute I decided to go, she figured that there was no longer any need for Xiumi to come as well, especially given that rural customs frown upon an unmarried girl showing her face among strangers. Meiyun has a thorough, calculating mind. Xiumi knew something was amiss but didn't understand. I simply watched from the sidelines.

Xiumi stayed angry at her mother the whole way. She sulked and dawdled so far behind we nearly abandoned her. Meiyun and Baoshen walked ahead, while Lilypad and I followed in the middle. We would walk for a spell, then stop and wait for Xiumi to catch up. Yet every time we stopped, she stopped too. She was angry at all of us.

The girl doesn't say much, yet she has a sensitive, suspicious, and incredibly stubborn heart. Zuyan once said that while she might be cold, she could easily be won over. I thought to provoke her a little, to test her by throwing some fuel on the fire in the hope of its burning brighter, so I pretended to flirt with Lilypad.

Lilypad has the easygoing sensuality and shameless bravado of a former prostitute. My initial forays led to more explicit innuendo, and we began to play my false game for real. She started by pinching my arm and breathing too loud, then leaned over to whisper, "I can hardly stand it." I quietly lamented my own stupidity while pretending not to know what she meant. She was like a ball of wet dough—once it sticks to your fingers, it never comes off. If she dared to be this forward on a public road in broad daylight, who knows what she might do after nightfall. With those soft hips and full breasts, slender waist and perfumed skin, colorful clothing, honeyed voice, and tempting disposition, she really could be the consummate femme fatale.

She noticed my frequent glances back at Xiumi and asked if I were more interested in the one behind us. I gave a noncommittal response. The harlot shoved me gently and teased, "They say 'new shoes are nice, but they pinch the toes; sharp thorns hide beneath the garden rose.'" Her words made me momentarily dizzy with arousal, and I nearly lost control of my body and desires. I came very close to pushing her into the reeds and going at it tooth and claw.

At the base of the river wall, we turned onto a narrow path that wound through tree groves and tall reeds. With no one in sight, the harlot redoubled her assault of suggestion, constantly probing me for a response. Seeing I no longer paid her any attention, she abruptly asked, "What year were you born in?" When I told her I was born in the year of the pig, she clasped her hands together and cried out, making me jump. When I asked her what was the matter, she said that many years ago, a fortune-teller she had given food to told her that she would face disaster at middle age, and her only means of escaping it was to marry someone born in the year of the pig. Thus this woman's self-deluded cleverness reveals itself, that she might think to hoodwink me with such a patently ridiculous story. With her previous efforts thwarted, she resorted to her most dangerous trick: she plastered herself up against my shoulder and quietly giggled, "But I'm getting all wet under there."

Truly a vicious stratagem. Had I been a callow young man, or a superficial, soulless playboy, I would surely have sunk into the mud with her past all hope of escape.

Her shamelessness was so thorough I had no choice but to bark, "Wet, wet, wet, to hell with your goddamn wet!" Now frightened, she shrieked and scampered away, hiding her face in her hands.

Xiumi caught up with us at the ferry crossing. She wore a green floral-print shirt, navy-blue pants, and floral embroidered shoes. Even at a distance, the river breeze carried her remarkable scent to me. She had only to appear in my field of vision and I couldn't take my eyes from her.

In that moment, both Lilypad and Xiumi stood before me, and I examined each of them in turn. One seemed an apricot flower laden with fresh dew, the other an autumn lotus touched by frost; one a young deer, bleating by the brook, the other a mare bent over the grain trough; one a pine bough, replete with green needles and oozing scented sap, the other heavy timber cut into a door, and smelling only of varnish. The very picture of refinement and vulgarity in immediate contrast. Oh, Little Sister, Little Sister!

Soon the sail was raised and the ferryman bid us all aboard. A stiff southeast wind raised a heavy chop on the water, making the boat pitch hard. When I saw Xiumi sway unsteadily on the gangplank, I reached out to support her. I didn't expect her to slap my hand away angrily and snap, "I don't need your help!"

The rest of the party turned to look at her in surprise. Though my help had been rebuffed, my heart was filled with a wild elation.

Little Sister, ah, Little Sister!

After eating a hasty dinner at Chen's Rice Market, I walked back to our residence alone. Why did my mind feel so clouded, my feet so clumsy? Why could I not take my eyes off her for a second? Why did I see her shadow everywhere?

On the way back, I approached a rocky cliffside where a stream poured into a pool and an owl hooted. As my eyes and ears took in the scattered dots of lantern light and the low murmur of voices in conversation, the evening's drink hit me, twisting my stomach and throwing my mind into chaos. I sat down on a cold stone and breathed in the pine-sweet air of the mountain valley. If heaven cares for me, I thought, it will bring her to my side right now. Amazingly, just as I was thinking this she appeared.

I watched her emerge from the shop and dawdle on the road, apparently distracted or lost in thought. She spent a moment looking down into the valley, then turned down the path to where I sat. She was alone. Oh, Little Sister. My heart beat so fast it felt like it was about to jump out of my throat.

Ugh, Zhang Jiyuan, are you really so pathetic, is your spirit so paper thin that you would dissolve into jelly over a country girl? Remember how you once crossed hundreds of miles with a dagger in your belt before you slid it into that imperial overseer's breast; how you hopped a boat in Danyang and fled to Japan, surviving trials and traps that brought you to death's edge, and you were never so nervous? Remember when... I could remember nothing, because the beauty had approached.

Had I said nothing, she would have slipped right past me, and my once-in-a-lifetime opportunity would have vanished. Had I reached out directly to embrace her and she screamed, what would I have done? Desperate, I suddenly had an idea. I waited until she neared me, then sighed and said, "It seems that death has just visited this family."

What was I saying? It was absolutely ludicrous. Xiumi could have ignored me entirely, yet she stopped, and asked me, "Who told you that?"

"Nobody told me."

"Then how do you know?" She was full of curiosity.

I got up from the stone and said with a smile, "It's plain as day. And it wasn't just one person, either."

And then I exerted my powers of invention to the utmost, manufacturing a story about a dead child and Chen Xiuji's suicidal wife, and Xiumi actually bought it. We found ourselves walking side by side down the path through the bamboo grove. The path was only wide enough for one, yet she didn't avoid walking next to me. I stopped and turned to her, and she turned to look at me, a faintly bashful look in her eye. Suddenly the whole world was pristine, and the Milky Way glowed above us as bamboo shadows played in the dark hush of nature. Her breathing quickened, as if in anticipation. I'd be mad to take her in both arms and squeeze her until her joints popped, or eat her in a single bite like a sweet clementine, to quench many days of painful thirst. Good heavens, do you really think it possible? As I hesitated, Xiumi turned and continued on ahead. We were almost out of the bamboo grove. Zhang Jiyuan, when will you have a better time to act than now?

"Are you afraid?" I asked, stopping once more. It felt like something was stuck in my throat.

"I am."

I put a hand on her shoulder, on the smooth silk shirt now chilly with dew. I felt her sharp shoulder underneath. Suddenly, a vision of Meiyun's flat face rose before my eyes, sneering at me from the shadows as if to say: If you lay one finger on her, I will boil your bones to make soup...

"Don't be afraid." I finally patted her shoulder and took my hand away.

Back at the residence, we sat down on the doorstep and continued to talk. Xiumi told me that the day she carried a letter to Zuyan's estate, she saw a hunchbacked old man in a black cloth robe spying on her from the other side of the fishpond. I broke out into a cold sweat.

Could it really be him?

Many know him as "Steelback Li," a seasoned spy for the imperial court. Heaven knows how many ambitious young men have lost their lives because of him. In that case, Xia village is in grave danger.

I spent much of the night tossing and turning in bed. I rose at midnight and sat by the table, watching the moon filtering through the screen, listening to the sound of wind in the trees and the continuous roar of Baoshen's snoring. How can she have taken over my heart so completely that I am powerless to do anything else? That a country girl should cripple me like this. Just thinking of her face as she looked up at me makes all else feel utterly meaningless. Here on the eve of a great project—truly this autumn has become a season of life or death—how could I allow private desires to bury the fruit of over ten years of struggle? Have you forgotten the oath you took in Yokohama, Jiyuan? No, this will not do. I must reclaim my spirit.

———

Han Liu walked into the room. Her footsteps were always so light as to be inaudible; she could walk right up to someone without the person knowing, as if she had appeared out of thin air. She told Xiumi that Number Four, Qingshou, had sent men in a boat for her; they had been waiting for some time.

Xiumi closed Zhang Jiyuan's diary, wrapped it back up in its square of multicolored cloth, and stuffed it back under her pillow before standing up to brush her hair. As she looked at herself in the mirror, one lip curled in a wry smile. *Why should I brush my hair*, she thought, *as if I have some reason to make myself look pretty?* She tossed her comb aside and went to the basin to splash her face with water, then shook her head again. *Why wash my face?* She returned to her seat at the table. Body and mind were still absorbed in the world of the diary. She thought of the inexorable movement of time and felt the ache of loss.

A letter sat beside her on the table. Qingshou had sent it to her yesterday through a courier. The calligraphy was delicately styled, and its message simple, consisting of these few lines:

The magical herb weeps dew; the rare flower drops its petals. Your servant sighs with regret at what he has heard. Will prepare a cup of tea the following day with the hope of sweet conversation. Please do us the great honor of accepting. May

an easy current carry you, and a straight path see you home.
Many thanks! The Wasted Man, Qingshou

Wang Guancheng had called himself "Dead Man Walking," and
was regrettably already a dead man lying down; now here was "the
Wasted Man." It seemed the robber kings at Huajiashe each liked to
think up his own fancy epithet. Yet who knows what kind of man
Qingshou was. Upon reading the letter, Xiumi didn't know how to
react. She and Han Liu went back and forth about it without coming
to a clear resolution. In the end, Han Liu said, "Since I've never met
Qingshou, I don't dare speak to his character. The letter is certainly
polite enough. 'May an easy current carry you and a straight path see
you home' looks like an assurance that he's not going to harm you,
and 'the magical herb weeps dew, the rare flower drops its petals'
sounds like sympathy for the abuse you faced. If he's planning something bad for you and trying to lure you over, then even if you don't
go, he'll just come here. To put it bluntly, he could just send men over
here to tie you up and carry you off, and you still couldn't do anything
about it."

It was Xiumi's first visit to Huajiashe. Though she had stared at
it innumerable times from across the lake, it never looked like anything
more than a pile of trees and a pile of houses with a pile of white
clouds overhead. As the boat left the island and sped toward the village, she felt a deep rush of shame.

The boat drew gently up to what looked like a massive covered
walkway constructed of stripped tree trunks supporting a thatched
roof. Rudely built and in obvious decay, the walkway extended in
both directions in an endless, meandering line. The tree trunks were
warped and varied in thickness. Some of the willow trunks had absorbed so much moisture in the shade that they had sprouted tufts
of new green. The roof was thatched with reeds and wheat husks, and
scattered with rotten patches, some of which had fallen through to
expose the blue sky above. Sun and rain had blackened much of it
with mold, and every gust of wind raised black dust from its surface.
Underneath the roof, a stream of cobwebs festooned swallow nests

and beehives. A railing made of slender tree trunks lined both sides of the walkway, though several sections of it had already broken off.

Gazebos, positioned every hundred feet or so, were much more artfully constructed. Clearly designed as resting places for the villagers, they featured ornate carvings throughout their interiors. Depictions of the *Twenty-Four Legends of Filial Piety* (famous figures from opera), as well as auspicious animals like carp, dragons, and phoenixes adorned every pillar and ceiling. Some had stone tables and four stone stools, others had benches built into the walls. Each structure was paved with square black bricks, not a few of which had begun to loosen, mud squelching up through the cracks when stepped on. As she followed the two servants, Xiumi tried to step carefully, though she couldn't tell which bricks would sink into the mud and stain her embroidered shoes.

The sound of running water accompanied them the whole way. A current of clear water flowed along an aqueduct beside the walkway, cooling the air noticeably. Xiumi quickly realized that the walkway had actually been built to follow the aqueduct, and not the other way around. She recalled Han Liu telling her that Wang Guancheng had diverted the mountain springs to let water flow into every kitchen in the village so that every housewife could always have fresh water for washing and cooking.

Xiumi thought of a heated argument Mother and Father had had around the time Father fell sick. Father had impulsively decided to hire workmen to build a covered walkway in Puji, with the intention of connecting every home in the village, and even stretching into the fields. Mother exploded immediately: "Have you gone crazy?! Why do want to waste money on some worthless walkway?" Father rolled his eyes, paying no attention to Mother's anger, and smiled. "Because that way the villagers can be shielded from the sun and rain."

Father's absurd idea became one of Mother's favorite anecdotes in idle conversations for years afterward, and she always ended it with a hysterical laugh.

Yet when she was small, Xiumi couldn't figure out why the idea so wrong. When she asked Baoshen, he frowned for a moment, then replied, "Some things seem fine to imagine but idiotic to fulfill in real life." Xiumi still didn't understand. When she asked Ding Shuze, he told her that while a Peach Blossom Paradise might exist in heaven, you would never find one on earth: "Only a complete fool like your father would drive himself crazy imagining such a ridiculous thing. That southern nutcase in the imperial court, Kang Youwei, was even crazier than your father, fooling the emperor and misleading the court with his talk of 'Great Unity' and legal reform. Did he think that thousands of years of traditional law and order could be flipped around and changed whenever he felt like it?"

Yet here she was, finding Father's crazy idea manifested in a nest of robbers. The walkway seemed to reach out in all directions, linking every courtyard like an enormous, sprawling spiderweb. Beds of flowers and lotus ponds fed by the aqueduct adorned the walkway on both sides. Water lilies and Indian lotuses bloomed in the pond, their fleshy petals curling slightly under the intense summer sun as swarms of red damselflies dotted the water. Every household looked exactly alike, with the same quaint courtyard featuring a well and two vegetable patches. Every window pointed toward the lake, and even the hanging baskets blooming with flowers looked identical.

The landscape became more disorienting the farther they went. Xiumi felt as if she had walked a long way only to find herself back where she started. In one courtyard, she saw a girl in a red hemstitched robe drawing water from a well, while only a little farther onward, she saw another young girl of the same age, dressed in the same attire, her hair pulled into the same high braids, knocking cicadas from a tree with a bamboo pole. It seemed that "In Huajiashe, even bees would lose their way" was not just an empty boast.

After nearly an hour, they arrived at a clean and well-kept courtyard. It looked exactly the same as every other courtyard in the village, save for the two spear-wielding guards who stood outside the door.

"Here we are," one servant said to Xiumi. "Come with me, please."

The courtyard door was wide open. A path paved with crumbling bricks covered with thick moss led to the inner hallway. The two servants bowed, asking her to "please wait a moment," and retreated backwards from her.

The courtyard was narrow and dark, and so close to the main hall that it seemed a part of it. A straight row of thick pillars supported a sharply sloped roof. A wooden ladder poked out of the wall on the left-hand side, possibly leading into an attic, while a small door in the rear, shaded by bamboo, opened into another courtyard, from which could be heard the sound of flowing water.

A man in a long robe sat in the center of the hall with his back to Xiumi. His age was not obvious at first glance. He was playing go with a woman in white. She looked around forty years old, her hair tied in a high bun. One hand rested at her chin, while the long fingers of her other hand gently played with a stone on the table. It appeared that neither had taken any notice of Xiumi standing behind them.

A collapsed panel screen, painted in black lacquer and gold leaf, leaned against the far wall. Bamboo hooks hanging from the rafters above held bunches of red chili peppers as well as a birdcage with a parrot inside it, which carefully scrutinized Xiumi. Fresh bird droppings dotted the floor. A statue of the Bodhisattva Guanyin and a terra-cotta incense burner molded in the shape of a toad with an open mouth were displayed on an altar. The incense had long burned to ash, but Xiumi could still catch a whiff of arrowroot and snowbell resin.

Late-afternoon sunlight rose from the geraniums onto the western wall and from there into the canopy of a grove, saturating the leaves with red. Xiumi heard the woman say, "No need to count stones, you've definitely lost." The man didn't respond, but continued counting though it was indeed clear he had lost. When he demanded a rematch, the woman said, "We can play again in the evening. The poor girl's been waiting forever."

The man turned to look at Xiumi, then immediately stood up and said to the woman, "Why didn't you say anything when she arrived?" Turning back to Xiumi, he cupped his fist in greeting. "Welcome. Many, many apologies for the wait." Hurrying over to her, he looked Xiumi up and down a few times and mused, "No wonder. No wonder."

The woman in white laughed. "What do you think? I guessed right, didn't I?"

"Absolutely," the man replied. "The kid Qingsheng has good taste."

The man must be Number Four, Qingshou, but who is the woman? Xiumi wondered. Not quite understanding what they were talking about, she stood with her eyes trained on the ground, the fingers of her clasped hands rubbing against each other. Perhaps it was the presence of another woman that made her feel slightly less nervous. The woman approached her too, and took her arm in her hands, saying sweetly, "No need to be afraid, my love. Come with me."

Xiumi found a seat while the woman brewed her a cup of tea, a broad smile on her face. With a folded fan in his hand, Qingshou addressed Xiumi: "Young miss, we've invited you here today for the sole reason of asking you a few questions. By my honor I should have taken a boat to the island to visit you, but as you know, that place is so filthy I can't bear to set foot on it. Having thought it over, I decided to ask my lady to write a letter of invitation to you, that you would grant us the honor of your company over tea. I hope you will forgive the abruptness of my actions."

Hearing this, Xiumi figured the woman in white must be his wife. Qingshou spoke in a deep voice, with a slow, measured tone that revealed an inner fortitude. The sight of his slightly furrowed brow and upright demeanor, which suggested that he was not a deceitful man, relaxed Xiumi further.

When Qingshou saw Xiumi would not raise her eyes or speak, he pushed a teacup toward her with his fan, and invited her to "please take tea" in a cold, affectless voice.

An attendant stumbled through the front door, then stood in the middle of the room to report, "This evening makes seven days since Number Five's wake. His people sent someone inviting the master to drink with them tonight."

Qingshou waved his fan at the attendant and frowned. "I won't go."

The attendant did not leave, but asked nervously, "Then what will I tell them?"

"No need to tell them anything. Just say I'm not going."

As the attendant turned to go, the woman in white stopped him. After pausing briefly to think, she ordered, "You can tell them that your master has caught a fever and has a toothache, and can't drink."

After the servant left, Qingshou said to Xiumi, "In the two months since you arrived at Huajiashe, our little village has been the scene of many strange events, to the point of bad news cropping up every hour. I'm sure you've heard much about this. First, our chief met his end when someone struck him down in his own home. Number Two was poisoned soon after, and exactly one week ago, Qingde was murdered in the livestock pen—"

"He's dead too?" Xiumi interjected.

Qingshou and the woman in white shot each other a glance, as if to say, *She's finally opened her mouth.*

"He and two goats were chopped into pieces." Qingshou chuckled, and went on: "His servants tried to collect his body, but how could they in that condition? In the end, they had to shovel everything into a coffin, goat manure and all, just so they could have the ceremony and get him in the ground. Even an idiot could see by now that there's more than one killer, and each one of them is merciless.

"Had we not reached this state of emergency, I would not be so rude as to disturb your seclusion. I must admit that ever since the head man was killed, I have been trying to draw my own conclusions, yet I have been proved wrong every time. In the end, I feel like I'm trapped in a dream; I have strained my brain nearly to bursting in my search for answers, yet come up with nothing.

"When the chief died, my thoughts turned first to Number Two. It's long been an open secret that he coveted the chief's position. Wang Guancheng first took to his bed with an illness a full six years ago, and it looked like he would die quickly. Who could have imagined that he would hold on for six more years, and just last winter, even recover enough to walk around? In early spring, just after the last ice on the lake had melted, we found him swimming in the frigid water. Later, he was heard several times in the village saying that his Peach Blossom Spring on earth had become a putrid whorehouse, and that some even had the gall to kidnap nuns. Since heaven had decided to cure him overnight, he was going to rectify the social contract. No wonder Number Two got nervous. He had been the de facto leader ever since Wang fell ill and couldn't possibly avoid responsibility for what Huajiashe had become. Besides, he was only four years younger than Wang Guancheng, so he knew he didn't have time to wait. So after he was killed, my wife and I were sure Number Two must have been the murderer.

"Who would believe that only days later, Number Two himself would die of poisoning. That checked him off our list. With him gone, we figured that among those remaining, Qingde was the most likely suspect. He used to be the Boss's military second-in-command, and while he was a lecherous man with an indiscriminate appetite, Wang never hesitated to punish him severely for his behavior. But back in the early days, when they were going after bandits in Fujian, he once saved Wang's life. Here at Huajiashe, he was the only one of us who could go in and out of the chief's home as he pleased, so taking the old man's life would have been particularly easy. I also heard that on the night of the chief's death, he braved a storm to visit the island in secret. A highly unusual act . . ."

The mention of that turbulent evening invoked a rush of shame and embarrassment for Xiumi; her gaze became more evasive, and she bent her head lower. The woman in white noticed all this, and hurriedly interrupted her husband's train of thought.

"We don't have to talk about that. Five is dead now, too, so he couldn't have been the killer."

"Yes, of course." Qingshou's grave countenance betrayed a total absorption in his own thoughts, and he occasionally prodded his forehead with the end of his fan. "But besides me, that leaves only Qingfu and young Number Six, Qingsheng, who are still alive. Recently, we had come to believe that the situation was gradually becoming clearer, since only two possibilities in our mind remained: either one of them was the killer, or both of them were—that is, they had banded together to exterminate the rest of us. Whatever the case, as you can see, I am next in line for the knife. If we do nothing but stand by and watch, we might not live through the summer. So instead, I have decided to strike first."

Having made this announcement, Qingshou fished a pipe from his pocket and put it in his mouth. Two female attendants each carried in a bowl of evening snacks: carefully prepared slices of steamed lotus root filled with sweet rice. The woman in white offered them twice before Xiumi could bring herself to try a bite.

"We've heard that aside from Number Five, Number Three also visited the island two or three weeks ago," the woman said. "I'm sure you're not eager to remember that moment, much less talk about it. And if you can't bear to talk at all, we won't force you. But the coup that's happening now threatens everyone in this village. And if you're willing to help us, we'd like to know what the two of them said when they were with you. Did they do anything out of the ordinary? Please, if you feel up to it, give us the whole story, beginning to end, without leaving out a single detail, particularly anything related to Qingfu. If we can safely eliminate him as a suspect, then we can focus on dealing with Little Six."

Xiumi contemplated the situation for a moment. Then she sighed, and was preparing to speak when a boy in shepherd's clothes and a straw hat barreled into the room as if bearing urgent news. Qingshou implored Xiumi with a "just a brief moment" and hurried over to the boy. Xiumi watched the shepherd boy stand on tiptoe so he could whisper in Qingshou's ear as he gestured outside with his crook.

After passing along his news, the shepherd boy left. Qingshou returned to the table, his expression impassive, and said to Xiumi, "Please continue, young miss."

Xiumi recounted everything that had happened to her on the island. When she described hearing someone laugh outside the hut's door as Qingfu was molesting his maid, Qingshou jerked so hard he spilled tea all over himself and made Xiumi jump. His face turned as white as a plaster mask.

"Who was laughing outside your door?" he asked.

"I don't know," Xiumi said. "Qingfu rushed out with his cook to look, but they searched everywhere and found nothing. But I don't think the person was actually outside the door."

"Where was he, then?"

"On the roof. I feel like he must have been on the roof."

"Number Three must have been scared to death, no?" the woman in white asked.

"He seemed to recognize the voice." Xiumi's gaze grew confused. "He kept saying, 'How could it be him?' As if he knew who it was but didn't want to believe it himself."

Qingshou and the woman in white once more exchanged a look as they said simultaneously, "Qingsheng?"

"I haven't seen him since I was brought here," Xiumi told them.

"Yes, we know," Qingshou replied. He had not yet recovered his composure. "Little Six was Number Two's own protégé, and a close confidant. He has brute strength but doesn't appear to have much for brains. If he really is the culprit, then how do you explain Number Two's death? 'Big trees give the best shade,' as the saying goes. He would never cut the very tree down that provided shade for himself while he still needed it. Besides, taking on five leaders on his own doesn't seem like the kind of thing Little Six could do...Curious, this is very curious!"

"Why don't we ask Carefree?" the woman asked facetiously, looking up at the parrot in the cage. "See what he thinks."

The parrot obviously could understand when it was being addressed. It lazily shook its feathers, then looked straight at its owner for a moment as if also deliberating the situation. Finally, it squawked out a quote from the ancient histories: "While the Qing brothers live, the city isn't safe."

"He's not wrong. Number Three and Number Six are both 'Qing brothers,'" Qingshou said with a bitter smile.

He and the woman in white shared a brief moment of laughter before worry spread across her face again. She reminded him, "Could it have just been a smoke screen? Qingfu pretending to be stalked by a killer so we wouldn't suspect him? He may act like an idiot, reciting poetry and quoting classical literature all day, but he has a clever mind. He has plenty of schemes behind those beady little eyes."

"I always used to suspect him," Qingshou replied gravely, as he stroked his beard, "but the scout told me just now that the ingrate has run away."

"Run away?"

"Away, away…" Qingshou nodded. "He took Crimson and Turquoise and left by the back road on a donkey. I expect he's crossed Phoenix Ridge by now."

"He got scared."

"Not just scared, he completely lost his nerve." Qingshou snorted derisively before resuming his somber expression.

"Could it really be Qingsheng?"

"If not him, do you expect it's me?" Qingshou asked from between clenched teeth. After a pause, he continued, "It's him, it's got to be him. He's the one who kidnapped her, and the smell of a woman drives him crazy anyway. I wonder why he never visited the island? Nor have we seen hide nor hair of him in the village these last few days. And how could he not know that Qingde and Qingfu already visited the island weeks ago? And why would he hold back for so long? It's him, it's him… The kid almost tricked me, too."

Qingfu's escape clarified the situation almost instantaneously and brought Little Six, Qingsheng, directly into Qingshou's line of sight. Like the island reappearing on the lake after the fog lifted, all obstacles had suddenly disappeared.

"I must be off." Qingshou tossed a quick glance at both women, stood up, and turned to leave.

"Qingshou!" the woman in white cried out anxiously after him.

"Qingshou!" the parrot in the cage called out.

Qingshou took down the birdcage and opened a small door; the parrot immediately jumped onto his shoulder and started nibbling his face. Qingshou gently caressed the parrot's feathers as he mumbled, "Carefree, Carefree, we once thought that escaping to Huajiashe would leave us safe and carefree. Games of go by day and books every evening. Who would have thought that even when you hide in your own bedroom, disaster comes looking for you?"

"If you ask me, I think we need to think about this for a minute," his wife declared.

"What's left to think about now?" Qingshou sighed. "If we don't kill him, he will inevitably come to kill us."

"Qingshou," his wife called to him with tears in her eyes, "why can't we be like Qingfu, and just fly away from here?"

"Fly away?" Qingshou turned to stare at her, then began laughing hysterically. He laughed so hard he had to bend over, tears flowing from his eyes as many months of repressed anxiety, suspicion, and terror poured out. "How can you say that? Even Little Six would feel let down. But if you really want to leave, you should take Carefree and go."

"When do you plan to do it?" asked the woman in white.

"This evening."

8

By the time Xiumi returned to the island, night had fallen.

Han Liu was waiting by the lamp with two bowls of pumpkin congee she had just cooked. She said she had spent the whole afternoon worried she would never see Xiumi again. "And there's also almost no rice left," she added, "though at least we have plenty of salt."

"What do we do once we eat all the rice?" Xiumi asked.

Han Liu assured her that there were still plenty of vegetables in the garden, plus the gourds hanging from the ceiling. She knew of several kinds of green plants on the island that were edible, and if things got really bad, they could slaughter the chickens.

Han Liu felt embarrassed saying this. She knew that taking life violated the laws of Buddhism, and she had always loved the chickens like her own children. Talking to them and playing with them had been her greatest pleasure when she was alone on the island. She had given each of them a name, all surnamed Han. And yet, as each new clutch of chicks hatched, she wouldn't hesitate to kill and eat them before they fully matured.

"It is sinful, it is sinful," she sighed. "But chicken soup is so tasty."

This latest brood of chicks had already started to lose their down, and their skinny bodies looked mottled and mangy. Tired from hunger, they strutted and shook themselves unsteadily beneath the table.

Xiumi described her trip to Huajiashe. The two remaining leaders would be at each other's throats that night, though there was no telling who would come away victorious.

"Do you know who the woman in white really is?" Han Liu asked, after scraping up some pumpkin congee with her fingers and putting it into her mouth.

"No, who?"

"Qingshou's aunt, his mother's younger sister. Heaven knows what kind of bad karma their ancestors handed down to them. She and Qingshou are close in age and used to play together when they were young. Then, when she turned sixteen, they slept together—and his parents caught them. He eloped with her, but their elder brothers from both sides, along with an uncle, chased them for years in hopes of bringing their heads back to placate the ancestors. Wang Guancheng not only took Qingshou in, he gave him the fourth seat at the table."

"And that didn't offend the villagers?"

"They say that in Huajiashe a man can openly marry his own daughter. Whether or not that's true I have no idea. The village is so remote that there's little communication with the outside world. For something like that to happen wouldn't be strange at all."

"There's still one thing I don't understand," Xiumi said. "If Wang Guancheng originally gave up his position to become a hermit so he could purify his mind and escape worldly suffering, how did he end up turning into a bandit?"

Han Liu chuckled bitterly and tapped her own chest. "He got trapped by his own idea," she sighed.

"What idea?"

"He wanted to build a heavenly paradise on earth," Han Liu explained. "The human heart is like a lily. It has as many divisions as the flower has petals, but as you pull the petals away one by one, you find a center hidden beneath them. That's what we mean when we say 'The human heart is hard to plumb.' Seeing through the illusion of birth and death isn't that difficult, the cycle of existence being beyond human control. But to see through the illusion of fame and fortune, and thus cast aside your desires, is much harder.

"Wang Guancheng desired nothing but to live purely among nature, with the dome of the sky as his roof, clothed in the stars, fed by the wind and rain, so he built a hut on an island. But his mind gradually changed. He decided he would make Huajiashe a place without hunger or poverty, where the people had no need to be selfish, lock their doors, or take what wasn't theirs. But fame and fortune still spoke to him. Wang Guancheng himself could lead an extremely abstemious lifestyle—bread and water and one set of clothes were all he needed, and he didn't care about money—but he was driven by the desire to win the respect of the three hundred–plus villagers in Huajiashe and build a reputation that would live on for generations after him.

"A village this far into the mountains doesn't have much arable land. Wang Guancheng wanted to build houses, dig aqueducts, and build his covered walkway, but he didn't have the money for it. As an ex-minister with experience leading military campaigns, the idea of stealing from the others naturally came to mind. But they only stole from rich merchants, never touched peasants, nor did they ever kill anyone. It worked out well in the beginning; clothing and jewelry were split evenly between all the residents, and fish from the lake were piled on the shore every day so people could take what they needed. Rural society here was simple enough to begin with, and Wang Guancheng's moral education really did make the people polite, productive, and altruistic. They greeted each other respectfully, fathers and sons loved and honored each other, husbands and wives worked as a team. People competed for the most worthless items from the raids so they could leave the good stuff for their neighbors, and they only took the smallest fish for themselves. The largest fish would remain on the shore in the sun and rot.

"But robbery isn't an easy task, and many of the larger villas they targeted had armed attendants, so success wasn't assured if a fight broke out. One year, they tried to rob a rich merchant in Qinggang, and not only did they return almost empty handed, they lost two good men. So Wang Guancheng thought of his old subordinates. Number Two was once the head of a provincial militia, Number Three was a garrison leader, and Number Five was a naval battalion commander. Of course, all three brought their own people. As imperial soldiers, they had to accept military rules and discipline, but then they became bandit kings. And while they may have shown some respect to the Boss at first, as time went on, how could Wang Guancheng control them? And then, of course, overwork took its toll on him, and once he became bedridden, inches away from death, he had to let them do as they pleased."

"Sounds like they're the ones who ruined everything," Xiumi said.

"Not entirely. Had Wang Guancheng himself not let the wolves in with the sheep, the village would still be what it was," Han Liu mused, picking her teeth. "Or, if he had simply kept to himself and lived out his days here on the island, Huajiashe would still be Huajiashe—farmers up at dawn and home at dusk. Though it would never have been glorious, it would have escaped this new disaster.

"At first, Huajiashe was nothing more than an idea. But the moment he reached out for it, set out to make it a reality, it moved beyond his control. Buddhism says that all things in the universe are born from the mind and made by it, yet no one expects that in the end, it all turns out to be an illusion that disappears before your eyes like a burst soap bubble. Wang Guancheng was committed to transforming Huajiashe into a world-famous Peach Blossom Spring, yet he ends up dying beneath the ax he taught his killer to swing and dragging the whole village into ruin. Do you smell that? It's like something's burning—"

Han Liu broke off and sniffed audibly, then got up and wandered around the hut with her nose in the air. "Where is that charred odor coming from?"

Xiumi took a turn around the hut, searching for the cause, then stopped in front of the north-facing window. The white window paper glowed orange, and she could see the glimmer of an occasional spark floating past the wooden frame. Han Liu jumped up from the table and ran to the window to open it. A mountain of flames had already engulfed the far side of the lake.

Xiumi stood next to Han Liu at the window, and the two leaned against the wall and watched in awe as the fire consumed the village. The smell of woodsmoke filled the air, and they could hear the crackle of burning timber. It seemed to burn fiercest in the village's northwest corner, where one house had already lost its roof and was reduced to naked pillars. Thick smoke curled and tore into itself as it rose and blew toward the island in a heavy cloud. Flame illuminated the covered walkway, along with the glassy border of the lake, the moored boats, the posts of the old bridge.

Human silhouettes also appeared in a black contrast so sharp they seemed right in front of Xiumi's eyes. Xiumi saw some elderly people standing on a far-off bank, watching the blaze as they leaned on canes; she saw naked children dashing between light and shadow while others watched from behind trees. The sounds of wailing and barking dogs merged together within the howling of the wind.

"Four and Six have crossed swords," Han Liu said. "And 'when the big cats fight, the little deer die,' as they say."

"Let it burn," Xiumi whispered through her teeth. "Let the whole place burn to the ground." She left her position at the window and went to the table to clean up the dishes. Regardless of what she had said, a small part of her worried for the woman in white. Those long, slender fingers and that mournful face, the birdcage hanging empty from the rafters and the talkative parrot all surfaced in her mind's eye. She felt a sharp pang of pity.

Of course, Wang Guancheng's dream bothered her the most. She suddenly felt like Wang Guancheng, Zhang Jiyuan, and her missing father were all one and the same person. Their figures and their dreams were like mist and clouds in the sky, evaporating into nothing at the first sign of wind.

Han Liu started to help Xiumi tidy up beneath the lamplight, after which the two of them boiled water for tea. As Han Liu tossed cordwood into the stove, firelight threw her heavy silhouette onto the opposite wall. Xiumi felt safe sitting near her. In fact, the very sight of Han Liu's red cheeks, full lips, and substantial upper arms made Xiumi feel safe. The two had sat together by the single lamp flame, beneath the collapsing roof with clouds of stars above, for countless nights already. Cicadas trilled ceaselessly by the lakeshore as the night cooled. Sometimes the two women didn't speak, yet even in those moments Xiumi felt at ease, as if she had nothing to worry about in the least.

Xiumi liked long-lasting, durable things that didn't break easily.

Han Liu was such a thing. Her breathing was rough like a man's, and when she snored, the whole hut snored with her. She smacked her lips and slurped when she ate rice congee, making quite a noise, but Xiumi thought it was nice. Back in Puji, making the tiniest sound during mealtimes always earned Xiumi a hard rap on the head with Mother's chopsticks.

When the heat of summer days became suffocating, Han Liu would walk around the house in nothing but her underwear, her full breasts rounding into the crook of her arm, her dark nipples and tan aureoles displayed before Xiumi's eyes all day. When she ate a plum, she'd eat the whole thing, chewing up and swallowing the pit. Xiumi would occasionally fantasize about how nice it would be to live with her on the island for the rest of their lives. The shocking realization that she had become attached to this tiny island on a lake would then tear her from this fantasy.

"Sister..." Xiumi began, untying her apron and tossing it onto a corner of the oven. Han Liu moved along the low wooden bench to give Xiumi room to sit down beside her. "Sister, what is the heart, really?"

"You're better off asking yourself that, not me," Han Liu said, laughing. She stirred the burning cordwood with her iron poker. "Saints and sinners don't have labels written on their faces. You'll meet some people who dress in fine clothes, have the best manners, and talk like poets, but inside they're as black as death, the worst kind of human in existence.

"Thoughts and desires are impossible to track—they change constantly, like the weather during the plum rains in May, to the point where you can't even be sure what you yourself are thinking. When the world is at peace, the human heart accepts the restraints of law and morality, becoming civilized through education, as if anyone could stand side by side with the Sage Emperors. But once chaos takes over, the bad spots in the hearts of those very same people burst like infected lesions, and even a Sage King can turn into an animal and do beastly things. You're an educated woman, you already know more about this than I do."

"If we survive this disaster, Sister, will you let me be your disciple? We can find a temple and spend the rest of our lives in prayer."

Han Liu smiled faintly but said nothing.

"Do you not want to? Or do I not have the wisdom for it?" Xiumi giggled, giving Han Liu's arm a shove. Still smiling, Han Liu shook her head. After a while, she explained: "I've broken my vows many times since they first brought me to this island. I couldn't be your teacher. If we get out of this alive and you still want to be a nun, I'll find you someone stronger in the faith to teach you. But my eye tells me you're no ordinary person, and you're not ready to leave the world. You may be destined for great things. Right now you're like a tiger in an open field, or a dragon in the marsh; the world is holding you back, and that's why you dream of leaving it. You can't take it seriously."

"Why would you provoke me? A girl with nothing, kidnapped by criminals and thrown into the mountains with a family who refused to help her—there's hardly any reason for me to be alive. What could I possibly do with ambition?" Tears brimmed in Xiumi's eyes.

"You might say that, but it's not what you feel," Han Liu replied.

"Well then, what do you think I'm feeling now?"

"If I tell you, you can't get mad at me," Han Liu said seriously.

"What's to be mad about? Just say it," Xiumi replied.

"Then I will." Han Liu turned to look at Xiumi, examining her face closely before continuing in a measured tone: "The fact is that you've had something on your mind ever since you got back from the village today."

"What?"

"You're thinking that Wang Guancheng was a failure, and that if you had been in charge of Huajiashe, you would have made sure everything was done right to make it into a real paradise."

Xiumi's eyes widened. Her hands and feet began to sweat, and a chill came over her before Han Liu had even finished speaking. Her focus turned inward: *I did have that thought today, but it was only a flicker. How could Han Liu have picked it up from a passing whim?* Xiumi's respect for Han Liu's powers of observation into the recesses of the human heart deepened. *Clearly this nun has a razor-sharp mind.* But to think that not only her every action but also her innermost thoughts had been exposed to Han Liu's keen eyes sent a nervous tingle through Xiumi's spine.

"I hate to say it, but if you had been in Wang Guancheng's position, the result would have been the same," Han Liu continued.

"How do you figure?" Xiumi asked with a laugh.

"Wang Guancheng was a scholar, a highly educated man; what could you think of that he couldn't think of? What could you do that he couldn't do, after working forty years in government, with battle plans and cities under his control? The ancients say that 'power equals work.' When you have one, you can do the other. Otherwise, you can imagine all the clever schemes you like, but what will it amount to beyond a life of dreams? Wang Guancheng dedicated his whole will to creating a heaven on earth, and he was still just chasing his own shadow. In the end, he merely built his own tomb."

Han Liu slapped the straw dust off her clothing and stood up to brew the tea. She gave Xiumi a pot, and the two continued to talk by the stove. Xiumi didn't go to bed until midnight. Glancing once more through the northern window, she saw that the fire in Huajiashe had burned out completely, total darkness reclaiming the world.

9

Xue Zuyan killed yesterday. Night before last, a brigade of soldiers set off from Meicheng under cover of darkness to surround his villa, as Zuyan and his concubine were sound asleep. The garrison lieutenant had been a childhood friend of Zuyan's, and killed him quickly during the struggle that morning. Li Daodeng was born in Xia village, and probably worried that if Zuyan were taken alive to Meicheng, he might give up local names under torture. Though he may be a running dog for the imperial court, he is a man of discreet and thorough action, and possesses both a strategic mind and a compassionate heart. Worthy of respect. They cut off Zuyan's head and carried it back to Meicheng in a crate, and dumped the body in the pond. Great works always require bloodshed; we must consider Zuyan's sacrifice appropriate, for both the time and place.

The hunchbacked fisherman Xiumi mentioned must certainly have been Steelback Li. That means our contacts in Xia village are already under surveillance.

Other committee members have proved themselves to be hateful cowards. They scattered like animals immediately after Zuyan's death, some running to other villages, others hiding in the wilderness. Zuyan's body floated in the pond for a whole day and night. After returning to Puji, I paid a fisherman thirteen taels of silver to recover the body, place it in a casket, and bury it in the valley behind the mountain. The money came from my own pocket; I'll accept reimbursement from the committee after our work is done.

Then went to reconnoiter with other members to plan our next steps. Didn't expect to find that all had lost their nerve, and those who had not already run made every excuse to avoid me. Finally made it to Zhang Lianjia's place in the northwest corner of Xia village in the middle of the night. The echo of my knocking resounded throughout the house, but no one came to the door. At last, a lamp flickered on in the bedroom. Zhang Lianjia's woman appeared at the door in her underwear and an open nightshirt. She asked me who I was and who I was looking for, but when I replied with our passwords she feigned confusion at first, then said, "The person you're looking for isn't in this house. Good night." Anger infused me with a burst of strength, and I slammed the door open and forced my way in. She didn't dare cry out after the door hit her, merely rubbed her big boobs and whined, "Owww, that hurts, that really hurts."

I charged into their inner chambers to find Zhang Lianjia lying on the couch in a dressing gown, smoking a pipe. His eyes were half-closed, and he didn't even acknowledge me. I asked him to help me contact members for another meeting to discuss our current situation. He turned his narrow gaze at me and sneered, "I fear you've got the wrong man. I'm just a peasant, I don't know anything about any committee." I reprimanded him strongly for being a coward and playing dumb in the face of danger. Didn't expect him to stand up and pull out a shiny butcher's knife. He raised it to my face and stormed toward me: "Get out! If you stay, I'll take you to the magistrate."

At that point, all I could do was leave; had I kept arguing, he might really have sold me out. Ah, Zhang Jiyuan, never forget the hopeless feeling of that moment. The day the revolution succeeds, we swear to wipe out all of these cowards from the map, starting with Zhang Lianjia and his harlot wife. Her legs certainly are white; tell me, how does a farmer end up marrying such a good-looking woman? Kill them, kill them both. I will take her flesh off piece by piece to satisfy my grievance.

Meiyun acting differently toward me lately. Obviously trying to force me out. But where can I go now? Can't return to Meicheng, Pukou still too dangerous. Best choice would be to catch a steamer out of Shanghai to Yokohama, then to Sendai. But where could I get the money for the trip?

Absolutely no communication from Dapples. He has been gone for over a month, no idea what's happened to him.

Meiyun came upstairs, crying unceasingly. She swore she would absolutely never let me go if the situation didn't demand it. My temper was long gone, and I had no interest in lovemaking. We sat awkwardly for a moment, until both of us finally got bored. She asked me if there was anything I still wanted to say or do; I thought it over, then told her I only wanted to see Xiumi one more time. She shoved me hard and stared at me with a look of hate and alarm, nodding her head until my scalp tingled and my hands started sweating. She replied icily, one word at a time: "Tell me what you wish to say, and I will make sure she knows."

I said in that case, I would go without seeing her. Meiyun stared at me blankly for a second, then went downstairs. To my surprise, she sent Xiumi up anyway.

If only I could persuade her to join us, how wonderful that would be!

Little Sister, oh, my dear Little Sister, my good Little Sister. My little white rabbit, I want to kiss your pouty little lips, and lick the soft down above them; I want to touch every bone in your body; I want to bury my face in your armpit and sleep until daybreak. I want you to plant yourself in my heart like a seed, I want you to pour forth milk and honey like a sacred spring; I want you to wet my dreams like a spring rain. I want to smell your fragrance every day—the scents of powder, of fruit, of soft earth in the rain, of a warm horse barn.

Without you, what good is revolution?

The body of the woman in white appeared the next morning. When Xiumi walked down to the shore, Han Liu was already guiding it in with a bamboo pole. The woman wore a pearl necklace and a pair of embroidered shoes with silver clasps that sparkled in the morning sunlight.

The rest of her body was naked. Burns the size of copper coins dappled her flesh like smallpox lesions. Her skin was pale white tinged with green. Half a night in the lake had swollen her face slightly. Her breasts had been cut off. Shreds of charred grass and leaves covered her body, which floated in the murky water like a cup dropped in a tankard of unfiltered beer.

Her slender, fine-boned fingers had been pounded into mush—no longer would those fingers grasp a go stone. The triangle of dark hair between her legs bloomed in the water like river grass; no longer would it give anyone pleasure.

"Vile sin, vile sin, vile sin!"

Han Liu seemed incapable of saying anything else.

Fire had consumed about a third of Huajiashe. Roofless houses lay like dead animals whose stomachs had been hollowed out by insects, tendrils of smoke still drifting from charred remains. A southerly wind blew the ash floating on the water to shore. A deathly quiet reigned.

And in a flash the village had a new leader. Qingshou had lost the battle. His aunt had been tortured. They made him watch as they tied bells to her nipples (bells that had been wrapped around her ankles) and jabbed her with hot pokers that made her jump and cringe. They ordered her to smile, and when she refused, they stuck the hot pokers on her face and into her belly button until she couldn't endure it any longer, and she smiled. They ordered her to talk dirty, but she wouldn't, so they smashed her fingers one by one with a nightstick. When they got to her ring finger, she obeyed. She said all the lewdest things she could imagine, all while staring imploringly at her husband. Qingshou had been tied securely to a chair and could do nothing more than stare back at her and shake his head as a signal for her to stay strong. But she couldn't withstand the pain. She did everything they told her to do until Little Six got bored and cut off her breasts with a sharp knife.

Xiumi heard about all this later on.

Qingshou's death was much more straightforward. They stuffed his mouth and nose with mud until he couldn't breathe. He pissed himself, kicked his legs a few times, and died.

She heard about that later as well, when Little Six, the new leader of Huajiashe, sent men over to the island with wedding invitations. He had decided to marry Xiumi.

10

THE WEDDING was held soon afterward. Seated once more inside a crimson wedding palanquin, Xiumi felt herself returning to that moment four months earlier when Lilypad had helped her into the palanquin seat. A thick fog had descended that morning and covered everything—the village, the forest, the river, the boat. She had fallen asleep. It felt as if this were the very same morning. Could it be that she had never run into the bandits, never been kidnapped to Huajiashe and imprisoned on a tiny island on a lake, never witnessed a chain of strange events and brutal murders in the village—everything, everything just a dream she had dreamt while napping in the palanquin?

Yet the reality she now faced was that she was about to get married. She was sitting in a boat on her way to the other shore. Lake water flowed under the gunwale; white shorebirds circled close to the water surface. The wooden rudder creaked loudly as the boat floated toward the village.

They arrived at their mooring. Through the thin red gauze over her window, Xiumi could see two naked children standing on the beach, staring at her party with fingers in their mouths. She saw trees, burned-out gazebos, courtyard walls, ponds, and sections of the covered walkway, everything decorated bright red. Water still burbled along the aqueducts.

Celebratory firecrackers had been going off for a while, and the air was tinged with the acrid yet pleasant smell of gunpowder. The palanquin turned into the alleyways, which were so dark and narrow that raising the window blind revealed only wet stone walls. Of course, there was also Han Liu, who walked to the left side of the palanquin in a pair of new blue pants. Emerging from the alleys, they headed west through a grove of trees before the palanquin halted and was shakily set down. Han Liu opened the palanquin door and reached inside to lift Xiumi out, announcing, "We're here."

They had come to the village's ancestral memorial hall, the only edifice to survive Wang Guancheng's reforms. It was built of dark gray bricks, which the generations had covered with invasive moss. A pair of stone lions guarded the front door, red wedding bows tied around their necks. Seven or eight grand dining tables stood in the outer courtyard, replete with meat and vegetable dishes of all kinds, while a team of cooks in aprons chopped more meat on a stone slab close by. A slow stream of people moved in and out of the front door, mostly women carrying dripping-wet baskets or bleeding chickens.

Above the drainage ditch at the far corner, a butcher was slaughtering a pig. He held his knife in his teeth as he lifted a ladleful of cold water and splashed it onto the pig's neck. The animal kicked and squealed, aware of what was about to happen. The butcher pushed his knife smoothly into the pig's neck, and a thick stream of blood spurted up, splashing loudly into a bronze basin. Xiumi gasped, having never seen a pig killed before.

A heavily rouged old woman walked up to her, bowed in greeting, and instructed her to "follow me" before leading her through the back door of the memorial hall, her thick waist rocking above her bound feet. Behind the wall was a square skywell paved with black stones, an apricot tree, and a well with a pulley. The doors and windows of both side chambers were plastered with red paper bearing the character for "happiness." The scent of mold and dead water assaulted Xiumi's nose the minute she walked in; yesterday's heavy rains had clogged the gutters. The old woman fished a key out of her pocket, opened a door, and led her inside.

This must be the wedding bedroom. A single wooden latticed window on the eastern wall let in little light. A large, freshly carved marriage bed gave off the strong scent of varnish. Its curtains and mosquito netting were new, too; two floral-print bedrolls had been laid out on it side by side, along with a pair of embroidered pillows. A makeup table and two chairs, mirror-bright with a new coat of paint, stood close to the bed. A small oil lamp burned on the table. The single window looked out onto the back wall of a private household; when Xiumi neared the window and stood on tiptoe, she could see past the hedge into the rear courtyard, where an old man was using a chamber pot.

The old woman said, "When the Boss was fighting with Number Four two weeks ago, his estate burned down, and they haven't finished rebuilding yet. The rooms in the memorial hall are a bit older; we hope you can put up with it for a few days." She poured Xiumi a cup of tea, then brought her over a plate of sweets.

Han Liu addressed the old woman several times, but the other pretended not to hear her. Eventually, two young maids in spring-green clothing came in and stood at attention beside the door, their eyes downcast, hands at their sides. The old woman turned to Han Liu and said coldly, "Auntie, if you have no more business here, you might as well return to the island."

Knowing she couldn't stay, Han Liu stood up and looked at Xiumi with tears in her eyes. "Does the young miss remember what I told her yesterday?"

Xiumi nodded.

"If you can endure a month, you can endure four years or forty; that's all there is to it. Suffering will always be a fact of life. Now you're with Number Six, the new chief, so be careful to obey him at all times so you don't have to receive pain for no reason."

Xiumi assented through tears.

"In the future, if you have the chance, come visit me on the island."

Han Liu sobbed, and her half-open lips quivered, as if she had something more to say. After a heavy pause, she pulled something wrapped in yellow silk out of her pocket and stuffed it in Xiumi's hand, saying, "Just a little thing, a keepsake in case we don't see each other for a while." She patted Xiumi's hand a few times, then turned and left.

Receiving the object, Xiumi felt a deep pang of foreboding. Her heart beat hard, then sank into her gut. She hurried over to the oil lamp and unwrapped the folds of cloth. There it was! The entire room began to spin; Xiumi teetered, then cried out as she lost her balance. The frightened old woman rushed over to hold her steady.

It was another golden cicada.

Xiumi staggered to the doorway, where the two serving girls reached out their hands to support her. She peered out the door: the sky over the memorial hall was still an ashen gray, as if portending another rainstorm. She saw the apricot tree and the well in the sky-well—Han Liu had disappeared.

The incredibly lifelike cicada looked exactly like the one Zhang Jiyuan had left her, with delicate wings unfolded, as if it were about to lift gracefully into the air. Except for its bulging eyes, which were made of black onyx, the rest of it appeared to be pure gold. Xiumi had learned from Zhang Jiyuan's diary that a very limited number had been forged—some said eighteen, others sixteen, and not even Zhang Jiyuan knew the exact count. They functioned as secret tokens used by the leaders of the Cicadas and Crickets Society to connect with one another. Rank-and-file members would never see one. It was said that the object would trill like a real cicada in times of emergency, but this of course was just a fairy tale. Han Liu was a simple nun from the mountains—how did she come to possess such an important treasure? Could it be that she too...

Xiumi gently ran a finger over the object's glimmering gossamer wings. No longer did she gaze on it with tenderness as she once did; on the contrary, she viewed it as a possible herald of bad fortune, like a living thing formed from the essence of the natural world and perfectly capable of trilling with its wings or flying away at any moment. Xiumi stared at it intensely, as thoughts, feelings, and memories chased each other in a rising whirlwind in her head, which began to throb with pain. She stared until exhaustion shut her eyes; she collapsed on the makeup table and fell asleep.

She awoke to find herself lying in bed still in her clothes. Darkness had fallen outside. Ripe dates and peanuts, dyed red, hung on individual strands of silk tied to the mosquito netting. She sat up, her head still sharply throbbing. The old woman sat on the edge of the bed and watched her with something like a smile on her dried-walnut face. Xiumi got out of bed and walked to the makeup table, where she tied up her hair carelessly and took a sip of cold tea. Her heart was still pounding.

"What time is it?" she asked.

"Late at night," the old woman replied. She pulled a pin from her hair to trim the oil lamp.

"What's that noise outside?"

"They're singing opera."

Xiumi stopped to listen. The sound of the music emerged from somewhere behind the memorial hall. It grew softer and louder as the wind took it. The piece was "Han Yu Snowbound at the Lantian Pass," which she knew well. It sounded like a large audience was attending; she could hear the clinking of cups, the bubble of voices talking and playing drinking games, the patter of fast footsteps, and even the occasional whine of a dog. Looking out the window, Xiumi saw bamboo trunks bend in the whispering breeze as a diffuse evening blue settled like fog. Four high-stemmed candles on the makeup table had already burned halfway down. A large serving platter next to the candles contained a small bowl of rice-ball soup, two vegetable dishes, and a plate of fruit.

"The boss just stopped by to visit the young miss, but he saw you were asleep, and didn't want to wake you," the old woman said.

Xiumi made no reply. When the old woman mentioned "the boss," she must have been referring to Qingsheng.

It was three or four in the morning when the party ended.

Qingsheng's appearance came as a surprise. He kicked down the bedroom door and stumbled in, alone and unarmed, to the surprise and fright of the yawning maids at the door. Xiumi assumed he was drunk. He staggered over to her place on the bed and put one foot up on a chair, like an opera clown. Then he just stared at her, a foolish smile on his face.

Xiumi turned her head away, but Qingsheng grabbed her chin and wrenched it back to him, face-to-face.

"Look at me . . . look at my eyes. They're gonna close in a minute," Qingsheng commanded, his voice charged with a sense of enormous physical agony.

Xiumi had no idea what he meant, and stared at him in stunned silence. Pea-size drops of sweat ran down his cheek, and his breathing grew louder. His expression made her think of Zhang Jiyuan on the night they stayed at Chen's Rice Market in Changzhou. He had looked at her as if he desperately wanted to say something, yet couldn't reach past a secret pain.

Xiumi caught a powerful whiff of raw flesh, so strong she couldn't help gagging. She couldn't figure out the source of it. She glanced around the room: the old woman and maids were long gone; the memorial hall was tranquil and still. Moonlight flooded the skywell and the apricot tree. The whole place glowed with an ominous silence, like a mausoleum.

"Want to hear a riddle?" Qingsheng asked playfully. "You have to guess a character. The clue is: a corpse with two knives stuck in."

He said that he had met a traveling Taoist fortune-teller that morning in the village. The man was rattling a tortoiseshell drum and waving an Eight Trigrams flag when he stopped Qingsheng in the street and asked him to solve a riddle: a corpse with two knives stuck in. Qingsheng couldn't figure it out; nor could his bodyguards when he asked them. The fortune-teller laughed. "That's good. If you can't guess it, that's good. Bad news if you could." He didn't look like your average priest, though. For one, he had six fingers on his left hand.

Xiumi's chest tightened when she heard this detail, but there was no time to feel frightened.

"I thought that once I killed all thirteen members of Qingshou's family, the massacre in the village would be done," he told her. "Didn't expect that he'd called his people over to kill me while I planned to kill him. We both had the same idea. After the Boss was killed, I drove myself crazy trying to figure out who had done it. Then Two and Five kicked it, Three ran away, and there was no one left but

Qingshou, so I figured it must be him. 'First come, first serve; come late, tempt fate,' as the saying goes. I just walked out the front door when I ran into him and his crew. They set fire to my house.

"We locked horns, and all hell broke loose. I fought him from the alleyway right down to the shore; heaven helped me snag both him and his whore of an aunt. Heh-heh . . . I held it together for four whole months, looking over my shoulder every single minute, and now I thought I could finally relax. I played with her for a while until I got sick of it, then I cut off her tits and fried 'em up for dinner and tossed her body in the lake. I wasn't too hard on old Number Four. I just stuffed him with mud and let it go at that.

"I thought it was all over. I killed his cook and his florist, I even killed that parrot he had hanging in a cage, and then I burned down the house. I thought I'd finished it. Who could have known the real mastermind hadn't even stepped out of the shadows!"

Qingsheng's eyes opened so wide they seemed ready to shoot out of his skull; heavy beads of sweat continued to form on his broad forehead. She heard him working hard to keep breathing, as if he were trying to inhale her body through his nose. The shadow of a human form flickered past the doorway. Qingsheng noticed it as well, and snorted. "The courtyard looks empty, but the whole place is full of spies. But they don't dare to come in, they're afraid of me! As long as I'm alive, as long as I can breathe, they don't dare come in. They poisoned my beer and stabbed me twice. I'm a dead man walking now. But they don't dare come in.

"Too bad I still don't know who killed me . . ."

Qingsheng grunted ruefully, then asked Xiumi, "The riddle . . . you figure it out yet?"

When Xiumi didn't respond, he grabbed her hand and put it on his waist. Her fingers touched something solid and round—it was the wooden handle of a knife. The blade had completely entered his belly. Her hand dripped with blood.

"That one's not the problem. There's another one in my back, touching my heart. My heart's about to stop beating. It hurts. I'll die unsatisfied . . ."

His voice grew weaker, fading almost to a whisper; she watched the lids of his huge eyes close and open, then slowly close again. His hands began to shake.

"My heart's about to fall," Qingsheng said. "You know what that means? When your heart falls, that's when you die. Brief, very brief, but it's the most unbearable moment of your life. It happens to everyone, no matter how you die. It doesn't hurt, honest, it doesn't hurt, it feels like panic...like I can hear my heart talking. It's saying, 'I'm sorry...I just can't keep beating, not even one more time...'"

Qingsheng tipped backward and fell heavily to the floor. Immediately he jumped back up, then fell down again before he could find his balance. He tried a few more times before giving up. His body shivered feverishly, and he flopped around on the floor like a freshly slaughtered chicken.

"I'm not gonna die, I won't," Qingsheng growled as he ground his teeth together. Coughing up a wad of bloody phlegm, he raised himself up to say, "They can't kill me that easily. Bring me a cup of tea to drink."

Xiumi had retreated to the opposite end of the bed in fear and covered her face with a curtain. She knew that the poison in Qingsheng's system was taking effect. A short sword stuck out between his shoulder blades, a bright red tassel dangling from the hilt. He spat out another mouthful of bloody sputum, and began to crawl on his hands.

"I want water. My chest hurts like hell."

He looked up at Xiumi and kept crawling. *He's crawling toward the table for some tea*, Xiumi thought. He made it to the edge of the table and tried to stand without success. He bit down hard on the table leg. A chunk of wood broke off in his teeth with a snap.

That marked the end of his strength. Xiumi saw his legs kick a few more times. He let out a raucous fart and died.

This gave Xiumi the answer to the riddle. A body with two knives stuck in it was the character for "ass."

11

"I'LL JUST call you Big Sister," the stable boy said.

"Then what do I call you?" Xiumi asked.

"Stable Boy?"

"That's your real name?" Xiumi turned her head away. Her lips tingled with pain, as if he had bitten them.

"No, it's not my name. I don't have a name. But since I was Number Five's stable boy, that's what everyone in the village calls me." He lay on top of her, breathing hard as he licked her ears, eyes, and neck.

"You're what, twenty?"

"Eighteen," the stable boy replied.

His panting sounded like a dog's. His body was dark and slick as an eel, and his hair was stiff. He buried his face in her armpit, his body quivering. He whispered repeatedly, "Mama, Sister, Mama, you're my real mother..." He said he liked the smell of her armpit because it smelled like horse sweat. He said that the first time he saw her in the boat, his heart sliced open. All he wanted to do was to look at her, to look at her face. He couldn't get enough of just looking.

Memories of that moonlit night surfaced in Xiumi's mind: lake water gurgling beneath her; the tall reeds parting and closing, then parting again. The stable boy staring at her. She remembered his tender, adolescent eyes: wet, clear, disheartened, and pained, like a river beneath the full moon.

Qingde had been dozing beside him. The stable boy grinned stupidly at Xiumi, showing his white teeth, thinking Qingde wasn't aware. Yet whenever Xiumi stared back, he would immediately blush and look away, and play with the tassel of his machete. He had propped one foot on the table, revealing a shoe with a hole that exposed his toes. He didn't stop staring and smiling at her the whole night. Later on, Qingde dumped the burning ember of his pipe onto the stable boy's palm, searing his skin and making him jump in pain. But after Qingde had fallen back asleep, the boy had licked his lips and kept on smiling and staring.

The stable boy held her so hard his fingernails dug into her flesh as his body continued to quiver.

"I just want to hold you like this and never let go. Even if someone put a knife on my neck, I wouldn't let go," the stable boy said. He looked even more like a child when he spoke.

"You've already killed five of the six leaders, is there anyone left to kill you?" Xiumi asked.

The stable boy didn't reply. His lips had already reached her breasts. The tongue that licked her sweat was hot, though the breath he drew was cold. He avoided touching her nipples at first, not because he didn't want to, but because he didn't dare. He fumbled around, obviously unsure of what to do. Xiumi felt herself grow dizzy. Her eyes glazed over, and her body stiffened like a drawn bow. Locking her legs straight, she pushed her toes as hard as she could into the baseboard of the bed as her body filled like a stream flooded with meltwater in the spring.

"I couldn't have killed them back then...couldn't have even imagined it. I couldn't look Number Five in the face, so how could I think of killing him? Besides, I couldn't have done it if I wanted to. He burned me with his pipe, made me drink horse piss and eat horse shit plenty of times. I wouldn't try to kill him just for burning me once."

"Then why—ouch...gently—then what...what exactly happened?" Xiumi asked. She actually kind of liked this young stable boy. His body smelled like mud and fresh hay.

"That was the day I met Dapples."

"Dapples?"

"Yeah, Dapples. He'd traveled from a long way away. He came to Huajiashe to tell fortunes for people."

"Does he have a sixth finger on his left hand?" Xiumi asked.

"How did you know that? Do you know him, Sister?"

Of course Xiumi knew him. Zhang Jiyuan had mentioned this mysterious figure in nearly every page of his diary. He obviously harbored some grand, secret mission. Now it seemed he had arrived in Huajiashe.

"He showed up dressed as a Taoist priest who could tell your fortune for a fee, but that was just a disguise. He's really one of the heads of the Cicadas and Crickets Society. They planned to attack Meicheng, but didn't have enough people, especially those who could use Western weapons, so he found his way to Huajiashe, hoping he could persuade the leaders to join him. Number Two was still in charge back then. When he heard what they wanted to do, he asked Dapples why the hell they wanted to attack Meicheng. Dapples said, 'In order to establish the Great Unity.' Number Two snorted and replied that Huajiashe had already created the Great Unity, and Dapples could crawl back to wherever he came from.

"After Number Two slammed the door on him, Dapples went to Three and Four, but they all said the same thing Number Two did. It must have been hard for Dapples; he had orders from his superiors to find support in Huajiashe, and it wouldn't have been easy to have to go back with nothing to show for it. So he started wandering around the village, trying his luck, and ended up at Number Six's house. He tried to get Number Six to listen to his whole speech on revolution, but Six had an awful temper. He hadn't even finished talking when Number Six said, 'Revolution, revolution, go revolve on your mother's cock!' and kicked him in the crotch so hard his feet left the floor. Dapples crawled around on the floor for a while and hissed at Number Six: 'If I don't get a pound of flesh for this, you'll never be rid of me, you wait and see!' Number Six just laughed at that, then ordered his people to strip him naked and toss him out. So not only did Dapples not make any friends, he was shamed in public and had to walk away naked.

"He returned again this spring, wearing his priest outfit, carrying a tortoiseshell drum and performing the fortune-telling act. He had also grown a beard, so no one recognized him. That day I had led the horses to the lake for a drink. I saw him walking back and forth along the shore, like he'd lost something. I asked him what he was looking for, and at first he wouldn't tell me, but when it seemed he really couldn't find it, he asked me if I'd seen a golden cicada. I thought he was playing a joke on me; cicadas are everywhere in the summer, swarming in the trees, but whoever heard of a golden one?

"He paced along the shoreline for a while, then sat down on the sand and watched me water the horses without saying anything. Then he stood up again, walked to the pier, and boarded a boat. I watched the boat weigh anchor, raise its sails, and set off, heading south. If he had continued on, nothing would have happened, but although the boat faded into the distance, it then started to grow bigger again. He had made the pilot turn around. Once it moored, he hopped off the gangplank and walked straight for me. He asked me, 'Young man, is there a tavern in Huajiashe?' I told him yes, that we even have two. He narrowed his eyes and looked me over carefully, then said, 'Young man, I think we were fated to meet each other. How about I buy you a cup of ale?'

"I told him that the tavern wasn't a place an ordinary stable boy could frequent. Dapples slapped me so hard on the back my knees went weak, and said, 'Why do you always think of yourself as a stable boy? Haven't you ever imagined becoming Huajiashe's chief some day?'

"Hearing him ask that question out loud scared me. If it had come out of my mouth and someone had heard me, I'd lose my head. So I started making excuses to leave. I lied and said that Number Five was waiting to get his horse back, because he needed it for a long trip. When Dapples saw me move away, he said, 'Not so fast, let me show you something,' and he took his bundle off his back. I thought he really was going to show me something, but when he opened the bundle there was only a shiny dagger inside. He put it to my stomach and whispered forcefully to me: 'Either we team up and kill the leaders here and you take over, or I will end your life with this blade right this minute. It's up to you.'

"Big Sister, I only want to be with you. Why does my heart hurt so much? The more it hurts, the tighter I want to hold you, but the tighter I hold you, the more it hurts, and I just feel like crying. I don't want to be chief. I just want to be able to see you all day, every day.

"So I gave up and followed him to the tavern. I tied the horse in the grove of trees next to the building, and we went in and drank quite a bit. There were too many people inside, so it wasn't a good place to talk. He didn't say anything, just toasted me a lot and gave me many looks, as if he was telling not to be afraid. After we got really drunk he lead me into a grove of trees, and we sat down in a sunny spot. I wasn't as afraid of him as I had been before; I guess that's why they call it 'liquid courage.' Dapples filled his pipe and lit it, then passed it to me. I took a couple of puffs, and my heart kind of settled down.

"Dapples started explaining things to me. He said that no one was born ready to be an emperor, but if you dreamed of being one, you could be one. If you dreamed of being chief, you could be the chief. And if you only dreamed about being a stable boy...

"'Then you'd feed horses your whole life,' I finished.

"That made Dapples happy. He said, 'See, I knew this kid had some brains!' After a pause, he told me, 'You know, being the chief is a pretty good life. You can have whatever you want and do whatever you want.' That reminded me of something. I told him that the village had just kidnapped a girl—I meant you, Big Sister—and if I could be the chief, could I make her mine? Dapples said, 'Of course, of course she'd be yours. You could screw her eighteen times a day and spend every minute next to her, and no one would ever say no.'

"He also said, 'Not only would she be yours, but any woman in the whole village could be yours if you wanted.' I said that I didn't want any of the village woman, only the one they recently kidnapped. Dapples laughed and said, 'Well, that's your choice.' Hearing him say that, especially after all the drink we had, I felt like I really could do it. But there were six leaders, each strong and capable, and they had bodyguards and servants—how would we be able to kill them? 'No need to worry about that,' Dapples said. 'We're in the shadows and they're in the light. Even if there were twice as many, we could still kill them all. Besides, you wouldn't need to do any of the killing—I'll bring people in for that. You just need to show us in and talk to us before you do anything.' Then he cut his own hand with a knife and passed it to me to do the same. I cut my hand and we shook.

"Then he said, 'Now that our blood flows together as one, you are an honorable member of the Cicadas and Crickets Society. There's no going back for you, either. If you desert us, betray us, or leak any information, I'll flay you alive and stretch your skin to make a drum that I can beat on for fun.'

"He made me take an oath. I repeated the words back to him without thinking. Then he reached into his bag and pulled out four silver ingots. Heaven help me—whole ingots, not just loose silver pieces. I'd only seen one of those before in my whole life. My mother fished it out of the bottom of a box after my father died so we could pay for his coffin. She had saved it for years. When Dapples pulled out four of them at once, I knew he was no ordinary guy, and he really wasn't joking about killing the leaders. He said, 'Hold on to these for the time being. They'll come in handy when the time is right.' Then we parted for the night.

"Soon they really did come in handy. Dapples made me give the first one to Wang Guancheng's governess. When she received it, she looked at it closely, weighed it in her hand, and bit one corner. Then she smiled and said, 'With this, I could take you up a mountain of swords or through a sea of fire faster than a horse could carry you.' Dapples brought in five guys to kill Wang Guancheng, sneaked them into the village at midnight, and I escorted the governess to meet them in one of the boats. She said the best time to carry out the plan was early in the morning. Wang Guancheng usually locked his door in the evening before he went to bed, so no one could get in. Dapples said they could lift the tiles on the roof and come down through the rafters. After a lot of discussion, they still decided to strike when he went into the courtyard at dawn to practice his martial arts. They didn't expect the governess to slip in early while he was washing his face and cut him down with the ax she had hidden in his room. How the old lady mustered that kind of strength is a mystery. So yeah, it's fair to say we killed Wang Guancheng.

"Dapples left again with his people after that. He said we'd wait a week or two, then take down another one. He said it was the safest, surest way to do it. The chief's death threw the whole village into chaos and sowed fear in everyone's hearts. But who would suspect a stable boy like me? So we took advantage of the confusion to poison Number Two, chop up Number Five, and scare Number Three into running off. We knew Four and Six would be the hardest to deal with, because their defenses tightened as the bodies piled up. We didn't expect that they'd go after each other before we went after them. Big Sister, why are you whimpering?

"Sister, my dear Sister, what's wrong? You're scaring me; I can see the whites of your eyes. If something's wrong, just tell your stable boy. Tonight we'll be husband and wife, and I'll do anything you say from this day on. I'll love you and only you. Now I'm the chief and you're my queen. We're leading an attack on Meicheng next month. Dapples says they have about three hundred people, and if you add a hundred and twenty from Huajiashe, we can definitely take the city. And then we can move into the magistrate's mansion and live in comfort. Dapples says that even if we don't succeed, we can hide in Japan until things settle down. Do you know where Japan is? Dapples says he's never been there either . . . Sister, what's wrong with you? What are you yelling for? Sister, loosen your grip a little . . . when you hold me that tight I can't breathe!"

Part Three
LITTLE THING

I

THE PRINCIPAL stepped out from behind a black lacquered screen, a careworn expression on her face. The cold light of the poorly lit room barely illuminated the wooden chair and makeup table, the screen, the carved wooden bed, and the long side table set with flower vases, making everything look as hard as iron. Only the silk fabric draped loosely over her body emitted softness. A single step and her clothes parted the air with a swishing sound. Her face was as pained as her sigh; even when she hiccuped, you could smell the sadness on her breath.

Tiger couldn't see her face clearly. It rippled and changed like the moon reflected in water, or like clouds passing over a wheat field. Still, he could feel her piercing gaze watching him.

"Tiger, come over here."

The Principal called his name in a near whisper. She didn't look at him but faced her vanity mirror as she arranged her hair in a high bun. Tiger drew near her. Her robe wasn't white, but apricot yellow, embroidered with tiny flowers. The intoxicating scent of powder hung in the air.

"What happened to your face?" the Principal asked, still without looking at him, a silver hairpin in her teeth.

"I got stung by a wasp yesterday."

"You'll be okay," she said, smiling coyly. It was the first time Tiger had ever seen her smile. "I'll squeeze a little milk for you to put on it, and the swelling will go away."

Wait...what? Tiger started. Had he misheard her? He stared at the Principal blankly, his heart pounding. *But, but, but …* The Principal reached under one arm and deftly released a silver button at the top of her green-hemmed robe, from which she brought forth a milky breast.

"Principal …" Tiger shivered in fear, then suddenly felt himself falling.

He opened his eyes to find himself lying on the long slope of a grassy hill. He had put out the Principal's horse to graze. The sun had already transformed into a red fireball that shimmered between the trees. His torso was damp with sweat, and the breeze from the mountains chilled him. For a brief moment, he stayed immersed in the dream, his head clouded and his heart racing.

If it's true that everything comes from somewhere, then where do dreams come from? Tiger wondered. It felt as if the Principal's dark, powder-scented bedroom floated somewhere high among the clouds, and he had slipped and fallen all the way down into the waist-high grass on the hillside. Could the process possibly be reversed? Could he wake to find himself back inside a dream, with the Principal undoing her buttons and flashing that alluring smile … ? Tiger's fantasies made him nervous. The chirping of crickets, the blood-soaked forest below him, and Black Dragon Temple, crouching like a bullfrog among the trees, felt illusory.

Tiger got up from the grass to pee. Gazing down the mountainside, he could see the new roof over the temple. No monks had lived under that roof for generations; the temple once served as a temporary shelter for traveling priests and beggars. There used to be a pond in the front courtyard, and an earthen opera stage next to it where troupes from Anhui and Hangzhou performed. After the Principal returned from Japan, the temple roof was retiled and the outer wall restored. Two side wings were added, and the whole place renamed Puji Academy. Tiger still hadn't seen any students there, only crowds of unfamiliar, bare-chested men who went in and out as they pleased, humming as they walked, and practiced with weapons inside the temple.

Little Thing sat on an old horse on the public road behind the temple. He was kicking his heels and clucking his tongue insistently, but the horse didn't move, turning his head sweetly up at the sky as if thinking about its own problems.

Most of the villagers called him Little Thing, though most of the elders called him Little Master. Some less well-intentioned people called him Little Bastard behind his back. He had shown up at Puji with the Principal as a two-year-old, barely able to talk, sleeping soundly inside his wrapping on the porter's back. Old Madame Lu said he was a foundling the Principal had adopted on her way home, and most of the villagers believed her. Still, as the child grew to three, then four, the Principal's likeness became clearly evident in both his facial features and his personality. Someone in the village let loose the rumor that the child might have been the product of the robbers' "firing squad" at Huajiashe.

The local tutor Ding Shuze always took an active interest in other people's business. Once, when Tiger and Little Thing were playing by the river, Ding Shuze ambled over to them with his cane and squatted down beside Little Thing. He took the child's hand and asked, "Do you remember who your father is?" Little Thing shook his head and said he didn't know. "Then do you remember your family name?" Little Thing shook his head again and said nothing. "How about I give you a name, then?" Little Thing neither agreed nor refused, and continued to kick the sand on the shore.

"This town we live in is called Puji, so let's just call you Puji. Puji's a good name; if you end up being prime minister one day, it'll sound grand. And it's a perfect dharma name if you become a monk," Ding Shuze said with a chuckle. "And you can take your grandfather's family name, so you can now be Lu Puji. Don't forget it."

People still called him Little Thing.

The Principal never paid any attention to him, even when she passed him on the street. Little Thing didn't dare call her Mama, so he called her Principal along with everyone else. Madame Lu loved him the most, and never called him Little Thing; to her, he was

"Little Deedlydo," "Heart's Blood," "Little Fartypants," "Little Cotton Ball," "Little Foot Warmer," and so on.

"I'm kicking him as hard as I can and he still won't gallop. What's going on?" Little Thing called to Tiger in frustration as the latter descended the hillside.

"Good thing he won't. If he really did bolt on you, you'd fall off and smash yourself into mincemeat," Tiger admonished him in an adult's tone of voice. "You're too small to ride yet, anyway." He grabbed the reins and led the horse toward the corral by the frog pond.

"I fell asleep just now on the hillside," Tiger said with a yawn, "and I had a dream."

Little Thing wasn't interested in his dream. Sitting on the horse's back, he waved his little fists and said, "Guess what I have in my hands?" Before Tiger had time to reply, he opened his fists to show him: a dragonfly, or at least the crushed remains of one. Little Thing grinned stupidly.

"I dreamed about your mother…" Tiger started to say, unsure of whether or not to tell him the rest of it.

"Who cares?" Little Thing snorted. "I dream about her every night."

"Well, that's just from looking at your little photograph of her."

Little Thing owned a single rare object that was his most prized possession: a small photograph of his mother, taken in Japan. It was so valuable to him he didn't know where best to keep it; sometimes he put it in his undershirt pocket, so that he could look at it whenever he wanted to, and sometimes he stored it under his pillow. Once, Magpie almost destroyed it when she washed his clothes, soaking it in water, pounding it with the pestle, and wringing it out with her hands. By the time Little Thing fished the photo out, it had been reduced to a hard nub of paper. Little Thing attacked Magpie, biting and kicking like he'd gone mad, until Madame Lu found a solution: she soaked it in water again until it opened up, then patted it flat and left it to dry by the hearth. Though the face in the picture was now impossible to recognize, Little Thing still valued it with his life, and he no longer dared to carry it around with him. Any mention of the event made the old woman sniffle mournfully. "The poor baby almost never says anything when you mention his mother. I thought he didn't miss her, but what child doesn't miss his mama?" She repeated those same words over and over again whenever the incident came up.

Tiger led the horse to the fishpond for water, then back to the stable. Little Thing had already thrown an armful of hay into the feeding trough. The two boys scraped the horse manure off the soles of their shoes onto the edge of the wooden threshold, then closed the stable door. Night had fallen.

"What do you think 'revolution' means?" Little Thing suddenly asked on their way home.

Tiger considered it for a moment, then responded sincerely, "Revolution is really just doing whatever you want to do—hit whomever you want to hit, sleep with whomever you want to sleep with."

He stopped, turned to Little Thing with a mischievous excitement in his gaze, and asked in a quavering voice, "Tell me: Whom do you want to sleep with most?"

He figured Little Thing would automatically say "Mama." Instead, Little Thing looked at him with deep suspicion, thought for a moment, and said, "Nobody. I sleep by myself."

Approaching the village entrance, they saw the blacksmith brothers Wang Qidan and Wang Badan, hands on their swords, interrogating a traveler. They shoved him back and forth as they asked him questions, spinning him between them. The traveler carried a long wooden pole on his back; he must have been a cotton fluffer. After the brothers finished their fun, they cuffed the man a few times and sent him on his way.

"What did I tell you?" Tiger said smugly. "You slap whomever you want to, and sleep with whomever you want to."

"But why did they question him?" Little Thing asked.

"They have orders to interrogate suspicious people."

"Who's suspicious?" Little Thing persisted.

"People like spies."

"What's a spy?"

"A spy is . . ." Tiger pondered this for a moment. "A spy is someone who pretends not to be a spy."

Feeling a little confused himself, Tiger added, "But how could there be so many spies around? The brothers are just looking for an excuse to beat someone up for fun."

They conversed until they stood at the front door of their home. Magpie and Baoshen had been looking everywhere for them.

That night at dinner, Madame Lu couldn't stop sighing and shaking her head. Though she was only in her fifties, her hair had turned completely white, and she spoke and moved like an old woman. Her hands trembled so much that she could hardly hold her bowl and chopsticks; she wheezed and coughed as she breathed. She suspected everything, though her memory for past events had crumbled and she frequently repeated herself or recalled things haphazardly. She often talked to her own shadow, not caring if anyone else heard her. These conversations usually opened with one of two customary lines: the first, "This was all my fault"; and the second, "This is all retribution!"

Opening with the first line meant she was about to scold herself. But what exactly had she done wrong? Tiger never could figure it out. Magpie had said that Madame Lu regretted allowing a young man named Zhang Jiyuan to stay with them. Tiger had met Zhang Jiyuan, and heard he was a revolutionary. For that, they tied a stone to him and threw him into the river; or as they said in the village, he was "sent down to pluck lotuses."

If Madame Lu started with the second line, she was complaining about the Principal. This was the subject she chose that night.

"This is all retribution!" She angrily wiped a bead of snot off her nose onto the table leg.

"I married her off properly, making sure she received the best of everything—new clothing, bedding, jewelry. Who would have thought she'd run into bandits! I didn't know anything about it until her husband's family sent word the following day. The village elders all said that bandits usually cared most about the ransom, that someone would come around in a week or two at the most asking for money, and all I would have to do was pay to get her back. So I waited and waited for days on end, unable to eat or sleep, just staring at the door until my eyes dried out for six whole months, and not a single goddamn word!"

At this point in her tirade, Little Thing would always giggle deviously. He thought hearing his grandmother swear was funny.

"And then my own daughter claims that I wasn't willing to spend the money to get her back! If anyone had actually showed up to ask for a ransom, would I care an ounce about a little silver? And for her of all people, to have the nerve to accuse me ... Even if we had zero savings I would have sold every inch of land and stripped the house for timber to get her back. Baoshen, Magpie, were either of you ever approached by someone asking for ransom?"

Magpie lowered her head with a morose "No one. Not even a shadow."

Baoshen added, "I would have brought the money to their doorstep myself, no matter if they showed up or not. I wore out six or seven pairs of sandals asking around for Xiumi without uncovering a single clue. Who knew she was right over there in Huajiashe?"

Tiger didn't know where this Huajiashe was, but his dad made it sound like it couldn't be too far from Puji. Magpie and Baoshen comforted and cajoled Madame Lu until she wiped away her tears, stared diffidently into the corner for a while, and finally picked up her bowl and ate.

Little Thing must have been exhausted from playing all day, because he slumped onto the table and fell asleep before finishing his dinner. Madame Lu ordered Magpie to carry him upstairs to bed, then sent Tiger into the kitchen for water to wash the young child's feet. But by the time Tiger arrived upstairs with some hot water, Little Thing was already awake and wrestling playfully with Magpie.

"Are they really going to attack Meicheng?"

"Who?"

"The Principal and all those guys."

"Who told you that?" Magpie asked in alarm as she fluffed the comforter. Her waist, hips, and breasts looked so soft; even the shadow she threw on the opposite wall seemed soft.

"I heard Lilypad say it," Tiger replied.

He and Little Thing had overheard Lilypad talking about it with some people by the pond; they were on their way to collect the horse from the stable around noon. Tiger's eyes liked to follow Lilypad, too. Her butt was much bigger than Magpie's. These past few days, it felt like the sight of any woman, no matter who, made him nervous, dry mouthed, and starry eyed.

That can't be true, can it? Magpie asked herself, her cheeks noticeably paler. She had only the tiniest measure of courage and could be frightened by her own shadow.

In the end, she said, "Kids like you shouldn't pay attention to grown-up things. If you hear something, keep it behind your teeth, don't go blabbing around."

Once she finished with the comforter, Magpie tested the water temperature with a finger, then picked up Little Thing to wash his feet. Little Thing splashed his feet in the basin, getting the floor and Magpie's clothes wet, but she didn't grow angry. She even tickled the bottoms of his feet. Little Thing giggled wildly and dove deeper into her arms. He could even snuggle his face into her bosom however much he wished.

"Do you think ... the Principal really is crazy?" Little Thing asked after he finished laughing.

Magpie rubbed his head with a cold, wet hand and laughed, "Silly child. Everyone else calls her Principal, but you can't. You should call her Mama."

"Is Mama really crazy?" he asked again.

Magpie paused, unsure of quite how to respond. "Most likely. Possibly. It's a good chance. Look at this, look at this now ... you put holes in these socks."

"But ... what happens to people who go crazy?" Little Thing blinked his big eyes at her, unwilling to let go of the question.

"You're not going crazy, why worry about it?" Magpie smiled.

Tiger sat down in front of the basin, took off his shoes and socks, and extended a foot toward Magpie. "Wash my feet, too," he said with an impudent smile.

Magpie pinched the meat of his calf. "Wash them yourself." She carried Little Thing to bed, where she helped him take off his clothes, tucked him in tightly, and leaned over to kiss him on the cheek. Finally she topped off the oil in the lamp, because Little Thing was afraid of the dark. As she left, she turned to remind Tiger: "If he kicks the blanket off at night, cover him up again."

Tiger nodded as he always did, while thinking, *I sleep until the sun's up, and every morning the pillows and blankets are all over the floor—how am I supposed to pay attention to him?*

Yet that evening Tiger couldn't sleep at all. Not long after Magpie went back downstairs, he heard Little Thing grinding his teeth. No matter how he lay, the first thing he saw when he closed his eyes was the scene from his dream on the hillside. It made his whole body burn, but when he tossed the covers away, he got cold. Wind hissed against the window. Visions of Magpie's face, the Principal's open shirt, and Lilypad's round butt floated through his mind. Every time he moved, the new straw in the mattress beneath him rustled, as if someone were talking to him.

2

XIUMI returned home from Japan during the first snowfall of winter. The air wasn't particularly cold, and the wet flakes of snow that fell from the apricot-yellow clouds carpeting the sky melted before they touched the ground. Lilypad was the first to meet Xiumi outside the village. She helped her down from her horse, brushed the melting snowflakes from her clothing, wrapped her in her arms, and wailed.

She had good reason to do so. Before Xiumi's marriage, they had been as close as blood sisters. That pain should accompany the moment of their reunion was entirely natural. What's more, Lilypad had secretly sold the family's tithes of the harvest that year to a middleman from Taizhou, and was once again facing the prospect of being driven out by an employer. Madame Lu had a soft heart and was reluctant to send away a longtime servant with no family or place to go, especially in such dangerous times. Then a letter arrived from Xiumi. Years of silence after the kidnapping had led everyone to believe she was no longer alive; Madame Lu had already bought her a votive at the Buddhist temple. No one expected this long-lost family member to reappear out of thin air. Lilypad concluded that heaven had sent Xiumi back to save her.

She said this openly, in front of everyone. According to Magpie, the news arrived while she was cooking in the kitchen. Lilypad jumped up on a bench and clapped her hands, exclaiming, "The Bodhisattva protects! Heaven has sent someone to save me."

Xiumi didn't share Lilypad's enthusiasm. She merely patted her lightly on the back a few times, then pushed her away and set off for home, her riding crop still in hand (leaving Lilypad to lead the horse).

Xiumi's absentminded reaction left Lilypad at a loss. Whether or not this young woman could serve as her protector, one thing was obvious: Xiumi wasn't the Xiumi of ten years ago.

Three porters with shoulder poles and a fourth with a backpack followed them. The three shoulder poles bent low under the weight of the heavy cases; their carriers shrugged their shoulders often and breathed hot steam. Little Thing snoozed happily inside a heavy cotton quilt as he rode high on the fourth porter's shoulders; soon, the old women and girls from the village gathered around, petting and tickling him.

Tiger followed his father through the whole production of welcoming Xiumi. His father cautioned him more than once to refer to Xiumi as Big Sister, but Tiger never got the chance to say it. Her eyes swept over the two of them without the slightest pause, proving that his "big sister" no longer recognized him after so many years. Her gaze seemed distant and distracted. When she looked at people, she didn't really look at them; when she chatted with her fellow villagers, she never really said anything, and when she laughed, she did so to hide her annoyance.

Baoshen, who was well known for his servile, deferential behavior, hid himself and his discomfort by helping one of the porters carry a shoulder pole.

Madame Lu awaited Xiumi in the family shrine room by the incense table. She wore a straight-hemmed jacket of brocade silk that she usually reserved for New Year's, and she had brushed, oiled, and perfumed her hair. As Xiumi approached the shrine room, the old lady began to tremble, smile, and weep. But Xiumi raised one foot over the high doorstep before she suddenly stopped and examined her with suspicion, as if trying to figure out if the woman standing before her really was her mother. Then, she asked bluntly, "Ma, where am I sleeping?"

The tone of her question sounded like she had never left Puji, completely unbalancing the old woman. Madame Lu took a moment to recover, then forced a smile and said, "My dear daughter, you've come home. This is your home, you can sleep wherever you like."

Xiumi retracted the foot that had crossed the doorstep and replied,

"All right. Then I'll stay in Father's chambers." She turned and left. Madame Lu's mouth hung open in astonishment. This was their first reunion, not one unnecessary word exchanged.

In the hallway, Xiumi bumped into Baoshen and Tiger. Tiger's father, who always embarrassed his son to no end, smiled obsequiously and fiddled with his wrinkled trousers with one hand while patting his son on the back with the other, as if trying to slap out some kind of greeting.

"Heh-heh, Xiumi, heh-heh, ah, Xiumi…" Baoshen stuttered.

Now Tiger felt embarrassed for his father.

Xiumi, however, walked right up to Baoshen with a smile on her face that recalled her former energy, naiveté, and girlish mischief, and cried out, "Oh, Cockeye!"

Her greeting carried a heavy metropolitan accent. Having just witnessed Xiumi's cold reception of her mother in the shrine room, Baoshen didn't expect to be addressed in such an intimate way. He imagined that the Xiumi standing before him was the same trouble-maker he knew ten years ago, who would sneak into the accounting office to mess up his abacus, put spiders in his tea while he was napping after lunch, and beat on his forehead as she rode on his shoulders through the New Year's temple fair. Unprepared for such affection, he couldn't keep two dusky tears from rolling down his cheeks.

"Baoshen, come here," Madame Lu called from the shrine room. Her voice sounded restrained and deeply confused. Its falling pitch suggested she was anticipating many changes about to take place.

Xiumi stood in the courtyard, ordering the porters to move her luggage into the studio. Lilypad joined in, pointing and giving orders with a hand on her hip, though the only person who listened to her was Magpie. Tiger watched Magpie scamper upstairs with a brass basin and a rag to clean the upper chambers.

Baoshen and Madame Lu couldn't keep up with what was happening before their very eyes. The fourth porter walked straight up to them to hand off Little Thing, who slept soundly within several layers of heavy clothes. When Madame Lu received him, his little eyes above his bright red cheeks opened up and looked straight at her, but the child neither cried nor screamed. Caring for him at least gave Madame Lu something to do for the time being.

She would later regret her laxity. Allowing her daughter to take up residence in that accursed studio seemed an unwise move. The building had come to embody ill fortune over the years, after her husband, Lu Kan, lost his mind while residing there, and Zhang Jiyuan's six-month stay there before he was killed. Nor could Madame Lu forget that if she had not ordered it rebuilt, the wolves would never have come into the fold and carried her daughter off to Huajiashe. It had remained locked and empty for a decade, moss covering its stones and ivy racing upward toward the roof. In the evenings, clouds of chittering bats circled the eaves.

After Xiumi moved into the studio, she didn't come out. Lilypad delivered her meals, always strolling back downstairs with confidence and an indifferent demeanor toward the others, including her mistress, to whom she no longer always paid close attention.

"I tell you, that little tramp is in Xiumi's corner now. Now that she's got coattails to ride, she's lost all her manners," Mother liked to complain to Baoshen.

Though she was angry, Madame Lu softened her tone when she spoke to Lilypad, preferring to swallow her irritation in the off chance she might learn more about her daughter.

"What's she got in all those boxes?" she once asked with a forced smile.

"Books," Lilypad replied.

"What does she do up there all day?"

"Read."

Days passed one after the other, and Madame Lu's anxiety increased. With Xiumi apparently going down her father's road, insanity seemed the only probable destination. "The day she came back I saw that look in her eyes, the same one her father had before he went crazy," Madame Lu declared. She and Baoshen discussed the matter thoroughly. Eventually, she insisted on going back to the same old method she had tried with Lu Kan: hire a Taoist priest to capture the evil spirits.

The priest was a cripple. He arrived with his spirit compass, magic flag, and toolbox, and immediately noticed a powerful evil presence hanging over the studio. When he asked Madame Lu if he could enter, she hesitated. Her daughter was a woman of the world, after all; she had even lived in Japan. What if she saw this priest and threw a fit? Madame Lu told Baoshen to decide. His replied, "Since the man is here, let him try his luck."

The priest swung himself upstairs on his bad leg. Strangely, the studio fell as silent as a sleeping baby for the rest of the afternoon. After about four hours had passed, Madame Lu got desperate, and ordered Magpie to sneak upstairs to check on them (she no longer gave orders to Lilypad). Magpie crept carefully upstairs, then returned right away to report: "The priest is sitting at the table across from her, just talking and laughing."

This news only deepened Madame Lu's suspicions. She looked at Baoshen, who looked back at her in confusion. "Extraordinary," she exclaimed, "that she gets along with a priest!"

The priest rocked his way downstairs around nightfall and hobbled out the door without saying a word. Madame Lu and Baoshen chased after him, expecting to find out what had transpired, but he merely smiled and kept walking, refusing the payment they had agreed on. As he crossed the outer threshold, he turned and left them with one final word: "Well . . . it looks like the great Qing empire is about out of time."

Tiger heard his words very clearly. In the past, anyone who said such a thing could expect the sword for himself and his whole family. For a lowly priest to say it so carelessly now must be a sign that the government really was on its way out.

Madame Lu's anxieties, however, were not misplaced. In fact, Xiumi's situation was far more serious than she had anticipated.

Two weeks passed before Xiumi emerged from her room. She showed up downstairs with an expensive-looking leather purse in one hand and a folded Western-style parasol she had bought in Japan under her elbow, and set off in the direction of the ferry. Two days later, she returned with two young guests, and from then on, the estate became her hotel, a constant stream of visitors coming and going. Baoshen eventually figured out what was happening and said privately to Madame Lu, "You said she was following in the old man's footsteps, but it doesn't look like that to me. In my opinion, she's turned herself into a second Zhang Jiyuan. The dead man's spirit never left us!"

Fortunately, Little Thing was a clever, sensitive child, and could offer some comfort to Madame Lu through her fear and unease. She spent every day by the boy's side, while Xiumi forgot about him completely. Madame Lu liked to hold him in her arms and talk to him, unconcerned whether he understood or not: "That first night your mother was home, I saw a new star twinkling in the west. I had hoped it was a good omen—didn't expect it to mean disaster."

Xiumi left the estate roughly once a month, for anywhere between two and five days at a time, just as Zhang Jiyuan once did. Nobody knew where she went. But careful observation revealed to Baoshen that she always departed the day after the courier brought her mail.

The courier, a young man of about twenty, had a gentle and civil disposition. He replied to Baoshen's oblique queries with careful evasions, refusing to say more than he deemed necessary. "Someone must be sitting in the shadows and giving orders through the courier," Baoshen analyzed for Madame Lu. But who could be giving the orders?

By the end of that summer, a few villagers informed the family that Xiumi had been in close contact with gang members from Meicheng. Tiger had heard a few such names mentioned more and more in recent years, leaders like Xu Baoshan and Long Qingtang. They sold opium and salt on the black market, and even dared to raid government silk-merchant ships on the Yangtze River in broad daylight. How could Xiumi possibly be involved with such people? Madame Lu couldn't bring herself to believe any of it at the time.

One evening, during a heavy rainstorm, typhoon winds from the south rattled the windows and clawed the roof of the estate until the sound of shattering tiles could be heard. An urgent banging on the front door woke Tiger around midnight. He and his father still shared a bedroom in the eastern chambers. Tiger sat up in bed to find the lamp already lit and his father gone. Tiger crept out the bedroom door and into the front courtyard, where he saw Magpie holding a lantern, standing next to Madame Lu by the stairs underneath the eaves.

The courtyard door had been flung wide open, and Xiumi stood in the skywell, wet from head to toe. Four or five men stood with her around three large wooden crates that looked like coffins. One of the men, still panting from exertion, motioned to Baoshen and said, "Go get a couple of shovels." Baoshen brought them two iron shovels and, wiping the rainwater from his eyes, asked Xiumi, "What's in the crates?"

"Dead people," Xiumi replied with a smile, as she tucked her hair behind her ear.

She and the others took the shovels and left. The rain continued unabated.

Baoshen circled the crates many times, trying to peer between the boards, and finally called Magpie to bring the lantern closer. Magpie was far too frightened to move, and so Baoshen retrieved the lantern himself. Tiger watched his father crawl on top of the crates, lantern in hand, and look inside, moving his head at different angles. Finally he stood up and walked resolutely toward Tiger. His teeth chattered vigorously; his lips and hands trembled; a steady stream of foul language poured out of his mouth. Tiger couldn't recall hearing his naive, sincere, earnest father ever utter a curse, but the terror of this particular shock brought out all his stored-up profanities in a single rush.

"Fuck, fuck, fuck . . . Motherfucker! They aren't fucking dead bodies, they're goddamn fucked-up motherfucking guns!"

Madame Lu felt she could not endure it any longer. She had to put an end to her daughter's idiocy, saying, "Guns aren't something you fool around with." Her first priority was to talk to someone experienced, who knew Xiumi. After long consideration, the person she settled on was Xiumi's old teacher, Ding Shuze. Coincidentally, before she paid him a call he showed up at her door.

Ding Shuze had gotten old; his hair and beard had whitened, and he wheezed when he spoke. He tottered into the estate, leaning on his wife for support, and demanded to see Xiumi.

Madame Lu hurried over and said in a low voice, "Mr. Ding, this strange daughter of mine isn't the girl she once was. Her temperament has changed for the worse..."

"That's fine, that's fine..." Ding Shuze replied. "Just bring her down and I'll talk to her."

Madame Lu thought for a moment, then cautioned him again: "You know, my daughter has been back for a while now, and I've barely seen her myself. She...doesn't recognize people anymore."

Ding Shuze rapped the bricks on the floor with his cane with visible impatience. "That's not a problem. I'm the one who taught her to read, remember? You just go get her."

"That's right," added Zhao Xiaofeng. "She might be able to ignore other people, but she can't ignore her old teacher. Go tell her to come down."

Mother looked over to Baoshen for assurance; Baoshen looked at his feet and said nothing. As Mother wavered, Xiumi walked downstairs. She had pinned her hair up in a high bun, held in place with a black silk veil. She still looked half-asleep. A middle-aged man in a scholar's robe accompanied her, carrying an old oilcloth umbrella. The two entered the front courtyard, chatting enthusiastically as they walked, passing Ding Shuze and the others without so much as a glance in their direction.

It was too embarrassing for Ding Shuze. His lips snarled in anger, then he smiled and let out an empty laugh, mumbling to Madame Lu, "Seems she...doesn't recognize me..." His wife, always the quicker of the two, rushed forward and grabbed Xiumi by the sleeve.

"Excuse me! What do you think you're doing?" Xiumi turned and asked sharply.

Ding Shuze, still blushing, took a few steps toward her and inquired, "Xiuxiu...do you still remember this old man?"

Xiumi replied with a sideways glance and a half smile, "Why wouldn't I remember you? You're Mr. Ding."

She turned back to the stranger and the two continued on.

Ding Shuze's mouth fell open; he was too stunned and humiliated to speak. When the pair reached a fair distance, he shook his head and murmured to himself, "Unbelievable, unbelievable . . . such a pity, such a pity, and such a disgrace! So she did recognize me after all, and yet she won't speak to me. By what right . . . ?" Madame Lu and Baoshen tried their best to comfort him with flattery, leading the old couple into the living room for tea, but Ding Shuze wouldn't have any of it, and said they'd be leaving.

"I can't think . . . I can't think . . ." he growled as he waved them off. "If she doesn't want to treat me like her teacher, then I have no choice but to pretend she never existed."

"Exactly. Why should we waste the effort?" Zhao Xiaofeng egged him on. "We're leaving. No need for us to come back."

Filled with disgust, they swore they would never darken the Lu family's threshold again, an oath obviously sworn in aggravated haste—as during the next three days, Ding Shuze showed up at the estate seven or eight times.

"Just like a sleepwalker," Ding Shuze said, after recovering his usual affected composure. "There's a pale light in her eyes that makes you shiver every time she flashes them at you. She's the spitting image of her father before he went crazy, if you want my opinion. Either her soul has left her body, or she's been possessed. Either way, she's mad."

"Yes, definitely crazy, no doubt," Zhao Xiaofeng chimed in with absolute certainty.

"To think that her old man, all those years ago, should be so shortsighted as to lose his job and be sent home, then had no sense to cultivate his mind and take care of his body properly as he aged, instead dabbling in books about utopian delusions until he drowned in it and insanity overtook him. It's as pitiable as it is laughable. Now, as the state falls into disarray, rebellion stirs everywhere; disaster lurks around every corner, in every difficult act at every moment, and morality vanishes. Dispassionate heaven has freed the madmen from their cages—"

"Let's just put aside her sanity for a moment," Madame Lu interrupted. "We need to think of some way to stop her from carrying on like this."

Her admonition quieted Ding Shuze immediately. The four of

them sat in an awkward silence punctuated only by aggrieved sighs. Finally, Ding Shuze said, "No need to act too hastily. Let's see what kind of a fuss she makes first. If things reach a point of no return, there's still an easy way out..."

"And by that, Mr. Ding, you mean..." Madame Lu looked blankly at him.

"Spend some money to hire a few hands from out of town to strangle her."

Xiumi really did raise no small amount of trouble in the village. The band of followers around her grew larger the longer she stayed in Puji. Aside from Lilypad (Madame Lu: "That whore has become a full-time first lieutenant for her"), the group now included the ferryman Tan Si, the potter's assistant Xu Fu, the blacksmith brothers Wang Qidan and Wang Badan, Baldy, Yellowtooth, Sun Waizui, Walnuts Yang, the widow Ms. Ding, and the midwife Chen Sanjie (Magpie: "All the shady characters"). Beggars, strangers who drifted among Meicheng, Qinggang, and Changzhou also filled their numbers, until Xiumi had amassed a decent army. The problem had expanded faster than Ding Shuze could have predicted. He observed on more than one occasion, "If it keeps up like this, she'll strangle all of us before we ever get close to her."

The group started a "Foot-Freeing Society," and went door-to-door demanding everyone's fealty to their new directive. Madame Lu didn't know what "foot freeing" meant, so she asked Magpie. Magpie replied, "It means not letting girls bind their feet."

"Why wouldn't they let girls bind their feet?" Madame Lu replied, confused.

"That way you can run faster," Magpie said.

"You arrived with big feet anyway, so there's nothing for you to worry about," Madame Lu said with a grin. "Now, what do they mean by 'independent marriage'?"

"That's marrying whomever you want," Magpie explained, "without needing your parents' approval."

"Without even a matchmaker?"

"No matchmaker either."

"But how can you get married without a matchmaker?" Madame Lu's confusion deepened.

"Oh, you know. It's like, like…" Magpie reddened to the ears. "Like Walnuts Yang and Ms. Ding doing it…"

"What happened with Yang Zhonggui and Ms. Ding?"

"Walnuts took a liking to Ms. Ding, so he tied up his bedroll and moved into her house, and they just… got together."

A "Puji Self-Governance Board" appeared soon after the Foot-Freeing Society. Black Dragon Temple was completely renovated, its walls reinforced and plastered, timber beams and roof tiles replaced. Two new side wings were added. Xiumi and Lilypad moved in permanently. There, they set up a nursery, a library, a medical clinic, and a nursing home. Xiumi and her subordinates held all-day meetings in the temple. She had drawn up a vast reform plan that included irrigation ditches to route water to the fields directly from the Yangtze River, a cafeteria, so that the entire village could eat together, and an array of other infrastructure developments, including a funeral home and a jail.

Yet the good and simple residents of Puji rarely visited the temple. With the exception of Xiumi's own son, the nameless Little Thing, few local children were sent to the nursery. Eventually, even Little Thing was spirited back to the Lu estate by a servant acting on Madame Lu's orders. The residents of the nursing home mostly consisted of old drifters or abandoned elders from neighboring villages. The clinic was little more than a sign on a door. Xiumi had hired a doctor who had studied in Japan and could allegedly cure illnesses without even taking your pulse, but sick villagers still consulted Dr. Tang; others preferred to lie in bed and wait to die rather than try the new cures advertised at the Self-Governance Board. The irrigation project began with Xiumi's order to dig a hole in the great river's embankment with the intention of guiding water into the fields below. The massive inflow of water, however, nearly ripped the embankment apart, and the whole village almost flooded in one disastrous instant.

As time passed, money became an issue.

When Xiumi produced a list of necessary expenses and sent people door-to-door asking for contributions, the wealthy families in the area suddenly disappeared. The Wang brothers managed to find a silk merchant—they hung him in the cowshed and beat on him for a night, then sent him home naked.

Gradually, Xiumi changed into a different person. She became noticeably thinner, and dark circles formed under her listless eyes. She grew tired and rarely spoke, until rumors spread that she had caught some sickness. She spent her days locked in the top floor of the *garan*, the main temple building, in a room with windows covered with black silk because she disliked sunlight. She had trouble sleeping, and neither ate much nor bothered with her appearance. She often fell into a daze, staring out in space, and she saw no one save Lilypad and a few select others. It seemed like she was punishing herself for something.

A night watchman visited the Lu estate to report that he often saw a figure wandering among the trees by the temple at night, sometimes staying out until dawn. He knew it to be Xiumi, but didn't dare get close. "Because what if…what if she…"

Madame Lu knew what he wanted to say. By that time, everyone in the village believed Xiumi to be a madwoman. Locals who saw her on the road openly treated her like one, skirting as far around her as they could. But the night watchman's visit pushed Madame Lu to a grave decision: she would go to the temple directly to have a long, serious talk with her daughter.

Under cover of night, she went alone with a full basket of eggs to the *garan*. But no matter what she said, or how intensely she pleaded, Xiumi refused to speak. Finally, as tears streamed from her eyes, Madame Lu said, "Mama knows you need money. I can tear down the house and sell the land; I can give you all the money we have, but you must tell me clearly what it is you're doing. Where are these strange ideas coming from?"

Xiumi finally opened her mouth. "I'm not doing anything, just having fun!" she replied with a mirthless laugh.

Her response sent her mother wailing. She twisted her clothes, tore her hair, and slapped the bricks on the floor with both hands, crying, "Oh, my daughter! You really have lost your mind!"

Shortly afterward, Xiumi threw out all her grand designs. She no longer sent people around demanding that village girls unbind their feet, called no more meetings, and halted any further progress on the irrigation plan. She ordered someone to take the Self-Governance Board sign down and cut it up for firewood, and had it replaced with another sign: PUJI ACADEMY.

This delighted the local gentry to no end. They saw it as a good omen, a sign that Xiumi was returning to a life of moral rectitude; they started to praise her, saying, "She's finally started an honest career, establishing a school to enrich the younger generation—a real blessing!"

Madame Lu also thought it evidence of Xiumi's improving health. But Ding Shuze wasn't convinced. He told her bluntly, "If she's really getting better, you can paste my name under the hole in the outhouse. She's not starting a school, she's just changing her approach. It's nothing more than a new look to fool people—the worst is yet to come, mark my words! Besides, what qualifications does she have to start a school? A stubborn, empty-headed little girl calling herself a principal—it's ridiculous!"

3

TIGER woke to find the sun high in the sky. He heard Little Thing calling to him from downstairs; the boy was chewing on a meat-stuffed bun while peeing against the wall. Magpie was washing bed-curtains by the well, stepping on the fabric as it soaked in a basin. Her feet were bare and her pants rolled up to her knees.

"You don't have to take the horse out today," she told him as he came downstairs. "Lilypad just stopped by to tell us you don't have to go."

"Again? How come?"

"The grass on the hillside has dried up, and it's getting colder," Magpie replied.

"What's the horse going to eat?"

"Give him bean meal, I guess." The bed-curtains ballooned under her feet. "Besides, even if that horse starved to death, what would you care? Always sticking your nose into everything."

Her calves were so white they looked almost blue; Tiger couldn't look away.

After breakfast, Tiger asked Little Thing what he wanted to do. "I'll go wherever you go," Little Thing told him. But Tiger didn't know where to go. The adults were occupied with their own business: his dad clicked his abacus in the office, while Madame Lu and Hua Erniang sat in the skywell, basking in the sun and talking absent-mindedly as they cleaned cotton bolls, separating the white boll from the husk and picking out the black seeds, which already lay in a mound on the table. Little Thing leaned up against Madame Lu's hip as he played with a wisp of cotton with his fingers; Madame Lu put down her work and pulled him into an embrace.

"Once all this cotton is clean, I might as well have a last dress made." Tears welled up in her eyes.

"Now why would you go and say something unlucky like that?" Hua Erniang replied.

Madame Lu simply sighed.

"What's a last dress?" Little Thing asked as he and Tiger circled the pond outside the house.

"It means grave clothes."

"Well, what are grave clothes?"

"Clothes dead people wear," Tiger explained.

"Who died?"

"Nobody." Tiger looked up at the sky. "Your grandma's just saying that, anyway."

The wind last night had swept the sky clean of clouds, leaving behind a pure, limitless blue. Little Thing said he wanted to go to the river to see the boats. In the fall, the waterways in the delta flowed shallow and narrow. White spikes of river reeds poked out of the exposed mud, as did the rust-red sheaths of sweet flag with its long, fuzzy leaves.

They reached the ford and found the ferryman, Tan Shuijin, mending sails. The river was calm, the sun warm. Gao Caixia sat in a wooden chair by the door of their house, wrapped in a heavy cotton quilt. Though her face was wan and sickly, a forceful stream of mumbled curses emerged from her mouth. She called the Principal a vicious slut and a witch, who had cast a spell that kept Tan Si by her side. Word in the village was that Gao Caixia's anger about her son had made her sick. Tan Si stammered when he spoke. For many months now, he had been spending his days at the academy; like his father, he was a good go player.

The father and son were the only two in Puji who really knew how to play go. Those who boarded the ferry to play already knew the pair by reputation. It was said the district magistrate in Meicheng once sent over a palanquin to pick them up so that they could stay and play at his office for a few days. But now the stammering son played go only with Xiumi. He lived at Black Dragon Temple, and wouldn't visit the boat for months on end. His mother said that just looking at Xiumi sent him into a stupor.

Gao Caixia and Tan Shuijin paid little attention to the two boys. Though Little Thing clambered all over the boat, and intentionally splashed water onto Shuijin's back, the old man ignored him. Even when Little Thing started to throw clods of mud at him, he only smiled faintly. He looked so feminine as he worked his needle and thread. Tan Shuijin didn't say much, but he was as bright as could be. His memory had as many rooms as there were holes in his net. When the Principal tried to divert water from the Yangtze into the fields and almost destroyed the embankment and flooded the town in the process, the entire village simply stood and watched, wailing in despair. The Principal was scared speechless. Tan Shuijin calmly rowed a boat to the damaged dike and knocked the bottom out. The craft sank across the hole and stopped the outgoing flow of water.

The boys eventually got bored of playing by the river. Little Thing blinked his big eyes at Tiger and said, "Let's go play at Black Dragon Temple!"

Tiger knew that he was thinking of his mom.

Viewed from the front, the temple looked deserted. Grass and reeds covered the earthen opera stage out front, where clouds of dragonflies hovered in the air. The front door was shut, but peering through the doorway they could see a whole company of people busily engaged. Tiger watched a group of unfamiliar, shirtless men drilling with swords and spears. Another group of people practiced throwing a rope into a tree and climbing up it as fast as they could. Little Thing lay motionless on the ground and watched through the crack beneath the door.

"Do you see her?"

"Who?"

"Your mom!"

"I wasn't looking for her," Little Thing replied.

Despite saying this, he became too embarrassed to keep watching. He walked over to one of the stone lions at the gate and climbed up so he could slide back down. But the game got old quickly. "Let's go," he said.

"Okay, but where?" Tiger asked him, turning his head upward. His heart felt as vast and empty and anchorless as the sky.

They could hear the springing-thumping sounds of the cotton fluffers working in the village. Tiger suddenly remembered the traveler he had seen the previous evening. "Let's go watch them fluff cotton."

"But we don't know which house they're in."

"Dummy, if we follow the noise we'll find it sooner or later, won't we?"

Tiger first thought the sound was coming from Grandma Meng's house, but that turned out to be untrue. Grandma Meng was sitting under her courtyard eaves in a well-polished black leather coat, playing mahjong with three others. When she saw the boys approach, she put down her tiles, stood up, and waved them over.

"Come here, Little Thing, over here," she called out cheerily.

As they walked through the door, she greeted them with a handful of sugar-coated fried dough twists, which she had Little Thing put in his shirt pocket. "Poor thing, poor thing," she muttered as she sat back down to her tiles.

"Poor thing, poor thing," the other three chimed in. "Such a sad life for a child."

"I get one, and you get one," Little Thing said as he passed a dough twist to Tiger.

"What about the extra two?"

"We'll bring them home so Grandma and Magpie can have some."

The two stood at the head of the alley and gobbled up their fried dough twists. Tiger then realized that the sound of the cotton fluffing was coming from Miss Sun's house. Miss Sun had been killed by outlaws before Tiger moved to Puji. Her old man had a stroke shortly after, and was bedridden for six months before following her to the

grave. The house remained abandoned for year, the front door hanging open. Tinkers and carpenters passing through the village sometimes
worked and slept there.

As the boys rounded the fishpond by the front door, the sound of
the fluffer suddenly ceased.

"I'm sure I heard the noise coming from inside the house. Why is
everything so quiet now?"

"Let's just go have a look. But, but, but..."

"But what?"

Little Thing's gaze shifted between the two remaining dough
twists, then veered upward as if he were doing some difficult calcula-
tion. "If I have two more left, and I give one to Grandma, that leaves
one more. Do I give it to Magpie, or to your father?"

"What do you think?"

"If I give it to Magpie, Baoshen will be mad; if I give it to him,
Magpie will be mad."

"So what'll you do?"

"I think the best way is to not give it to anybody, and I'll eat it
myself."

"Then eat it."

"I'm really going to eat it."

"Go ahead."

Little Thing munched away without hesitation.

The weed-choked courtyard was empty and quiet. The eastern chamber, where the kitchen had once been, featured a slowly collapsing
roof and a door that hung off its hinges next to the threshold covered
in grass. The guest room stood at the farther end of the courtyard.
Its door was open, but the bright sunlight in the courtyard made it
look murky inside. Bedrooms stood on either side of the guest room.
Each had a small, inward-facing window covered by red paper, which
was badly torn and fading to gray. A derelict wooden plough and
milling frame slowly decayed in the long grass.

Tiger found a table made of two doors laid across a pair of benches in the guest room. It was piled high with cotton. The fluffer's wooden bow leaned upright against a wall. Threads of cotton covered every surface of the room: from the rafters to the tiles and pillars, and all over the walls and the face of the oil lamp. How long the fluffer had been gone was a mystery.

"Weird," Tiger said. "I heard that *bang-bang-bang* sound just a second ago, how could he disappear so fast?" He plucked the string of the bow; its metallic *boing* made Little Thing flinch in alarm.

"He just went out for lunch," Little Thing said.

The door to one of the bedrooms was wide open, a spiderweb bridging the gap to the doorjamb. The door to the other room was closed. Tiger pushed gently against it; it felt like the crossbar was down. *The cotton fluffer might well be in that bedroom,* he thought. *But what was he doing in there?* Tiger beat on the door a few times and called "Hello? Hello?" but no one stirred.

"I have an idea," Little Thing announced.

"What is it?"

"I should eat this last one, too!" He was still thinking about the fried dough twists.

"Didn't you say you were saving it for Grandma?"

"If she asks about it, I'll just say Grandma Meng never gave us any. What do you think?"

Tiger laughed. "Dummy, if you don't tell her, why would she ask you?"

"Then I'm gonna eat this one." Little Thing stared intently at the dough twist.

"Eat it, eat it." Tiger waved an impatient hand at him.

Tiger noticed a small table in one corner of the guest room. A metal water pipe, a tight roll of paper to hold an ember, a mask, a bowl of cold tea, and a wooden cudgel were spread out on the table. Beside the cudgel Tiger found a green bandanna and a fine-toothed bamboo comb, the kind that women used for parting their hair. His heart sank; he picked up the bandanna and comb and held them to his nose—a faint trace of perfume still lingered. He had seen the bandanna before but couldn't remember where. He looked back at the closed door, and his heart began to race as the thought occurred to him: What if there were a woman in there? And if the cotton fluffer was in there too, what were they doing at this time of day?

"Let's go." Little Thing had finished his dough twist and was licking grains of crystallized sugar off his palm with an air of sublime satisfaction.

They left the house, one behind the other, Tiger glancing behind him as they walked. By the time they reached the street Grandma Meng lived on, Tiger heard the *boing-boing thud-thud* of the fluffer's bow ring out again.

"That is so creepy." Tiger stood still and turned to Little Thing. "Right after we left, the fluffer started up again. So why did he lock himself in the bedroom?" *Nobody lived in that house, so where did the woman's bandanna and comb come from? Whom did it belong to? And why did it look so familiar?* Tiger brooded over these questions as he followed Little Thing home. Of course, he was mostly inventing fantasies of men and women alone together. A host of women's faces floated in his mind's eye. He even thought of quickly going back to check for sure.

"Hey! What do you think . . ." Tiger caught up with Little Thing, grabbed his shoulder, and asked in a low yet breathless voice, "What do you think a guy and a girl would be doing, locked up in a room together in the middle of the day?"

"What else would they be doing? Fucking," Little Thing replied.

Approaching their front door, they encountered a stooped old woman who held hands with a child on each side of her as she peered into their courtyard. "Yeah, this is it," they heard her say.

"Who are you looking for?" Little Thing asked, walking closer to the old woman.

She turned and looked at Little Thing for a brief second, then walked straight into the courtyard without replying. Once the three of them passed the outer door into the skywell, they fell to their knees and started moaning so loudly they frightened Magpie into a near panic as she was putting up the curtains she had just washed.

The woman was in her sixties or seventies, her hair mostly gray; the children kneeling on each side of her looked five or six years old. They met Baoshen's insistent questioning with more wailing. Then the three of them started to sing. The old lady beat time on the bricks with one open palm as she wiped the snot from her nose onto her shoe with her other hand. Seeing that neighbors and passersby had begun to poke their heads around her doorway in curiosity, Madame Lu hastily sent Baoshen out to close the door, while she addressed the old lady: "Please rise, Grandmother, and come talk inside. How can we help you if we don't know what the problem is?"

Madame Lu's exhortation made the woman wail even louder. The children both looked at her, as if confused. Baoshen's sensitive ears had already picked up enough clues from the old lady's song to form a rough idea of what happened.

"Tell me, who defiled your daughter?"

The woman stopped crying and looked up at Baoshen. "These poor children haven't had a grain of rice in their bellies for three days..."

So that was it. They had come for a meal.

Madame Lu, finding an opening in the conversation, immediately sent Magpie off to the kitchen for rice. The three guests, with Baoshen leading them, went into the kitchen and were seated around the table.

As the guests ate, Madame Lu asked, "So someone defiled your daughter? What happened?"

The old woman continued shoveling food into her mouth and said nothing. Finally, she managed a mumbled reply. "I just know he's from Puji, has a gold tooth in his mouth, kills pigs for a living. I don't know what his name is."

Mother looked at Baoshen and mumbled, "Yellowtooth?"

Baoshen nodded, let out a long sigh, and said with a smile, "Grandmother, if it's Yellowtooth you're looking for, you have the wrong house."

"I know it," the old lady replied. "Let me have a few more bites, and I'll tell you the whole story, from beginning to end."

The old woman said she was from Changzhou, and lived on the far bank of the Yangtze. Her son had been a medicinal herb harvester until last summer, when he fell over a mountain cliff and died, leaving behind a young wife and two children. The wife was fair skinned and healthy, with an appealing countenance. They managed to scrape by on a few acres of land until the following spring.

"On Tomb Sweeping Day, my daughter-in-law went to tend to my dead boy's grave. It started to get dark on her way back, and just as she passed the old pottery kiln, a group of men jumped out of the woods and attacked her. The poor girl went hysterical. They dragged her into the old kiln and raped her until dawn. Half-dead, she miraculously dragged herself back home that morning. When I saw her clothing torn so badly it couldn't even cover her tits, I knew what had happened. I brought her some water, but she wouldn't drink; she held on to me and cried from morning until night.

"Then she shook her head and said, 'Mother, I don't want to live anymore.' I asked her who had done it. She said they were from Puji. The one with the gold tooth in his mouth was a butcher, and she had never seen the other two before. Then she started crying again.

"When she had cried herself to exhaustion, I said, 'Child, if you really have your heart set on dying, I can't stop you. It's the only road for us women who have been through something like this. But like the ancients say, "If an ant can survive, why can't a human?" Somebody breaks your teeth, all you can do is swallow the blood; not only that, if you leave the three of us behind, with me so old and your children so young, what are we going to do?' I begged and pleaded with her until she stopped talking about it.

"She stayed in bed for a month or so, and then she got up and started to work again. And if that had been the end of it, well, so much the better. But then that worthless son-of-a-bitch Yellowtooth has to run his mouth about what he did; he has to get drunk, has to throw a fit at his uncle's house, has to boast in public about screwing some guy's widow. He said that three of them did it together, and really tickled the little whore good. Well, the news spread in the village, and reached her parents' ears, and then there was nothing else the poor dear could do but die. She visited her family, and neither her father nor brother would see her; they obviously wanted her dead.

"Three days ago she walked into my room, dressed up in her finest clothes, and asked me, 'Should I jump down the well or hang myself?' I couldn't argue with her anymore, so I said, 'It's all the same in the end.' She had no way out. The tears dripped down her cheeks like pearls from a string.

"She said, 'Mother, I can't bear to leave my children, but I have no choice but to close my eyes and do it.' I told her that death is just the last of a thousand troubles: 'Grit your teeth and you'll endure it. But better to hang yourself because if you ruin our well, where are an old woman and two toddlers going to get water?' Her son was sound asleep next to me. She peeled off the blanket and kissed his bottom several times; then she left. She didn't hang herself or jump down the well—she jumped off a cliff."

Silence flooded the room after the old lady finished; Magpie and Madame Lu wiped away tears. After a pause, Baoshen chimed in: "In that case, you should report him to the magistrate or look for Yellowtooth yourself."

"Buddha's brother!" The old lady clapped her hands together. "We arrived in Puji this morning to look for Yellowtooth. He wasn't home, and his mother's an old, blind woman pushing ninety. She said, 'Yes, Yellowtooth is my son, and he is a butcher, but he hasn't come home in two years; he hasn't brought back as much as a marrow bone for the dogs to gnaw on. So if he wants to act like he doesn't have a mother, then I'll just pretend I don't have a son. Whether or not he's killing pigs or people, none of it has to do with me. Every debt has its owner and every bill comes due, so if he beat and raped your daughter, you should go to the magistrate. Chasing after an old bag of bones like me won't do you any good. If you want my bones to boil in your soup, you can have them.'

"Well, there wasn't much I could say to that. I left the blind lady's house and walked to the center of the village, not knowing what to do; the three of us started to cry. A fellow who had journeyed from the south and was carrying buckets of night soil found us there. He took pity on us and asked why we were crying. So I told him the whole story. He thought it over, then said, 'Yellowtooth doesn't sell meat anymore; he spends his time performing weapons drills over at Puji Academy, though nobody knows why.'

"I said, 'Okay, then we'll go to the academy.' But he stopped me and said we'd never be able to get in. I asked him why, and he said that the academy was full of senseless people. I replied, 'If the students are senseless, can you expect a sorry old peasant like me to have any sense?'

"'That's not how it works,' he said to me, 'but I don't have time to explain it to you.' Then he sat down on his shit buckets and thought about it. In the end, he told us that we should come here and settle with you. He said Yellowtooth was one of your daughter's subordinates. If he works for her, then your daughter must be a butcher too, correct?"

The assumption made Magpie snort with laughter. Madame Lu glared at her, then said bitterly, "If only she were a butcher, it would be a blessing for all of us."

4

WAKING from their afternoon nap, Little Thing and Tiger discovered that the old woman and her children were still talking to the adults by the hearth. Madame Lu could sense the grandmother's unwillingness to leave; she sent Magpie into her chambers to fetch a few handfuls of loose silver and some used, yet still presentable sets of clothing. To this she added a scoop of soybeans and a scoop of rapeseeds, plus half a bag of wheat, so the old lady would have something to plant next year. At which point the old woman kowtowed to the mistress and happily went home to Changzhou, her two grandchildren following behind her.

Minutes after the party had left, Madame Lu began to complain of a headache. She leaned against a wall, her head in her hands, an "oh, no..." escaping from her lips as she slid to the floor. Baoshen and Magpie rushed to her side and lifted her into a comfortable chair; Madame Lu asked them for a bowl of sugar water. When Magpie reappeared with the bowl, Madame Lu wheezed a few times, then coughed up a mouthful of blood. Baoshen and Magpie panicked. After they quickly helped the mistress to bed, Baoshen flew out the door in the direction of Dr. Tang's house. Little Thing, scared half to death, yelled at his back, "Run faster, Baoshen! Run as fast as you can!"

Hearing his cry brought Madame Lu to tears. A moment later, she opened her eyes, rubbed Little Thing's head, and reminded him, "He's not 'Baoshen' to you, child. You should call him Grandpa." She looked at Tiger and said to him, "Take him out to play, don't let him sit here frightened." But Little Thing wouldn't leave. As if suddenly remembering something, he bent over Madame Lu's side and whispered something in her ear. The old lady laughed.

"Can you guess what this child just asked me?" she said to Magpie.

"What did he say to make the mistress so happy?"

"Happy?! He asked me if I was going to die."

Turning to Little Thing, she explained, "Whether I die or not isn't really up to me. You can ask the doctor in a minute." Then she added, "Of course it isn't really up to the doctor either. You'll have to ask the Bodhisattva."

"What is death?" Little Thing asked her.

"It's like when you have something, and then all at once it's gone."

"But, but...where does it go?"

"It just disappears, like smoke in the breeze."

"Does everybody die?"

"They do." She thought for a moment. "Your grandfather liked to say that we are all just stewards of our lives. He meant that your life is like a thing someone has put in your hands to take care of. Sooner or later, they'll come back for it."

"Who comes to take it?"

"Well, that's Yama, the god of death, of course."

Magpie finally dragged Little Thing away from the bedside and placed him in Tiger's hands. "Take him out to play—don't let him stand here all day saying unlucky things."

Tang Liushi walked in. He asked Baoshen, "Where's the blood the mistress coughed up? Let me see it." Baoshen brought him into the guest room, where Magpie had already sprinkled wood ash over the bloodstain. "Was the blood red, or black?" the doctor asked.

Baoshen replied, "Red, the color of new paint on a temple door."

Tang Liushi nodded, then bent over and sniffed the blood. He smacked his lips, shook his head, and muttered, "Not good, not good..." Then he went to see his patient.

Madame Lu lay in bed for a full week. The doctor changed her prescription twice, but it didn't seem to help. The second time Tiger and Little Thing went in to see her, they could hardly recognize her. The smell of medicinal herbs permeated every room in the estate.

Villagers dropped by to pay their respects, as did her own relatives from Meicheng. Baoshen and Magpie always seemed to be sighing and shaking their heads.

Once, Tiger overheard his father saying to Magpie, "If the mistress really does pass away, my son and I can't stay here in Puji." Magpie bit down on her handkerchief and started to cry. Tiger finally realized that Madame Lu might really be in trouble.

That night, Tiger was forcibly shaken out of a deep sleep. He opened his eyes to find Magpie sitting by his bed, looking very nervous. "Get dressed," she said urgently, then turned away, still trembling.

"What's going on?" Tiger asked, rubbing his eyes.

"Go wake your godfather up. The mistress coughed up blood again, a whole bowlful of it, and her face is turning purple."

"Where's my dad?"

"He went to Meicheng, remember?" Magpie reminded him, then turned and scurried down the stairs.

That's right, his father had gone to Meicheng that afternoon to buy wood for the coffin. Grandma Meng had said to him that if he needed timber, the apricot tree outside her house was ready to cut. Baoshen considered it, then replied, "Best to go to Meicheng for something better."

Little Thing was still sound asleep. As Tiger deliberated whether or not to wake him up so that they could go together, Magpie shouted at him from downstairs to hurry up.

Tiger ran down and out into the street. Stars filled the canopy, while the moon slowly sank in the west; it must have been well past midnight. He followed the alley that would take him to the rear of the village. Neighborhood dogs barked one after the other as he passed more houses. Tang Liushi lived at the border of the mulberry field at the village's far end. He was the sixth-generation scion of a family of traditional doctors, but a wife and two concubines hadn't been enough to give him a son. Once, Baoshen asked Madame Lu to offer Tiger to Doctor Tang as a godson, so he could pass on his family's trade. Madame Lu was too respectable to be refused outright, so Tang Liushi said, "If you could trouble your clerk to bring his son around, I will read his face."

That had been New Year's Day two years ago. Two weeks later, on the day of the Lantern Festival, Baoshen dressed in his best clothing and marched happily to Tang Liushi's house with his son and a lacquered gift box. But when the doctor saw the two of them, he chuckled and said, "Cockeye, I assume you're making fun of me because I can't have a son."

"How could I be?" Baoshen protested. "It's a win-win situation, everyone profits. The Tang family medical tradition needs an heir, and the boy will learn a trade he can feed himself with later in life."

Though Tang Liushi had promised to read Tiger's face, he gave him little more than a quick glance before saying, "From the looks of him, your boy would do better learning how to butcher pigs with Yellowtooth."

Baoshen didn't know whether to laugh or get angry.

The doctor paused, and continued, "I'm not trying to mock you. Look at the heavy eyebrows, the powerful frame. Studying medicine would waste his talent. A military career seems much more promising. I expect he could rise to be a garrison commander no problem."

It was obviously just an excuse, but Baoshen took him at his word, and walked home just as content as he had left. He said that while Doctor Tang did write bad prescriptions on occasion, his judgment of potential was as sharp as a razor. His "garrison commander" prediction even inspired Baoshen to speak to his son in a different tone of voice than he had before.

That night, Tiger arrived at the doctor's front door and knocked. Many minutes passed before lamplight rose inside. In a surprising display of clairvoyance, Tang Liushi didn't ask who was at the door, but simply coughed a few times and called out, "Go home. I'll be right behind you."

As Tiger walked home, he thought anxiously, *The doctor sent me home without even asking who it was* ... What if he goes to someone else's house by mistake? He was trying to decide whether or not to turn back when, as he passed the fishpond next to Miss Sun's old house, he heard the front door creak open. He knew that an itinerant cotton fluffer was squatting in the house, but what was he doing up at this hour?

Through the trees, he could faintly make out the silhouettes of two people leaving the house. A woman said with a childish lilt, "You're really a pig?"

A man replied, "I was born in 1875."

"You better not be lying to me."

"Oh, dearest, do the math yourself and you'll see. Why would I lie to you?" The man put an arm around the woman's waist and pulled her in for a kiss.

Could it really be her? What was she doing here? Tiger asked himself.

It was obvious that the two of them were quite familiar with each other, and that there was more to him than met the eye. The conversation, though, didn't make much sense to Tiger. Zodiac signs? Year of the pig? Tiger's heart beat loudly as he thought of the bandanna and comb he had found inside Miss Sun's house a few days earlier. So it really was her.

He heard the woman push the man, saying, "You're getting me all wet again."

The man snickered.

The woman crossed behind the pond, coming directly toward Tiger. He had no time to hide, so he marched quickly on his way. She had clearly discovered his presence, her footsteps behind him quickening. Then she started to run.

The woman caught up to Tiger just as he reached the alley that passed Grandma Meng's house. She put a hand on his shoulder; his whole body froze. The woman put her face close to the back of his neck and whispered, "Tiger, what are you doing out here so late at night?"

Her voice touched him with soft, weightless tendrils, like fog.

Tiger said, "Getting the doctor to come check on the mistress."

She wrapped her arms around him. He could feel the heat of her body on his face, though her fingers were cold. "Were you listening to the two of us just now?" she asked him in a voice that seemed like both a sigh and a moan, though it was so low that Tiger had to hold his breath to hear her clearly.

"Tell your big sister the truth. What did you hear?"

"You asked him if he was a pig..." Tiger said.

His brain wouldn't work and his body wouldn't move, so he stood still and let her move him.

"Do you know who he is?"

"A cotton fluffer."

For a moment, she was silent. Then he felt her fingertips slide over his lips and jaw: "Haven't seen you in a few days, and you're already growing a beard." Her fingers played over his throat: "And you've grown an Adam's apple!" She massaged his shoulders: "What a strong boy you've become."

Tiger felt a little dizzy. Though he couldn't see her face in the darkness, her fingertips, her voice, the breath from her lips both mortified and intoxicated him.

"Such a good boy..." She pressed her hips tightly to his back, as her hands flowed down over his shoulders like water. Tiger slowed his breathing to make it easier for her fingertips to find their way smoothly under his shirt collar. She caressed his chest, his stomach, his ribs. Her fingers were so cool and soft and sweet.

"You can't tell anyone about what's happened tonight, my dear," she murmured in his ear.

"I won't..." Tiger replied. His voice sounded different, like he was crying. Quietly he promised himself that he would agree to anything she asked of him; no matter what she wanted him to do, he would do it. "I wouldn't tell for anything," he added after a pause.

"Call me Big Sister..."

He called her Big Sister.

"Call me your favorite Big Sister..."

He called her his favorite Big Sister.

"You mustn't talk to anyone about this. Your sister's life is in your hands now..." She suddenly let go of him and turned to look behind her. They both heard the sound of coughing not too far away. Tiger knew it was Tang Liushi finally catching up to him.

She kissed him on the cheek and whispered, "Someone's coming... Come to the academy tonight." Then she smiled and padded sinuously away, disappearing into the grove of trees in front of Grandma Meng's house. Tiger continued to stand locked in place, his mind empty. The whole affair had ended before he even had a chance to understand what was happening—like a dream, yet stranger than a dream. He felt a part of himself ache with a painful swelling.

"I said you could go home without waiting for me," Tang Liushi said as he arrived at the end of the alley, a wooden box under his arm. "The truth is, it doesn't really matter if I go or not. Your mistress isn't going to make it. After taking that prescription I wrote for her yesterday afternoon, if she had slept through the night, there would still be hope. But I went to bed with my clothes on, and I knew it was you when you knocked on my door." The doctor nattered on as he shuffled unevenly toward the house.

Then he asked Tiger, "Where did your father go?"

"He went to Meicheng to buy coffin boards," Tiger replied.

"It's just about that time," Tang Liushi said with a nod. "Though maybe a little soon still. I expect she has five or six days left in her."

As they entered her bedroom, Tiger saw Hua Erniang sitting next to Madame Lu, applying a cold cloth to her forehead. The mistress's face looked swollen and noticeably shiny, as if it had been rubbed with wax. Seeing the doctor come in, Hua Erniang addressed him, "Just now, when she opened her eyes, I spoke to her, and she didn't recognize me."

Tang Liushi sat beside the bed, picked up the mistress's wrist to take her pulse, then shook his head. "'We all must pass through the iron gate and rest inside a loaf of earth,' as the poem goes. At this point, even if I were the best doctor in the world, there is nothing I could do." Instead of examining further or prescribing new herbs, he opened his box and removed his water pipe, then crossed his legs and began to smoke.

The smoke smelled wonderful to Tiger; he suddenly no longer felt so worried about Madame Lu's sickness. The people before his eyes, the events happening around him, nothing seemed related to him. Everything felt different.

Tiger left Madame Lu's room. He sat for a while under the inner eaves of the courtyard, absorbed in thought, then went into the kitchen and drank two bowls of cold water. His heart was still beating fast. Going back upstairs, he lay in bed with his clothes on, thinking of nothing but her. He kept asking himself the same question: *If Tang Liushi hadn't showed up, would she have…*

Little Thing turned over in bed and announced, "It's going to rain."

Tiger knew Little Thing was talking in his sleep. But then he heard the pattering of raindrops on the tile roof. The shadows of trees on the window paper began to sway as the wind rose.

Tiger decided to wake Little Thing. He would explode if he didn't talk to someone. But Little Thing was impossible to wake, even as Tiger tickled him, shook him, slapped his face, and breathed on him. When he sat him upright, he discovered that Little Thing could sleep sitting up. So Tiger pinched his nose shut and waited. Little Thing took a gasping breath in through his mouth, rubbed his eyes, and giggled. He really did have such an easygoing disposition—no matter what you did to him, he never got mad.

"You remember that cotton fluffer?" Tiger asked him.

"What cotton fluffer?"

"The foreigner, the one living in Miss Sun's house."

"Yeah, what about him?" Little Thing looked blankly at him.

"You remember how we saw that green bandanna on the table when we were in Miss Sun's house—"

"What bandanna?"

"And there was a bamboo comb, too."

"Bamboo comb?"

"I'm going to tell you a secret, but you can't tell anybody."

"Okay, I won't tell."

Little Thing lay his head on his pillow, turned back over, and went back to sleep. The rain thundered down on the roof. After a gust blew the oil lamp out, Tiger could see that it was already dawn.

"That bandanna was Lilypad's." Tiger heard himself whisper these words in the half light, half darkness of the early morning.

5

THE RAIN continued until midmorning. Baoshen returned from Meicheng covered in mud, with a hired donkey cart full of timber as well as a couple of carpenters. The carpenters unloaded their tools in the skywell and started hammering and sawing away. Wood shavings soon carpeted the skywell floor.

Ding Shuze and his wife stopped by to see the mistress and talk to Baoshen about a headstone and epitaph. In a side wing, Hua Erniang surveyed bolts of cloth with a seamstress hired to make the mistress's burial clothes. Grandma Meng was everywhere at once, carrying cups of tea for the guests in one hand and her metal tobacco pipe in the other. To everyone she met she said, "When the mistress dies, that's another empty seat at the mahjong table."

Other visitors sat in the guest room, smoking, drinking tea, and chatting. The seamstress worked energetically and somewhat happily away, marking lines for cuts and hems on the cloth with her triangular tailor's chalk, her measuring tape dangling around her neck. In fact, everyone but Magpie seemed to be in excellent spirits. Though Madame Lu had not yet died, she slept alone in her room, no one noticing her absence. Which meant no one was looking after Little Thing. He and Tiger played among the guests as they pleased, once slamming into Grandma Meng so hard she dropped a porcelain teacup, which shattered on the floor.

"If you really need something to do," Baoshen said to his son, "why don't you go split some kindling in the rear courtyard instead of getting in everyone's way?"

Bursting with energy, Tiger took his father's suggestion, leaving

Little Thing and heading to the rear courtyard. In what seemed like a blink of an eye, he appeared again, walking toward the front door with a slingshot in his hand.

"Didn't I send you to split wood?" Baoshen asked.

"I split it all."

"Then go stack it in the woodshed."

"It's all stacked."

"That fast?"

"Go look for yourself if you don't believe me."

Baoshen looked his son up and down for a moment, then shook his head and continued on with his task.

Tiger kept looking up at the sky only to see the sun not moving, motionless. Time was passing too slowly for him. Deep within the domestic commotion, he could hear the sound of fluffing cotton. He knew it concealed a secret—a secret as fragile and ephemeral as drifting clouds. He worried that something might happen before nightfall to dash his hopes. *Was it real? Could such things really occur? Would she take all her clothes off?* he asked himself over and over again. Pondering these questions made him nervous.

Someone pushed him gently from behind. It was Magpie. She was carrying a wooden bucket to the well.

"What are you daydreaming about? Come help me draw some water, my back's about to break."

She handed him the bucket so she could twist her knuckles into the small of her back. As Tiger drew water, a cold draft of air from the well made him realize his cheeks were burning. He passed the full bucket to Magpie, but when she grabbed it, he didn't let go. He thought he heard Lilypad's voice in the darkness saying, *You're getting me all wet again.* What would it be like if Magpie said that? He stared at the little blue flowers patterning Magpie's shirt and the fine hairs on her arm.

"Let go of it, you idiot." Magpie gave an annoyed yank that sent water sloshing out of the bucket and onto the ground. "What's wrong with you today? Did they put something in your food?" She

looked at him with a confused and suspicious eye, as if she didn't
know him.

With great effort, Tiger made it to evening. After putting Little Thing
to bed as early as he could, he sneaked down the stairs. At the foot
of the staircase, he ran into his father.

"I thought you went to bed. What are you doing down here?"

Luckily for Tiger, Baoshen was too preoccupied to seriously attend
to his own question. He was meeting with the heads of a couple of
opera troupes, who were offering their services for activities after the
funeral. "No opera," Baoshen replied impatiently. "The world's falling
apart all around us. No opera." He locked his hands behind him and
strode out to the rear courtyard.

The coffin was almost finished. Tiger watched a carpenter scraping down the plaster that sealed the joints; soon it'd be ready to
paint.

Tiger walked through the front gate, then paused to get his bear-
ings, as if he were on the cusp of a great decision. He inhaled a long
breath and set off for the academy. What would he say if he met
anyone on the way? Should he knock if the door was closed? What
if he knocked, but they didn't let him in? All kinds of worrying questions crowded his mind, each as intractable as the next. Fortunately,
the initial questions didn't need to be answered—he met no one on
the road, and the academy door was open when he arrived. As he
stepped through the temple's entrance, he seriously wondered if he
might be dreaming.

Inside, all was quiet and calm. Lights were on in every building.
A few human shapes passed through the mist, and he occasionally
heard the sound of coughing. He crept around the outer wall of the
herbalist building, which was connected to the courtyard wall of the
Guanyin Bodhisattva hall, and found the kitchen. He knew Lilypad
was in charge of things there. Oddly, he didn't run into a single soul.
The kitchen was a rectangular building that people said once fed over

a hundred monks a day in its heyday. Tiger arrived at the kitchen door. Before entering, he asked himself once more: *Do I really have to do this?* It was too late to turn back. He had only to touch the door and it opened.

He interrupted a meeting. Eight to ten people, including Lilypad, were sitting in the cafeteria. A man in a scholar's robe reprimanded the others in an unpleasant foreign accent. His voice wasn't loud, but Tiger could tell that he was angry. He was the only one standing up; the others seated around him in the room, including the Principal, had expressions of morbid guilt on their faces. The foreigner didn't appear to notice Tiger's entrance, as he was too busy cursing out the assembled party: "This is shameful! This is truly shameful!" Tiger could see the Principal's face was burning with embarrassment.

Tiger didn't move in the doorway, unsure of whether to go or stay. He noticed Lilypad trying to shoo him away with stern eyes. When the foreigner finished cursing, he sat down and picked his teeth. Then the Principal stood up. She began by acknowledging that she assumed full responsibility for what happened at the academy, since she had been unable to control her subordinates. Then she looked at Tiger— or looked through him, as her gaze didn't seem focused on him. Her eyes glittered like knives; her face looked inhuman.

Just as Tiger was beginning to panic, he heard the Principal ask, "What does everyone think, do we kill him or not?"

A man in an old felt hat seated at the other end of the table chimed in, "Kill him, kill him...We have to kill him."

Tiger's legs shook, and he protested, "Kill me? You— Why do you want to kill me?"

He spoke at the same time another man said, "At this point, it's all we can do."

"Then we'll proceed accordingly," the Principal said nonchalantly. "Where is he?"

"I already brought him in; he's locked in the stable," Wang Qidan piped up.

Tiger let out a sigh of relief. *So it's not me they want to kill. Who could it be then?*

The Principal finally noticed him. "Tiger," she called out, her voice threatening.

"Yes…" Tiger replied, completely unnerved; he looked desperately at Lilypad.

"What are you doing here so late at night?" Her voice was quiet yet formidable. Tiger's gaze didn't move from Lilypad. He wet his pants.

"Tiger, did something bad happen at home?" Lilypad prodded, her eyebrows raised.

Tiger calmed himself, then replied, "The mistress is sick. They sent me to ask you to come home."

"What about Little Thing? He didn't come with you?"

"He's asleep."

Tiger didn't expect her to ask after Little Thing; he started to relax a little.

The Principal regarded him in silence, then said, "Go home. I'll be there in a bit."

Lilypad followed Tiger out of the cafeteria.

"Who knew you're smarter than you look?" she whispered to him. Perhaps sensing that his body was still shaking, she put a hand on his shoulder. "That scared you pretty bad, huh?"

"Who…who…who are they going to kill?"

Lilypad chuckled. "What do you care? It's not you, anyway."

Stumbling his way home, Tiger went straight to his father's office instead of going to bed. The light was on, and he could hear the clicking of the abacus. Stopping in the doorway, Tiger looked at his father and blurted out, "Dad, I just heard something that will scare you."

Baoshen stopped his work and looked up at his son to ask what the matter was.

"They're planning to kill someone!" Tiger said shrilly.

Baoshen stared at him, then waved in annoyance. "Get out, out… Best for you to be in bed, not raising hell and throwing my accounts off down here."

Tiger didn't understand how his father could be so composed; he betrayed nothing of the panic and nervous profanity of when he had found the guns in the crates. He left his father's office and, entering the front courtyard, ran into Magpie and Hua Erniang, who were just exiting Madame Lu's bedroom with an oil lamp in hand. Tiger stepped in front of them and announced, "They're going to kill someone."

Magpie and Hua Erniang looked at each other, then burst out laughing.

"Well then, let's hope they do it," Magpie said as she cupped her hand around the flame to protect it from the wind.

"What does it have to do with you anyway?" Hua Erniang asked. Then she added, "Looks like Yellowtooth won't live to see morning. Not keeping his mouth shut really did him in."

So it was Yellowtooth they were going to kill, and Baoshen, Magpie, and Hua Erniang knew about it long ago. Only he had been left in the dark.

6

TIGER later learned that when the old woman from Changzhou arrived in Puji with her grandchildren, Yellowtooth was cooking herbal medicine for his mother at his home. He was well known for being a filial son. When the ferryman Tan Shuijin heard that the old women and her two grandchildren were looking for him, he hurried to tell Yellowtooth the news: "Three people from Changzhou have come to Puji, and it looks like they want your blood."

Yellowtooth seemed unconcerned. He tapped his chest and said to Shuijin, "So what? An old lady and two kids. I'll kick the three of them out the door."

His blind mother, reacting with the circumspection that comes with age and experience, confronted her son. "Don't lie to me: Did you do it?"

"I did," Yellowtooth replied.

The old lady sent him up to his room. "Hide and don't make any noise. I'll send them off first, then I'll deal with you later."

Yellowtooth obeyed his mother's order, sequestering himself quietly in a corner of the upstairs room. Soon the old lady and her grandchildren arrived at their door, crying and wailing. Although the mother couldn't see, she could tell by the visitor's voice that the old woman was honest and straightforward, and somewhat timorous, and so with a mix of false innocence and persuasive lies, she succeeded in sending her away. After closing the door, the blind woman put her ear to it, listening to the visitors leave, and called her son downstairs only when she couldn't hear them anymore.

"Son," she said, "the money you gave me from your butchery work is all in the camphorwood chest by the head of my bed. I haven't touched a single cent of it. I had meant it to be used toward finding you a wife, but now you must take it, along with a change of clean clothes, and run. Run as far away as you possibly can, and don't return for six months, or at least a year would be better."

Yellowtooth laughed. "Ma, what are you talking about? As if I should be afraid of them? I don't need to run anywhere. If they dare to knock again, I'll kill them."

"Your old mother may not know anything, but I lost my parents when I was six, got sold as a child bride, married your father at fourteen, and was a widow by the time I was twenty-six. I might be blind, but I remember every awful thing I've been through. Listen to me, son: Despite everything that has happened already, I had a dream last night. I dreamed a flock of white herons landed on your father's grave. It's a bad omen, and I'm afraid it has something to do with you."

"You're letting your imagination run away with you, Ma," Yellowtooth told her. "Times have changed. The world's changing, chaos is the law. And Puji's been revolutionized."

"I hear you going on day after day about revolution this and revolution that, running around raising hell with a certain girl from the east side of the village, not even doing the job your father and grandfather taught you—"

"Revolution's about killing people, and not much different from killing pigs—just a pale knife in and a red knife out. Once we've taken down Meicheng and killed the governor, I'll move you into his mansion."

Seeing that her son wouldn't leave, the blind woman thought for a moment, then tried a different approach.

"Judging from her speech, the old lady doesn't seem like the type to cause a scene. Her daughter-in-law dies because of you, and she comes straight to us instead of the magistrate—that means she wants money more than anything else. If you don't want to take my advice and wait things out somewhere else, at least take half of the money in the chest upstairs and have someone you trust pass it to her. 'Money melts misfortune,' as the old saying goes. You can ignore everything else I've said, but not this—you must do it."

Yellowtooth made a show of assenting to his mother's wish. He helped her drink her medicine, then went out to gamble.

A few days passed, and the old lady stopped reminding her son to send the money. Then one afternoon, Yellowtooth came home reeking of alcohol. The moment he stepped through the door, he said to his mother, "The Wang brothers bought me drinks today at lunch, but it didn't feel right."

"What's wrong with a couple of friends treating you to drinks?" his mother asked.

"Nothing, but then as we were drinking, Wang Qidan pulled a rope out of his back pocket and said, 'The two of us have something we've got to do, brother—I hope you won't hold it against us.' I couldn't tell what he meant by it."

"What happened next?"

"The two of them got drunk and passed out on the table."

His blind mother rolled her eyes back in her head, slapped her thigh, and sobbed: "You fool, you fool! How did I give birth to such an idiot? They've put the blade right up to your throat and you still can't see what's going on!"

"Why...who would want to kill me?" Yellowtooth rubbed his throat uneasily.

"Child, don't you understand? The brothers weren't buying you drinks; they were setting a trap for you."

"Why would they buy me drinks if they wanted to trap me?" Yellowtooth asked.

"Stupid, with your strength, even the two of them together couldn't take you sober. They had to get you drunk first, otherwise they could never do it. Thank goodness they got themselves drunk, too, otherwise you'd be dead already."

"But I have no business with them...Why would they want to kill me?"

"It's not what they want. Someone else sent them to do it."

"So...you mean the Principal?" This unpleasant thought dragged

Yellowtooth halfway out of his drunken fog. "Why would she . . . why would she want to arrest me?"

"To atone for the Changzhou incident."

Yellowtooth's face turned pale. The chair he leaned his hand against creaked as he gripped it harder.

"How strange," the old woman noted. "You're always swaggering around the village like a demon incarnate, not afraid of anything. Yet just mentioning that little girl turns you into a clump of nerves."

"Ma, what the hell am I gonna do?"

"Well, since the brothers couldn't do it, someone else will try next. Get your things together now, and leave the village at nightfall. Walk me to the kitchen; I'll bake some flatcakes for you to take with you."

That evening, a barber stopped by their house, shuffling up to their front door with a wooden tool chest under his arm. Yellowtooth recognized him as Lame Xu from Xia village. Yellowtooth hadn't had a haircut in over a month, so he figured he might as well get a trim before fleeing. He bartered the barber down to a reasonable price and plopped into a chair to get started.

After draping a cloth over Yellowtooth's chest, Lame Xu reached into his toolkit for a straight razor. He pressed the gleaming steel to Yellowtooth's throat and whispered, "Keep still, brother. You're a butcher, you know what this edge can do. If you don't move, I won't move."

Yellowtooth sat motionless under the knife, completely paralyzed with fear. Several people stormed in through his front door and tied him up. Wang Qidan patted his shoulder, saying, "We were supposed to nab you at lunch today, but my brother and I got a little too thirsty and almost messed up the whole plan."

Ignoring the bitter entreaties and curses of the blind old lady, they carried Yellowtooth off to the academy.

According to the villagers, if Yellowtooth had been able to control his tongue, he would never have faced death.

The night they took him away, his old mother pawed and stumbled her way across the village to Ding Shuze's house and fell to her knees at his front door.

When Ding Shuze found her, he said, "Your son committed a heinous and intolerable crime, offensive to both gods and men. Even if the court had taken him, he would still be put to death."

"How can you only hear that old woman's side of the story? How do you know her daughter-in-law really did kill herself because of my son? How do you know she didn't die of consumption? And that the clever mother showed up in Puji to blackmail us?"

"The truth was revealed through your son's own lips," Ding Shuze replied, "and now both culprit and evidence remain. That he not only should be lecherous and rapacious but brazen enough to boast of it later makes the crime utterly inexcusable. There is nothing more to say."

"My Yellowtooth may be a horribly bad man, but he did have one good quality: He knew how to respect his elders. Say nothing of what he did for me, I know that you and your house received plenty of the best cuts of every pig he slaughtered," the old lady continued to protest.

"If that is your purpose here, wait and I will settle all the family's accounts with you. Whatever we owe you I will pay and close this account."

The blind woman laughed through clenched teeth. "Sounds like an easy enough way out for you! Pay your account if you like, but there's one debt you'll never be able to settle. Remember how you treated me in the days before I went blind? Not even a week had passed after my poor husband died when you came groping around my house. And me still wearing my mourning dress, how could I have had the energy to refuse you? 'Nothing makes one horny like a wife in mourning,' eh, you worthless creature? Don't you play the spotless saint with me now! You ran me ragged, if I hadn't thought to save the interest on this bloody account for my ancestors, I would have swung myself from the rafters years ago! So don't you grab your prick and lose your memory now."

Her words filled Ding Shuze with such anger, shame, and frustration, he could barely speak.

His wife was washing dishes by the stove and heard every word that was said. When the situation reached the boiling point, she hurried out of the kitchen and addressed the blind woman cheerfully: "Come now, a couple of old folks like you digging up your youthful indiscretions out loud in broad daylight, what will the neighbors say? Our nephew's business is our business, there's no doubt. How can we stand by and let him be seized for no reason? You just go home now and don't worry: we'll take care of everything." She helped the blind woman rise from her knees, sending her off with more gentle assurances.

Ding Shuze was still staring into the courtyard, shaking his head and mumbling: "Dragged through the mud, just dragged through the mud..."

"Drag your mother's ass through the mud!" Zhao Xiaofeng snapped, and slapped Ding Shuze across the face so hard she raised a welt.

Ding Shuze spent the night drafting a bail guarantee and acquiring signatures from a few respected members of the local gentry. The following morning, he went to the academy to bail out the prisoner. Xiumi wasn't around that day; she had left the potter, Xu Fu, temporarily in charge.

"Principal ordered his arrest," Xu Fu told Ding Shuze. "I can't give him to you until she gets back."

"Xiumi was my student—she doesn't refuse me anything," Ding Shuze lied. "Just let him go."

Xu Fu replied, "If that's the case, teacher, we'll beat him first so he learns his lesson."

When Yellowtooth heard they were letting him go, his attitude changed. "Beat me? Which one of you dares to beat me? Wang Badan, get over here and untie me... Now, you little shit, or I swear you'll regret it."

Wang Badan looked at Xu Fu uncertainly. The latter had a painful toothache that commanded most of his attention. He waved a hand and said, "To hell with it. Do him a favor and untie him, and we'll make sure he sends us a pig's head next time he's working."

Further emboldened, Yellowtooth stuck out his chin and roared,

"Some real bullshit to harass me and lock me up for! I'll tell you right now, what happened to Miss Sun those years ago was all me too! I fucked her and killed her, and had a good time doing it! And what are you gonna fucking do about it?"

Ding Shuze could hardly believe his ears; Xu Fu was scared speechless. A minute later, Xu Fu stood up and bowed to Ding Shuze, saying, "Mr. Ding, if what he says is true, it means he has another murder to answer for. I don't dare make the call—I can't let you have him."

Ding Shuze could only laugh bitterly, shake his head, and leave again.

Wang Qidan and Wang Badan were the first to be tasked with killing Yellowtooth. But Wang Qidan pulled a face and claimed he couldn't bring the ax down on someone he knew so well. They hired another executioner from outside the village, a peasant who also had no experience killing people. One evening, the peasant dragged Yellowtooth out of the stables and marched him out to a secluded spot. He whispered to him, "Brother, I know you've got a blind mother at home to worry about, so once I hack through these ropes, start running and I'll pretend to chase you for a while. After you get away, don't come back for at least a couple of years."

"It's funny," Yellowtooth replied, "you got a piece of the action too when we gave it to that cunt in Changzhou. So how come I get arrested and you're off the hook? Shut up and cut these ropes off me, my arms are getting numb."

The executioner raised his eyebrows in alarm, and immediately sank his knife into Yellowtooth's back. Yellowtooth screamed, then cried out, "Stop, brother, stop! I have something to say...!"

"And what is that?"

"You can't kill me," Yellowtooth grunted as blood oozed through his teeth.

"Why not?"

"Because... because... if you kill me, everything will go dark."

The executioner didn't reply; he found the hollow space under Yellowtooth's collarbone, aimed the knife, and drove it in halfway up the handle. When the blade entered, Yellowtooth's neck stretched straight out and his eyes bulged. When the blade slid back out, his neck relaxed and his eyes finally shut.

7

IT WAS Tiger's first visit to the *garan* shrine. The tall and imposing building was still poorly furnished—a simple wood-frame bed against one wall and a long table with a single oil lamp for the whole hall. That was it. Why would the Principal be lighting lamps in the middle of the day?

Almost no external light filtered into the enormous room. The windows that stretched across the main hall's eastern and western walls, along with the wide door that led to the Heavenly King shrine in the back, had been bricked up. The skylight above had also been covered with a black curtain. Upon entering, Tiger could smell unswept dirt in the chilly room cloaked in shadows.

The temple didn't resemble his dream at all. There was no lacquered black screen with gold inlay, no sharp-angled pearwood furniture, no gold-rimmed mirror, no blood-red vase of flowers. He noticed the shabbiness of the Principal's bed, its mosquito netting patched in several places, the bed held together with ropes, its old sheets a jumbled mess. A pair of black cotton shoes rested on a rude wooden footstool beside the bed.

The Principal was dressed in a light cotton jacket with a red floral pattern, wisps of loose cotton padding bursting through the seams. The only aspect of her that matched Tiger's dream was the sadness of her expression. You could even smell sadness on her breath. When Tiger's gaze fell on an uncovered bedpan in one corner of the room, he felt a pang of pity for her. He still couldn't bring himself to look her in the eye.

"Come to me," the Principal said in a husky voice.

She directed him to sit at the edge of the bed, then turned slightly his way and asked, "Do you know why I've asked you here?"

Staring at his feet, Tiger stammered, "I...I...I don't know."

The Principal stared at him silently. Tiger could feel her eyes peeling back his skin.

"How old are you?"

"What?"

"I asked you how old you are."

"Fourteen."

The Principal smiled. "No need to be afraid. I only wanted to talk."

She spoke like she had something in her mouth. Tiger looked up to see a silver hairpin between her lips; the Principal was putting up her hair. He could almost smell her breath—not fragrant at all, and a little sour, like the smell of yams.

"Talk about what?"

"Anything," she replied.

She started to ramble, and Tiger listened, though it sometimes felt like she didn't really care if he were listening or not. She said she couldn't sleep, she could never sleep. Only when she walked by the river alone and smelled the fresh water did she feel sleepy, but once back in bed, the feeling disappeared. She said she hated sunlight. She said that only dead people who had turned into ghosts hated sunlight. Then she chuckled sardonically and slapped Tiger's shoulder. "Look at me. Do I look like a ghost to you?"

Tiger merely trembled.

"Don't be afraid. I'm not a ghost," she said with a laugh.

She said she couldn't be sure the work she was doing wasn't a mistake—or even worse, a joke. She mentioned a place called Huajiashe. She said there was a tomb there, with a headstone that was carved with an inscription written by someone as sad as herself. Sometimes she felt like they were the same person.

She said that one evening in Yokohama, she was walking down an empty street and ran into someone she didn't expect. It gave her such a shock, she sat right down on the pavement. It was inconceivable, absolutely inconceivable.

"And who do you think it was? Take a guess."

"Um... I don't know." Tiger shook his head. He imagined that if he shook it a few more times, she might let him off the hook.

She talked about the strange dreams she had been having. She was sure that everything she dreamed about was real. Sometimes you wake up from dreams, but other times you wake up inside them, and you realize the world you had been living in was itself a dream. Her speech gradually lost logical coherence. Had she really sent a messenger out for him so she could tell him all this nonsense?

"I don't understand what you're talking about," Tiger interrupted her for the first time in his life. "Why are you telling me all this?"

"Because no one else will listen to me say it," the Principal replied. "Not a day, not a minute passes when my head doesn't hurt. As if it were being fried in oil. Sometimes I just want to smash it into a wall."

"Are you really going to attack Meicheng?"

"Yes."

"But... but why do you want to attack Meicheng?"

"Because the only way to forget something is to do something else," the Principal said.

"What do you want to forget?"

"Everything."

"So what do they mean by 'revolution'?" Tiger asked after a pause.

"Ah, revolution..." The Principal rubbed her temples, as if her head had started to hurt again. "Revolution is when no one has any idea what they're doing. You know you're making revolution, it's true, but you have absolutely no idea what's going on. It's like..."

The Principal closed her eyes and leaned against the wall before continuing, "It's like a centipede that crawls over the walls of Black Dragon Temple every day. It knows every part of the temple, every crack and cranny, every single brick and tile. Yet if you asked it, 'What does Black Dragon Temple look like?' it couldn't answer you. Understand?"

"Yes, that's true," Tiger agreed, "but there has to be someone who knows what revolution is. Even if the centipede doesn't know what Black Dragon Temple looks like, the hawk would know."

"You're correct. The hawk knows," the Principal replied with a smile. "But I don't know who the hawk is—who is up there giving the orders. He sends a messenger to Puji regularly, always the same person. Sometimes it's a written message, other times it's by mouth. The messenger's extremely private. It's impossible to persuade to him to give us more information. We've tried before. But I've never met the person who gives the messages. Sometimes I feel like a centipede myself, one that's been trapped underneath a magic tower..."

The Principal slid off topic again, and Tiger gradually lost the thread. Yet she seemed more delicate to him now, despite her babbling, and not at all like the intimidating madwoman he thought she was.

"Okay..." She breathed in sharply and adjusted her bearing, raising her voice as she addressed him. "Enough of this nonsense. How old are you, Tiger?"

"Hmm? Didn't you just ask me that?"

"Oh, did I? Then forget it." Xiumi continued, "Let me ask you a serious question."

"What?"

"You're lying to me about something," the Principal declared. "Tell me what it is—there are no strangers here."

"I don't know what you're talking about."

The Principal asked with a short chuckle, "You came into the kitchen awfully late last night. Were you supposed to meet someone?" Tiger couldn't hide his nervousness. "I...um...I...I came to get you, the mistress was sick, I came to ask you to come home, she was dying, I—"

"Tell the truth!" The Principal was scowling now. "You may only be a child, but you've already learned how to lie."

Her eyes were wet, her gaze both threatening and gentle. The fact that she could spot deception so easily meant that not only was she not crazy, she was very much alert. Tiger felt like she could hear his thoughts while he was thinking them.

"A cotton fluffer came to the village..." he began his reply.

The sound of his own voice startled him, as if the words hadn't been spoken by him but had escaped his lips of their own accord. He hesitated, still unsure whether he should tell her everything that happened that night.

"A cotton fluffer? From where?" the Principal asked.

"I don't know."

"Keep talking. What about the cotton fluffer?"

True, where exactly had the cotton fluffer come from? What was he doing in Puji? How did he meet Lilypad? And why did she ask him if he was a pig? Why did Lilypad get so nervous when she saw Tiger, and why did she tell him "Your sister's life is in your hands"? This last question raised a cold sweat on his back.

"Principal, what's your zodiac sign?" Tiger looked up at her and asked.

"Monkey, why?" The Principal looked at him in puzzlement. "You just told me that a cotton fluffer had come to the village."

"He...he...he, uh, he fluffs cotton really well!" Tiger blurted out, having finally made up his mind. He pursed his lips together hard, as if worried that opening his mouth one more time might allow the secret to slip out.

"All right, that's enough. Get out of here." The Principal sighed and shook her head.

As he emerged from the darkness of the temple, the sharp glare of the summer sun reminded Tiger that it was still daytime outside. A cacophony of voices filled his head. He plodded toward the temple gate. As he passed under the eaves of the pharmacy, a figure popped out of the shadows behind him. It was Lilypad. He knew it was her without having to look back. He knew from her scent. He couldn't figure out where she had been hiding; in one hand she carried a bunch of wet scallions.

She caught up with him in a few strides. Tiger's heart was already racing. He continued walking with her next to him.

"Look to the west," she said in a lowered voice.

Tiger looked in that direction. He saw the temple's high outer wall, and the branches of an even taller locust tree that reached over the wall from the other side.

"Do you see that locust tree?"

Tiger nodded.

"Can you climb trees?"

"Sure."

"Good. If you climb the tree, you can reach the top of the wall easily. I'll leave a ladder on the other side. Don't let anyone see you. Come tonight, don't be late." Lilypad hurried off.

Tiger looked up once more at the canopy of the locust tree, which contrasted sharply against the infinite blue sky. An old sparrow's nest sat on one of the branches like a promise. Amidst this tranquility, he could hear the rushing of his own blood through his veins. For the first time in his life, he felt an irresistible urge to smoke.

Returning home, he sat down on the stone lip of the inner courtyard wall and waited for the sun to set. He had already planned to leave through the back door of the rear courtyard. There could be absolutely no mistakes, otherwise his chest would surely explode and he would die. He couldn't risk even the slightest error. To ensure no one would hear him pass through the door, he sneaked into the rear courtyard to apply some soybean oil to the hinges. Only after testing it a few times and confirming that it would make no sound did he finally relax.

8

THAT EVENING, Tiger slipped out of bed and crept his way downstairs and into the rear courtyard. As he had planned earlier that day, he took off his shoes and carried them in one hand as he tiptoed toward the back gate.

He drew the bolt, opened the door, and slipped outside. Aside from the occasional barking of dogs, he heard no sounds indicating knowledge of his presence. He knew he was in the middle of the first important act of his life. He felt no need to hurry to the academy; at this juncture, there was no point in hurrying anything. He made his way to the riverbank. The narrow stream, grown thick with sweet flag and cattail, ran straight into the Yangtze. Fronds of sweet flag beneath the moonlight looked withered, and rustled like old leaves in the breeze.

He sat by the river a long time, looking between the moon suspended among the trees like a cloth floating on water and its shattered reflection on the river surface as the current breathed cold air on him. He wanted to think clearly about what was going to happen, but a vague, inexplicable sadness interrupted his train of thought.

The locust tree grew right next to the temple's outer wall. He easily climbed the tree and threw a leg over the top of the wall. Some distressed wasps circled closely around his head. Only after he climbed down the ladder did he sense the stings slowly swelling on his face. They didn't hurt so much.

The discovery of the ladder made him smile. His heart felt light; a salty taste rose from his throat. The moonlight lit the way to her door, which sat ajar. He smiled again.

He wondered whether or not to knock; the door opened wider and a hand reached out to pull him inside.

"It's late," Lilypad said in a low whisper. "I almost thought you weren't coming."

She put an arm around his neck, and he could feel her hot breath on his cheek. She grabbed one of his hands and placed it on her chest. Her breathing quickened.

A softness filled Tiger's hand. He quickly moved it away, but she grabbed it and put it back in its place. She licked his cheek and his lips, bit his nose and the corners of his ears, and moaned something he couldn't quite hear over her panting.

She really is a whore, Tiger thought.

She told Tiger to pinch her, so he pinched her. She asked him to do it harder; he said he was pinching as hard as he could. He smelled her sweat, which reminded him of a stable. He heard her say in his ear, "You can do whatever you want." Then she was frantically helping him take off his clothes, asking him to call her "Big Sister, Sister, Sister, Sister, Sister..."

After they had gotten naked and embraced under the covers, Tiger heard himself say, "I'm gonna die." His body felt like it would melt away in an instant. Silently, he began to cry. In the darkness, he heard Lilypad giggle and reply, "Yes, it's true—this isn't much different from dying."

She climbed on top of him, pinching, twisting, and biting. He lay flat on the bed, his whole body as taut as a bowstring. She gave him orders, which he followed obediently, and taught him how to say things that appalled him. He watched her waist lift and smash down on him over and over again in waves. She clenched her steel-strong thighs around him and ground her teeth as she pinched his shoulders. The sight of her head lolling back and forth terrified him as he lay beneath her frightened and confused. Lilypad, her eyes closed, occasionally whispered, "Good boy, good boy, good boy..."

Frigid moonlight streamed through the screen windows onto the bed. Lilypad's pale, naked body looked like it was covered in frost. They lay next to each other, motionless and silent for a long time. The sweat on their bodies evaporated quickly in the night breeze, leaving the smell of their sex behind. The smell no longer embarrassed him. It was on her neck, her elbows, her stomach, her armpits. He also could smell a faint perfume drifting in the air. He couldn't tell if it was from the osmanthus trees in the courtyard, or the powder on her cheeks.

Lilypad covered him with a blanket and tucked him in like a child, then got out of bed. Her naked flesh rippled like overflowing water. She hunted around the room until she found a metal tin, bringing it to the bed as she climbed back on top of him, her body now cool and smooth like a carp. She opened the tin, took something out, and stuffed it into Tiger's mouth.

"What's this?" Tiger asked.

"Rock candy," she replied.

The crystallized sugar crunched loudly between his teeth. He felt secure and relaxed, like he didn't need to think about anything.

Lilypad said that when she worked in the brothel in Yangzhou, they would give a piece of rock candy to every customer after he was finished; it was a house rule.

Tiger asked how they received their customers. Lilypad patted his cheek gently and said, "Exactly like we were doing just now." Tiger held her more tightly.

Trying to please her, Tiger told her that when the Principal called him to the *garan* shrine that day, he hadn't said anything.

Lilypad blinked her eyes a few times and replied, "But you must have said something; otherwise she wouldn't have sent Wang Qidan out this afternoon to arrest him."

"Did they get him?"

"He had already left a while ago," Lilypad said.

She asked Tiger about the details of his meeting with Xiumi. He carefully answered each question she asked. In the end, she sighed with relief. "A close call! She's the smartest person I've ever met. It's almost impossible to tell what's going on inside her head. She never stares directly at you when she's looking at you, so she can see right into your bones before you realize she has her eye on you."

The way Lilypad was talking about Xiumi suggested they weren't the close confidantes the villagers perceived them to be. It seemed they kept a close eye on each other. But what could each suspect of the other?

"You said she's smart," Tiger said thoughtfully, "but everyone in the village says she's crazy."

"Sometimes she really is crazy."

Lilypad grabbed his hand and brought it to her breast. The nipple stiffened until it felt like an unripe mulberry or a button knot. Lilypad cried out softly a few times, then continued: "She wants to turn the people of Puji into one person, with everyone wearing the same clothes and living in the same houses. Nobody would own any of the land, as everyone would own it. Everyone would farm together, eat together, and go to bed at the same time. Every person would have the same possessions, and every house would get the same amount of sunlight, rain, and snow. Everyone would smile the same way and dream the same dreams all the time."

"Why does she want to do that?"

"Because she thinks it will make everyone's frustrations disappear."

"But . . . but I think her way would be kind of nice," Tiger interjected.

"Nice my ass," Lilypad replied. "This is the kind of crazy stuff she thinks up when she can't sleep. Everybody has fantasies like that every once in a while, but you usually just indulge them for a moment then forget about them. Nobody except a psychopath would actually try to realize them."

After a pause, she went on, "Although, she's definitely not the only psychopath in the world, otherwise why would so many people be running around calling for revolution?"

She mentioned Zhang Jiyuan, and all the strangers coming and going in the academy. "But the way I see it, the Qing empire won't fall. And even if it does, someone else will name himself emperor."

After whimpering, she turned to kiss his lips. Even her breath smelled sweet.

For some reason, Tiger thought of the cotton fluffer again. "So, the cotton fluffer: When did he leave?"

"Day before yesterday," Lilypad said. "He's a nomadic artisan, he doesn't stay in one place for very long."

"But I heard Magpie say that we had a whole pile of cotton for him to fluff."

"Other cotton fluffers will come to the village."

"That evening, why did you ask him if he was a pig?"

Lilypad narrowed her eyes, as if he she hadn't heard the question, and asked him with a mischievous smile, "If I were twenty years younger, would you want me as your wife?"

"I would!" Tiger replied.

"Want to 'die' one more time? It'll be dawn soon."

Tiger thought for a moment, and said, "Okay."

She told him to roll on top of her; he hesitated, then did as she commanded. She told him to slap her and choke her, and so he choked her until her throat gurgled and he could see the whites of her eyes. He feared that if he really gripped her hard, he would strangle her. She made him call her a whore, a dirty bitch, a filthy slut, a village bicycle, a common fuck, telling him to repeat each name after she said it.

Finally, she started to sob.

9

ONE MORNING, after ten days of sleep and delirium, Madame Lu opened her eyes. She ordered Baoshen to help her sit up and Magpie to the kitchen. "Boil me a little date-sugar tea. Don't forget the honey."

Magpie rushed downstairs and back to the bedroom with the tea. After Madame Lu finished the cup in a flurry of gulps, she declared that she was hungry and asked for a bowl of pinched noodles. Magpie and Baoshen exchanged looks; then Magpie hurried back to the kitchen to roll dough. The mistress's abnormal behavior inspired a sigh of relief from the entire household. They thought it was a sign she was recovering. But Doctor Tang Liushi didn't share their enthusiasm.

When Tiger came to his house with the news, Tang Liushi was sitting in a bamboo chair, wiggling one foot and humming snatches of opera.

"She's done for," he said, not bothering to move. "It's her last burst of energy. Go tell your father to prepare everything for the funeral. I doubt she'll last more than half a day." He went back to his aria: "I crossed swords with Yang Lin not long ago, now they've banished me way out to Dengzhou..."

Back home, Tiger told his father what the doctor had said.

"How could that be?" Baoshen replied. "She just ate a whole bowl of pinched noodles in one sitting."

Madame Lu called for Magpie again. "Bring me some hot water."

"Hot water?"

"Mmm... I want a bath."

"Madame, how can you think about taking a bath now?"

"Just do it. If you wait too long, it might be too late."

Magpie and Hua Erniang bathed her, helped her into a clean change of clothes, and got her back into bed. Madame Lu asked Baoshen if the coffin was ready.

"It's long been finished," Baoshen told her, "we're just waiting for the last coat of paint to dry."

Madame Lu nodded. She closed her eyes and leaned against the folded duvet behind her. Some minutes passed before she opened her eyes again and told Baoshen, "Go get Little Thing for me. Have him stand in the doorway so I can see him one last time."

"Little Thing is already here," Baoshen said. He waved a hand, and the people standing in the doorway moved away to reveal the boy behind them. His shins were covered with mud that had dried in the sun, and he had torn a hole in the seat of his pants so wide that his round butt cheeks peeked through. Madame Lu began to cry as soon as she saw him.

"This far on in the year and where's his jacket?" she scolded Magpie. "His pants are ripped, and he's not even wearing socks."

Turning to Baoshen, she said, "The boy is almost five years old and he doesn't have a real name. Think of something now."

Baoshen told her that Mr. Ding had, in fact, already named him Lu Puji. Madame Lu considered this, and agreed, saying, "Fine, we will call him Puji." She turned back to the boy and cried silently as she regarded him. She said to him, "Child, Grandma has to leave."

"Where are you going?" Little Thing asked.

"To a faraway place."

"Really far?"

"Really far."

"You should wait until you're better first, then go," Little Thing said.

"If I were getting better, I wouldn't need to go," Madame Lu said with a smile. "Will you miss your grandma after I'm gone?"

"Of course!"

"Then come to my grave so you can talk to me."

"How can I talk to you if you're underground?"

"When the breeze passes through the grass and the trees, they'll make a sound. And every sound around you will be Grandma talking to you. When you have time, come talk to me. And when my grave gets washed out by the rain, don't forget to bring a spadeful of dirt to rebuild it."

"But what if Grandma misses Little Thing, what will she do?" Little Thing asked, suddenly realizing a problem.

"Your name isn't Little Thing anymore. Your name is Puji. I'm going to call your name and you respond. Puji, hello..."

"Yes," Little Thing answered.

She called his name three more times and he answered each time.

Magpie's eyes were already red from crying, and both Baoshen and Hua Erniang were wiping their eyes with their sleeves. When Little Thing noticed that everyone else was crying, tears and snot began to dribble down his face, too.

"If he hadn't brought it up, I would have forgotten. Magpie," the mistress ordered, "open the drawer on my large dresser. See if there's a small lacquered box inside. If you find it, bring it to me."

Magpie opened the dresser drawer and rooted around until she found the box, the cover of which was decorated with a colorful design. Madame Lu took the box and looked it over, saying to Little Thing, "If Grandma misses you, all I have to do is open this box and sniff it."

"What's inside?"

"All your little nail parings from when Grandma cut your nails as a baby. Fingernails and toenails. I couldn't bear to throw them away. Today, I'm going to take them with me." Madame Lu sighed as she stared at Little Thing. "Go out and play now. Grandma has to go."

Madame Lu started to pant and turned her head toward one side of the room, then the other in an effort to catch her breath. Soon she began to vomit. Though clearly distressed, neither Baoshen nor Hua Erniang knew what to do, and could only stand helplessly and watch. Tiger heard Hua Erniang whisper, "Her heart is falling..."

Convulsions rippled through Madame Lu's body so violently that the joints of the bed creaked. She complained that her blankets were crushing her, and cried, "I'm going to suffocate!" Magpie hesitated briefly before pulling the blankets away. Tiger saw Madame Lu in her blue-striped pajamas, noticed her pallid ankles crossed uncomfortably, like wooden dowels, one on top of the other. She kept kicking the baseboard as she clenched her hands tightly into fists. Her lips turned red then white, purple, and finally black as her mouth stopped moving.

"There it is," Grandma Meng announced. "Magpie, don't just stand there crying. Help me change her clothes."

But Madame Lu suddenly opened her eyes. They glittered as they carefully surveyed every person in the room. Then, clear as a bell, she said, "It's going to snow in Puji."

No one spoke. In the silence, Tiger could hear the subtle fluttering of snowflakes on the tile roof.

A pink foam oozed out between her lips, which quivered as a rhythmic clucking sound almost like a burp emerged from the depths of her body. Magpie poured two spoonfuls of warm water through her clenched teeth that leaked back out through the corners of her mouth, soaking the pillow. Magpie looked to Baoshen, but the latter could only sigh.

The convulsions resumed; her mouth opened and closed. Tiger watched as she tore open the front of her nightgown and wailed, "It's so hot, it's suffocating me! Take the blankets off!"

"I already did," Magpie said through tears.

The mistress dug long red lines into her throat with her fingernails. Her deflated breasts hung across each side of her chest. Her back and waist arched as she strained her legs and flexed her feet. She had a furious scowl on her face, as if she were angry with someone. Her teeth gnashed loudly. Her waist pitched and fell, waves crashing one after another on a lonely beach; she seemed determined to exhaust every last drop of her strength.

Gradually, her movements dwindled; her balled-up fingers relaxed, her clenched jaw dropped, and her body's excruciating tension dissipated. Her eyes stayed open wide. One ankle continued to spasm periodically, until it too finally stilled.

The Principal materialized.

She seemed to have been there for some time. The snowflakes on her clothing had melted and dampened her jacket. She stood alone and unnoticed in the doorway. She still looked as if she wasn't completely awake. She walked softly to the edge of the bed, and straightened madam's bent lower leg flat next to the other. She crossed her hands over her chest, straightened her clothing, and lifted her head to adjust her pillow. Finally, she closed Madame Lu's eyes. Then she turned to the others and said gently, "If you could please step out for a moment."

She locked herself in the room with the corpse and remained there until nightfall. No one knew what she was doing in there, and no one dared intrude. Neighbors and friends who came by after hearing the news crowded together beneath the eaves, under the walkway, and in the kitchen. Little Thing informed every new guest multiple times that "my grandma just died," but no one paid any attention to him.

Baoshen stood with his arms folded in his sleeves, occasionally looking up at the sky. They couldn't do anything but quietly wait.

Tiger sensed that the other villagers treated Xiumi with wary respect, most likely due to the awed terror that insanity usually inspires in people. Yet he felt like the last few days had transformed him into a completely different person. He felt no worries; Madame Lu's death seemed unrelated to him. He felt buoyant, at ease, possibly happy.

For the longest time it had been as if he were trapped inside a black box, the huge, edgeless sky over the village the box's lid. He'd seen only pieces and shadows of things and had no means to discover why everything around him was happening, or how invisible threads appeared to bind everything together into a single, many-layered mystery. Now he was a part of that mystery: the flame riding the lamp's hempen wick, the turning hawk in the sky, the scent of the body he savored so much—sweet, anguished, intoxicating.

At the lamp-lighting hour, the door to the bedroom creaked open, and Xiumi emerged. She looked much older and worn than before, though no sign of grief was visible on her face or in her half-closed eyes. Tiger thought she looked like she did the first time he saw her, when Baoshen brought him from Qinggang to Puji: deeply ensconced in a long and shadowy dream.

When Little Thing saw his mother, he ran and hid behind a pillar in the courtyard's covered walkway, then scampered farther down the walkway to hide himself behind Magpie's legs. The Principal didn't seem to notice him. When Baoshen led her into the skywell to inspect the coffin, Little Thing finally ran over and looked up at her, with his silly grin on his face, as if to say, *Here I am.*

Baoshen rubbed his hands together and asked what ought to be done about the mistress now.

Xiumi pursed her lips and replied, "Bury her." And added, as if finally remembering something crucial, "Oh, that's right, where were you planning to dig the grave?"

"In the daylily field, west of the village."

"No," Xiumi shook her head, "you can't bury her there."

"The mistress picked the place herself," Baoshen said. "She gave the order a few days ago, and hired a yin-yang geomancer to assess it."

"That's not my concern," Xiumi replied as her expression darkened. "You can't bury her in the daylily field."

"Then where do you suggest we bury her?" Baoshen asked obsequiously.

"It's up to you. Anywhere is fine, as long as it's not in the daylily field." With this, Xiumi turned and went back to the academy.

Tiger saw Grandma Meng give Hua Erniang a nudge and a meaningful look. She whispered, "Erniang, did you see her waist?"

An ambiguous smile creased Hua Erniang's face as she nodded.

What about her waist? Tiger looked at Hua Erniang, then back at Grandma Meng. Turning his eye to the door, he watched snowflakes dance across the lid of the casket. The Principal was already gone.

The snow fell harder on the night of the wake. Dry gusts of snow turned to softer, heavier flakes, like goose down, that blanketed the earth with a piling thickness.

In Ding Shuze's opinion, this unseasonable blizzard represented the anger of heaven above. He circled the coffin, tapping on the skywell floor with his cane, and cried, "Flagrant immorality! Most flagrant immorality!" Everyone knew whom he was talking about, but no one paid any attention to him.

Baoshen's mind wandered. *Why wouldn't Xiumi let them bury the mistress in the daylily field?* He repeatedly asked himself the question out loud as he turned it over in his mind, his muttering irritating Magpie to the point of her correcting him.

"Do you even need to ask? It's obvious!"

Baoshen walked around to where Magpie stood on the other side of the coffin, tapping his temple in confusion. "Tell me, then. What does it mean?"

"Someone else is already buried in the daylily field," Magpie said. "You really are an idiot."

That someone was Zhang Jiyuan. Ten years earlier, when they found his body locked in river ice, the mistress had publicly thrown herself on top of it and cried. Afterward, she hired an oxcart and transported his corpse back to the village. Baoshen had to tell her that ancient custom prohibited them from holding a wake or funeral for the corpse in their residence, because he was not a member of family, and had died violently in the wilderness. But Madame Lu stridently refused to listen.

She went so far as to threaten to fire Baoshen and kick him and his son out the door that same day. Baoshen was so frightened he kneeled down and knocked his head until it bruised. She paid no attention to Grandma Meng's earnest pleas, nor to Ding Shuze's long-winded pontifications—the black predictions from the fortune-teller also fell on deaf ears. When Magpie tried to add her voice to the chorus of protests, the mistress snapped, "Bullshit!"

Only Xiumi moved her to change her heart. She said nothing, merely curled her lip and snorted derisively, and the mistress's cheek turned gray. She ordered a bamboo funeral tent set up outside the house by the fishpond, burned incense by the coffin for twenty-one days, and hired Taoist and Buddhist priests to recite sutras for the dead soul. She had the coffin interred in the daylily field at the west side of the village.

Magpie's explanation inspired a faint glimmer of understanding in Baoshen's brain, but he scratched his head and admitted, "I still don't quite get it."

"If you still don't get it that's too bad. Honestly, what an idiot."

Magpie's words brought Tiger back to that one evening many years ago when he had climbed the studio steps in pouring rain, lamplight darkened to yellow smudges. He recalled seeing the mistress's naked ankles hanging over Zhang Jiyuan's shoulders. Her moaning had mixed with the moans of the wind outside.

Tiger lowered his gaze to the icy coffin below him. His heart felt empty. After all these years, he could still recall the sound of her breathing.

Why had Xiumi not allowed them to bury her mother in the daylily field? Magpie suggested the answer was hidden in events that had transpired more than a decade earlier. As subsequent events would prove, though, her answer was mistaken.*

*In August 1951, the first list of revolutionary martyrs from Meicheng County was officially published. Zhang Jiyuan's name was on it. His remains were thereby ordered to be relocated to the Puji Revolutionary Martyrs' Cemetery. Zhang Jiyuan had originally been buried in a daylily field on the western side of Puji village, but years of negligence as well as several severe floods had flattened the grave mound completely. As the location of the coffin could not be accurately identified, the excavation team dug up the entire field. In addition to Zhang Jiyuan's coffin, the team also discovered three wooden crates, which turned out to be filled with German-made Mauser repeating rifles. Upon excavation, the firearms were already rusted and unsalvageable. They eventually joined the collection of the Meicheng Historical Museum.

10

THE FUNERAL procession took place the morning of the following day.

A new grave site had been marked out in a cotton field not far from the daylily field. Baoshen planted a Himalayan cedar tree, an osmanthus tree, and some swallowtail bamboo along its borders. He patrolled it nightly after the burial, setting out every evening with a hurricane lantern and an ax, and coming home to bed only after first light.

Preparations were under way for his move back to Qinggang. Baoshen's sadness was visible and unremitting; sometimes he cried alone in his office.

Should he take Little Thing with him? He couldn't decide.

Baoshen declared he would watch over Madame Lu's tomb for the forty-nine-day mourning period, then head back to Qinggang. He didn't dare wait any longer. Each time Magpie heard him say it, she would hide in the kitchen and cry. Tiger knew she had no place to go.

One evening Baoshen went to guard the grave, but returned early. Magpie asked what brought him back so soon. Deep distress twisted Baoshen's countenance, and he swore nonstop, as if profanity were the only thing that could relieve his agitation.

"Fucking motherfucking ass-fuck, someone was there, fucking scared the shit out of me."

"Who was it?" Magpie inquired.

Baoshen sighed. "Who could it have been but her?"

He said that after arriving at the grave, he had filled his pipe and lit it. Before he finished the plug, he saw a shadow flicker by on the far side of the grave site. "I thought I was seeing a ghost at first!" he exclaimed. Then he figured it was a trick of the eye, until the silhouette advanced toward him. It had long, unkempt hair and a darkly yellow face, and said to him in a rough voice, "Don't be scared, Cockeye. It's me, Xiumi."

Xiumi walked to Baoshen's side and sat down next to him. "Will you let me have a drag of your pipe?" she asked.

Baoshen passed her the pipe with a trembling hand; she took it quietly and began to smoke. Her posture suggested she had plenty of experience smoking. Baoshen recovered from his shock and asked, "So you're a smoker, too?"

Xiumi smiled. "I am. I've even smoked opium before, if you can believe it."

After she finished the plug, she knocked the pipe against the sole of her shoe and passed it back to Baoshen. "Fill me another, will you?"

Baoshen refilled the bowl. When Xiumi lit it, he saw that her hands, lips, and body were trembling.

After one long pull, she asked him, "Is the deed for the estate with you?"

"The mistress kept it," he replied.

"Find it for me when you get home and send Tiger over to the academy with it tomorrow."

"What do you want the deed for?" Baoshen asked.

"I've sold the family land," she said tranquilly.

"Which land did you sell?" Baoshen asked in surprise, as he jumped to his feet.

"All of it."

"Xiuxiu, you...you..." Baoshen couldn't hide his distress. "If you sold all the land, what'll we all live on?"

"What do you care?" Xiumi retorted. "Besides, aren't you and Tiger going back to Qinggang anyway?"

According to Baoshen, the sight of her as she stood up terrified him. He once again suspected he was talking to a ghost, and he walked around her a few times in blind confusion, and asked softly, "Young lady, young mistress, are you really Xiuxiu? I'm not talking to a ghost, am I?"

"Do I look like a ghost to you?" Xiumi laughed.

Her laughter only confirmed Baoshen's suspicions. He backed up a few steps and fell to his knees in front of the mistress's grave, knocking his head on the earth in supplication. After his second bow, he froze—a pale hand had descended on his shoulder, and a husky voice said, "Turn around and look at me carefully."

Baoshen didn't move. "One question will tell me if you are a ghost or human."

"And what's that? Ask me."

"You said you sold all the family land. Do you know exactly how much land we have?"

"Thirty point eight-five acres."

"The family's land stretches from here to as far as eight miles away. How could you know its boundaries if you've never been concerned with the planting?"

"Lilypad knows. She took me around to see it all the day we sold it."

"And may I ask what family within twenty miles of here could possibly afford to buy it?"

"I sold it all to Long Qingtang, in Meicheng. It won't be long before he sends someone by for the deed."

"Have you signed it over yet?"

"I have."

"Why are you selling it, anyway? The land has been passed down through your family for generations."

"I need the money."

"How much did you sell it for?"

"That's none of your business," Xiumi said emphatically, her tone suddenly sharpening.

Baoshen broke out in a sweat despite the winter chill. He knew that the man Xiumi referred to, Long Qingtang, was the head of the Anqing Brotherhood, and a first lieutenant to the overlord Xu Baoshen. He controlled the black market salt trade and the brothels from

Yangzhou to Zhenjiang. How could such a man be acquainted with Xiumi?

After that night, Baoshen lost his will to speak. He left the house before the dew evaporated, and returned after it had formed again in the evening. With his hands clasped behind his back, he walked every inch of the family's land. When he finished, he locked himself in the office and didn't come out.

The sight of Little Thing brought him to tears. He would hold his small face in his large, calloused hands and lament, "Puji, Puji, you're as broke as a beggar now."

On the day of the sale, three palanquins crowned with green velvet arrived in Puji. Long Qingtang's majordomo, Feng Mazi, showed up at the estate with two able-bodied assistants. Baoshen stacked the account ledger, tenant-farmer list, and deed neatly before them, and it was done. Feng looked through everything while grinning so broadly he hardly closed his mouth. His task completed, he looked at the dispirited Baoshen and said, "Conventional wisdom says that 'a field will know ten farmers in a hundred years, and every sale renews it.' Even oceans change to mulberry fields; that will always be the way of things. But don't allow yourself to feel too depressed. As you have done such a beautiful job of handling the accounts, I hope you'll consider bringing your family to my master's household in Meicheng and continue to oversee this land for us."

Baoshen stood, tears brimming in his eyes. "I am extremely grateful for such a generous offer. But your servant has spent fifty years following Minister Lu from Beiping to Yangzhou to his final abode in Puji. Now that the family's fortunes have turned and its integrity ruined, a servant as withered and worthless as myself cannot hope to serve such an august person as your master. I only wish to return to my old home to live out my final years in . . ." Before he could finish, he broke down in sobs.

Feng replied, "We remain responsible to those who afford us our livelihood. If the steward wishes to refuse a second master's meat, I wouldn't dare force the matter. There is one more thing, however—a small favor I hope you will grant me."

"If it's in my power, I'll do whatever I can."

Feng turned the heavy ring on his finger and said, "I've heard that the Lu family owns a rare treasure, an object called a 'Double-Phoenix Crystal Basin' that supposedly can tell the future. Would it be possible to bring it out, so I can see it with my own eyes?"

Baoshen replied, "Ever since the head of the house first ran away, the family's fortunes have only declined. The few pieces of jade jewelry he owned were pawned off long ago, and the silver pieces broken up for spending money while he was still here. Now that the land is changing hands, all that's left is a run-down house, never mind any valuable antiques."

The majordomo pondered in silence for a moment, then stood up and smiled politely. "Before setting out for Puji, I overheard the governor, Long Qingtang, say that the Double-Phoenix Crystal Basin was an exceptionally rare object in the possession of your estate. Curiosity spurred a hope that I might see it for myself while I was visiting. But given what you have said, I think it's time for me to take my leave."

After seeing off the majordomo, Baoshen stood in the skywell and wondered aloud to himself, "Feng said something about a priceless antique, but I've been here for years and have never heard anything…"

Magpie, who was hanging laundry out to dry, overheard Baoshen's musings and replied, "Was he talking about that old enamel basin? I heard that the master bought it off a beggar years ago."

"What basin?" Baoshen asked.

"A beggar was using it as his begging bowl. The mistress said the master fell in love with it at first sight and set his heart on buying it. But the beggar wouldn't give it up. That is, until the master forked out two hundred taels of silver for it. The master used to admire it every day up in his chambers. The mistress used to say that buying that basin might have been the beginning of his sickness."

"Where is the basin now?" Baoshen's expression changed dramatically.

"Probably still up in the studio."

"Bring it down for me, and be careful. I want to have a look at it."

Magpie dried her glistening wet hands on her apron and went upstairs. Moments later she came back carrying something that looked like a salt crock. Two phoenixes, glazed green, were carved into its enameled-copper surface. Years of disuse had left it dusty, with cobwebs covering the lid and mouse pellets stuck to the base.

Baoshen wiped it clean with his sleeve and set it down in a sunny spot to inspect more closely. "This is just a common begging bowl. I don't see anything special about it at all."

"If the master adored it, he must have had his reasons," Magpie said.

"Well, there are two phoenixes, just like Feng Mazi said. But where does the 'Crystal' part come from?"

"Who's left to tell you, now that the both the master and the mistress are gone?" Magpie asked.

"But how could Long Qingtang know that we had a thing like this here?" Baoshen pondered. "I fear there's a story behind all this."

Over the next several days, Tiger often found his father sitting in the sun, his gaze focused on the basin.

"Looks like you're going crazy, too," Magpie snapped, after Baoshen's behavior finally exhausted her patience. She snatched the bowl from him and took it into the kitchen, where she used it to pickle cabbage.

In those days all kinds of rumors spread through the village about Puji Academy. Meanwhile, during days of heavy snow, the organization started to fall apart. Tiger heard someone say that Xiumi had intended to use the money from selling the family estate to buy guns, but her overseer at the academy, Xu Fu, simply ran off with the money without completing the purchase. Someone saw him climb onto a raft and set off down the Yangtze. Later, some boatmen passed along information that Xu Fu had opened an apothecary in the city of Nanjing and had taken three wives.

Xu Fu's escape inspired several new developments. Walnuts Yang and Ms. Ding visited the *garan* late one night to announce that they were leaving. It came as an unpleasant surprise to Xiumi, who asked in disbelief, "Zhonggui, you're leaving too?"

Walnuts told her that when he joined her, his life hadn't been worth a damn; he was a bachelor without a roof over his head or a pot to piss in. Then the Principal was good enough to marry him to Ms. Ding, and they built a little house and tilled an acre of abandoned farmland. Though they weren't rich, it was enough to live on. But now that she was pregnant, messing around with guns and swords wasn't such a good idea, especially with frequent news of the court sending the army out to suppress rebellions. So the two of them discussed it and decided they would set down their swords for plowshares for good. They hired someone to write a statement for them, and here they were, ready to cut all ties to the academy.

Though their statement was unpleasant to hear, it was also the naked truth. And it revealed by contrast why Zhang Jiyuan the revolutionary had listed "those who possess hereditary estates" as the first of his ten targets for execution. Xiumi had puzzled over that issue for years after reading the diary, and understood it only now.

Soon Baldy also left the Academy. He had been one of the staunchest supporters of the Self-Governance Board back in the early days, and his oath of entry was by far the most lyrical, composed of quoted opera lines about his head being smashed, meeting the sword with his neck, yellow sands covering his face. The harshness of his words made it sound like the real thing. So his unannounced departure hurt Xiumi deeply, while also waking her up to the severity of her situation. About a week later he returned, but as no prodigal son. He marched happily into Xiumi's room, much to her surprise, with a pig's head and its large intestine. When Xiumi asked him where he had been, he replied as if performing an operatic soliloquy:

"Today, I'm filling Yellowtooth's vacancy. Yellowtooth's death left the few hundred residents of Puji without a butcher, and I've decided to take up that vocation. Business officially opens today, and I'm offering the Principal a taste of fresh pig's head and innards."

In less than two weeks, the academy lost half of its residents. The artisans and beggars from beyond the village, as if by agreement, rolled up their blankets and disappeared together overnight. The worst was the carpenter, who cut down one of the temple doors and carried it off with him. Aside from Lilypad, Sun Waizui, Wang the cook, Tan Si, and the brothers Wang Qidan and Wang Badan, only twenty or so others remained, and they were all shaking their heads and hatching their own plans. But worse news was still to come. Two other organizations in Guantang and Huang village that had promised to act in solidarity with Puji sent emergency messengers to report that government battalions had made surprise raids on their meetings. The heads of many revolutionary leaders had been sent to the court, their bodies chopped into pieces and strung above their village. Hunks of human meat froze in the winter air as they dangled overhead like New Year's sausages.

Wang Badan had long considered leaving the academy, but he didn't know how his brother felt. He worried Qidan might laugh at his cowardice. The truth was that his brother was of exactly the same mind.

Though they were twins who spent nearly all their time together, each kept his own counsel and harbored his own private suspicions. The quiet mistrust between them gave the false impression that the other was perfectly satisfied to stay at the academy. But the growing tide of unsettling news, particularly Baldy's desertion, made it impossible for Wang Badan to uphold their pretense any longer.

One day, when the two were drinking in the village tavern, Wang Badan summoned enough courage in his alcohol to stammer out a tentative question to his brother.

"Hey, you ever think about going back to work at the forge?"

Wang Qidan allowed himself a quiet sigh of relief as this one question washed away months of repressed frustration and suspicion, yet still smiled impassively as he replied to his brother, "You afraid, Badan?"

"Of course not." Wang Badan blushed and looked askance.

"Well, you might not be afraid but I sure am." Wang Qidan refilled his brother's cup, and continued, "It's now or never. Let's get out of Puji, and go as far away as we can."

On the question of where far away they could go, the two held different opinions. Badan believed the best course was to seek out their father's brother, a cloth merchant, in Meicheng, while Qidan thought they would have better luck with their aunt's family in Tongzhou. When neither was able to convince the other, they decided instead to go all the way to Nanjing and appeal to Xu Fu.

At the first crow of the rooster the following morning, the brothers slipped out the academy doors and headed for the ferry through a heavy snowfall. Their plan was to cross the Yangtze River to Changzhou, then continue on to Nanjing. They got to the ferry just as Tan Shuijin was raising sail, but when Shuijin saw the brothers, he slid the gangplank back out and waved at them to board. The brothers jumped into the boat to meet a startling scene: Sitting across from them, smoking his pipe, was the academy cook, while another man leaned back with closed eyes against a duffel bag he had propped over the gunwale. That man was Sun Waizui.

Sun Waizui originally came from Taizhou but had lived a wanderer's lifestyle for many years. He had been one of Zhang Jiyuan's staunchest allies after the latter came to Puji. He and the other three men all looked at each other in tacit understanding.

The old cook was the first person to break the silence. Opening the front buttons of his jacket, he pulled out a pair of bronze ladles, a small cleaver, and a handful of soup spoons, also bronze. As he looked these items over, he sighed, "Well, after two years at the academy, the monkeys run when the tree falls, and all I'm left with is this worthless stuff."

The other three laughed.

Sun Waizui admitted that the Principal had treated him well, and in a time like this, when the academy needed people the most, he shouldn't be running away. But he had received a letter from home only a few days earlier saying that his eighty-year-old mother had been bedridden since last fall and was waiting to see him one last time. So he had no choice but to leave.

Ferryman Tan Shuijin, who sat behind them, working the oar, sighed and added, "Some men run to the cities in the dead of night, some travel home through snow and sleet. Only my own stupid monkey leaves good work at home so he can keep chasing a delusion."

Of course Shuijin was talking about his own son, Tan Si.

By the time Tiger heard about the situation from Lilypad, the New Year was nearly upon them. Lilypad said that except for herself and Tan Si, only fifteen or so people were left at the academy, and most of them were beggars who had fled south from Anhui. Baoshen had been spending all his time preparing for the New Year's party.

"Why don't the beggars run?" he asked Lilypad.

"Where would they run to in all this snow? At least there is hot congee and steamed bread for them at the academy."

Tiger asked, "Why didn't you run? And what about Tan Si?" But Lilypad merely smiled.

When Tiger's questions began to irritate her, she poked his nose and retorted, "At your age, you're still too young to understand what's really going on."

He also heard that the Principal's hopeless situation was actually making her feel better. She spent her days reading inside the *garan*, or playing go with Tan Si, as if nothing had happened.

A row of winter plums grew by the *garan*'s outer wall. A sudden dip in temperature plus heavy snowfall caused them to burst into bloom, and the Principal spent hours standing outside, gazing at the flowers. When Lilypad gave her the news of the Wang brothers' unexpected departure, Xiumi simply smiled and waved a newly cut sprig of plum blossoms in front of Lilypad's face. "Smell this—they're sweet."

It seemed to Lilypad that the Principal's mood had improved greatly. The darkness in her countenance had disappeared, her skin looked fresher, and she had put on some weight. Even weirder was the time she entered the kitchen unannounced to say seriously to Lilypad, who was cooking, "I can sleep at night now."

She said she had never felt so carefree at any point in her life, as if she had nothing to fear or worry about. As if she had been locked in a long, dark dream, and was only now waking from it.

"But...but...but..." Tiger protested uneasily, feeling as if the thick snowflakes outside the window, the warm fire in the hearth, Lilypad's alabaster body, were utterly empty, "how can that be?"

Lilypad slapped his naked behind and laughed. "You're still too young to understand this sort of thing."

11

LITTLE Thing stared at his mother's photograph again.

Oversoaking, sunlight, and the hot air of the stove had made the paper hard and brittle; the image had grayed so much her face was nearly unrecognizable. Little Thing never mentioned his mother to anyone. When others talked about the Principal, he pricked up his ears and listened quietly, his eyes darting back and forth like a squirrel's. But whenever anyone mentioned the Principal's illness or called her crazy, he would blurt out, "You're the crazy one."

He looked at her photo only when he was alone, as if it were an illicit act. Magpie used to say that though Little Thing didn't speak much, he knew exactly what was going on. She said she had never known such a clever little kid. Once, Madame Lu overheard her saying this, and the old lady whacked her sharply on the head with a back scratcher. Madame Lu strictly prohibited anyone from saying Little Thing was smart, because she believed the old village wisdom that smart children don't live long.

New snow fell every day, covering the entire landscape in a sheath of blinding white. Baoshen said he had never seen so much snow in all his years in Puji. With nothing else to occupy his time, he cut a few lengths of fresh bamboo in the courtyard so he could make a New Year's lantern.

They had finished the holiday shopping early that year. The two legs of pork Baoshen had bought from Baldy, the new butcher, hung along with several fish beneath the eaves, frozen hard as iron. Grandma Meng had sent a basket of walnuts, two pumpkins for the sweet sticky-rice cakes, and a ladleful of sesame seeds. Ding Shuze had sent them two sets of New Year's couplets, four pairs of peachwood good-luck charms, and a New Year's wreath made of cut paper. The main thing they needed now was a red lantern.

Baoshen sat by the fire and sighed despondently as he tied the bamboo ribs together. He said he feared this would be his last New Year's in Puji. He said he would make it the best party ever—they would want for nothing, settle for nothing. Once the old year passed, they would pick up and leave for Qinggang.

After the Principal sold the land to Long Qingtang, Baoshen eventually decided to take Little Thing with him. One day, he called Little Thing over to where he was sitting, pressed him gently between his knees, and said, "Puji, do you want to go with us to Qinggang?"

Little Thing blinked his eyes and tugged at the hairs of Baoshen's beard without agreeing or refusing. Instead, he asked, "If I went to Qinggang, would I need to be your son?"

Baoshen laughed out loud and rubbed the boy's head. "Silly child, I'm nearer to being your grandfather than your father."

Magpie by far was in the worst position, having nowhere to go. She suggested several times to Baoshen that what the hell, she might as well go with the rest of them to Qinggang. Baoshen never responded. He knew she was only saying it; she would need to be married off at some point. Grandma Meng had brought her to the house originally, so she counted as family. Recently, the old lady had sent word to certain matchmakers to find Magpie a husband, but the heavy snows had closed the roads and year-end festivities kept people too busy for a match to be found.

The only thing Magpie could think to do was embroider shoe soles as if her life depended on it. Baoshen joked that she had soled enough shoes already for Little Thing to wear until he died. Then he cursed himself for speaking of ill fortune, spat twice on the ground, and slapped himself on the cheek, which made Little Thing giggle.

Baoshen's hands shook so much as he tied the lantern frame that he snapped several bamboo ribs in succession. He felt it a bad omen. Mentioning it to Magpie encouraged her own suspicions; she told him that she had punctured her hand several times with her embroidery needle.

"Do you think something's going to happen over there at the temple? Everybody's saying that the government's cracking down on revolutionaries."

She was thinking about Puji Academy, but Baoshen worried about other things.

As the day before New Year's Eve arrived with clear skies, Baoshen was covering his holiday lantern with red paper and writing characters on its surface when the sound of singing drifted to his ears from outside the courtyard. The voice sounded like an old woman's. At first, neither Baoshen nor Magpie paid much attention, and assumed she was a beggar singing New Year's blessings for money. Baoshen even hummed along for a while, yet the more he listened to the lyrics, the more uneasy he felt. Slowly Magpie stopped her work, and stared blankly at the wall as she listened, a half-stitched sole in one hand. Partly to herself she said, "Why do I feel like she's singing about actual stuff that has happened to us? Her lyrics seem to be all about our family."

Understanding dawned on Baoshen's face. Looking seriously at Magpie, he replied, "Singing? She's only singing out of one side of her mouth. She's cursing us, trying to draw blood with every line."

"How could she know so much about our personal business these past few years?" Magpie asked as she wrapped the remaining thread around the sole. "I'll give her a couple of buns and send her away."

Magpie put down her work and went out, only to return a few moments later with the buns still in her hand. She said to Baoshen, "We thought it was a beggar. Guess who it really was?"

"Who?"

"The blind woman!"

"Blind woman from where?"

"Yellowtooth's blind old mother. I offered her the buns but she wouldn't take them, just turned around and walked away with her cane without saying a word."

Baoshen paused, the calligraphy brush still between his fingers, then wondered aloud, "What would she be doing that for?"

As evening neared, Magpie offered to go burn spirit money at Madame Lu's grave. She said the old woman's singing had made her anxious; one of her eyelids wouldn't stop twitching. When Baoshen asked her which eyelid, she replied, "Both of them."

Baoshen thought for a moment, then said, "Take Tiger with you." When Little Thing heard that Tiger was going, he whined so much that Magpie had to take him, too. The three were about to leave the estate with a basket of spirit money when Baoshen ran to the front door and called after them, "Burn a few for Zhang Jiyuan, too."

Little Thing clamored to be allowed to carry the basket; Magpie feared he would get too tired, and told him no. But Little Thing insisted. He yanked it out of her hands, proclaiming, "I can carry it, I'm really strong!"

Holding the basket in both hands, Little Thing plowed through snow that nearly reached his waist, keeping up a decent pace as he blundered along. Hua Erniang complimented him on his strength as he plowed by, spurring him to go faster.

When they reached the grave, Magpie first undid her bandanna and spread it out on the snow, directing Little Thing to kowtow to his grandmother. Then she took the paper money out of the basket, found a place protected from the wind, and struck a match. As she burned the paper bills, she prayed under her breath, as if the mistress really could hear her. Flaming bills made a crackling sound as they fell onto the snow. Tiger heard Magpie say to the grave, "After the New Year, Baoshen is taking everyone to Qinggang; even Little Thing is going with them. And I will need to leave Puji after the year is over."

"When we're all gone, who will be left to burn money for you here?" Magpie asked, then began to weep loudly.

They continued on to Zhang Jiyuan's grave. His grave mound was much smaller and lacked both a headstone and fence. The snow in the daylily field was so soft and loose that Little Thing couldn't pull his legs out after sinking in.

Magpie said that the mistress was always the one to visit Zhang Jiyuan's grave; who could have imagined that this year, she would need someone to visit her own? Then she started crying again. Tiger tried to comfort her when he saw Little Thing point into the distance and yell, "Look! What's that over there?"

Tiger followed his finger to where the sun sank between the two mountains and shimmered like molten iron in a crucible. The high road to Xia village snaked around the side of one mountain and stretched toward them. A western wind kicked up loose snow and blew it around wildly. Tiger heard the sound of galloping horses.

"Magpie, Magpie, look!" Little Thing cried out.

Magpie straightened up and looked out toward the high road. A solid black cloud of military cavalry with rifles on their backs were barreling down the road toward Puji. In a flash, horse after horse flew by them. Every soldier wore robes of black cloth and a conical helmet topped with a bright red tassel that flailed wildly; the soldiers jostled and cursed each other as they urged their horses on down the mountain and toward the riverside.

"Bad news!" Magpie cried as she stared in horror.

Tiger's heart sank, and a feeling of desperate helplessness overcame him. Rumors of approaching soldiers had proliferated so widely in the village during the last few days that Tiger had gotten sick of hearing them. He didn't expect that when the soldiers finally did appear, they would still scare the strength from his body. Behind him, he heard Magpie shout, "Little Thing! Where's Little Thing?"

She was turning in circles, as if she were looking for a lost needle. The sight of more soldiers than she had ever seen in her life had frightened her into a frenzy of confusion. Tiger turned around and spied Little Thing immediately.

He was bounding over a snow-covered cornfield like a rabbit, headed in the direction of Black Dragon Temple. He had already reached the edge of the high road. Tiger saw him fall face-first into the snow several times, but he picked himself up and kept running.

"Go, go grab him, Tiger, go now!" Magpie wailed.

As Tiger started off, he heard Magpie exclaim, "Huh? My legs— why won't my legs move?" When he turned back to her, she yelled, "Forget about me! Go catch Little Thing!"

Tiger ran down the mountain. He could hear the pounding of the horses growing closer. By the time he caught up with Little Thing by the temple gates, the boy was so tired he was retching; he heaved a few times without vomiting anything, then said between ragged breaths, "They've come to take Mama . . . Go, run as fast as you can!"

Little Thing could barely move his legs. Tiger took his hand and half-led, half-dragged him through the front door of the academy. Fortunately, they ran immediately into Lilypad, who was heading outside with a bucket, perhaps to draw water from the fishpond. "They're here . . . they're here . . ." Little Thing cried, and Tiger echoed him, "They're here . . . they're here!"

"Who's here?" Lilypad asked. "What happened to you two, what's going on?" The questions barely escaped her mouth when they heard the *pop* of a rifle. Several more pops followed in quick succession, Lilypad flinching after each one.

"Come hide with me in the kitchen, now!" Lilypad tossed the bucket away and rushed back inside. Tiger followed her to the kitchen, where she crawled inside the firebox of the cold oven and waved him over. Tiger realized Little Thing hadn't come with them. He called out a few times but got no response, and though he wanted to go back out for him, the soldiers had already made it through the front gate. Unseen rifles were firing in all directions; a bullet broke through the kitchen window and shattered a porcelain water basin, sending water everywhere. Tiger stood frozen in the kitchen for a moment, then remembered Little Thing. He was just about to open the door when Lilypad rushed out and locked him in her arms. "You fool, bullets don't recognize kids."

Moments later, the firing ceased.

Tiger carefully opened the door and stepped out of the kitchen. The first thing he saw was a mound of black stuff in the middle of the snow; it was a pile of fresh horse manure, still steaming. Poking his head around the corner of the cafeteria wall, he saw a handful of corpses lying haphazardly on the snowy ground and a soldier collecting dropped rifles.

Tan Si was rolling around on the snow, clutching his stomach and groaning with pain. A soldier walked up to him and drove a knife into his chest. As he tried to pull it out, Tan Si gripped the handle with both hands and held it there, until another soldier walked over and swung the butt of his rifle down onto his head. He immediately relaxed his grip and groaned no more.

Tiger found Little Thing.

He lay facedown in the drain canal beside the covered arcade. As Tiger approached him, he could hear the gurgle of fresh meltwater as it trickled past him. Tiger touched his hand—still warm. Turning his little face to him, he saw Little Thing's eyes were moving, as if he were thinking hard about something. He even stuck his tongue out to lick his lips. In the years that followed, Tiger would tell his father many times that when he found Little Thing in the drainage ditch, he was still alive. His eyes were still open. He even licked his lips.

Little Thing's body felt soft all over. The back of his cotton jacket was soaked with blood. Tiger called out his name, but he didn't answer. Only the corners of Little Thing's mouth moved silently, as if he were going to sleep. His eyes stopped moving and lost focus—Tiger could see more white than black. Finally his lids drooped, and his eyes narrowed into slits.

Tiger understood that it wasn't blood that dripped out of the hole in Little Thing's back, but his whole spirit.

A man who looked like an officer walked over, squatted down next to Tiger, and turned Little Thing's head over with his riding crop. Then he looked at Tiger. "Do you recognize me?"

Tiger shook his head.

The man explained, "A few months ago, a cotton fluffer came to your village. You remember, yes? That was me!" The man gave Tiger a self-satisfied smile and slapped his shoulder. Strangely, Tiger wasn't scared of him at all; the man seemed born to be a cotton fluffer and nothing else. Tiger pointed to Little Thing, motionless on the ground. "Is he dead?"

"Yeah, he's dead," the man sighed. "Bullets don't have eyes."

The man stood up and began pacing around the snowy courtyard with his hands behind his back. He obviously had no interest in Tiger, or in the prostrate body of Little Thing.

Tiger could feel Little Thing's hand get colder, and he watched his cheeks turn from pink to blue. The Principal appeared soon afterward.

She stumbled out of the eternal darkness of the *garan,* pushed and goaded by several hands, her hair falling in a mess around her shoulders. She looked at Tiger and at the bodies strewn around her without a hint of shock. Tiger wanted to yell at her, "Little Thing is dead!" But no sound came out when he opened his mouth. None of the people took any interest in Little Thing's death.

The officer stepped forward and cupped his fist in greeting. The Principal stared at him coldly. Tiger heard her say, "The captain before me must be Long Shoubei?"

"You are correct," the officer replied politely.

"Then may I ask, who is Long Qingtang to you?"

The Principal's tone was casual, and betrayed not the slightest trace of nervousness. Did she not know that Little Thing was dead? His little arm had already begun to stiffen. Melting snow from the eaves above occasionally dripped onto his nose, shattering into tiny crystalline droplets.

The officer hesitated, obviously caught off guard by the Principal's demeanor. Then he nodded to himself as if to say, *She has a sharp eye!* and replied with a smile, "That would be my father."

"So Long Qingtang has sold out to the Manchu court?"

"No need to put it so unpleasantly." The officer's smile didn't change. " 'Smart fowl choose their roost wisely,' as they say."

"In that case, you could have taken me any time. Why wait until today?"

To Tiger, the question seemed to suggest that the Principal had been waiting for the soldiers to come arrest her. He couldn't understand why she would say such a thing. Little Thing's fist had stiffened shut. Blood no longer flowed through from him, but his brows stayed knitted together.

The officer laughed so heartily you could see his teeth and gums. When he had laughed his fill, he said, "Why else but to make sure we secured those thirty-plus acres of land! My father's a shrewd businessman. He always does his homework first. He said that every day you held on to the estate was a day we couldn't take you." His voice drifted off from the exhaustion of laughing.

Tiger heard the Principal make a *hmmm* sound, as if to say, *Ah, now I understand.*

Tiger noticed his father. Baoshen stood at the front door of the temple, his entry barred by crossed rifles, trying to crane his neck to see inside the hall. Tiger moved Little Thing's body so that the water from the roof wouldn't drip onto his face. Evening fell as usual. A raptor circled in the gray sky above.

Tiger heard the Principal say, "One more question I would like answered honestly."

"Ask away."

"How old are you, Long Shoubei?"

"Your servant was born in 1875."

"So that makes you a pig?" The Principal's last question gave the officer a nasty shock. He grimaced, taking a few breaths to respond. "That is correct. So, it appears you know everything. Everyone calls you crazy, but in my own humble opinion you're the most cunning woman in the world. How unfortunate that you should never find your moment."

The Principal said no more; she was standing on tiptoe and casting her eye around as if looking for someone. Tiger knew whom she was looking for.

Then she squatted down and, carefully, deliberately, examined the pile of horse manure on the ground. She scooped up two handfuls of it and rubbed the manure evenly over her face, until her eyes, mouth, nose, forehead, and cheeks were covered. She performed this action silently, as if it were compulsory and of the highest importance. The officer didn't stop her, but watched and paced back and forth impatiently. The academy was deathly quiet.

Only when a soldier approached to whisper what looked like a serious message in his ear did Long Shoubei nod lazily to his subordinates and command, "Tie her up."

Several soldiers ran at once to where Xiumi was crouched on the ground and yanked her to her feet. Her wrists were bound tight, and they escorted her off to Meicheng.

Lilypad also left Puji that evening. Long Shoubei hired a palanquin to carry her in a wide arc around the village and on to Meicheng under cover of night.

12

LITTLE Thing lay naked on a clean bedsheet. His body looked shorter and slighter than it had when he was alive. Magpie carried in a basin of hot water and cleaned the blood from his body. She didn't cry; her face remained wooden, devoid of any anguish or grief. As her rag touched the shoulder blade that the bullet had shattered, she asked softly, "Does that hurt, Puji?" as if he had never died, as if all she had to do was tickle his armpit and he would giggle uncontrollably.

Hua Erniang turned out Little Thing's pockets and found a wooden top, a feathered *jianzi* shuttlecock, and a sparkling gold cicada.

Grandma Meng knew the second she saw it that the cicada was no ordinary object. A tentative bite revealed that it was real gold. "How odd...Where did he get his hands on a cicada like this?"

Grandma Meng passed the cicada to Baoshen, and told him to keep it safe. Baoshen looked it over carefully from red-rimmed eyes, and sighed. "A child's treasure. Bury it with him—I don't care if it's gold or brass."*

---

*In November 1968, Meicheng County took steps to reform funerary practices in response to the government-directed movement to modernize old customs. A public cemetery was constructed in Puji. During the process of transferring remains from the old tombs to the new location, villagers accidentally discovered a golden cicada among a pile of bones in a cornfield on the western side of the village. Village elders confirmed that the bones belonged to the son of the revolutionary martyr Lu Xiumi; the boy had been shot by Manchu soldiers when he was only five years old. Yet the Lu family had neither direct descendants nor proximate relations. The cicada passed through several hands and was finally given to a barefoot doctor named Tian Xiaowen. An elderly jeweler melted it and reworked the gold into a ring and a pair of earrings for her. Dr. Tian became ill and passed away not long

Once Magpie had dressed Little Thing, Baoshen carried him on his back and the party went out into the winter darkness to bury him. Little Thing's head dangled over Baoshen's shoulder as if he were asleep. Baoshen turned and kissed his face, then said, "Puji, Grandpa's going to send you home."

Grandma Meng and Hua Erniang were holding on to each other, weeping. Magpie didn't shed a tear; she and Tiger brought up the rear on their march toward the grave. Tiger could hear his father continuing to whisper to Little Thing, as the first traces of morning light appeared around them.

Baoshen said, "Puji, Grandpa knows how much you like sleeping, so here you go now...We'll let you sleep for as long as you want."

Baoshen said, "Puji, your grandpa is a good-for-nothing, a worthless man no better than a pig or a dog, Puji. The whole village called your mama crazy, and even Grandpa said it too, but Puji never did. Whenever you heard them say it, it hurt you, didn't it, Puji? When the soldiers came, Puji was the only one who thought to go warn Mama. Puji ran into the temple when the bullets were flying, but he wasn't afraid. Puji didn't run or hide, he just wanted to let Mama know. Puji, Mama didn't even look at you when you were lying in the ditch, but all you wanted to do was save her."

Baoshen said, "Puji, you mustn't blame your grandpa or resent him. The year is almost over—tomorrow is the first day of the New Year. Baoshen can't make you a coffin in the middle of winter when the ground's frozen. I couldn't make you one even if I wanted to, because the family's so poor now. We'll wrap you up in a reed mattress and send you home."

Baoshen said, "This mattress is brand new. We made it last fall out of fresh Japanese gentian. Oh, it smells sweet! And it's never been used. We've got all the toys you like to play with—your top, your iron hoops, your mud whistle...that's right, and the cicada. Grandma Meng said it's made of real gold. We'll send all your things with you,

---

after. On her deathbed, she told several people that she could hear a small child whispering in her ear.

nothing left behind. Except for the most important thing, that picture of Mama you liked to look at so much. Grandpa couldn't find it anywhere. Where did you hide it?"

Baoshen said, "Puji, we couldn't find a priest to call your soul back, so Grandpa will do it for you. When Grandpa calls your name, you respond.

"Puji!

"*Here!*

"Puji!

"*Here!*

"There we are... as long as you reply, it means your soul has come back."

Baoshen said, "If you miss Grandpa, come visit me in a dream. And if you see your Grandma Lu down there underground, tell her Baoshen is a fool, Baoshen is worthless, Baoshen deserves to be chopped into little pieces..."

Baoshen lay Puji on the reed mat next to the grave, then rolled him inside it. He had only just tucked in the edges when Magpie approached and opened the mat again. Baoshen closed it back up and Magpie reopened it. She did it two more times. She neither cried nor said anything, just looked blankly at Little Thing's face. Only after Baoshen gritted his teeth and ordered Grandma Meng and Hua Erniang to hold her back did Magpie allow him to put Little Thing's body in the shallow earth.

Once they finished shaping the burial mound, Baoshen asked, "May I kowtow to him?"

Grandma Meng replied, "He passed on first, which makes him your senior in the spirit world; and besides, no matter how young he was, he was still your mistress's child."

Baoshen knelt and touched his head to the ground three times in front of the grave. Grandma Meng and Hua Erniang did the same after him. Magpie continued to stand there, motionless and seemingly lost in thought.

"The poor miss has certainly been scared witless by what happened last night," Grandma Meng said.

As the party walked back to the village, Magpie suddenly stopped and cast her gaze around her as if looking for something. Then she thought for a moment and asked, "Hey...where's Little Thing?"

Tiger and his father left Puji in April of that year, during the greening of spring willows and lush grasses and the fragrant explosions of peach blossoms. Baoshen said that the Lu family's misfortunes all started the year the master transplanted an orchard of peach trees to the estate; their color and fragrance possessed a wicked allure. By the time the caressing rains and whispering breezes of the Tomb-Sweeping Festival arrived, even the well water carried the faint flavor of peach petals.

Yellowtooth's blind old mother believed that Xiumi and Lilypad were a pair of peachwood fairies who had attained human form after a millennium of Taoist cultivation but became infected with demonic energies. The old woman transformed and embellished the story of Puji Academy in the dramatic verse of southern provincial drum-singing, traveling around the local villages with a pair of young female apprentices, performing her narrative on street corners.

The theatrical retelling featured the old woman's son, Yellowtooth, as the human incarnation of the mythical demon hunter Zhong Kuei. A tragic hero, he infiltrated the heart of demonic legions wielding only a pair of butcher knives, passing through bitter tests of heroism before being murdered by the witches' black magic. Unexpected death on the very eve of his righteous triumph caused hot tears to fall from his mother's eyes.

The theatrical version of Lilypad, meanwhile, was as alluring and destructive as any legendary Helen of Troy, a filthy, reprehensible whore without morals or pride who forged secret plans with Long Shoubei to cajole the Lu family into selling their land before finally betraying her mistress. Her portrayal relied heavily on absurd detail and an excess of colorful, immodest language. That said, the tale gave Tiger the basic arc of the real story.

Other details still confused him, though. If Xiumi knew she couldn't trust Lilypad, why did she hold back and pretend not to see anything for so long? Also, what was the story behind Xiumi and Lilypad both asking Long Shoubei if he was a pig?

Upon arriving in Meicheng, Xiumi was incarcerated in the county prison. Her personal history with Long Qingtang along with his receipt of a bail guarantee drafted by Ding Shuze and signed by over forty local dignitaries spared her from immediate execution. In his letter, Ding Shuze argued for clemency for two reasons: one, that Xiumi's mental illness made her incapable of understanding what she was doing; and two, that she was already four months pregnant.

The magistrate consented to stay her execution until after the child was born.

Tiger knew it was Tan Si's baby. Tan Si's father, Tan Shuijin, spent months pulling every string he could to try to get custody of his grandchild, hoping to salvage the family's broken lineage. But nothing came of his effort. In those days, he heard more than once from Baoshen and Magpie that there would be yet another Little Thing.

In the summer of the last year of the Xuantong emperor, Xiumi gave birth to a child in prison. It was taken from her custody by order of the magistrate and given to the wet nurse of a prison guard. The day before Xiumi was scheduled to be strangled, Sun Yat-sen led a military uprising in Wuchang that drew support from every corner of the nation and coalesced into the revolution that would bring down the Manchurian dynasty. On a stormy night in October, Long Qingtang killed the magistrate alongside all thirty-plus members of his family and announced Meicheng's independence from the empire. While revolution brought new forms of chaos and bloodshed every day, Long Qingtang traveled among Wuchang, Guangdong, and Beiping, forming ties to the new faces of power. Hidden away in a dark corner of prison, Xiumi was entirely forgotten; only one old prison guard continued to bring her food and water each day.

But these events happened much later.

Before Tiger left Puji, he and his father paid a final visit to Madame Lu's grave to say farewell. In Baoshen's words, they were leaving Puji forever. Magpie, with nowhere to go, stayed behind to watch the estate. In fact, she would remain on the property for the rest of her life, through old age to her death. Thirty-two years later, Tiger returned to Puji in the summer of 1943 as a captain in the New Fourth Army's advance column and set up camp in the village.

He found Magpie as an old woman in her sixties. She had never married and couldn't remember much about her past life. Mention of former events rarely elicited any response beyond a head shake or a smile and a nod, and one could sense the ruin and disappearance of her own personal history. The trunk of the chinaberry tree in front of Little Thing's grave had grown as wide as a rice bowl; the field of daylilies dazzled the eye as always. Tiger sat under the chinaberry tree and thought painfully of the past. The whole world had changed around him, but Little Thing was still five years old. No matter on what day or in what era he thought of him, he was always five years old.*

But this, too, happened much later.

After Tiger and Baoshen returned to Qinggang, Baoshen bribed the prison guards in Meicheng to let him see Xiumi. He visited the prison a total of three times; on his first two visits, Xiumi refused to see him, providing no explanation. On the third visit, she at least accepted his gift of new clothes, yet the two did not meet face-to-face. Instead,

---

*In August 1969, Tiger was removed from his post as director of the Meicheng Regional Revolutionary Committee and punished as a class criminal in one of many struggle sessions taking place across the region. He returned to Puji four years later for what would truly be his final visit. He found his last resting place among the ruins of the old Lu family estate, hanging himself with his belt from the carrying timber of the studio. He was seventy-six years old.

Xiumi sent the guard back with a white silk handkerchief, on which was written a short couplet:

> Unused to the wind that snuffs my candle in dreams,
> I endure the batter of rain on my window when I wake.

Baoshen read the lines but couldn't make much sense of it. News of Xiumi grew scarce after that, and Tiger heard nothing more about her.

Part Four
FORBIDDEN SPEECH

I

XIUMI spent three months in the Meicheng county jail before being transferred south of the city to an abandoned guest house filled with cotton. A Western-style garden villa in a nearby valley served as her last residence as a prisoner.

The villa, ringed by a wrought-iron fence topped with iron spikes, was originally owned by a female missionary from the United Kingdom. The powerful silence of unvisited forests enveloped the villa night and day. Its garden featured Chinese gazebos, crooked walkways and brick-lined paths, and a bronze statue of an angel on a fountain. Years of exposure to the elements had turned the angel's skin bright green. In order to convert the pious Buddhists to her own Christian faith, the sixty-two-year-old missionary had immersed herself in Buddhist studies, even teaching herself Pali. Five years later, she converted to Buddhism. In 1887, she wrote a letter to the bishop in Scotland, openly proclaiming that "Buddhism is superior to Christianity in every respect." God's wrath followed soon afterward. In July 1888, a sudden outburst of mob violence claimed her as a victim. Her body was found in a sparsely populated temple north of Meicheng, having been subject to "horrifying brutalization."

The garden villa separated Xiumi from all contact with the outside world save the calls of birds and evening thunderstorms. She found it a perfect arrangement. Day after day of quiet repose and mournful leisure suited her clouded brain and tired body very well. Truly, no place could compare with prison. The carefree state enforced by the loss of one's freedom she experienced as deep relaxation.

After the revolution, Long Qingtang threw himself into new

struggles for local power. By the time he remembered the captured revolutionary from Puji, Xiumi had been imprisoned for a year and three months. Long Qingtang felt no desire to cause her further harm; on the contrary, he frequently sent people to check on her and send her tea, expensive snacks, and household items. Xiumi returned or gave away most of these gifts, keeping only an inkstone and inkstick, a goat-hair writing brush, and a book on raising silkworms for herself.

Long Qingtang, acquiring a general impression of her state of mind and her interest in silkworm trees, thought to encourage her studies, and sent her Fan Chengda's famous treatises *My Village Chrysanthemums* and *On Plums*, Chen Si's *The Crab Apple*, Yuan Hongdao's *History of the Vase's Heart*, and Han Yanzhi's *Tangerine Record*. Reading the books inspired in Xiumi mixed feelings of hatred and gratitude toward Long Qingtang. That autumn, not long after Xiumi was allowed to move freely about the garden, Long Qingtang sent her several bags of plant bulbs. Among these were a few that looked like a cross between garlic and narcissus, which she planted in the sandy soil around the fountain. In the early days of the following spring, their green shoots broke through the ground, and as the days passed they grew into tall, thick stalks topped with heavy buds that a few spring rains helped open into blue and purple blossoms. Xiumi had never seen such beautiful flowers before.

Flowers and plants gave her a degree of pleasure she felt she didn't deserve, driving her back into a deep sadness. Even the faintest scent of happiness disturbed her calm and stirred up memories of a humiliating and furious past, especially of the child she had given birth to in prison. She never even had the chance to look at his face.

He had been born only a few breaths away from death. In the confusion of that night she still vaguely remembered an old woman with a red flower in her hair and dressed in coarse black felt taking him away from her. Maybe they buried him, or maybe he was still living; Xiumi heard nothing and asked no one about him.

After her body recovered, she summoned an alarming force of will to train herself to forget the child, along with all the people she had known and the events she had experienced. Every face—whether of Zhang Jiyuan, Dapples, the stable boy at Huajiashe, or the tireless revolutionary activists she had met in Yokohama—became indistinct in her mind, turning faint and distant, ready to dissolve at the first breeze. Reflecting on her own past once more, she felt like a fallen leaf caught in a river, trapped in the current and dragged through the water before she could even make a sound. Her life had not been voluntary, nor wholly compulsory; she couldn't say she despised it, yet it had never brought her any comfort.

When Baoshen came to visit her, she refused to see him, replying only with a line of verse: "Unused to the wind that snuffs my candle in dreams, / I endure the batter of rain on my window when I wake." When Long Qingtang sent orderlies inviting her to the opera, she sent a written reply: "My mood is no longer suited for any kind of pleasure." It felt like the final ritual farewell to her past, a final acceptance of self-torment. Punishment and self-abuse afforded her an appropriate comfort while overwhelmed by grief. Her life had no objective except the enjoyment of sorrow.

Now the only problem was her impending freedom. She felt like the news had come too quickly. She didn't know where her true resting place might be.

The day before her release, Long Qingtang came to visit her. It wasn't their first meeting, but it would be their last. His role had recently changed from acting provincial governor to president of the Meicheng regional branch of the Progressive Society. While he didn't know that Xiumi had become completely mute, he was forgiving of the latter's silent indifference. Of course, he did suggest that she stay in Meicheng and work alongside him. He even offered her a new position on the spot: director of the Agricultural Encouragement Association.

Xiumi thought for a moment, then laid out paper and ink and replied with a couplet:

While spring's embrace makes the crab apple a fine nest for
  swallows,
When autumn passes the mountain elm is already empty
  of cicadas.

Long Qingtang's cheeks flushed when he read it. Nodding, he
replied, "Then what do you plan to do once you're out of prison?"
Xiumi wrote, "At this point, a beggar's life suits me best."
Long Qingtang smiled. "I doubt that would be appropriate. You're
too pretty, and far too young."*
Xiumi didn't reply. She decided to return to Puji, which, of course,
was the only thing she could do.

High summer had arrived; merciless heat sapped Xiumi's weakened
body of strength. After lunchtime, an enchanting tranquility descended
on the town. Everything seemed new and unfamiliar to her: the
leaning shop fronts and the rows of black roof tiles on the verge of
collapse; the white clouds piled high above tiled roofs; the listless
water sellers; the fat farmers asleep beside carts of melons; the children
chasing each other through the alleys and sword-fighting with bamboo switches, which made a hollow whizzing sound through the air
like the vibrations of a temple bell.
This was her first exposure again to the sweet disorder of the real
world, a chaotic mess in which everything still existed in its given

---

*Long Qingtang (1864–1933), scion of a wealthy family of salt merchants, entered
the mafia in 1886 as an operative for the Treasure Shade Triad, and gradually took
over the illegal salt trade in the Yangtze River delta. In 1910 he was appointed acting provincial governor in Meicheng and assumed control of the local military garrison. After the Republican Revolution he entered politics, and served as deputy
chief strategist for the Patriotic Citizen's Commission to dethrone Yuan Shikai. In
1918, he retired from military service and went to Shanghai to become an opium
smuggler, eventually rising to the top of the city's mafia hierarchy. In 1933, his con-
spiracy with Huang Jinrong to assassinate Du Yuesheng, Chiang Kai-shek's
staunchest mafia supporter, was exposed when the assassination attempt failed,
and he was tied to a stone and thrown into the Huangpu River.

place. She felt a deep sense of reassurance walking at a measured pace, examining her surroundings, her mind empty. Only the buzzing flies acknowledged her presence.

The road from Meicheng to Puji passed through ten or so villages of different size. Though by now cooking beneath the noonday sun, Xiumi could still recall a few of their names. She had heard them recited in nursery rhymes as a child, and they abided in a tender and inviolable place in her memory. Her mother would take her to visit relatives in Meicheng, seating her in a palanquin, in a wheelbarrow, or in a basket on a porter's back; she would peer through the red curtain of the palanquin at the strange people in the street as she listened to her mother sing:

Out of West Gate Village through East Gate Village
From Qianxi Town to Houxi Town
And the barrows in between...

Perhaps it was the familiar melody, or the sudden wave of half-estranged sensations assailing her, or the hazy image of her mother's face floating against a dense forest that brought tears of remorse to Xiumi's eyes. She was no revolutionary, nor was she her father's successor on his hunt for a Peach Blossom Paradise or a young woman staring out at the sea from a wooden house in Yokohama; she was a baby, dozing in a cradle that rocked its way down a rural avenue in the early morning. It was painful for her to think that by the time she realized she could begin her life anew from within the depths of her memory, that life had already concluded.

When she stopped to beg for water in a village called Douzhuang, the locals thought her nothing more than a deaf and mute beggar. Her exaggerated gestures attracted a large crowd, many of whom were children. They threw clods of earth at her to see how she would react. Her submissiveness and silence piqued their curiosity, and they followed her, making faces and screeching as they circled her. They tried scaring her with caterpillars, leeches, wasps, dead snakes, and other unrecognizable animals; they used slingshots to fire pellets at her face, and even tried to push her into the reed-filled bogs by the road-side.

Xiumi kept up her steady pace on the road, not speeding up or stopping to look around, not showing the slightest trace of anger or elation on her face. Eventually the children—confused, disappointed—tired themselves out and stood by the bog to watch her pass into the distance.

Once she was alone again, Xiumi stopped by the roadside. She thought of Little Thing, how he had collapsed in the drainage moat in the temple courtyard, frigid meltwater murmuring around his small, inert body. Black lines of blood extending slowly across the snowy ground until one of the pillars of the covered arcade blocked their advance. Even in that moment she'd known that it wasn't only blood that flowed out of his skinny body but the whole of his child's spirit.

"I'm such a fool," she whispered under her breath.

She reached West Gate Village just as evening fell. On the county avenue leading up to the village, the road thick with dust, she ran into a hunchbacked old man.

Xiumi observed at first glance that he was a real beggar as well as a seasoned and inquisitive old lecher. He fell in close behind her, following her like her own shadow without saying as much as a word. Nor was he impatient to act. The stench of his body followed her, too, even reaching her nose when the two lay down some distance from each other in a threshing field to sleep for the night.

A cool night breeze blew away the daytime heat. One by one the windows in the village went dark, and the stars lit up in the sky. The beggar lit a fire in a pile of reeds and bitter artemisia to drive away mosquitoes. Each studied the other's face in the firelight. The beggar pointed to a pile of straw not far off, and said the only thing he would say to her: "If you need to pee, go behind that straw pile, don't hold it in."

Grateful tears brimmed in her eyes. *Why am I crying so easily?* she wondered, as she fought to control her emotions. *This isn't a good sign.*

She awoke the next morning to find the beggar gone. He had left her a hollow gourd full of clean water, half a cucumber, and an old sock full of bad rice that emitted a pungent odor. A beggar's gift was a true gift, yet she had no way to repay him. Had he wanted to have her the night before, she probably would have let him. *It isn't my body anyway; let him ruin it if he wants.* Giving herself voluntarily to such an ugly, filthy old man would have been impossible. Yet only impossible things were worth trying now.

2

Xiumi arrived home in Puji. Her first impression was that the rooms and courtyard of the family estate had shrunk, the place far more cramped and dilapidated than the grand quarters she remembered. The courtyard walls leaned under their own weight, while the mortar at the top of the walls curled up in sharp, brittle triangles like tallow-tree leaves, or like a crowd of butterflies. The wooden pillars and stone pedestals were full of cracks. Black columns of ants marched back and forth through the old beehives and up the walls in long, twisting lines.

Chickens and ducks ran wild around the courtyard. One of the rooms in the eastern wing (the room in which Mother had taken her last breath) had lost its inner-facing wall, which had been replaced with a fence made of poplar and locust boards to corral an old, black-dappled sow. Her litter of spotty piglets pranced around the pen, then stopped immediately upon hearing the sound of footsteps, pricking up their long ears.

Xiumi watched a large white goose with a reddish-brown crest at the top of the courtyard steps carry its heavy abdomen slowly down toward her. The bird shook itself briefly, then emitted a spurt of liquid feces that dripped down the stone stairs.

Good heavens. Xiumi shook her head and sighed as she walked into the rear courtyard. *Magpie's masterpiece—a domestic barnyard scene.*

Aside from a few duck boxes in the bamboo grove, the rear court-yard was essentially the same. Arboreal shadows floated across every surface of the abandoned space; a row of sparrows looked down from the wrought-iron railing of the studio.

Magpie must have heard about Xiumi's release from prison because the courtyard had been swept. A pile of rotting leaves and dry grass was piled in one corner; a fine layer of sand had been sprinkled on the stairs of the studio to prevent slipping. Xiumi studied the side door through which her father had disappeared over ten years ago. That narrow doorway had become her most significant memory, the central pivot around which all her memories turned. She had relived that sunlit afternoon innumerable times, searching for something that might explain the enigma of an instantly vanishing present. The oilcloth umbrella, almost completely destroyed, still stood in its original place by the door. Insects had chewed away the oilcloth, leaving only the bare ribs. She could clearly recall her father picking it up and opening it right before he went out, leaving her with that eerie, timid smile and his last words: "It's going to rain in Puji very soon." After more than a decade of neglect and exposure, this umbrella wasn't necessarily any more decayed than Father was the day he had walked out that door.

Silence filled the estate; Magpie wasn't there. Xiumi climbed the stairs to the studio and pushed open the door—not much had changed, including the smell of mildew she knew so well. A white porcelain vase on the dresser by the head of the bed contained a newly picked lotus blossom. For some reason, the sight of the flower brought tears again.

When Magpie returned, Xiumi was fast asleep.

Magpie had left early that morning for market day in the neighboring village with a full basket of eggs to sell and returned home with every single one. At noon, she bumped into Walnuts Yang's wife, who whispered in her ear, "The Principal's back." News of her imminent release had reached Magpie's ears almost two weeks earlier, but the Principal's actual return agitated her. She hurried home with one hand covering her basket of eggs. The old ferryman Tan Shuijin met her as she neared the front entrance to the village.

His hunch had become more pronounced. Clasping his hands behind his back, he looked obviously displeased, and hailed her with "So the madwoman is back?"

He took a few more steps toward her and continued, "I hear she came back alone?"

Magpie understood the real meaning behind his questions. The first implied that he was still upset about the brutal death of his son; the second that he was thinking of the unborn baby Xiumi had taken with her. Poor Shuijin had secretly hoped Xiumi had brought his family's child with her. The bump in her belly had been the last glimmer of light in his old age. But if she had returned by herself, where was the child?

Upon returning to the estate, Magpie first locked herself in the kitchen to catch her breath. She was too nervous to see Xiumi yet; her heart was beating uncontrollably. She hadn't spoken to her in years, after all, including during Xiumi's time with the academy, when she rarely deigned to even look at Magpie.

At dinnertime, Magpie made a bowl of noodles and carried it up to the studio. Pausing at the head of the stairs, she clenched her teeth and screwed up her face in grotesque expressions to give herself the courage to go inside. She found Xiumi deep asleep, lying on her side with her face toward the wall, her clothes and shoes still on. Magpie set the bowl of noodles down gently on the chest of drawers, then held her breath as she backed slowly out of the room, closed the door, and went downstairs.

Magpie spent the entire night in the kitchen heating and reheating water, expecting her mistress to come downstairs for a bath. Yet the lamp in the studio stayed dark. When she tiptoed back upstairs the next morning, she was surprised to discover Xiumi still asleep, her body turned away from her. She had at some point eaten the bowl of noodles. Lifting the bowl and chopsticks, Magpie found a scrap of paper with writing on it hidden underneath. After she returned downstairs, she examined the writing every which way until her vision blurred, but she could make no sense of it. Her spirits fell as she thought, *Did she forget that I can't read? That means her sickness hasn't gotten any better.* But Magpie worried that the note might include an urgent errand her mistress wanted her to accomplish immediately. She deliberated for a moment, then took the note to Mr. Ding's house.

Ding Shuze had been bedridden for six months. Word around the village was that he had reached the end of his days and wouldn't live to see the harvest. Yet by the time the year's harvest passed and Ding Shuze ate noodles made with the fresh flour, his condition hadn't changed. And of course he wouldn't get better. He lay curled on his bamboo mat like a giant shrimp, constantly wetting one end of it with drool.

Having read the note Magpie passed to him, he slurped back a mouthful of saliva and raised three fingers.

"There are three sentences." Ding Shuze had lost almost all of his teeth, and his breath whistled as he talked. "The first one says, 'I am no longer able to speak.' That means she's gone mute, she can't talk. That's number one."

"Why can't she talk anymore?" Magpie asked.

"That's hard to say," Ding Shuze replied. "It's clear enough here on the paper: 'I am no longer able to speak.' She's gone mute. As the saying goes, 'The halls of the courthouse run deeper than the ocean.' She's lucky enough just to have come out alive."

"That's the truth," interjected his wife. "People who go to prison always endure all sorts of punishment. Turning you mute is one of them. They must have fed her a special serum to do that, maybe her own earwax, and then she couldn't talk anymore. It's an easy thing to do. If you're not careful and you accidentally eat your own earwax, it can turn you into a mute, too."

"What else did she write?" Magpie asked.

"The second sentence says, 'The front courtyard is yours, the rear is mine.' That means she's splitting the family estate with you: The front half is yours, the back half is hers, and never shall they overlap. The third sentence . . . She wants you to tear down the duck boxes in the bamboo grove."

"She must hate me for turning the house into a pigsty and letting all those animals run around." Magpie's expression turned disconsolate.

"She can't blame you for that," Mrs. Ding replied. "After she sold every last inch of the family land, and with no savings left to support you, how's a girl like you going to feed herself without a few animals? And besides, all that time in prison has made her useless, and if she can't work, she's going to have to rely on you, won't she? So no need to worry about that. Since she's given you the whole front courtyard, you should do what you want with it and keep what you want in it. Say nothing of chickens and ducks, you could keep a man there and she'd never say anything."

Magpie blushed all the way down to her neck.

In the days that followed, Magpie visited the Ding household so many times that, in Mrs. Ding's words, "you're going to walk our doorstep right into the ground."

Most of the notes were lists of things Xiumi wanted Magpie to buy for her on market day, like writing brushes, ink, and paper. Other notes involved simple household issues: "Chamber pot leaking, should fix immediately," "Last night's soup too salty, can you make it milder?" "No need to dust the studio every day, once every two weeks suitable," and "Chickens crowing at sunup, very very annoying, why not kill them all?"

This last note elicited a condescending snort from Ding Shuze. "Truly an addle-headed child. Only roosters crow at dawn, the hens don't crow at all, why slaughter all of them? Looks like her old revolutionary habits die hard. Keep the hens alive to lay eggs; if you kill the rooster, send me a bowl of broth."

When Magpie brought over chicken soup the next day, Mr. Ding said, "If she could hear the rooster crowing, it means her ears aren't deaf, she's just mute. So if you have to tell her something, just say it to her directly. No need to have me write everything down for you. These old bones can't take so much bother anyway."

The most peculiar note read: "Please gather the following items as soon as possible for later use: outhouse liquid from last year, powdered sulfur, pond mud, tofu dregs, several freshwater crabs."

Ding Shuze snorted, then shook his head. "What could she want all this random stuff for?"

Mrs. Ding read the list with the same confusion. "If you keep giving her what she wants, she might ask you to pick stars from the sky tomorrow. If you want my opinion, I think you should just ignore her completely."

But Magpie had already decided to do what she asked.

When she went to the fishpond for mud, she leaned too far over the bank and fell in, almost drowning. Once she finally clambered out, she didn't dare go near it again, and so dug up some of the harder mud from the drainage ditch in front of the house, mixing in water as if she were making dough until she achieved the exact stickiness and appearance of mud from the pond. Tofu dregs were easy to acquire—the tofu maker on the west side of the village had a plentiful supply. As for last year's outhouse liquid, she figured she could just as well take a few fresh scoops right from the basin, since Xiumi could never smell the difference between last year's and this year's. Fresh water crabs were common enough in the ditches and rice paddies, so she sent the village children off to collect them for her until she had a whole basketful. The hardest thing to track down was the powdered sulfur, whatever that meant; she asked around the entire village, but not even the assistant at the herbalist's knew what that was exactly. In the end, she bought a string of firecrackers, unwound their twisted caps and poured out the gunpowder inside, mixing it with yellow sand until she thought it looked like "sulfur powder."

Once Magpie had gathered everything on the list, she set out the items in a neat line along one edge of the studio's stone foundation, then retreated behind the door of the front courtyard to watch what happened, her curiosity overpowering. A little after noontime, she saw Xiumi sleepily descend the studio stairs; she watched her sniff each of the containers, then roll up her sleeves and spring into action with a childlike excitement.

It turned out that she wanted to grow lotuses.

The family had always kept lotus plants, raising them in two tall, widemouthed basins of blue-and-white Ming porcelain. The plants had been Baoshen's responsibility, and they bloomed at the height of summer every year. The late mistress had often used the wide, fleshy leaves to wrap meats and sticky-rice cakes for steaming. Xiumi could almost remember the sweet, green smell of the leaves as they cooked. As the first of the winter snows drew near, she would watch Baoshen cover the basins with a wooden frame that he filled with a thick layer of straw to protect the submerged roots.

The basins had stood neglected ever since Baoshen left Puji, and Magpie had assumed the lotus plants inside had long since dried up. When she had gone to tidy up the studio for Xiumi's return, though, she was amazed to find a single scrawny red flower blooming in one basin. It floated over the black water amid a handful of stunted leaves that had either dried up and curled or had decayed and rotted. The water smelled foul, and stink bugs crowded around the edge of the basins; the bugs flew off in a cloud of armor and wings that peppered the face of anyone who passed by. Magpie snipped the lone flower and brought it upstairs to the studio, where she had placed it in a white vase with water.

So Xiumi had decided to play with the two lotus basins. She mixed the tofu dregs, mud, and sulfur powder together in a wooden bowl, then added the outhouse liquid and mixed some more until she got an even texture. She let this concoction sit in full sunlight while she moved on to the basins, pulling out the weeds, cleaning out the insects, removing the stale water with a wooden ladle. Soon she dripped with sweat, her breath quickened, dots of mud spattered her face.

By sunset, Magpie could no longer restrain herself, and she emerged from her hiding place and barged into the rear courtyard to help. Xiumi was packing the new mud from the wooden bowl around the roots of the lotus plants; seeing Magpie approach, she kicked a wooden bucket next to her and gave Magpie a look. Magpie understood immediately: Xiumi wanted her to fetch clean water from the pond. Magpie hustled outside and returned with a full bucket of water. As she watched Xiumi pour it slowly and deliberately into the basins, she blurted out, "Why do it that way?"

She received no response to her question.

Passing by the basins a month or so later, Magpie was astonished to find them choked with fleshy, bluish-green leaves the size of her hand. Flowers of pale white and deep red had pushed through the crowded borders, and gave off a faint fragrance. Magpie stood by the flower basins until nightfall, unwilling to take her eyes off them. She remembered hearing Baoshen say that the master's lotuses were all rare strains he had cultivated for decades, and she had to admit that they were easy to fall in love with. The freshwater crabs climbed above and below the leaves, making the stems quiver in the water. When the breeze blew through the flowers, they rustled gently.

The next morning, Magpie found another note while she was upstairs cleaning. When she gave it to Ding Shuze, he laughed and patted her head. "Silly child, she wrote this for herself, it's not related to you at all."

When Magpie asked what she had written, Mr. Ding replied, "These words here—'pond rose,' 'Indian bean,' 'sacred lily,' 'water lily,' and the rest—are all types of water flowers, while these here— 'Gilded Edge,' 'Silverpink,' 'Peach Dew,' 'Snowskin,' 'Winegold,' et cetera—are names of other flowers. It's a word game educated people play by themselves to free their heart and clarify their thinking. It has nothing to do with you."

Ding Shuze rubbed his beard for a moment and mused, "The seasonal flowers and fragrant grasses have long been compared to beauties of the fairer sex, as they can improve one's nature and understand speech. The orchid resides in the tranquil valley, the chrysanthemum hides in fields and hedges; the winter plum piles fragrant snow on the mountainside, while bamboo fans its green airs across the scholar's window. Only the lotus endures the shame of life in filth and bottomless mud, yet it emerges from there without stain. Its moral character is pure and restrained, its nature warm and gentle. Perhaps the tribulations of an ill-starred life have drawn Xiumi to the fair lotus as a symbol? Nevertheless, one observes in her ambitions a hermetic tendency toward seclusion. Such a pity, such a pity..."

Magpie haltingly replied, "Mr. Ding, I didn't understand a single word of what you just said."

A hungry glimmer flashed in Ding Shuze's dirty eyes. He stared at Magpie and said slowly, "If you want to understand what I said, I can help you with that."

Magpie couldn't quite tell what he was suggesting, so turned to look at his wife. Mrs. Ding explained, "We see you running in and out of here, carrying scraps of paper with crazy scribbles on them as if they were imperial edicts, and you're frightened of every word. This won't work out for the long term—it's exhausting for you, and even more so for us. I shouldn't say this, but if the teacher passes away one day, are you going to dig him up from his grave and ask him to help you write back? The teacher and I talked it over yesterday evening, and we decided he might as well teach you to read and write a little. With his experience and learning, it shouldn't take you much longer than a few months before you can read everything she writes. What do you think?"

Magpie glanced over at the skeletal old man on the bed and the spit stains on the walls and floor and felt deeply uneasy. With the teacher's wife staring at her from under arched eyebrows, waiting for a reply, she grimaced and started to say, "If you could just give me time to consider it..."

"What's to consider?" Mrs. Ding asked bluntly. "Mr. Ding is one of the great minds of his age. Had luck been with him, he would have become a general or a first minister in the imperial court. That he should be willing to lower himself this far is your own good fortune. You couldn't find an opportunity this good if you went hunting at night with a lantern. And if you don't want to accept, there's no need for you to come to this house for help anymore."

The mistress's strident tone flustered Magpie into giving her nervous consent. As the phlegm all over the floor made the full kowtow ritual inconvenient, Mrs. Ding put a hand on her head and pushed her into three ceremonial bows toward her new tutor. Once Magpie had officially become his student, a new ferocity seized Mr. Ding's spirit. He raised himself up from the bamboo mat until he could sit with his back against the wall and proclaimed, "By convention, I should charge money to teach you to read. But since you have no savings, I won't ask you for my standard tuition. Every day, once your hens have laid eggs, I want you to bring one of the big eggs with you whenever you come by. One or two a day should be plenty."

With a troubled heart, Magpie left the Ding family household and went straight to her neighbor Hua Erniang to discuss the situation with her. Hua Erniang was spinning thread beneath a window, and she pedaled her wheel and worked as she listened to Magpie. She replied with a laugh, "One egg every single day? The old devil has some nerve just thinking of it. You know, the proverb says that 'Reading is the mother of all confusion.' Nothing's more important in this life than clothing and feeding yourself. And you're a woman. It's not like you're about to go sit for the civil service exam—why waste your energy on learning to read? My opinion is that you should ignore all this business of his."

Magpie left Hua Erniang's place and went to see Grandma Meng. As the latter was an old acquaintance and the closest thing she had to family, plus could read a little herself, her opinion was naturally quite different. She said, "Learning a few words isn't a bad idea. You could use them to organize your accounts or whatever when you sell the piglets. He doesn't want tuition from you, and thirty eggs a month isn't really that many. Ding Shuze never had any children, and he's surely eaten up all his savings by now—he's really in a sad state. I expect he can't even remember what an egg tastes like."

Grandma Meng's reply assured Magpie, and she went every day thereafter, rain or shine, to Ding Shuze's house for reading lessons. The first two months passed uneventfully, but as time wore on, a new concern arose. Ding Shuze had a habit of touching her head with his dirty fingers, or of leaning or pressing against her as if by chance. At first, Magpie held her tongue in the interest of saving face for her elder, but Ding Shuze's behavior grew more appalling as time progressed, and he began dropping suggestive comments into their conversation. While Magpie couldn't always grasp the meaning of the embarrassing things he said to her, the look in his eyes told her everything she needed to know. The mistress was an infamous virago; if Magpie told her it would inevitably start some kind of trouble, which could turn into a public embarrassment. So she repressed her revulsion and pretended not to understand him. Once, Ding Shuze started talking about Madame Lu and Zhang Jiyuan; when he got to the racy part, he grabbed Magpie's hand and massaged it, calling her "Mama" in a low whisper.

Magpie had no choice but to complain to the mistress. She didn't expect Mrs. Ding to giggle and laugh. "Your teacher's halfway underground already. If he squeezes you a few times or says some dirty things, as long as it's not too outrageous, you might as well let him."

3

THE STUDIO was built above a pile of boulders collected from Lake Tai. A hexagonal gazebo with a stone railing stood on the slightly lower western side of the property. Besides a stone table and stools, the gazebo contained no other furniture. Two pillars displayed a couplet engraved in Father's handwriting:

> Sit facing the trees beyond the window
> Watch shadows turn across three sides

After her release from prison, when she wasn't tending her lotuses, Xiumi spent most of her time reading inside the pavilion. The uncommitted life of the recluse provided the peace she had always dreamed of. When her eyes tired, she would lie down on the table and nap for a stretch. In the afternoon, she watched the shadows slowly traverse the western face of the courtyard wall; as the weeks passed, she learned to tell the time based on their movement.

As with a sundial, using shadows to tell time requires one to account for the vicissitudes of each season and its transitions, as well as for the balance of day and night. Father once created a shadow calendar for the courtyard that incorporated such considerations. As with all of Father's writings, it had been carefully bound with a cover by Baoshen.

If the sunlight passed through the vegetation—like the morning glories, Japanese banana trees, or loquat branches—the shadows made calculating time more difficult, as each plant grew differently and produced inconsistent sizes and numbers of flowers from year to year.

Had Father merely wanted an accurate measurement of the passage of time, he could have ordered an hourglass, yet that wasn't his solution. Only the truly solitary make a careful study of time; for those who have been driven to idleness by internal torment, the situation is not so different.

Overcast or rainy days irritated Father because they made a mess of his diurnal calculations. The darkness of early dawn closely resembled evening, while the warm sunlight of an autumn afternoon could be mistaken for the new brightness of April. This confusion happened especially when one woke, consciousness still unsteady, and the scene surrounding the gazebo lured one into an immediate judgment.

Father spent countless nights sitting in the gazebo, gazing at the field of stars above him, naming the ones with visible permanence. The names he gave the stars were adopted from various sources, such as animals, flowers, and even family members or people he knew. One excerpt from his journal read:

> Baoshen and the Sow stare at each other across the Milky Way, with four stars between them: Jasmine, Ding Shuze, Ego [himself], and Goat. Ego doesn't shine brightly early on and can be very hard to see. Jasmine, Goat, and Ding Shuze stand in a triangle. Baoshen and the Sow stand South and North; they sparkle more brightly than all the other stars in the sky.

Long passages of Father's journal detailed his vibrant impressions of the passage of time. He believed that while the web of time woven by the many phases of the changing seasons, the life cycle of vegetation, and the succession of day and night appeared on its surface to be immutable, it was in fact completely reliant on the vastly different perceptions of each individual. For instance, although one hour barely exists for someone sleeping, it can feel endless to a woman in the middle of a difficult birth. Furthermore, if the sleeper has a dream within that same hour, the situation changes again. Father wrote:

Today's dream felt almost without end. All that I saw within the dream was different from the present world. A past life? A future life? I woke feeling disturbed, this emotion turning into sadness, until I found myself crying.

When he quietly followed the movement of shadows across the wall, time appeared to freeze, and "an inch or so of difference felt like a hundred years." But after a brief nap on the stone table, "I was hurled forward into evening, with darkness closing in on all sides, and my robes already damp with dew—I knew not the hour."

Besides his observations of the night sky and his detailed records of time, his journal also included various accounts, poems, and songs, as well as fragmentary, nearly incomprehensible jottings. The final entry was dated the last day of the lunar year 1878. In very small characters, Father wrote:

Heavy snows tonight. Time thrown into tangled knots, like spiderwebs or hemp strands. Nothing, nothing to be done.

Between the gazebo and the courtyard wall lay a narrow strip of open ground where Father had first planted his flower garden. Magpie had recently hoed the soil and replaced the grass and weeds with patches of garlic and spring onion and a row of chives. Only the roseleaf raspberry trellis remained where it had been originally placed, still intact, though the roseleaf had dried up long ago. Brown creeper vines still hanging on the frame shivered when the wind touched them.

Magpie came out to the rear courtyard just about every day at noon to pull up scallions and garlic. Every time she crouched down, she would raise her eyes toward the gazebo; if Xiumi was watching her, she would flash a smile. Her cheeks were pink and she moved intently, blowing by like a gust of wind, or flickering in and out of sight like a shadow. She seemed to be in a hurry all the time. Besides harvesting scallions and garlic, she fetched wood from the shed, and also climbed the studio steps to help Xiumi clean her chambers, or to give her some seeds or bulbs she bought at the market.

In the evenings, when the setting sun turned the grasses and vines on the western wall a fiery orange, Xiumi would come down from her room and stand concealed among the roseleaf trellis, the wood-shed, and the bamboo grove. If the courtyard had not been swept before the last rainfall, the heavy carpet of decaying leaves cushioning her feet and the bright green clumps of moss filling the spaces around her would enclose her in a verdant tranquility.

Once the lotus flowers withered, Xiumi thought of chrysanthe-mums; sadly, all she could find were a few wild clumps hiding in the corners of the courtyard wall. Their alternate leaves and tight clusters of buds bloomed pale white or yellow, like the color of jasmine, without fragrance. Xiumi very cautiously dug one up and transplanted it into a terra-cotta pot, which she placed in a shady spot beneath the studio. Though she cared for it faithfully, it died in a mere few days. Meanwhile, flowering plants like asters, nadina, shameplants, eupa-torium, and others grew everywhere. Wang Shimao in *On Learning to Garden* called each of these plants chrysanthemums—"timber chrysanthemums," "Bodhisattva chrysanthemums," "brocade-ball chrysanthemums," et cetera, though none actually belong to the chrysanthemum family. At the height of autumn, the petals of all these flowers fell. The red persimmon trees, the two sweet olive trees, and the yellow cockscombs seeded in late October, when the bright-est spot in Xiumi's vigilantly supervised courtyard was the impatiens along the courtyard wall.

After many years on their own, the row of impatiens seemed on the verge of disappearing, their red stems exposed and their leaves torn into sawtooth edges by the beaks of hungry chickens. Xiumi combined yellow earth with fine sand and packed the mixture around the roots, which she then nourished with the rinse water from rice, along with chicken manure and ground soybeans. She killed the earthworms with lime. After a month's worth of work, when the autumn breezes turned cool and the first frosts approached, their leaves turned from yellow to green. After a cold shower of rain, they actually flowered—

a spectacular panoply of purple shades interspersed with red. Single blossoms opened first, too spare to make an impression. Xiumi nipped off the withered buds at evening and tied the plants to bamboo stakes. The cluster of opened flowers gradually thickened, until new stamens and pistils crowded together in soft spheres and blooms raced up every stalk, their colors flagrantly alluring.

In those days, Xiumi would spend whole afternoons crouching among the impatiens, forgetting herself as she gazed at them, as if lost in deep thought. One night in late September, she drank a little too much tea in the evening, and lay awake long after dark. At midnight, she abandoned the pursuit of sleep and got up, throwing on some clothing and descending the stairs with a lantern in hand to check on her flowers. A night breeze gently stirred the petals and leaves, making the beads of dew on them glitter. Beneath the gleaming surface, the ground at the edge of the wall was the domain of insects. That world teemed with active life, as lacewing flies, crickets, ladybugs, spiders, and goldwing beetles flapped and clambered among the stalks, wings ruffling. These insects charmed Xiumi immediately, particularly one shiny Japanese beetle, which rode its partner's back in a slow ascent up the stalk of a flower. Meanwhile, an innumerable party of ants carried a gigantic flower petal in a stop-and-start procession that reminded Xiumi of the flower-wreath bearers in a funeral.

Although this realm of insects was isolated, it was as wholly sufficient in every aspect as the world of humans. If a diving beetle were to find his path blocked by fallen flower petals, might he accidentally wander into a Peach Blossom Paradise, like the fisherman in the story?

Xiumi felt as if she herself were an ant lost among the flowers. Every facet of her life was inconsequential, quotidian, and without meaning, yet also permanently visible, and unforgettable.

She remembered how she often saw Lilypad collect impatiens petals in a clay bowl, add a pinch of potash alum, and mortar them into a paste. Then she would sit against the courtyard wall with her legs crossed and paint her fingernails with the paste. As she painted, she would say to Magpie, "You're washing the dishes tonight. I'm just doing my nails now, and they can't get wet."

She remembered Mother explaining that they were called impatiens because they were, in fact, impatient—once their seedpods filled out like green plums in early fall, they would explode when you touched them, the pod curling up like a fist while black seeds shot out everywhere. Mother once slid the burst pods onto her earlobes, one per ear, like a pair of earrings. "This is your wedding jewelry," she said. Xiumi could even recall Mother's warm breath tickling her ear as she said it.

She remembered how the village doctor, Tang Liushi, used to go around collecting flower petals and seeds when the fall mornings grew colder, to brew into medicinal tinctures. According to the doctor, the serum he made with impatiens could cure difficult pregnancies, white spots on the throat, and several other maladies. But Xiumi's father didn't put much stock in impatiens as an herbal cure; his opinion was that generations of quack doctors had been fooled by Li Shizhen's *Compendium of Materia Medica*. After all, it was said that Tang Liushi's first wife had died of complications during pregnancy.

She remembered that her teacher, Ding Shuze, also grew impatiens at home, only his were grown in pots, not along a wall. His cloudy eyes grew distant and distracted every time they flowered. He said that impatiens were pretty but fragile at heart; beautiful, and as bewitching as any peach or plum blossom, but could be content with a quiet birth and death in a secluded corner, uninterested in flaunting their colors or attracting bees, giving them an aura of virginal modesty.

I see, now I understand . . .

These past events, which Xiumi had not consciously brought forth, or even thought she had experienced, now tumbled one after another in her mind. She saw how poignant and incontrovertible even the most mundane details could be as constituents of her memory. Each one summoned another in an endless and unpredictable sequence. And what was more, she could never tell which memory particle would sting the soft places in her heart, make her cheeks scald and her eyes brim with tears, just as the gray embers of the winter hearth do not announce which one of them can still burn your fingers.

4

As AUTUMN advanced, the number of visitors to the estate increased. Some arrived in traditional Manchu gowns and vests, and did a lot of bowing and scraping, while others strutted in wearing expensive Western suits and addressed everyone as "Miss" this or "Missus" that. Pistol-clad soldiers and cane-wielding scholars all dropped by, frequently with protective entourages; ragged beggars also showed up in torn clothes and wide straw hats to shield their faces. Xiumi refused to see anyone.

Magpie ran back and forth passing notes between the two sides. Most of the visitors, on reading Xiumi's response, would shake their heads, sigh, and leave disappointed. Some stayed firm, demanding that Magpie pass several notes for them, yet they soon discovered that Xiumi would stop replying. Then they'd wait until their tea went cold and evening fell, and eventually would have no choice but to leave.

Magpie initially treated the visitors with the utmost politeness, offering a seat and a cup of tea; when they left, she would see them off and apologize on behalf of her mistress. But once she saw how each visitation wiped out Xiumi's appetite for days and even invited fits of silent tears, Magpie began to view the guests with contempt and active disgust, her patience gradually wearing away. She stopped announcing new arrivals to Xiumi, and stonewalled each visitor with the announcement that "the mistress isn't at home," while pushing the guest physically out the door.

Where did all these people come from, anyway? Magpie wondered. Why did they want to see her mistress? And why did Xiumi refuse to see them without even asking who they were? She asked these questions directly to her teacher.

Ding Shuze replied, "Most of them are probably old acquaintances of Xiumi's, people who kept close contact with her before the revolution. After the first two attempts failed, Yuan Shikai became the man of the hour, and the activists from the southern parties scattered—some to Beiping and some to other places. A few played their cards right and got reborn as military governors, chiefs of staff, or colonels. Others fell into the underworld, or hid in the ranks of commoners and beggars. Some are probably coming to ask her for help, some to flaunt their newfound power and strut their stuff on their home streets, and some are probably only here on personal business, for no other reason but to see an old friend. Of course, all these reasons might just be excuses. Doubtless, her beauty is the real reason so many of them have come from so far at such considerable expense."

"Do you really think Xiumi is that beautiful?" Magpie asked curiously.

"To be honest, she is beautiful to a degree that these tired eyes have rarely witnessed. Even after she's shut her door and turned away from the outside world, she still attracts a swarm of wandering bees and butterflies." Ding Shuze stole a glance at Magpie, then took her hand in his and patted it gently, whispering, "But you, my dear, are easy on the eyes as well..."

At the start of winter, a middle-aged man in a felt hat found his way to Puji following the tail end of a silent blizzard. He looked around forty-five, with a wild mustache and beard that spanned half of his face. He entered the estate covered with snow from head to foot. His padded jacket had worn through at the shoulders, so that the cotton lining puffed out, and he wore only thin trousers and cloth shoes. The buttons on his jacket had all fallen off; it was secured with a length of white cord tied hastily at the waist. He walked with a slight hitch in his gait, and carried an old bag made of woven reeds in one hand. He started shouting for Xiumi to come out and talk to him the minute he strolled through the door; while he waited, he warmed his fingers with his breath and stamped his feet. When Magpie received him with the usual excuses, he opened his round eyes wide and declared in a stentorian voice, "You just go tell her that I have six fingers on my left hand and she'll see me."

Hearing this, Magpie retreated into the rear courtyard.

Xiumi was arranging freshly cut sprigs of winter plum in a vase, their heavy scent permeating the room. Magpie repeated to Xiumi what the man outside had said to her. Xiumi continued to arrange the flowering branches, as if she had heard nothing at all. Every blossom that dropped onto the table she picked up and put into a bowl of clear water. Magpie watched the blossoms float in circles like little golden bells; she didn't know what to do.

She returned to the front courtyard moments later with a made-up excuse. "My mistress is feeling poorly today, so she can't see guests. You should probably go home."

This made the guest furious, and his beard shook as he said, "What? She won't see me? Not even *me*, for God's sake? You go back and tell her it's Dapples. Dapples!"

Magpie hurried back upstairs to relay this new information. But Xiumi seemed to pay even less attention to whether it was Dapples or Apples or Maples than she had before, and simply stared at Magpie without saying anything. So Magpie returned to the visitor once more, shaking her head in silence. She expected that such a surly, impatient man would surely fly into a profane rage at her refusal. Instead, his temper deflated. He tossed his cattail bag onto the floor and rubbed his forehead in confusion. After a long pause, he reached into a pocket of his jacket with a trembling hand and brought out a small object wrapped in a handkerchief, which he passed to Magpie with a smile. "If your mistress can't see me, then I'll be on my way. But please give this to her. The country's a republic now; I have no need to hold on to this cursed thing, so I'll leave it with her. She can always sell it for some cash in an emergency."

Magpie accepted the object and ran upstairs. Xiumi was busy separating the stamens of her plum blossoms with a sewing needle, her lips pursed in something like a tight smile. Magpie put the object on the table and went back downstairs without addressing her, but when she reached the bottom, Xiumi came racing down after her, the handkerchief in her hand. By the time they both passed the guest room, they could see Dapples had left.

Magpie opened the cattail bag and found a couple of strips of dried fish, a string of preserved sausages, and a few sections of bamboo shoots. Xiumi stood in the front doorway and looked out. The snow was falling fast already; no human form was visible through the flying flakes.

The handkerchief held a golden cicada, exactly identical to the one buried with Little Thing.* *Who knew that two rare objects so completely alike could exist!* Magpie thought. The cicadas were an intimation to Magpie of the size and mystery of the outside world. All the doors to that world seemed closed to her, and she knew neither where they led to nor the reasons why they existed—just like her mistress's silence.

Who was the middle-aged man Dapples? Where had he come from? What did the cicada stand for, and why did it make Xiumi cry to see it? And why did she forgo a perfectly good life as a rich man's wife to go mess around with revolution? Needless to say, Xiumi's world was utterly inaccessible to Magpie, even at its farthest reaches. It seemed to her like everyone was surrounded and tied down by a

---

*Zhou Yichun (1865–1937), known as Dapples, went to Japan in the summer of 1898 to study. He returned to China in 1901 and devoted himself to revolutionary activism, cofounding the Cicadas and Crickets Society with Zhang Jiyuan, Tong Lannian, and others. Zhou orchestrated a successful outlaw uprising at Huajiashe in 1905, then led an assault on Meicheng in the spring of the following year, besieging the town for twenty-seven days before being injured and subsequently captured. After the Republican Revolution, he was hired as a staff officer in Gu Zhongshen's Yangtze River Army. One year later, in December 1912, he returned to Huajiashe and opened a school. In August 1937, as the Japanese army advanced on Nanjing, he and a handful of students with long rifles barricaded the road. When his ammunition ran out, he continued to shout down the enemy before dying of multiple gunshot wounds.

whole assortment of causes, and she was no different. The moment Xiumi tried to escape from her cloistered world, her efforts evaporated like a drop of water on hot iron. Outside the window, snow was falling and falling, faster and faster, and the multitude of snowflakes seemed uninterested in her questions.

By the time of Dapples's appearance, Magpie had already learned to read many words; as her teacher said, she was already "half a literary lady." Before her studies had started, she spent most of her time with the pigs, geese, ducks, and chickens, or running between the market and the milliner's or the rice chandler's, and never thought herself unhappy. Once she learned to read and write a little, new problems started to crop up.

Xiumi began spending more time in the front courtyard. When Magpie cooked meals, Xiumi helped her keep the fire going; when she went to feed the pigs, Xiumi followed along to watch. That winter, the sow had another litter of piglets, and Xiumi spent the entire evening with her in the overpowering stench of the pigpen. Every time another piglet was born, Magpie would smile, and Xiumi would smile with her. It appeared that they both liked the animals. Xiumi washed the blood off the newborn piglets with a cloth soaked in hot water and wrung out so as to avoid burning their tender skin. She even picked them up and rocked them to sleep like babies.

Xiumi was already used to washing her own clothes, cleaning her own room, and dumping her own chamber pot. She later learned to plant vegetables, hull rice, make sticky-rice cakes, cut shoe patterns, and sew shoe soles. She even learned to tell the difference between male and female chickens at a glance. She still didn't speak.

One day, Magpie went to the market and didn't come home until after nightfall. To her astonishment, she found Xiumi waiting for her in the lamplit kitchen with dinner already made. Her face and hands were black with soot. Though the rice was burned and the vegetable dishes much too salty, a tearful Magpie energetically shoveled the food into her mouth until her stomach nearly burst as a show of gratitude. Afterward, Xiumi pushed her out of the kitchen so she could do the dishes, and ended up knocking a hole in the iron wok with the spatula.

Magpie observed that Xiumi was growing a little plumper, and her cheeks glowed a healthy pink. She would frequently stare at Magpie for no reason and smile. She just wouldn't talk; nor had she taken a single step outside the estate since her arrival from prison. Even when Hua Erniang's son got married and repeatedly invited Xiumi over for celebratory drinks, she merely smiled in reply.

One quiet winter evening after the day's work, the two sat together in the main hall doing needlework. Though the northwest wind howled outside, the fire in the stove burned brightly. The two women would occasionally look over at each other and smile; the room was so quiet you could hear the snowflakes brushing the window paper. Magpie looked out at the snow filling the windowsill and thought, *Wouldn't it be so nice if she weren't mute and could talk to me? I have so, so much to tell her. If Xiumi wanted to, I could stay with her like this until dawn.*

A new desire stirred in Magpie's breast, and turned into a daring idea. Mr. Ding had been teaching her for nearly six months, and she could write a number of words now. Why not write down what she wanted to say on paper, and talk that way? If she wrote anything wrong, Xiumi could correct it for her. It would help her learn faster. She blushed deeply as she sneaked a look at Xiumi. Xiumi noticed the color in her cheeks and turned her eyes up to her with a quizzical expression.

Magpie's idea kept her excited the rest of the night. Finally, by noon of the following day, she could hold it in no longer. She clenched her teeth, breathed in deeply, and scampered up the penthouse stairs to Xiumi's room. She lay a piece of workbook paper in front of Xiumi, on which she had written: "What do you want to eat this evening? I wrote these words myself."

Xiumi stared at the paper in awe, then looked back at Magpie with disbelief. She ground her inkstone in some water and picked up a brush. Turning to look once more at Magpie, she very carefully wrote a single character in reply.

One look at the character Xiumi had written made Magpie's eyes cross. She picked up the paper and took it back to her room to study, but she could not for the life of her figure out what it meant. It made her angry. She felt like Xiumi must have intentionally written a really difficult character for her; she thought Xiumi must be confusing her intentionally as a way of teasing her. The character contained so many strokes, like a hurricane of sweeping black lines. No human could read a character like that! Maybe not even Mr. Ding.

When Magpie showed the character to her teacher, Ding Shuze pulled his wooden back-scratcher out through his shirt collar and rapped her hard on the head. "How do you not know that one, bonehead! It's the character for 'congee'!"

5

FOR THE sake of Magpie's studies, she and Xiumi began a written correspondence. Xiumi assiduously corrected her miswritten characters and grammatical errors. Their conversations generally focused on trivial aspects of daily life: crops, meals, planting flowers and vegetables, and of course the market. Eventually they moved on to different subjects, which introduced new information, such as:

> —It's snowing again today.
> —It sure is.

> —The neighbor's new wife has pockmarks on her face.
> —Does she?
> —She does.

> —Mr. Ding is sick again. He has an open sore on his back.
> —Oh.

Most of their exchange was surely inspired by boredom. Midwinter days were short and the nights long, and Magpie needed to talk about something to endure the loneliness. Yet Xiumi often provided only perfunctory, one- or two-word answers. Xiumi would occasionally start an exchange herself, with questions like, "Do you know where I can get a winter plum tree around here?" She was still thinking about flowers. But this was winter—the vegetation had long since withered and died back, the earth covered in layers of ice and snow. Where would she ever find a plum tree?

Conversing through a writing brush made Magpie happy; there was something strangely exciting about it. But as the two of them spent more and more of their time together, she found that situations in which conversation was truly necessary didn't arise so often. Eye contact was much more efficient than talking, and there were plenty of times when one look was all one of them needed to know what the other was thinking.

It was still snowing on New Year's Eve; Magpie and Xiumi were busy preparing the traditional celebratory meal for the following day. Afterward, the two of them lit the charcoal bricks in the brazier in Magpie's bedroom and crawled into bed. Though a frigid wind blew outside, the bedroom stayed toasty warm, red reflections of the fire dancing on the walls. Magpie had never been so close to Xiumi's body. She had come to think of Xiumi like an infant who needed her care and protection; the idea brought her security and peace. The room got so warm and the two of them lay so still that soon Magpie began to sweat. Fortunately, a cold draft seeped through the molding around the skylight above and floated down right above her nose.

When it turned midnight, and New Year's firecrackers popped through the neighborhood, Magpie still couldn't sleep. She felt Xiumi's toes brush against her upper arm. Assuming it was unintentional, she pretended not to notice, until moments later she felt her arm being poked again.

"You still awake?" Magpie asked her, completely ignorant as to what Xiumi wanted.

To Magpie's surprise, Xiumi tossed her covers off and crawled over to her end of the bed. The two lay shoulder to shoulder as Magpie's heart raced. Charcoal snapped loudly in the basin; snowflakes rushed onto the roof tiles. She sensed through the darkness that Xiumi was crying. Extending a hand to touch her cheek, Magpie felt fresh tears. Xiumi reached out and touched Magpie's face, too; she gently pulled Xiumi's head to her chest.

Xiumi curled into her embrace and sobbed until her whole body shook; Magpie patted her shoulder until Xiumi's distress slowly subsided and she fell fast asleep. Magpie, though, stayed awake. Her shoulder fell asleep under the weight of Xiumi's head, and her long hair tickled Magpie's nose, yet she didn't move, forcing herself to remain perfectly still. When Xiumi had touched her face a moment earlier, Magpie felt a weird, complicated sweetness—something very, very deep in her had been affected. She had never experienced such emotions before. Only when a rogue snowflake that had slipped through the skylight dropped onto her cheek did she realize how hot her face had become.

When Magpie woke up the next morning, she discovered that Xiumi wasn't in bed. She dressed herself and went into the kitchen. Xiumi, wearing a cloth apron, smiled at her with her head cocked to one side—a smile that looked different from any other she had given her. Magpie opened her mouth to speak, but her heart was so full she became dizzy and no words came out. She sighed to herself and wondered, *What's going on here?*

Neither of them said much that first day of the new year, though they spent the day together. Wherever Xiumi went, Magpie followed her, and vice versa. One of them could be in the front courtyard and the other in the rear, and soon they would find themselves sitting next to each another.

In a flash, three years passed.

A shower of rain one evening brought with it an unexpected peal of thunder. Xiumi enthusiastically copied out a line of poetry for Magpie to read. It went: *Beyond the lotus pool echoes distant thunder.*

Magpie had a taste for literature by then. Although she didn't know that Li Shangyin had written the line, she knew it was poetry—the stuff scholars made up after dinner when they had nothing better to do. She took the paper and studied the line closely until she finally began to understand the meaning of the words. Though the pond outside didn't have any lotuses, there were a few ducks in it currently shedding their feathers, and the thunder in the sky was real enough. Such an ordinary, insignificant sentence, but when you thought about it long enough, there really was something ineffable about it. The more she pondered the verse the more she liked it. The air felt fresher in her nostrils, and she couldn't help but admit to herself that maybe not all the poets in the world were idiots. Maybe all their chanting and rhapsodizing had a higher purpose hidden within.

Magpie quietly asked Xiumi if she would teach her to write poetry. Xiumi ignored her at first, but Magpie wore her down. Xiumi thought for a moment, then wrote the first line of a couplet for Magpie to match: *Apricot flowers spring rains southern banks.*

Magpie received this as if it were a priceless treasure; she took it back to her room to plumb its mysteries. Just looking at the line made her feel good. Apricot flowers were a common enough sight in the village; Grandma Meng had an apricot tree outside her door. As for spring rains, well, those started to drizzle down in early March and just kept falling. "Southern banks" here obviously meant the southern banks of the Yangtze River, the area around Puji and Meicheng. But the meaning of the three images seemed to change the instant you placed them together in one line, like making a painting you couldn't physically see but only imagine. *How wonderful, wonderful! Who knew poetry could be so easy.* Magpie laughed to herself. She felt she could write this kind of poetry too if it merely consisted of putting three random things together.

That night, Magpie lay in bed and thought until her brain nearly fell out of her skull. Then she sat up and threw the blankets around her, scolding herself for acting crazy from just trying to think of a single line. Around midnight she finally constructed a matching couplet, but when she counted the characters in her line, it didn't match the length of Xiumi's. Her line ran, *Rooster hen and chicken eggs.* Even after she cut out the "and," it still looked off; she thought it was horrible. Xiumi's line was so refined and refreshing, and hers? It smelled vaguely of chicken shit.

Exhausted, she slumped over her makeup table and fell sleep. She dreamt of a rooster and a hen that clucked incessantly. The hen laid an egg. Her dream felt heavy, and long. When she lifted her head, morning had arrived. Lamp ash covered the table, morning light filled the room, and a morning chill gripped her whole body.

A white porcelain bowl with a few newly picked purple bayberries had been placed on the table; Xiumi must have come over at some point. *Why didn't she wake me up?* Magpie wondered. She picked up a bayberry and put it into her mouth, and while sucking on it, she noticed her rooster poem on the table. Her face flushed, and in the midst of her burning embarrassment, she thought of a good line. Perhaps out of fear that the words would fly out of her brain like a bird, she hurriedly ground some ink, unfurled a new sheet of paper, and wrote it down. Before the ink had dried, it was on its way to Xiumi. But Xiumi was suddenly nowhere to be found. Magpie stormed around the courtyard, calling her name and complaining, until she finally discovered her underneath the roseleaf trellis. Flowers had bloomed from the thirty or forty pots and now covered the bottom of the trellis; Xiumi was pruning stems and leaves with gloved hands and a pair of scissors. When Magpie handed over her line of poetry, Xiumi first looked at it in surprise, then turned to look at Magpie, as if unable to believe she had really written it: *Lamp ash winter snow endless nights.**

That evening, Xiumi brought Magpie down a copy of Li Shangyin's collected poems from the studio library. It was one of Father's few thirteenth-century woodblock-printed editions, its pages of tiny printed characters chaotically interspersed with Father's own handwritten marginalia, in-line notes, and poetic responses. But clearly, Li Shangyin's poetry was still too difficult for Magpie to understand at that stage. Immortal maidens seemed to float in and out of the lines as they pleased, and Magpie couldn't make sense out of much

---

*Shen Xiaoque (1879–1953), also known as Magpie, was born in the Shen family court in Dapu village, Xinghua Township. She moved to Puji around the turn of the century. Never married, Magpie learned to read in her thirties, and later composed over three hundred and sixty poems. Her poetic style, informed by classical masters like Wen Tingyun and Li Shangyin, is known for its metrical sensitivity, buoyant lyricism, and formal virtuosity, and occasionally touches on Buddhist and Taoist themes. Her collection *Lamp Ashes* is still extant.

of the verse. She lay on her bamboo mat in the sweltering summer heat, flipping through the pages, picking out lines about rain and snow that spoke to her: "Your red chambers look colder through the rain," "Our emissaries not yet returned across snowy peaks," "A spring of soft rains misting my roof," and so on. While she couldn't quite tell what the ancient poet was talking about, it was the perfect distraction from the torturous climate.

Late one night, while a sudden downpour drummed the roof above her, Magpie came to a poem called "Untitled," with the line "Golden toad bites the lock; burning perfume enters." For some reason, old Master Lu had drawn little circles beside "golden toad." Magpie recognized the character for "toad," though it was a rare one—why would the master want to highlight it? In the margin next to the poem she found a brief note:

> Golden cicada
> Enters—any woman, even the most faithful or virtuous
> Who is Zhang Jiyuan?

This startled her. Granted, Magpie couldn't fully grasp the meaning of the original poem (what did he mean by "golden toad bites the lock, burning perfume enters" anyway?), but the master's annotation, though nonsensical, did suggest a connection between the line, Zhang Jiyuan, and the gold cicada figurine. Magpie recalled that Zhang Jiyuan had arrived in Puji after the master went crazy and ran away—so how could the master have known about him? And why "golden cicada"? Of course, the characters for "toad" and "cicada" were pronounced the same way, and perhaps that was the reason. But thinking of the cicada that Little Thing took to his grave and the one the strange visitor had left them years ago produced a cold lump in her stomach.

Thunder and lightning crashed outside as the storm surged directly above them. Magpie's single lamp flickered amid layers of phantasmal shadow. Was Master Lu's insanity somehow connected to Zhang Jiyuan? Magpie couldn't bring herself to think about it further; it almost felt like the old man was standing right behind her. She closed the book, feeling no desire to open it again, and huddled quietly beside the table. Once the rain let up, with the book clutched in her arms, she ran to the back of the estate to talk to Xiumi.

Xiumi was still awake, seated at her table and staring blankly at the enameled-copper basin Magpie had used to ferment pickles. After her return home, Xiumi had emptied it, cleaned it out, and taken it back to the studio. She had a weird look in her eyes and her face was a greenish hue. Opening the book, Magpie flipped to the poem "Untitled" and pointed out the note to Xiumi. Xiumi took the book and gave it one indifferent glance before closing it and tossing it aside. Bitter resentment was apparent in her frigid expression.

She turned once more to the basin. She flicked its side lightly with a fingernail, then bent her head to bring her ear closer. Ripples of sound expanded into the rain and empty darkness like the peals of a temple bell. Xiumi tapped the basin over and over, as tearstains smeared the heavy layer of powder on her cheeks. Then she looked up at Magpie and stuck her tongue out like a willful child.

At that moment, Magpie felt as if Xiumi had transformed into her original self.

6

MAGPIE had visited Mr. Ding's house less often the last few years. She still stopped in on holidays and sent him the large eggs he liked so much every month without fail. Naturally, this gave Ding Shuze no cause to complain, but Mrs. Ding still came running to the estate every now and then to fetch her, each time stumbling over her bound feet in awkward haste and yelling, "Quickly, quickly, your teacher's in bad shape" the moment she stepped through the door. And each time Magpie would run back with her, only to find Ding Shuze lying in bed, humming an opera tune. Yet in November of that year, Ding Shuze really was in bad shape. Once again, Mrs. Ding came by with the news, but only got as far as "That old devil..." before she burst into tears.

Ding Shuze lay supine on his bamboo bed, his belly distended, skin tight as a drum. His bedroom was crowded with people: Dr. Tang, Hua Erniang, Grandma Meng, and two relatives who had traveled to see him stood silently by the bedside, waiting for Mr. Ding to breathe his last breath. According to his wife, the teacher had not had a full bowel movement since the height of summer. Eight straight days of drinking the broth Dr. Tang prescribed—a concoction of fibrous laxatives like aloe root, lotus leaf, and rhubarb—had no effect at all. His eyes half-closed, Mr. Ding had been panting and kicking his legs through the afternoon into evening. Eventually, even his wife couldn't bear it any longer; with tears in her eyes, she bent down and whispered in her husband's ear:

"Shuze, just let go. Holding on like this won't do you any good. If you go before me, at least you'll have someone to see you off. If I die first, you won't even have anyone here to feed you."

At his wife's exhortation, Mr. Ding obediently calmed down. And yet he managed to raise one trembling, emaciated hand to slap the mattress three times, causing everyone in the room to look at one another in confusion. But his wife knew him better than anyone else; lifting the mattress, she found a folded piece of bamboo paper. She unfolded it, and handed it to Grandma Meng to look at.

"Ah ... Mr. Ding wrote his own epitaph."

"That's just like him to be so thorough," Hua Erniang said with a smile. "There's no one else in Puji who can write one of those except for Mr. Ding."

"There are plenty of people who can write epitaphs," Doctor Tang replied with a mirthless half smile, "but my guess is that he didn't trust anybody else to do it for him. He had written tomb inscriptions his whole life, and when he got to his own, he couldn't leave it for someone else."*

The others continued to argue as Mrs. Ding threw herself over the body and began to cry. Doctor Tang took his pulse and announced, "He's cold."

*

*Ding Shuze wrote his own epitaph. The text is a perfect copy of the Tang dynasty luminary Chen Zi'ang's "Epitaph for My Younger Brother." It reads:

A solitary child, he was gifted with a courageous, upright nature and a beautiful brilliance that set him apart. Though serious and fastidious, he admired unrestrained originality; though honest and disciplined, he was not aggressively solitary. Having first mastered the classics of poetry and rites, he perused the histories and biographies, and immediately harbored dreams of bringing order to all things and rising above all others of his age. To that end, he never spoke a promise he wouldn't keep, or compromised his principles for temporary gain. He controlled his body and mind, committed himself to studying the Way, and revered morality. His female relations lived harmoniously, and his comrades acted with courtesy. In truth, he was strong in the accomplishment of justice, brave in the preservation of compassion, faithful in the support of enterprise, and determined in his adherence to morality. He made his decisions in his heart and acted of his own volition. Truly he was esteemed by all, and none dared to compare themselves to him.

The departure of schoolmaster Ding Shuze at the impressive age of eighty-seven gave the funeral proceedings something of a festival air. His wife's wailings, even at their most extreme, never strayed far from the mention of money. Local dignitaries paid for his coffin and engraved headstone, and also hired Buddhist monks and Taoist priests to perform the necessary rites. By chance, an opera troupe from Zhengzhou was passing through, so interested parties hired them to perform in the village for three days. Diviners and geomancers dropped by to contribute their ritual expertise, while friends and neighbors provided enough money and food to make the event exciting as well as respectable. The funeral lunch alone fed over thirty tablesful of guests, more than two hundred people.

Grandma Meng said to Magpie, "You were one of his official students, and a tutor for a day is a father forever, so they say, so you shouldn't avoid your responsibilities."

To which Mrs. Ding forcibly objected, "You know, by rights, Xiumi was a student of his, too."

Hua Erniang replied, "There's no use in picking a fight with a mute like her." So Magpie accompanied Grandma Meng and Hua Erniang to help with the Ding household, leaving home before dawn and coming home after nightfall, on top of her daily workload.

In the later hours of one such exhausting evening, Magpie decided to run home to check on things there. As she was leaving the Ding family's courtyard, she noticed a group of people in tattered clothing eating and drinking at a round dinner table beneath the trees by the wall. They were beggars who had followed the smell of food and drink to the party but couldn't be seated with the other guests, so the family had provided them with their own table, amply supplied with rice and simple vegetable dishes. Many of them shouted and pushed one another; one small child climbed onto the table to shovel rice from the serving bowl directly into his mouth.

But one beggar in a hempen robe and a battered straw hat with a dog-beating nightstick clutched under his armpit was sitting quietly as if thinking of something. Magpie thought it strange, and so examined him closely. After she got home and lit the fire under the stove, she suddenly felt like she had seen the beggar's face before, but couldn't remember where. She was so unsettled that she put the fire out again and returned to the Ding estate to look at him once more. But when she got to the house, the beggar had already gone.

On the day of the funeral procession, the strange figure reappeared. He was crouched under the eaves of a neighbor's house, his back against the wall as he wolfed down mouthfuls of steamed bread. The straw hat lay low over his face, and the nightstick was still tucked under one arm. His hands were bony and tanned almost to black. Magpie couldn't see his eyes. She definitely recognized him from somewhere. She continued to walk around with Grandma Meng, carrying a reed basket of flower corsages for the procession and helping to pass them out. The flowers were either white or yellow and made of paper. Magpie quietly went through a mental list of all the people she knew, but couldn't come up with a match; she decided to get near him and look more closely. Yet every step she took toward the beggar, the other moved a step along the wall away from her. As Magpie quickened her pace, the beggar did the same, and soon ran for the village outskirts while keeping one eye on Magpie. This meant not only that the beggar recognized Magpie, but also that he was afraid she would recognize him. She chased him all the way to the edge of the village; only when she saw him take the high road to Meicheng did she stop to catch her breath and rub her lower back as she watched him go. The incident bothered her for several days—she couldn't get the beggar's familiar visage out of her head.

He wasn't the only irritation she had to deal with. The second day after the funeral, an ill wind from somewhere blew in an epidemic of bird flu that killed every single one of the twenty-plus chickens she had worked so hard to raise. Magpie boiled and plucked them all, then brined about half, sending a few of these to Grandma Meng and Hua Erniang.

Grandma Meng laughed. "Mr. Ding sure is a lucky man—he dies, and every chicken in the village dies with him. Just think, if he were still alive, how would you get him his eggs?"

In August, the red dates ripened. Magpie awoke one morning to find Xiumi had gone out. She looked all around the estate for her, but Xiumi was nowhere to be found. Magpie counted the days and realized that today was market day; could she have gone to the market in Changzhou by herself? By noon, Xiumi still hadn't returned and Magpie couldn't wait anymore—she hurried off to the market alone. But the vendors were already closing shop when she got there. She peered into dark corners and asked everyone she knew if they had seen Xiumi—no luck. Dusk forced her to head home.

Entering the village, she saw Hua Erniang and her sons shaking dates off the trees. When the old lady noticed Magpie's beleaguered state, she motioned her over with a nod and a smile. She told Magpie that when she heard Xiumi had gone missing, she and Grandma Meng went to look for her.

"She hadn't actually gone anywhere; she spent the whole day sitting by Little Thing's grave. We convinced her to come back, and she's now home, lying down."

Hearing this, Magpie could feel her anxiety dissipate. As she walked home, she heard Hua Erniang say behind her back, "Isn't it a little late to finally be thinking of that poor child?"

Magpie found Xiumi fast asleep in the studio; only then could she finally relax. But something even stranger would happen that same night.

Magpie made dinner, but Xiumi stayed in bed and wouldn't come down. Magpie swallowed a few hasty mouthfuls of rice and went up to the studio to spend the night with her. Xiumi appeared to be crying: her pillowcase and the edge of her blanket were wet. Magpie thought, *Maybe she saw the village families visiting the graves for the Mid-Autumn Festival and couldn't help thinking of Little Thing.* The memory of Little Thing brought endless tears to her own eyes. She had heard that Xiumi had given birth to another child in prison, but no one knew if the child survived. The child would be around Little Thing's age if alive now. Ferryman Tan Shuijin had sworn it was the child of his son Tan Si, and tried to track the baby down as best he could. He said he'd even sell his boat if it meant getting the child back. But with the mother now mute, what could he do? She met his every word with closed lips and a steely expression. Magpie recalled these painful events and cried with Xiumi for a while. Then she took off her shoes and socks, blew out the lamp, and lay down beside her to sleep.

At midnight, a long, low moan reached Magpie's ears through her sleep.

The sound frightened her awake. Who was moaning? The sound had been low but clear, as if it came from a long way off. Magpie sat up in bed, lit the lamp, and turned to Xiumi. But Xiumi seemed fast asleep, her teeth grinding off and on. Now filled with suspicion, Magpie crept to the studio door and peered outside: the moon hung half-concealed behind clouds, trees swayed noisily in the wind, but there was no sign of anyone. Could her ears have tricked her, or had she heard the sound in a dream? Her heart still felt uneasy.

Magpie went back to bed and was about to drift off to sleep again when she heard Xiumi roll over and say in a clear, loud voice:

"Ahhh ... his face isn't warm, that's why the snow piles up."

This time Magpie heard every word, though she could barely believe her ears.

Too weird, too weird ... she can still talk after all! She wasn't mute! So she had been ...

Magpie sat in bed hugging her knees to her chest, her body chilled as if with fever. An hour or so passed and she listened to Xiumi's snoring abate and her teeth start to grind once more; Magpie's nerves slowly calmed down.

She tricked me for three and a half years! If she hadn't exposed herself by talking in her sleep, she might have kept it up for the rest of my life. But what did she mean, anyway? I'll have to sit her down and confront her when she wakes up tomorrow.

Yet when she ran into Xiumi under the roseleaf trellis the next morning, she abruptly changed her mind.

7

SPRING breezes returned in February and March, turning the water in the fishpond green during the incessant mist and rains. Water droplets fell like needles in bursts of showers from early March to the Tomb-Sweeping Festival in mid-April. When sunnier days returned, Xiumi discovered that the many potted plums she had planted under the roseleaf trellis had all bloomed.

The wild plums displayed only a few gently fragrant blossoms that burst through delicate buds and dotted their slender branches in a pleasing pattern. The wild hybrids, by contrast, produced many blooms with fleshy, layered petals and pale gold centers thick with fine stamens. The other varieties—the Hunan plum, Green Sepal, Mille Fleur, Mandarin Duck, Apricot Air, and the rest—reached outward in diverse bouquets of flower-laden branches that quivered in the breeze. Their colors ranged from reds and purples to soft whites, their scents from heavy to faint, yet all were growing enthusiastically and competing among themselves to be the greatest spectacle.

Several years of careful cultivation had resulted in over a hundred different flowering plants in the garden beneath the roseleaf trellis. In spring bloomed crab apples, plums, peonies, perilla, and rambler rose; in summer, hibiscus, hollyhocks, and pomegranates; in fall, royal jasmine, sweet olive, eupatorium, and impatiens; while winter featured the winter plum and narcissus. It was customary among the locals in Puji to grow narcissus in the winter. They would buy a bulb or two at the market, sometime after midwinter, placing each in a bowlful of water that they would fill with river stones and set beside a well-lit window; soon, flowers would bloom boldly against the snow outside. Winter plums were more difficult to procure. In his classic handbook *On Plums*, Fan Chengda notes that the winter plum is not actually a plum; it is named thus because it behaves so much like one, its honeycomb-shaped blossom opening in nearly the same season and smelling almost identical to a plum flower. Xiumi had reminded Magpie several times to keep an eye out for one on market days, yet years passed without either of them seeing a single specimen.

Near the end of winter the previous year, Magpie's nose caught the scent of their demure fragrance as she passed by Black Dragon Temple on her way to pull mustard leaves from the daylily field. She followed it to the collapsed remains of the *garan*, where three winter plums grew through the broken tiles. From these she cut a few flowering sprigs, which she brought back and arranged in a vase in the penthouse. The flowers were a deep yellow-orange, tightly packed, and so richly fragrant that even after their petals fell and the vase put away, their scent lingered for days afterward.

Xiumi knew that the winter plums at the temple had been planted by a monk, and the variety was known locally as Dog Louse. She could still recall the snowy scene at the temple when Mother took her out to cut a few branches each year after the New Year. Of course, she could never forget that the ruined temple was the old home of the Puji Academy, though it was one memory among others that Xiumi tried her hardest to forget, memories that can stab your heart at any unexpected moment, like a wooden splinter under your fingernail.

When Xiumi and Magpie went to the market in winter, they would often pass by an old man selling flowers in front of a Taoist temple. They noticed he never had any customers. While on occasion they stopped in front of the temple to see what he carried, they never even inquired about his prices, as he mostly sold common flowers and plants, nothing rare. One day, however, the old man called them over. He said he had an heirloom plum at his house, an old shrub he had bought in Shaoxing. He had tended it for sixty years. He said his home wasn't far, and would they want to come see it? Xiumi looked at Magpie, who looked back at Xiumi in a moment of mutual ambivalence. Yet they ended up following the old man home anyway.

He led them around the temple, through two narrow stone alleys and over a few small bridges that led to a clean and well-cared-for courtyard house. It was a decently sized property, bordered on three sides by a bamboo fence. There appeared to have been a large vegetable and flower garden in the inner courtyard, though the plants had long since withered. The place had clearly once belonged to a wealthy owner but had now fallen into the old man's solitary care. He walked them down the courtyard path to a thatched-roof gazebo, which sheltered an old plum tree. The tree's branches twisted in corkscrew curves that left an unforgettable impression of ancient, sinewy, uncompromising strength. Decades of sun and foul weather had brought it perfectly in tune with its environment. It filled the pot completely, its blooming branches twisted into every imaginable position, scales of green moss covering its bark like wrinkled skin. A delicate hanging moss draped long threads over several branches. The slightest breeze stirred the green hairs and made them billow in a most enchanting fashion.

"This flower has followed me all my life," the man admitted. "If I weren't worried about paying for my own funeral, I swear I'd never let it go."

Xiumi gazed at it with admiration and a powerful longing, but the old man wanted too high a price, and she had to back down. As the two women exited the courtyard the old man followed them and called them back, saying, "There's a lot of vulgar, superficial people here in Changzhou these days. The hermits and educated men who had real taste in flowers are all gone. The fact you two were willing to visit this broken house means you must genuinely love them. So if this plum tree suits your fancy, take it home with you. As for the money, give what you think is right. I can't tell you how many people have come by looking to buy this tree; I just couldn't bear to let it depend on a stranger's goodwill, so I never sold it. But now at my age, I take my socks off at night and don't know whether I'll be putting them on again the next morning. If this plum tree can find a good home, I'll rest easy." He sobbed faintly as he spoke.

Xiumi and Magpie fished all the money out of their pockets and gave it to him. Before handing over the tree, the old man stroked the plum's leaves with a shaking hand, obviously unwilling to let his lifelong companion go. He reminded them repeatedly of the tricks to watering it, pruning it, and feeding the soil, and he walked with them as far as the outskirts of Changzhou before waving goodbye and turning homeward.

Yet after the heirloom plum came to rest in Puji, despite Xiumi's constant and meticulous attention, it withered away and died in less than two months.

Magpie sighed. "I guess flowers really are exactly like people. It simply didn't want to be separated from its owner." Xiumi grieved silently. On a later market day, the two made a special trip back to the old man's residence, but found his place empty, the garden overgrown, and the door leaning off its hinges. Only dried beanstalks in the arbor rattled their brown pods in the wind. When they asked the neighbors about him, they said the old man had died some days earlier.

8

AT THE end of the summer, Puji endured its worst drought in over a hundred years. The village elders said that all the year's rain fell in the spring, and heaven didn't give them a drop more after July. The ground split and the river dried up as the sun spit fire that scorched the earth for miles around. Even the apricot tree that had stood in front of Grandma Meng's door for two centuries died. The many flowers beneath the roseleaf trellis in Xiumi's garden couldn't take the bitter cold of well water; they began to yellow and die, half of them gone within a month.

While the men, women, and children of the village knelt outside Black Dragon Temple to pray for rain, clever businessmen in town were already predicting the famine that would surely follow. They quietly hoarded foodstuffs, which drove up prices and inspired panic in the village. The day Magpie planned to take her piglets to the market, Hua Erniang said to her, "Who's going to have enough grain to feed a pig when people are starving?" Sure enough, the market was almost empty but for a handful of hungry-eyed strangers asking about the price of wheat; no one had any interest in buying her pigs.

In August, at the peak of the drought, locusts arrived. The first to see them was Tan Shuijin. The moment he found a handful of them in his boat, he ran toward the village, shouting, "People will die! People will die . . . !"

Less than three days later, a solid mass of insects swarmed up from the southeast, slashing through the sky like arrowheads and blocking out the sun. Farmers lit fireworks and ran through their fields with torches tied to bamboo poles, trying to drive them away. But the swarm only thickened, and soon the locusts flew into their hair, under their collar, into their mouths and ears. Many merely squatted down in the irrigation ditches and wept. Once the swarm passed, the villagers discovered that every single ear, fruit, and seed—not to mention the leaves on the trees—had been eaten.

The severity of the situation dawned on Mrs. Ding. She stood at the edge of the village, saying to herself repeatedly, "With all these locusts, what will we eat come winter?"

"Shit," Grandma Meng replied bitterly.

The depressed farmers broke out into raucous laughter. Only Tan Shuijin didn't laugh; he was too busy picking up dead locusts. He filled several burlap bags' worth of the insects, then brined them in a basin. Those pickled locusts would see him and his wife through the famine now upon them.

In the last two weeks of January, people started dying—Mrs. Ding included, though no one knew at the time it happened. The village thought of her only in early February, with the New Year's holiday drawing near. The body they found on her bed had already begun to mummify in the dry cold.

Magpie spent the days so hungry that, in her own words, she could have pulled the legs off the furniture and eaten them. Xiumi ate nothing but a small bowl of wheat-hull soup every day; she spent most of her time reading in bed, and only rarely came downstairs. But her expression showed neither panic nor suffering; in fact, she seemed happier than ever. Most of the things in the house that could be sold were sold.

Xiumi had long kept the golden cicada close to her, in the lining of her clothes. When she gingerly unfolded its handkerchief wrapping and passed it to Magpie, her eyes shimmered. Seeing the cicada reminded Magpie of Little Thing and of Xiumi's words while she slept: "His face isn't warm, that's why the snow piles up."

Magpie brought the cicada to the pawnshop, but the pawnbroker wouldn't take it. In fact, he wouldn't even look at it twice. He stuffed his hands in his sleeves and said dully, "I know it's gold. But gold isn't worth anything when people are starving."

Magpie had heard that Baldy's household still had some grain, so she lay down her pride and went to barter with him. Baldy had helped Xiumi build the Puji Academy, and later took Yellowtooth's place as the village butcher. After making enough money as a butcher, he opened his own grain shop.

Baldy was sitting in his bedroom doorway lighting a portable hand warmer when he saw Magpie step into his courtyard. He looked her up and down without speaking as she stood in the courtyard shifting her weight awkwardly, her eyes on the ground and her cheeks red. Finally, Baldy put down the hand warmer and sauntered up to her, a friendly smile on his face. He drew nearer and put his lips to her ear, whispering, "You've come to ask for food, yeah?"

Magpie nodded.

"At this point, I'm like the boils on a mouse's tail—the pus I've got isn't much."

Magpie turned to leave when she heard Baldy say, "Unless..."

"Unless what?" Magpie asked hopefully.

"You come inside and let me fool around with you. We can find you some food," he replied in a low voice.

Magpie couldn't have imagined he would be so vulgar. Embarrassment and anger sent her hurrying out of the courtyard toward Grandma Meng's house.

But before she had even walked through Grandma Meng's door, the crying of many children reached her ears from behind the wall. She turned and headed for Hua Erniang's house, entering without knocking.

Hua Erniang was sitting inside with her grandson on her knee, staring dumbly at the snowflakes drifting across her doorway and whispering, "It's okay, it's okay. If we must die, we'll die together, all of us together..." Hearing her words, Magpie pretended that she was just passing by and, without saying anything, went straight home.

Later that night, when hunger woke her up and drove her to peel some plaster off the wall to chew on, Magpie felt a twinge of regret. She should have just said to hell with it and let Baldy play with her like he asked. She sat up in bed and looked at Xiumi. "What do we do?" she asked.

Xiumi dropped the book in her hand, looked back at her, and smiled, as if to say, *What do we do? We die!*

Magpie rose early the next morning. But when she knelt down to light the kitchen stove, she remembered there was no food to cook, so she sat beside the stove and cried. The room began to spin in front of her. She recovered herself enough to halt the movement, only to see everything around her split into double images. When she stood up, the ground wavered beneath her feet. She knew she didn't have many days left. She filled the ladle with cold water, drank a few mouthfuls, and went to lie back down.

Passing through the skywell, she noticed something spherical and soft-looking on the ground against the wall. The previous night's snowfall had covered it. Magpie walked over and nudged it with her foot—a cloth sack. After brushing away the snow, she put a hand on the sack and squeezed; her heart skipped a beat. *Good heavens, it couldn't be?* She hurriedly untied the mouth. The bag was full of milk-white rice.

"Lord!" Magpie shrieked. "Where did this come from?" She looked up at the courtyard wall, then down at the ground again. Several roof tiles lay in fragments around the bag, suggesting someone had pushed it over the wall last night.

Without thinking twice, Magpie raced to the rear courtyard, her legs propelling her up the studio stairs with a strength she didn't know she still had. Bursting into the room, she called out to Xiumi, who was brushing her hair, "Rice! Rice! There's rice!"

Magpie's excitement infected Xiumi as well. She tossed her brush down and followed Magpie downstairs into the courtyard. Sure enough, it was a bag full of rice. Xiumi scooped up a handful and sniffed it, then turned immediately to Magpie and ordered, "Go get Grandma Meng and Hua Erniang over here now."

"Why them?"

"Just do it. I need to talk to them both."

Magpie made an assenting noise and turned to leave. Her excitement was so intense she felt nothing out of the ordinary about the conversation. But just as she put her foot over the threshold, she froze and looked back at Xiumi in shock. *Wait...wait...what? What did she say?*

She...she... Magpie's heart surged as tears rose in her eyes. *She finally spoke. She isn't mute. I knew she wasn't mute; how could a mute talk in her sleep?*

But now everything would be okay: They had food, and Xiumi could talk. Every worry disappeared. Magpie felt full of energy, as if she were strong enough to last another two weeks, or a month.

Perhaps it was her elation or the hazy confusion of extreme hunger that caused her to announce as she pushed open Grandma Meng's door, "Our Xiumi just said something!"

"She said something?" Grandma Meng replied feebly. She was scraping the bottom of her wok with a soup spoon, looking for flecks of old food but getting nothing but shards of iron.

"She did," Magpie replied. "She just started talking. She's not mute."

"Ah, so she's not mute. Well, she's not mute, she can speak, that's good, very good. Very good," Grandma Meng chattered to herself, then returned to scraping her wok.

Magpie stepped into Hua Erniang's house and said, "Erniang, I just heard our Xiumi talking a minute ago."

"Talking? So what if she's talking?" Hua Erniang was holding her grandson in her arms; the boy's cheeks were blue, and his hands shook.

"I always thought she was mute."

"She was mute?" Hua Erniang asked with no trace of feeling. She was obviously deranged with hunger.

Magpie walked homeward, utterly perplexed with her neighbors' reactions. Only when she reached her own doorway did she remember her most important item of business, and had to turn around and go right back.

Seeing the rice, Hua Erniang gushed, "Oh savior, savior, savior..." several times over before exclaiming, "Who could have the kind of money to offer such a rare thing these days!"

Grandma Meng asked, "My dear, where did you get this bag of rice?"

"I saw it in the courtyard after I got up this morning," Magpie told her. "I think somebody pushed it over the wall last night."

Xiumi chimed in, "Don't worry about where it came from, we need to feed people."

"It's true," agreed Grandma Meng, "feeding people comes first. What do you plan to do, my dear?"

Xiumi wanted to put the two women in charge of making rice congee, which they would serve every day in an equal amount to each villager. The community would hold on for as long as it could on this sack of rice. "You know, my dear," Grandma Meng confessed to Xiumi, "I hate to say it, but back in those days when you were crazy, doing your revolution and your communal cafeteria and playing with all those weapons, Auntie was awfully worried about you..."

Hua Erniang tugged Grandma Meng's sleeve to shut her up, then smiled and said, "But this will save the whole village. After the famine has passed, we'll have someone raise a monument to you."

The two old women teetered off on their small feet to spread the news around the village. Miraculously, the other villagers responded by bringing out handfuls of rice bran, wheat bran, and bean cakes. Some even offered their seed crop for the following year, while Baldy and his wife brought over a bag of white flour.

The old women made congee out of the rice from the bag and served it once a day in front of Grandma Meng's house. The sight of the village men, women, and children waiting patiently at Grandma Meng's doorway for their share filled Xiumi's heart with a mix of grief and pleasure. The riots she had worried about didn't occur; even when a few strangers and beggars lined up, the villagers didn't drive them away. Each person received one ladleful of congee; no one was left out. The scene reminded her of Zhang Jiyuan and the Great Unity he never got a chance to build, of her days at Huajiashe and the still-born Puji Academy, as well as the peach blossom fantasy Father took with him when he vanished.

One day, Magpie was helping Hua Erniang serve the congee. But when the final pair of hands held out a cracked bowl to them, there was no more left in the pot. Hua Erniang remarked, "That's a sad coincidence—we're only short your share."

Magpie raised her eyes and saw that the bowl belonged to the same beggar she had seen at Mr. Ding's funeral. Magpie stared intently, then said, "Where are you from? I feel like I know you."

Panicking, the beggar dropped the bowl and turned to run without even picking it up. Magpie chased the beggar with her big feet all the way to the river, thinking, *I'm going to find out who this is once and for all.* The beggar was losing steam, now pausing for breath, now bending over, hands on waist. Finally, as the two of them circled around a fishpond, Magpie stopped running and cried out, "Stop! I recognize you now, anyway. You're Lilypad."

Hearing this, the beggar stopped. After a stunned silence, she fell into a crouch and started to bawl.

The two sat on the edge of an abandoned mill wheel beside the pond and talked. Bright sunlight fell on their faces and warmed the air around them. Fresh meltwater trickled down through the teeth of the mill wheel and burbled into the river.

Magpie sat and cried with Lilypad for a while, then wiped her cheeks on her sleeve. Still sniffling, she asked her why she was dressed like a man, and how she had been living the past few years. Lilypad cried and said nothing.

"Didn't you get married to . . . to what's-his-name, Long Shoubei? How did you end up like this?" The question caused Lilypad to weep hysterically; she repeatedly wiped the dripping snot from her nose onto the edge of the mill wheel.

"Alas," Lilypad sighed, then said slowly, "it's just my destiny."

She told Magpie that after leaving Puji, she went to live in Meicheng with Long Shoubei. During her first year with him, Long Shoubei acquired more property elsewhere, and added another two concubines. After that, he never darkened her doorway again. Lilypad swallowed her shame and endured another three anxious months in his household, until Long Shoubei sent a young nephew to give her the news.

"He never actually said anything, just walked through the door and slammed his pistol down on the table. I knew my time there was up, so I asked him if he was driving me out. The messenger was only a kid, maybe eighteen or nineteen; he gave me a dirty smile, and I could smell the booze on his breath when he got close and said, 'No rush, no rush. Let me take a load off first.'"

Once she had been thrown out of Shoubei's house, Lilypad returned to her old trade, working in a couple of local brothels. At the first one, the madam eventually heard about her former husband and threw her out.

"Makes no difference if it's true or not," she told Lilypad. "In any case, you've been a man's wife. If Director Long finds out you're here, he might think I'm trying to humiliate him. And you're too old for this anyway."

Lilypad moved to another brothel, but the madam there said the same thing. She had no choice but to walk the streets with a bowl in her hands.

What was strange was that no matter what direction she traveled, the road always took her back to Puji. "As if Little Thing's soul were dragging me back," she said.

The mention of Little Thing made Magpie's heart ache. "For the most part, when you were at Puji Academy, the Principal was good to you..." Magpie bit her tongue, unable to complete the second half of the sentence.

"I know, I know..." Lilypad sucked in her breath sharply. "It's just my destiny."

She recounted her story of being on her own in the southwest and meeting a beggar on the road who had a starving child in tow. The child was clearly on his last legs, and pity moved Lilypad to give them a couple of steamed buns. As she walked away, the beggar stopped her. He said that the gift of a meal should be repaid with a lifetime of servitude, and though he wasn't good at much, he did have a knack for telling fortunes. After looking at her closely, he pronounced that she would end her life as a beggar and die on the roadside to be eaten by wild dogs. It wouldn't be hard to avoid that fate, however, as long as she married a man born in the year of the pig.

"Long Shoubei disguised himself as a cotton fluffer and came to the village to scout out the activities of the revolutionaries. I had no idea of his true identity. By coincidence, the Principal—Xiumi, I mean—had a painful toothache and sent me out to get Doctor Tang. When I passed Miss Sun's house, I saw the fluffer sitting out front resting, smoking his pipe. So I chatted with him. The sonuvabitch may be rotten right through, but he sure is handsome, and he knows how to talk. He had me hook, line, and sinker before I even knew what was happening. I swear I had no idea then that he was spying for the court. Back then, I wouldn't even have had the courage to betray the Principal for anything, even if my life depended on it. But then . . ."

"Did you decide to go with him because he was born in a pig year?" Magpie asked.

Lilypad considered this for a moment and nodded, then shook her head. "Not entirely. You've never been with a man so you don't know what the good part can be like. And that sonuvabitch sure was a fine piece of man meat—tall, strong, beautifully built. For women like us, once a man like that pinches you in the soft parts, it doesn't matter if you agree or not, you'll still make mistake after mistake for him until all you can do is close your eyes and let him move you any way he wants."

Magpie's cheeks turned crimson; she stared silently at the ground.

After a pause, Lilypad asked how Xiumi was doing, and if she had mentioned her at all upon her return. "Good question," Magpie replied. "All these years, she hasn't said a single word. I thought she had gone mute."

"She isn't mute, she can talk."

"How do you know?"

"I'm the only one who knows what she's thinking. She refuses to talk in order to punish herself."

"But why? I don't get it."

"It's all about Little Thing, right?" Lilypad said. "Back in the academy days, everyone thought she was crazy for ignoring her own son the way she did. But she was thinking about that boy every single day."

"How do you know that?"

"One day, when I was talking to her in the *garan*, I asked her, 'Why are you so cruel to Little Thing? No matter what, the boy is still the flesh of your flesh. How could you bear to treat him so badly?' You know what she said to me?"

Magpie shook her head.

"She told me that the moment she started down this path, she had accepted the inevitability of her own death, just like Master Xue and Zhang Jiyuan. The harder she was on her son, the less he would miss her after she was gone."

Magpie started to cry again. After finally controlling her tears, she asked Lilypad what she was going to do in the future.

"What will *I* do?" Lilypad turned the question around as if she were asking Magpie as well as herself. "I don't know. I'll take it one step at a time. But I'll never come back to Puji again."

Magpie had a forgiving, compassionate heart, and it pained her to hear Lilypad speak this way. In a tentative voice she said, "Maybe if I can talk to Xiumi about it, you can stay in Puji and live with us."

"Nuh-uh, nope," Lilypad replied. "Even if she did agree to take me in, I couldn't bear to look at her again. She may have been the one who sold all the family's land to Long Qingtang, but the idea was mine to begin with. And even though Little Thing didn't die by my hand, he did die because of me . . ." Something else suddenly occurred to her. "I heard she had another child while she was in jail?"

Magpie replied, "They said the baby was taken away three days after the birth. Nobody knows where the child ended up, or if it's still alive."

The two women talked from noon to the early evening. The northwest wind picked up, and Magpie realized her hands and feet had gone numb with cold. Lilypad collected her nightstick and put on her straw hat, readying herself to leave.

Not knowing what to say, Magpie blurted out, "If you ever get really desperate, you might as well come back to Puji."

Lilypad grimaced at her from over her shoulder and set off without replying.

As Magpie trudged home, her eyes red, she frequently cast her gaze back in Lilypad's direction. By the time she reached the estate, she spied Xiumi standing by the front gate waiting for her. Xiumi looked at Magpie, then out into the vast, windswept wilderness behind her, and asked, "So Lilypad isn't coming home after all?"

9

TWELVE years passed.

By late fall, the rice crop had been cut and harvested, and the shaved paddies lay under a gray-white layer of frost. The copses of tallow trees by the roads and streams turned red overnight. Their white berries dangled on the branches like snow, or willow catkins, or plum blossoms.

Xiumi said that the rice in the fields was ripe, its time had come and it would soon be cut. Xiumi said that the tallow trees were turning red. Once their leaves dropped and their berries blackened, the winter snows would begin.

Her words materialized out of the blue; Magpie could merely guess at the feelings behind them. The weather was unbelievably perfect— days without a breath of wind, the sky a boundless field of blue—truly an "autumn spring," as southerners called it. Time seemed to halt under the warm sunlight. Flocks of geese passed occasionally over the treetops. Xiumi said that after the geese passed, the winter crows would soon follow. Her pronouncements seemed to carry a heavy implication. Fortunately, Magpie had become accustomed to hearing them, so that while they still surprised her, she no longer thought about them much.

For over ten years, Xiumi had tended her flowers and plants in the rear courtyard. Pots, basins, and buckets of various sizes filled the open space corner-to-corner in a chorus of leafy hostas, peonies, perilla, bush cherries, rhododendrons, sweet chrysanthemums, and winter plums. From the roseleaf trellis to the studio stairs and the vegetable garden, from the foot of the courtyard wall to the border of the bamboo grove, no spot remained empty.

Though her vow of silence had been broken, Xiumi still didn't speak very often. With autumn far along and the chrysanthemums in full bloom, Xiumi copied out chrysanthemum poems as she remembered them for Magpie to read when she needed a brief distraction. Yet Magpie frequently found their messages disturbing, such as:

> The hermit's hedgerow is like the Peach Blossom Paradise:
> After these flowers open, no others will bloom.

Or:

> At times, looking back with a drunken eye,
> I mistake the dreaming hermit for the man who found the
> orchard.

Or, on another occasion:

> Yellow stamens and green stalks like years past;
> Hearts hold fruitless cries of regret.

A hundred anxious thoughts seemed tangled in Xiumi's breast. One day, as they pruned branches in the courtyard, Xiumi asked Magpie, "You've heard of a place called Huajiashe, yes?"

Magpie nodded.

"Do you know how to get there?" Xiumi prodded her.

Magpie shook her head.

Magpie had never in her life traveled farther than the market in Changzhou. She raised her head to look at the sky. Huajiashe was like a wisp of white cloud up there—you could see it, yet it was as distant as a dream. Magpie couldn't understand why Xiumi would suddenly want to go back there.

She said she wanted to see the little island again.

As Xiumi was determined to go, Magpie had little choice but to ask around the village for directions to Huajiashe and prepare dry rations for the trip.

A nice, long trip might be a good thing, Magpie thought. *It might distract her a little and ease her worries.* A few days later, Xiumi asked Magpie to send someone out to tend to the grave mounds for Madame Lu and Little Thing. Once that was done, the two of them set off.

Magpie prepared three days' worth of dry rations. In her opinion, three days was already too long—more than enough time to reach every corner of the earth. Xiumi refused to hire a rickshaw at any point in the journey, no matter how tired they were. They walked at a steady pace, crossing valleys and mountains; Magpie noticed that Xiumi cried frequently, and that her interactions with others, her gestures, were noticeably slower than normal, causing Magpie's anxiety to escalate again.

They asked directions in each village, drank water from each well, got lost seven or eight times, and passed a week of nights in unfamiliar peasant huts. Xiumi suffered from dysentery for a stretch on the road, and babbled through the night in a fever-induced delirium. Magpie ended up having to carry her on her back to continue on. When they arrived at Huajiashe at noon on the eighth day, Xiumi was asleep, her head resting on Magpie's shoulders.

Xiumi opened her bleary eyes, which instantly overflowed with tears again. They appeared to be standing near a tavern at the village entrance. Its faded and fraying banner, which hung over a window, rose and fell in the breeze. No patrons were in sight. The New Year's couplets, originally written on bright red paper and glued to the door frame, had apparently faded first to pink, and on to their current ashen gray. A young girl in a floral-print cotton jacket sat on the doorstep, rolling skeins of yarn, and repeatedly raised a watchful eye toward the two travelers.

The mountainside village looked much smaller and more run-down than Xiumi remembered. The blackened ruins caused by the fire those many years ago still stood out starkly in the surroundings. The covered walkway that connected each home had been dismantled long ago, leaving only shallow, round postholes on either side of the road. Whenever a gust passed through it raised clouds of dust.

The forest behind the village had been almost completely cut down, leaving the mountainside bald. House after crumbling house looked like it might topple at any moment. The streams of clear water still running along the aqueducts and the cooing of a few pigeons that circled over the gray tiled roofs were the only signs of life.

As they prepared to keep walking, the window of the tavern opened, and a middle-aged woman's plump, somewhat puffy face emerged.

"Here to eat?" she asked.

"No, thank you," Magpie replied with a smile.

With a crisp *smack*, the window closed again.

They found their way to the lakeside. The island, barely an arrow's flight away from the village, was nothing more than a dark smudge on the water's surface. The house that Xiumi and Han Liu had inhabited for a year and three months was gone, and the island now bristled with mulberry trees. Aside from a single fisherman on the water bringing in his nets, there seemed to be no one else around.

They waited on the shore until noon passed, when the fisherman finally docked his boat. Xiumi asked if he would take them out to see the island. He examined both women suspiciously for a long moment, then said, "Nobody lives out there."

Xiumi replied, "We'd just like to go have a look. Would you be able to ferry us over?"

"Nothing to see out there. Only mulberry trees, not a single person," replied the fisherman.

Hearing the fisherman's refusal, Magpie pulled a banknote out of her waist pocket and passed it to him. On seeing the money, the fisherman made no move to take it but quietly replied, "If you really want to go, I'll just row you over. Don't worry about the money."

The two women boarded the boat. The fisherman told them that the island was exactly the same as when he first arrived at Huajiashe. However, he had heard people say that there used to be a house there with a nun living in it. But at some point, the house was torn down, and he had no clue where the nun had gone.

"So that means you're not local?" Magpie asked.

The fisherman said he had married into his mother's sister's family five years ago. He fished the lake every day and had never seen anyone on the island. Only the village women went out to the island in the spring, after their black-haired silkworms emerged from their eggs, to collect mulberry leaves.

He said his wife had also raised four or five baskets of silkworms. Once, the worms were hungry late one night, and his wife begged him to go out to the island with a lantern to pick some leaves. She didn't know that eating mulberry leaves swollen with dew would kill silkworms. The next morning, they dumped all the snow-white worms into the lake. He said he loved the noise silkworms made when they ate; it sounded like rain.

Looking up at the two women, the fisherman asked, "And where is home for you? Why do you want to see the island?"

Xiumi didn't reply; she was gazing at the dark expanse of the mulberry orchard. The wind rattled the stiff, green leaves.

As the boat glided closer to the island, Magpie spied the ruins of an old foundation through the trees. Xiumi let out a deep sigh, then said, "Enough. We're not getting off. Take us back."

"Why change your mind now?" the fisherman asked.

"This isn't an easy place to get to after eight days of travel," Magpie implored. "Let's just get out and stand for a while. At least it'll put something to rest."

"I've seen it before. We're going back," Xiumi replied. She spoke softly, in a hard, emotionless tone that silenced any argument.

They decided to leave Huajiashe that same day.

A black-capped sampan took them back to Puji by water. The boatman said that if they were lucky and there was a tailwind, they could make it to the Yangtze River by noon the next day. Xiumi lay in the chilly darkness of the tiny cabin and fell asleep to the sound of water flowing past her head. Soon, tall reeds began to tickle the cabin's roof, making a crisp hissing noise. She dreamed once more of the tiny island sequestered by lake water, the blue face of the tomb in moonlight, the mulberry orchard, and the shards of wall plaster and roof tiles scattered on the earth. Of course, she also dreamed of Han Liu. Heaven knew how many times the two of them had sat beside the window, chatting and watching the night's blackness fade as a trembling morning sun the color of molten iron rose over the lake and washed the trees by the shore with red. She heard Han Liu say at her elbow, "Every person's heart is an island, trapped by water, sequestered from the world."

But where was Han Liu today?

Sometime around midnight, a dusky yellow glow lit the cabin. Xiumi threw her jacket around her as she sat up and peered outside: A convoy was passing by. Every boat glowed with a single lamp—Xiumi counted seven. The boats were connected to one another with an iron chain. Seen from afar, they looked like a line of travelers carrying lanterns down the road.

A wind rose, and the stars above twinkled. It was certainly a clear autumn night. Xiumi shivered as she watched the convoy of boats float into the distance; tears welled up in her eyes. She knew she had encountered not a passing convoy, but her own self of twenty years earlier.

*

One winter morning, Xiumi woke up in the studio just like always. The cold air was unbearable, and she couldn't bring herself to throw off her blankets. The sun rose. Magpie called up to her from the vegetable garden. She said, "The winter plums under the roseleaf trellis have all bloomed!"

Xiumi dragged herself out of bed and approached the dresser to brush her hair. She noticed that a spiky rime of frost coated the copper basin sitting on her table. She recalled that she had used it to wash her face the previous night and must not have dumped all the water out, so the bottom and sides had iced over. She cast a careless glance into the basin, but then didn't look away. A sudden, profound shock contorted her expression.

In the mosaic of lines drawn by the frost, she saw a face—the face of her father. She couldn't believe her own eyes. Father appeared to be stroking his beard and smiling. He was sitting on the ground at the edge of a broad avenue, playing go with someone.

The light in the studio was far too weak. Xiumi dropped her wooden comb, picked up the basin, and carried it outside to the gazebo. Sitting on one of the stone stools, she held the basin under a ray of morning sunlight that shined over the tops of the trees by the eastern courtyard wall and examined it closely. Another person was seated across from Father, but she could see only his back. They both sat in the shade of a large pine tree. The foothills of a mountain rose gently behind them, and a flock of sheep appeared to be grazing on the slope. Beside the two figures stretched a wide, open highway that bordered a powerful river on its opposite side. The two people, the pine tree, grass, river, and sheep all stood out in crisp, fully lifelike detail.

A car was parked on the edge of the highway. One of its doors was open, and a passenger (a bald man) had one foot outside the door, as if he were about to get out. His face was indistinct but definitely familiar to Xiumi; the more she scrutinized it, the hazier it grew. The frost crystals were melting under the sunlight, gradually, irreversibly disappearing.

The ice pattern that faded before Xiumi's eyes was her past and future.

Ice is delicate, just like people. Xiumi felt a painful wrenching in her chest, and she leaned on a pillar to recover her breath. With her back against the pillar, she quietly died.

In April 1956, the governor of Meicheng County* was riding in a new Jeep down the mountain road that led to the Puji Reservoir. By chance, Governor Tan noticed two elderly people sitting cross-legged beneath a large pine tree playing go, and he ordered his driver to stop the car. His secretary, Miss Yao, was sitting next to him, sucking on hard candy and enjoying the scenery. When she heard the governor order the driver to pull over, she touched him gently on the arm and asked with a smile, "Is that go bug of yours biting again, Governor?"

*Tan Gongda (1911–1976), previously named Mei Yuanbao, was Lu Xiumi's second son, removed from her custody at birth by the wife of the prison guard Mei Shiguang. He lived for many years in Pukou. Just before Mei Shiguang passed away in 1935, he revealed to his adopted son the actual history of his birth. The boy's real father was purported to be Tan Si of Puji, though this was impossible to prove. In 1946, Tan Gongda was appointed chief political officer for the battalion of the New Fourth Army's advance column that encamped in Puji. In 1952, he was made governor of the county.

OTHER NEW YORK REVIEW CLASSICS

For a complete list of titles, visit www.nyrb.com or write to:
Catalog Requests, NYRB, 435 Hudson Street, New York, NY 10014

J.R. ACKERLEY My Dog Tulip
RENATA ADLER Speedboat
AESCHYLUS Prometheus Bound; translated by Joel Agee
ROBERT AICKMAN Compulsory Games
LEOPOLDO ALAS His Only Son *with* Doña Berta
CÉLESTE ALBARET Monsieur Proust
DANTE ALIGHIERI The Inferno
KINGSLEY AMIS The Alteration
KINGSLEY AMIS Dear Illusion: Collected Stories
KINGSLEY AMIS Lucky Jim
KINGSLEY AMIS The Old Devils
KINGSLEY AMIS One Fat Englishman
KINGSLEY AMIS Take a Girl Like You
ROBERTO ARLT The Seven Madmen
U.R. ANANTHAMURTHY Samskara: A Rite for a Dead Man
IVO ANDRIĆ Omer Pasha Latas
WILLIAM ATTAWAY Blood on the Forge
W.H. AUDEN (EDITOR) The Living Thoughts of Kierkegaard
ERICH AUERBACH Dante: Poet of the Secular World
EVE BABITZ I Used to Be Charming: The Rest of Eve Babitz
EVE BABITZ Slow Days, Fast Company: The World, the Flesh, and L.A.
DOROTHY BAKER Cassandra at the Wedding
J.A. BAKER The Peregrine
S. JOSEPHINE BAKER Fighting for Life
HONORÉ DE BALZAC The Human Comedy: Selected Stories
HONORÉ DE BALZAC The Unknown Masterpiece *and* Gambara
VICKI BAUM Grand Hotel
SYBILLE BEDFORD A Legacy
SYBILLE BEDFORD A Visit to Don Otavio: A Mexican Journey
MAX BEERBOHM The Prince of Minor Writers: The Selected Essays of Max Beerbohm
MAX BEERBOHM Seven Men
STEPHEN BENATAR Wish Her Safe at Home
FRANS G. BENGTSSON The Long Ships
WALTER BENJAMIN The Storyteller Essays
ALEXANDER BERKMAN Prison Memoirs of an Anarchist
GEORGES BERNANOS Mouchette
MIRON BIAŁOSZEWSKI A Memoir of the Warsaw Uprising
ADOLFO BIOY CASARES Asleep in the Sun
ADOLFO BIOY CASARES The Invention of Morel
PAUL BLACKBURN (TRANSLATOR) Proensa
CAROLINE BLACKWOOD Corrigan
LESLEY BLANCH Journey into the Mind's Eye: Fragments of an Autobiography
RONALD BLYTHE Akenfield: Portrait of an English Village
HENRI BOSCO Malicroix
NICOLAS BOUVIER The Way of the World
EMMANUEL BOVE My Friends
MALCOLM BRALY On the Yard
MILLEN BRAND The Outward Room
ROBERT BRESSON Notes on the Cinematograph
DAVID BROMWICH (EDITOR) Writing Politics: An Anthology

VARLAM SHALAMOV Sketches of the Criminal World: Further Kolyma Stories
ROBERT SHECKLEY Store of the Worlds: The Stories of Robert Sheckley
CHARLES SIMIC Dime-Store Alchemy: The Art of Joseph Cornell
MAY SINCLAIR Mary Olivier: A Life
SASHA SOKOLOV A School for Fools
BEN SONNENBERG Lost Property: Memoirs and Confessions of a Bad Boy
VLADIMIR SOROKIN Ice Trilogy
NATSUME SŌSEKI The Gate
JEAN STAFFORD The Mountain Lion
RICHARD STERN Other Men's Daughters
GEORGE R. STEWART Names on the Land
JEAN STROUSE Alice James: A Biography
HOWARD STURGIS Belchamber
ITALO SVEVO As a Man Grows Older
HARVEY SWADOS Nights in the Gardens of Brooklyn
MAGDA SZABÓ Abigail
MAGDA SZABÓ The Door
JÁNOS SZÉKELY Temptation
SUSAN TAUBES Divorcing
ELIZABETH TAYLOR You'll Enjoy It When You Get There: The Stories of Elizabeth Taylor
TEFFI Tolstoy, Rasputin, Others, and Me: The Best of Teffi
GABRIELE TERGIT Käsebier Takes Berlin
HENRY DAVID THOREAU The Journal: 1837–1861
ALEKSANDAR TIŠMA The Use of Man
TATYANA TOLSTAYA White Walls: Collected Stories
LIONEL TRILLING The Liberal Imagination
KURT TUCHOLSKY Castle Gripsholm
RAMÓN DEL VALLE-INCLÁN Tyrant Banderas
CARL VAN VECHTEN The Tiger in the House
SALKA VIERTEL The Kindness of Strangers
ROBERT WALSER Jakob von Gunten
ROBERT WALSER A Schoolboy's Diary and Other Stories
MICHAEL WALZER Political Action: A Practical Guide to Movement Politics
SYLVIA TOWNSEND WARNER The Corner That Held Them
SYLVIA TOWNSEND WARNER Lolly Willowes
ALEKSANDER WAT My Century
LYALL WATSON Heaven's Breath: A Natural History of the Wind
MAX WEBER Charisma and Disenchantment: The Vocation Lectures
SIMONE WEIL On the Abolition of All Political Parties
GLENWAY WESCOTT The Pilgrim Hawk
REBECCA WEST The Fountain Overflows
EDITH WHARTON The New York Stories of Edith Wharton
T. H. WHITE The Goshawk
JOHN WILLIAMS Augustus
JOHN WILLIAMS Stoner
HENRY WILLIAMSON Tarka the Otter
ANGUS WILSON Anglo-Saxon Attitudes
GEOFFREY WOLFF Black Sun
FRANCIS WYNDHAM The Complete Fiction
JOHN WYNDHAM The Chrysalids
BÉLA ZOMBORY-MOLDOVÁN The Burning of the World: A Memoir of 1914
STEFAN ZWEIG Beware of Pity
STEFAN ZWEIG The Post-Office Girl